REVOLUTIONARY KISS

Mary-Kate Summers

www.BOROUGHSPUBLISHINGGROUP.com

REVOLUTIONARY KISS
Copyright © 2021 Mary-Kate Summers

ISBN: 978-1-953810-27-4

For Gabriele, our guide

ACKNOWLEDGMENTS

We would like thank our husbands, family, friends and readers for their support and encouragement.

REVOLUTIONARY KISS

Prologue

November 1777

Everyone was dressed in ugly black gowns and coats. Now and then she caught glimpses of her father atop the steps, far across the broad avenue. Her mother held her hand in such a tight grip she could see little beyond the crowd of people swarming around her. She stood on tiptoe to try to see the coach. Hearing a slow rumble of wooden wheels, she could tell it was getting closer. People were curtsying and bowing as horse hooves rang along the cobblestones. Her father was standing closer, a beautiful spot of blue and gold color. Something urged her to run. Run from buildings melting in the hot sunshine as she held her arms out to him. She was almost there, reaching out, when an avalanche of screams descended on her: horses' wild neighs, then everywhere a blinding flash—

Nicole woke, her heart racing, her skin damp under her nightdress. In the still, dark room, the familiar dream was fading. She panicked, grasping at the memory. *No, you mustn't leave. Stay.* It was her mother now slipping from her. *Maman, help me. Where is Papa?* She could almost feel him taking her into his arms.

Squeezing her eyes shut, she felt a sense of urgency. There was something she needed to remember. Something important. If only she could—

From the far side of the dormitory came a whimper, like the whine of a puppy. It was so unexpected, so out of nowhere, that Nicole's eyes flashed open. She sat up. What was that strange sound? She knew every cough and sneeze of the other girls in the ward, every window rattle, every rat scratching inside the walls.

This was different. Puzzled, she tossed back her thin blanket and rose. She made her way in half darkness across the cold floor.

Coming closer to the whimpering, she paused. There in the corner, on what for months had been an empty cot, a new arrival was curled up and crying into her pillow.

Nicole drew closer until she made out a wisp of a girl with snowy white hair.

"Don't be sad," Nicole said as she knelt beside her.

The girl looked up with a tear-streaked face. "I want my *maman*," she whispered, her breath catching between sobs.

"Of course you do," Nicole said softly, smoothing hair from the girl's forehead. "We all miss our mothers. Do you have a papa?"

The girl shook her head. *No.*

"Neither do I," Nicole stated. With the sleeve of her nightdress, she dried the girl's tearstained face. "What's your name?"

"Aimée."

"I'm Nicole."

Aimée's bottom lip quivered. "It's my birthday."

The utterance startled Nicole, then excited her at such an amazing coincidence. "It's my birthday too," she whispered. "How old are you?"

"Eight."

"I'm eight as well," Nicole exclaimed in a burst of surprise. Catching herself, she lowered her voice. "That makes us sisters."

"Twins," Aimée replied with a sniff, her eyes beginning to brighten.

They shared a shy smile at the notion of twins who looked so different: Aimée fragile and sprite-like. Nicole tall and willowy. The girls grasped hands. Their fingers intertwined.

"I must go back to my bed sister Aimée," Nicole murmured, placing a small kiss on her new friend's forehead. "Tomorrow we'll eat breakfast together then clean the floors side by side. You'll see. It won't be so bad. I'll find you a gift, I promise. Will you be all right?" she asked, rising.

Aimée nodded. "*Bon anniversaire.*"

"*Bon anniversaire,*" Nicole whispered back, then with a backward wave, tiptoed away careful to avoid the squeakiest floorboards.

When she thought she'd made it safely to her bed, the hall door banged open. A streak of amber light cut into the room, revealing the outline of a gaunt woman wearing a puffed sleeping cap and night wrap.

"Who's up? You there. Stop."

The other girls were groggily awakening, though most pretended to be asleep or pulled pillows over their heads as the directress, holding her candlestick high in surveillance, marched down the center aisle.

Standing stone-still, Nicole watched as *Madame* Colére stopped, her eyes hardening.

"I'm sorry to have disturbed you, *Madame*," Nicole muttered.

"Nicole Vogel. Aren't you beggars enough of a nuisance without this sort of disobedience?"

"But, *Madame*, I only wanted to—"

"I heard voices. Who were you talking to?"

"No one. I had a dream…about my father. I remember he was wearing a *uniform,* blue and gold—"

Madame Colére reached out and slapped Nicole's face.

Nicole's eyes widened, her cheek blazing from the blow. She held back her tears. Never would she cry in front of this woman. *Ever.*

"Don't defy me. You lie to make yourself special with such a story."

"But I remember, I do. No matter what you say."

"Quiet."

Nicole shrunk inside as the woman's small black eyes flicked about her hair. *What was she thinking?*

Madame Colére lifted a strand up for inspection. "My, isn't it pretty how it shimmers with gold in the light." She stroked the abundant tresses. "Still, it's the color of wheat, wouldn't you say? Common. Nothing special."

"*Madame.*"

"It's time we corrected your disobedience, Nicole Vogel." The woman grabbed a handful of Nicole's hair at the nape of the neck.

"Please, *Madame*," she begged, wincing in pain.

"Stop it." The cry came from the darkened corner of the room. *Madame* Colére lifted her candle to reveal Aimée, sitting up in bed and watching them. Nicole shook her head for her new friend to say nothing, but it was too late.

Madame Colére had let go of Nicole's hair and was marching toward Aimée's bed. "You. New girl. Stand," she demanded, holding up the candlestick.

Looking like a dazed angel, Aimée rose, her pale blue eyes fixed on *Madame* Colére's face. Nicole could withstand *Madame* pulling her hair—she'd suffered much worse—but Aimée's terrified expression filled her with rage. "Leave Aimée alone," Nicole shrieked, running to her bedside. "It's my fault. I came to her."

Madame Colére's thin lips puckered. "So," she mused, eyeing them both. "A new little friend, hmm?"

"She's done nothing," Nicole cried.

"Fetch the scissors," *Madame* Colére ordered Aimée. "In the next room. The sewing basket. Hurry."

Seeing Aimée's panicked glance, Nicole nodded she should do as told. Aimée scurried off, limping lightly on a twisted foot. *Madame* Colére dragged Nicole by the hair to the middle of the dormitory, ordering everyone in the ward up on their feet. As the disoriented girls clambered out of their beds, *Madame* Colére held out a hank of Nicole's long locks and glared at Aimée rushing back with a huge pair of scissors. "New girl." *Madame* pointed a crooked finger an inch from Nicole's scalp. "Cut here."

Aimée's whole body shivered.

"Now," *Madame* Colére commanded. "Do. As. I. Say."

"Do it," Nicole whispered.

"Quiet," *Madame* Colére ordered. "Cut."

Feeling the heavy cold metal against her neck, Nicole closed her eyes. *Why does she hate me so?* Biting her lip to quell her pent-up rage, she said to herself again and again, *It wasn't a dream. It wasn't a dream.*

PART ONE

All Are Joined in the Cause

Chapter One

March 1789

Long ago, Nicole learned to do what she was told, quickly and without complaint. But it wasn't duty that prompted her to join Antoine tonight. These treasonous excursions through the dim side streets of Paris were a stand against tyranny. Regardless of the consequences.

At least that's what she told herself as she followed Antoine in his wild dashes past darkened buildings and around blind corners. How could she feel more alive than *this*, the wind whipping her hair about her face, her blood pulsing with excitement?

"Here," Antoine whispered, stopping at a wall beneath an overhang of trees. She pulled a paintbrush gooey with gray paste from her basket. He grabbed the handle and in one smooth motion smeared the wall, mindless of the ooze dripping down his ink-stained fingers. Nicole, her breath frosted by the air, stood back to observe him, his narrow-boned face grimaced in concentration as if no danger lurked in the shadowy alleyways. Such bravery gave her a sense of invincibility.

"Hurry," he urged.

She snapped to and unfurled a poster still smelling of ink, a message for King Louis XVI. With freezing fingers, she pressed it against the wall, careful not to tear the words that she now knew by heart:

Weak king, be brave. Don't listen to bad counsel anymore, neither from bad priests, nor from your villainous wife: one little push and the machine will roll.

Then they were off, looking for the next stone wall or building, any surface to post protests of the injustices done to Parisian citizens.

It had been almost a year since Antoine had brought her into his clandestine world of rights and equity. He'd helped her realize that someone like her, an orphan raised without hope, had a right to "pursue happiness," something he said the Americans demanded. So she'd decided she would do that.

No longer would she deny her talent.

In the orphanage her inner world of creativity had been her escape. It was how she'd survived. One day, she would create the most magnificent hats in Paris and sell them to the bourgeoisie—as they were now being called—not nobility, but an entire new class of merchants making a fortune in business and trade. With their wives as clientele, she could buy the finest materials. Until then, she would content herself to stay up late and stitch her designs using the leftover scraps from Gustave Baston's millinery. By day she'd deliver his old-fashioned bonnets to a dwindling number of customers, which was how she'd met Antoine Durand.

She'd been sent to deliver a dowdy brown hat to Antoine's aunt. He had answered the door and to her surprise sat and watched as she presented the hat to *Madame* Durand. Or *Charlotte*, as the woman insisted Nicole call her. She had liked Antoine at once. He and his young brother Sebaste were like her, orphans, but their Aunt Charlotte had raised them with a mother's tenderness.

Antoine's steadfast dedication to this hobbled-together family had touched Nicole so much that for the first time, alone with a man, she let down her guard. She found his company enjoyable, and he protected her from the insolent gazes of male strangers.

Antoine wasn't like them. Never once had he come close to making an improper comment. The Bastons approved of him as a "fine young fellow," and her dear friend Aimée thought he was right for her. Never could any of them have imagined that Antoine would introduce her to the secret underworld of a brewing revolution.

Antoine stuffed his paintbrush into the basket. "I think that's enough for tonight."

He looked over his shoulder. Alarmed, Nicole followed his gaze. That's when she heard it, too. Marching boots. Not far away.

"*Le Guet Royale*," he murmured, his gaze searching about the darkened streets.

Nicole's breath caught. Police? From which direction? The rhythmic clicking of thick-heeled boots drew nearer. A charge of panic flashed through her. After all these months, she'd never let herself believe they would actually be caught.

"Where can we hide?" she whispered. It would be impossible to outmaneuver the *Guet*, who patrolled their own local districts. This was their territory. Not Antoine's, and certainly not hers.

Antoine grabbed the basket. "*Dépêche-toi*," he ordered. "Let's go."

She sprung after him as he took off running. Her mind reeled in fear. What was she doing here in the streets being chased by the police? How could she have been so reckless? For the first time the thoughtlessness of their actions struck her. What about Gus and Sarah? Or Aimée? Innocent people she cared for. They could be hanged because of her.

"*Halte*. You there. Stop."

The command came from directly behind. Feeling the night closing around her, she ran faster, struggling with her heavy skirt, keeping her eyes on Antoine's back. She chased after him down one alley, then another, through the murky maze of streets with police commands to halt echoing from all directions. She thought her chest would burst as Antoine ducked behind a cart and yanked her down to crouch beside him.

Her heart pounded with such force she feared it would give them away. If only she could take deeper breaths, fill her lungs with air. Closing her eyes, she leaned her forehead against the cart and shakily inhaled as quietly as she could. Had they lost them? She couldn't bear to look.

"Over here."

She sat up in alarm. Antoine raised his forefinger to his lips. She nodded as footsteps came closer.

From her stooped position, Nicole peeked under the cart. Two pairs of black boots appeared. Ducking lower, she recognized the telltale red stockings of the *Guet*. Antoine grasped her arm, his fingers squeezing so hard she had to bite her lip to keep from crying out.

The moment stretched out. Her mind was frantic. Were the *Guet* playing with them? They must know they were on the other side of the cart.

"This way," a different voice boomed and in a scuffle, off the men ran. Nicole waited breathlessly feeling she would melt there while waiting to see if they would return. The scrape and clatter of boots echoed farther and farther away until she could hear only Antoine's heavy breathing.

"Have we lost them?" she whispered at last.

"I'm not sure."

She dared to peer around the corner of the cart. Never had the cramped and filthy streets seemed more welcoming. Not a soul lingered. "They're gone." She sighed in relief.

Antoine slowly released his hold. They sat catching their breath until he shifted closer, his lips hovering at her ear. "It seems, we are true enemies of the crown."

His breath fanned across her cheek. Nicole couldn't tell if her heart pounded from their close escape or from his nearness. "Can we be sure they won't come back?" she whispered, turning to read his expression. Despite the darkness, she glimpsed a satisfied smile on his lips.

"Those overfed lackeys?" Antoine smirked. "I'd say they're sprawled somewhere on the cobblestones, gasping for breath." His smile faded. "You know, I'm glad you're at my side in this struggle."

He abruptly leaned forward and, with the basket wedged between them, lowered his mouth to hers in an awkward kiss. Caught off guard, her first impulse was to draw back. But as his lips pressed against hers, she gave in to the moment. Still tingling from their near escape and wanting to intensify the thrill, she closed her eyes, trying to feel the same heart-pounding excitement for the kiss as she had for their adventure.

Something left her stiff, unyielding. She broke away, hoping Antoine could not read her doubt.

Without a word, he helped her to her feet. She couldn't meet his eyes. What was wrong with her? Her first kiss should have felt different. She wasn't sure how. But this lackluster feeling? Where was the thrill? The excitement of kissing your first love. Well, maybe not her love, not yet, but she cared deeply for Antoine.

If Antoine was disappointed, he covered it well. "We should go," he said.

Taking his hand, Nicole stood and faced him, slouching a bit as she did. She wished she weren't so tall. She wanted him to gaze down at her with that expression of self-confidence she admired. Perhaps he'd try another kiss. It would be better, she was sure. But he turned away and gathered up the basket of posters.

Wrapped up in their scarves braving the cold, they walked toward the *Rue Crémieux*, keeping step together as though the clumsy kiss had never happened. Instead they spoke softly of the success of the night. What had been pure terror faded into a sense of satisfaction at having escaped the *Guet*.

"We'll wait a few days before we go out again," Antoine stated.

"That would be wise," Nicole agreed, though she only half listened. Her mind was on the kiss. Why had it been such a disappointment? Unthinkingly, she touched her lips. They were cold, but she knew it wasn't from the night air. What was wrong with her? Everyone thought they belonged together.

She would try harder. Perhaps one day she could come to love him as a paramour, as a husband.

They stopped before the entrance of *La Fenêtre*, a café tucked into a row of narrow, two-story buildings crammed along a rat-infested street. Although women rarely went into cafés, Nicole enjoyed accompanying Antoine into them. She liked listening to the furious arguments and debates about the unjust conditions of their lives, thrilled to be part of something grand. But she'd had enough revolution for one night.

"Do we have to go in?" she asked. "After all that's happened, I'd like to go home."

"Nonsense. There's someone I want you to meet. Wait until he hears about our chase."

With that, he pulled open the door and ushered her in.

The aroma of roasted coffee greeted her. This close to midnight, most everyone had gone home, leaving the café empty except for two men in the corner. The one, a sandy-haired man with a finely clipped beard, sat with his elbows propped on the table, speaking with animation to his companion, who leaned back in his chair, his face obscured in shadow.

Antoine and Nicole entrance drew their attention. They watched as Nicole uncoiled her scarf and smoothed the tangled strands from her hair. Antoine, spying the men, took Nicole's arm and brought her across the room.

"Le Mansec, I see you made it," Antoine said in a warm greeting.

The man called Le Mansec took in the sight of Antoine's basket half filled with posters and a fat brush sticking out. "*Salut,*" he acknowledged. "It seems you've had a busy night."

"Giving the *Guets* something to do besides haul cartloads of prostitutes to the *Salpêtrière*." Antione chuckled and turned. "May I present Nicole Vogel, official gluer and paster, my dear companion without whom I could not complete this rowdy little sport."

With a small laugh Nicole held up her hands, her fingertips dotted with remnants of gray paste. Antoine placed his arm about her shoulders. "Nicole, this is the man I've been telling you about, Bertrand Le Mansec."

Nicole inclined her head. "*Bonsoir, Monsieur* Le Mansec." Perhaps it was the crooked smile half hidden beneath his beard, or the impertinent tilt of his cap, but Antoine's friend struck her as something of a rapscallion.

"Please, it's Bertrand among friends," he replied, doffing his cap as he stood to greet her. "I must say, I'm most delighted to hear of this misbehavior toward the king, especially from someone with such an innocent face."

"Don't forget toward the queen," Nicole added with a smile.

"A shame, Antoine," Bertrand chastised, "to put such lovely hands to sticky work."

Antoine grinned, pulling off his gloves. "I think she likes it. You should have seen her. She gave the *Guet* a good run tonight."

Bertrand indicated the man across the table. "This is my friend, Luc Chatillon. I've been trying to persuade him to join our cause."

Nicole turned her attention to the man now leaning forward from the shadows. He was quite handsome, his face tanned and angular, his wide mouth unsmiling. Evidently, he did not find their pastime amusing.

He rose and gave her a brief nod of acknowledgment. "*Enchante, mademoiselle.*"

"*Bonsoir,*" she replied.

She couldn't look away from the man's inquisitive brown eyes that seemed to stare into her thoughts, while at the same time withholding his own emotions. Flushing unexpectedly, she accepted the chair Antoine pulled out. She found herself seated between him and the unsettlingly attractive man sitting back into the half shadows.

Bertrand motioned for coffee. "Nicole," Antoine said, "everything will change with Bertrand joining our cause. He'll be our resource with news and the latest rumors. We'll be able to do more than paste up cartoons and ditties about the king and queen. We'll have facts and solid information for the newspaper."

"I see," Nicole said, scrutinizing the man. "How is it that you're such a great resource?" Even as she spoke, she could feel the seductive pull coming from Luc Chatillon, like the current she sometimes felt while bathing in the Seine. She'd never experienced such a feeling near a man, much less a stranger.

They were interrupted by the café owner, a balding man with a huge mustache. Nicole admired the way he wiped the table clean, fastidiously arranged her cup and filled it with steaming coffee then did the same for Antoine. Finishing with a prideful nod, the owner flung his towel over his shoulder and withdrew.

Taking a sip of dark, steamy coffee, she peered above the rim of her cup to watch the man disappear into the back room. It was good that Antoine insisted they come in. This was what she needed. Warmth and coffee, and the comfort of others.

"Bertrand has access to Versailles," Antoine said with a sense of personal pride.

Nicole set down her cup with a clink. "You can't be serious," she exclaimed. "However, are you connected to Court?"

Bertrand shrugged. "I have my avenues."

Curious, she glanced toward the man to her left, noting with interest his fine coat. He obviously came from wealth. Perhaps that was why he was ignoring them, tracing a woodgrain pattern on the table with the end of a spoon, his thoughts were clearly on something other than their conversation. She realized that as breathtaking as his face was, he was one of those men with little interest in his physical attractiveness, or in being in the middle of a debate. He seemed centered in his own thoughts. Something prompted her to draw him into the conversation. "What about you, *Monsieur* Chatillon, do you also associate with the nobility?"

Monsieur Chatillon looked up from his invisible pattern on the table. "Only if I can't help it." He smiled good-naturedly and Nicole realized he had been listening all this time. For some reason, she wanted to tuck a dark lock of hair that had fallen across his forehead behind his ear. Startled at such an impulse, she grabbed her cup and took a sip.

"Luc here might have something of interest to say," Bertrand baited. "He's returned from America only a short time ago. It seems he was quite taken with their freedom experiment."

That bit of information caused Nicole to sit back and openly study the man. "America?" she asked "How wonderful. What was it like? Is it true that everything and everyone is in chaos? Are there savages? Is it wild?"

He cleared his throat. "In truth, while there I saw only order. I visited one of the large cities, Boston. Besides enjoying the beauty of the harbor and the countryside, I found a true sense of fraternity among the townspeople. If poverty existed, I never witnessed it beyond the simple broadcloth coats and plain wooden houses. There were no gilded carriages with wigged footmen and plumed horses better fed than the children they passed on the streets. It was, to my eyes, the way men should live."

Everyone sat clearly enthralled by his description.

Abruptly breaking the mood, Bertrand scraped back his chair and rose. "What say, there's an old friend just arrived," he said. "I'll wager I can get a cigar from him. Pardon me."

Thinking about Luc Chatillon's words, Nicole grew somber. The romp through the streets pasting up posters now seemed childish and petty in light of the American struggle. How could the people of France ever unite in such a brotherhood? How could they convince an eight-hundred-year-old monarchy to change? The impossibility of it fell gloomily upon the three of them as outside the clock chimed midnight.

With a sigh, Antoine scooted back his chair. "Nicole, it's time. We must be on our way."

"Yes," she agreed. "Gus will be worried."

"Gus?" Luc asked.

Nicole was surprised by his interest. "The milliner, Gustave Baston."

"Nicole is his apprentice." Antoine gathered the basket from the floor. "Let's hurry before we're stopped for curfew. We've already had one near miss tonight. Let's not chance another. Especially carrying this treasonous evidence."

Nicole rose and pulled the basket from him. "Let me," she said, hiding it beneath her cloak.

Bertrand rejoined the group, puffing on a cheroot, a contented grin on his face. "Ah, leaving so soon? The night feels young."

"Old enough for us," Antoine said, drawing his scarf about this neck. "Thank you, Chatillon for an idea of a better way of living."

"We can't forget Americans sacrificed much for their freedoms," Luc said.

"Yes, this is all our duty," Antoine added gravely, then acknowledged Bertrand. "Le Mansec, I trust you'll join us next week."

"I've every intention of doing so," Bertrand replied.

Luc rose to stand a full head taller than both Antoine and Bertrand. His broad shoulders exhibited the fine cut of his coat, not the vibrant gold brocades of the nobility with sumptuous embroidery and expensive lace, but dark wool, with deep cuffs and brass buttons. Nicole liked the simplicity, and was unable to take her eyes from him.

"And you, Chatillon," Antoine said. "I'd like to hear more about your visit to a country that has no king."

"I would enjoy doing that." Luc glanced at Nicole, his eyes flicking to the basket ill-concealed under a thick bulge in her cloak. "On the condition *mademoiselle* allow me to relieve her of these posters. I'll be out of Paris in a few days. I can distribute them through the villages. Consider it my contribution to the Cause. I can give a report at your meeting next week."

Nicole hesitated, blushed, then looked to Antoine for direction. The request seemed to throw him off guard for an instant before he gave a curt nod. "Of course," he muttered.

Nicole pulled the basket from beneath her cloak. Luc drew close. "*Mademoiselle*. If you'll allow me." He held out his hand.

Unable to look into his eyes, Nicole handed over the basket, warm from her body, and filled with enough evidence to send its bearer to the Bastille.

Chapter Two

One of the endearing traits about Aimée Guerin was that despite her misshapen foot and her belly robust with child, she possessed a rare grace. Trailing a long black ribbon in one hand and a fluttering pink ostrich plume in the other, she wafted around the cramped millinery shop with the buoyancy of a fairy through a forest. "Will you be using these?" she asked, maneuvering through the maze of chairs, past shelves filled with dust-covered hatboxes, some tipped over without lids, until she glided to a stop before Nicole, who stood at a pine table working on a hat.

"Perhaps," Nicole said, her eyes focused on her task, her mind absorbed in an inward debate. She felt some apprehension. Would anyone like her hats? Her designs were so different from Gus's *grand partour* bonnets with their gay ornamentation.

Day in and day out she sewed frippery and flounces onto his worn-out creations without complaint. After all, her apprenticeship to Gustave Baston was a blessing. She wanted to help him in any way she could. Surely, though, that didn't mean spending her life making copies of old-fashioned bonnets like those worn in court for decades. Especially not now, after meeting Luc Chatillon at the café. Since then, she'd awakened early every morning, seized with the urge to design something new. A *chapeau*, a modern hat. And not just any hat, but one that *meant* something. Hats had become a way of speaking about society, about the state of the world and events of the day. And for some reason, Luc Chatillon's words about America had inspired her to do precisely that.

"I think this pink and black are striking together," Aimée declared.

"*Mm*," Nicole murmured, turning the half-stitched hat about to see it at all angles.

Aimée leaned on the table, trying to capture Nicole's eyes. "*Ma chére amiee,* wherever are your thoughts today?"

Nicole pulled a stitch and snipped the thread. "Look. It's almost finished." She held up a wide-brimmed, small-crowned creation made from scraps of the finest blue wool gathered from the refuse bag. Fussing with the scalloped organdy that circled the edges in a sheer cloud, she offered it up for opinion. "What do you think?"

"It's beautiful," Aimée gushed, her face filled with wonder. "I've never seen one like it. It is not a bonnet. But a bit like a man's hat, no?"

"It is, but different. Just wait." Browsing the shelves, Nicole plucked two elegant silk flowers off enormous bouquets protruding from Gus's bonnets. Under Aimée's gaze, she delicately placed them on the blue hat.

"How pretty." Aimée bent down to look closer.

"I can't forget this." From her pocket, Nicole pulled forth a fragile quail feather. "It's from a bonnet I found crushed in a box in the back room. Surprisingly, it survived."

Fascinated, Aimée watched as Nicole gingerly placed the feather amidst the flowers, and with a touch of glue, floated it above the blossoms as if untethered.

"Do you like it?"

"I love it. But what will Gustave say, you making hats like this in his shop?"

Nicole fussed with the hat. She'd worried about that. She would never hurt these people who meant so much to her. "I'm sure he won't mind."

"How could he?" Aimée asked. "Never have I seen a prettier hat. You can name it Beauty Hill. Or Sunrise Over the Meadow."

Nicole smiled. "It already has a name. It's called 'Boston.'"

"Bos-tone? What is that?" Aimée fluttered the ostrich feather against her cheek.

"A city in America. A place of brotherhood and *égalité*."

A puzzled look crossed Aimée's face. "Who names a hat for a city?"

"Oh, it's the latest thing. Truly."

"An American city? Why?"

Nicole stared at the hat. A simple question. The answer was anything but. She'd wondered if she should even say anything about Luc Chatillon. Had she ever kept anything from Aimée? Why did she feel so nervous?

"Nicole? Why do you name your hat for a city in America?"

Nicole gave a small laugh. "Come, join me. I want to tell you about someone I met."

Aimée said nothing as they crossed to a well-worn settee jammed in the corner of the room. "What is it, Nicole?" she asked with an expectant smile. "I can tell there is something. I know you better than anyone."

It was true. They had been best friends since Aimée's first night in the orphanage. Shortly after Nicole found an apprenticeship at Baston Millinery, Aimée had married Jacques Guerin, a cabinetmaker, and moved to his apartment, located close enough so they could visit. Hardly a day went by that they didn't see one another.

Nicole took a moment, unsure where to start. How could she tell her dearest friend, whom she told everything, about this man? She didn't even know why she felt uneasy. Ever since that night at the café, something fluttered in her stomach whenever she thought of Luc Chatillon. It seemed impossible to explain why she found him fascinating. Different.

With some apprehension, she decided to start on safe ground, telling her about their narrow escape from the *Guet*.

"This is terrible," Aimée cried, her hands cupping her swollen belly, her tiny feet dangling inches from the floor. "How could Antoine put you in such danger?"

"We are safe, don't worry," Nicole insisted, not sure she believed her own words. "What we do is important. Our country must change. Don't you feel it? It's our duty to make a better world for us and your child."

Aimée eyed the blush on Nicole's cheek. "Ah, this is about France then? Then why do I sense this isn't what you really wish to tell me?"

Nicole had to think. What precisely did she want to say about Luc Chatillon? Where should she begin? "There is something else that happened that night…when Antoine and I went to *La Fenêtre*."

Aimée's pretty white eyebrows lifted wistfully. "Oh, you and the cafés. Perhaps one day Jacques will allow me to go inside to see what they're like." She shrugged. "But I interrupt. Please tell me what's so important."

"I met a man." Nicole squirmed awkwardly, suddenly at a loss. What could she say about Luc? How could she explain? But then, remembering him—that smile, those deep brown eyes—her body softened. His words still rang in her ears. She could still smell his musky scent, the memory bringing a rush of warmth and excitement. "His name is Luc Chatillon. He was kind and...and wonderful." She reached out for Aimée's hand. "Oh, Aimée, when he spoke of America and justice he became so impassioned. I've never heard ideas like his."

Aimée withdrew her hand and crossed her arms. "I see. This man, is he handsome?"

Nicole remembered Luc standing tall in that fine coat, his relaxed demeanor as he said *enchante, mademoiselle*. Perhaps the most handsome man she'd ever seen. "Well, he is. He's strong and tall." Seeing the knowing look on Aimée's face, she stiffened and sat taller. "Oh, but there's so much more to him. He's well-mannered. And—" She stopped. "I don't know. There was something else. I can't explain it, Aimée. Simply sitting across from him, listening to him speak, made me feel alive, somehow."

The shaggy plume dropped from Aimée's fingers into her lap. "Antoine? Was he not there?"

"Aimée," Nicole entreated. "You know I care for Antoine. Deeply. But I don't love him, not in that way. I try, I pray to, but the mere sight of this man, this Luc Chatillon—" She stopped short, not sure how to go on. Her thoughts and feelings were jumbled, her skin growing prickly with a vague excitement. "If only you could have seen and heard him." She looked away from Aimée's intent stare. "I know you'd understand if you met him."

Aimée didn't respond, only jiggled her little booted foot and waited for more.

"Maybe it's a fantasy, but I believe he was interested in my thoughts. My questions. He listened so intently and answered with clarity and truthfulness." Nicole half laughed. "I actually felt he respected me. Do you think it possible? A man like him? He suggested as much, the way he looked into my eyes as if his words were only for me, saying he's coming next week to the café."

Aimée frowned. "That's quite bold, don't you think? Especially with Antoine there. Surely he knew you were together."

"Luc Chatillon *is* a bold man. Yet gentle, too. He has a quiet power. He captured *everyone* in the way he talked with such strength and passion about that American city, Boston."

"Boston?" Aimée nodded that she now understood about the hat. "This man who's all of these things, you've met him only this once? Perhaps for a few moments? Maybe you are still thinking of him, but do you know for sure he's unmarried?"

Nicole flushed. It had never occurred to her. "Married? Of course, he's not."

"Maybe betrothed to another?" Aimée pursued. "Do you know this for sure?"

"Aimée, please be happy for me," Nicole implored. "You have your love. Your passion. I'm happy you have it. Can't you wish a bit of happiness for me?"

"Of course, I want that for you, and more," Aimée demurred. "But what about Antoine? You know him. He loves you. He's a good man. If you are feeling something for another man, remember, it is nothing but a moment in time, not the lifetime of security and love Antoine can give you."

"Aimée, I honestly don't know why I don't love Antoine that way. The heart is not the head." She clasped Aimée's hands. "Don't you see I must follow my heart? I can't explain what's happening. I feel alive. Look, I've begun making my own hats. Please, wish me the best."

"You know I do," Aimée said, touching Nicole's cheek. "I wish you will marry the man of your dreams and—" The ostrich plume in her lap tremored. "Oh," Aimée exclaimed, looking up with surprise. "The baby wishes it too." She pulled Nicole's hands to her pregnant belly. "Can you feel it?" Nicole's lips parted in awe as she felt new life move.

At that moment, the shop door flew open, ushering in a gust of wind, along with a man in a tattered shawl, his woolen cap pulled over his ears. Gustave Baston slammed the door shut with such force it rattled the windows. He jerked off his cap to reveal a head of white hair thick as sheep's fur, with a bushy mustache and eyebrows to match. "A messenger," he shouted, holding up a large white card.

"Gus, what's happening?" Sarah Baston's voice rang out from the upstairs kitchen.

"Sarah, come here. Hurry."

Her heavy steps lumbered down the stairs, immediately followed by the silent descent of Midas, a long-haired ginger cat holding his magnificent tail aloft.

"What is it, Gus?"

He held up a card. "A livery boy was roaming about, looking for our shop." Gus turned to Nicole. "He brought a card for you, Nicolette."

"It's for our Nicole?" Sarah said, inspecting the thick card. "Why, it is. Look at this." She held it up. "*To Mademoiselle Nicole Vogel.*"

For one wild moment Nicole imagined she was being recalled to Legros, the orphanage. Her heart slowed with dread so that she could scarcely breathe as Sarah brought the card to her.

"What a beautiful hand, too," Sarah marveled. "Written by a lady, to be sure."

Nicole took the card bordered in a band of silver.

Madame Chatillon requests a viewing of sample chapeaux designed by Mademoiselle Nicole Vogel at three o'clock this afternoon at the Chatillon estate.46 Rue de Vangonne

She had to read it a second time to fully comprehend what seemed impossible to believe, and when she finally did, she was stunned. Luc Chatillon's mother wanted to see her hats? Luc must have arranged a showing. How had he found Gus's shop? She had to sit. It was too wonderful to be true. Luc Chatillon wanted her to come to his home. To meet his mother.

"Nicole, don't keep us in suspense," Aimée said. "What does it say?"

Nicole came to herself. "Oh, it's—" She held up the card. "Well, listen." She read aloud to the group, all of it, including the address at the end. Her fingers tingled. She was thrilled and terrified, both in equal measure, at the thought of seeing Luc Chatillon again, and of presenting her hats to a woman who could change their lives.

"A showing," Gus repeated. "How could we do it?" He plopped into his chair.

"And to a grand lady," Sarah marveled with a dreamy smile, her face reflecting her vision of a kitchen with pastries and cream, and abundant firewood for the stove.

Aimée came and took the card to read it. "Chatillon. Why, that's—"

"An acquaintance of Antoine," Nicole interrupted, giving her a signal with narrowing eyes. "It's an incredible opportunity, Aimée."

"You want this, Nicole?" Aimée murmured, handing the card back.

"Yes. Very much."

Gus pulled his pipe from his pocket. "There's much to consider here, Nicolette. How can we do such a thing? We have nothing for such patrons."

Aimée squeezed Nicole's shoulder reassuringly. "Ah, but you do," she said, limping to the worktable. "This one, you must." She lifted "Boston" up for their inspection.

Puzzled, Gus came to take a closer look. He held the hat at all angles, peering at it with curiosity. "Where did you get this?"

Seeing the look on his face, Nicole realized for the first time how her dreams in many ways were a rebuke of his passing world, his antiquated ideas. Her designs looked nothing like those produced in the Baston Millinery, bonnets that were little more than pieces of fabric pinned to the top of wigs tall as ship masts, and decorated with fat ribbons and colossal silk bows and strings and beads. Today's styles reflected a new customer. The common, ordinary woman. In newspapers Nicole had seen drawings of these latest *chapeaux*, sleek and modern, made to cover real hair, not perch atop an aristocratic wig.

"It's something I've been working on," she said as Gus stared at the hat with an unreadable expression. "But it's not finished."

"How can you say that?" admonished Sarah, brushing Gus aside to take the hat from him. "Look at how pretty it is. And so different." Her inspection progressed from curious to outright confidence in her judgment. "Do you have any others like these?"

Nicole looked about the shelves of bonnets she'd been working on for Gus these past weeks, her gaze landing on one of her own hats she'd finished several months before.

"There is one."

"Then let's see it," exclaimed Sarah.

Pulling it from the shelf, Nicole didn't know whether to feel guilty that she had made another hat in secret, or thankful she had one to bring today.

"It's lovely," gasped Sarah. "What a talent you are, my dear. Isn't she, Gus?" Nicole turned to Gus, who was gazing at yet a second hat from his shop that he'd not noticed before.

"Where did you say you met this woman?" asked Gus.

"I... I met her son. He's a friend of Antoine's." She didn't want to lie to Gus, but how could she say anything? Seeing Aimée wince, she felt a twinge of guilt and looked to her friend for understanding. But all she got was Aimée's roll of the eyes.

Gus took a thoughtful puff from his pipe. "Sarah, take the girls up for some tea. I'll stay here and box up the hats."

Aimée took Nicole by the elbow and whispered into her ear, "We must talk."

"Shhh. Not now," Nicole murmured. As they climbed the stairs, she looked over her shoulder at Gus studying the hats.

"Gus, be sure to tie down the lids with our best ribbons," instructed Sarah as she lumbered up before them. "It will be like opening a box of the finest chocolates. *Madame* Chatillon will not be able to resist."

***

Alone in the workroom, Gus puffed on his pipe, studying two most interesting hats. They certainly were unusual. And he had to admit they were well made. But he hadn't been in the business this long not to see the need for some changes. Setting the pipe aside, he pulled on his well-worn leather apron, tied it around his full-sleeved white shirt, and began gathering together boxes of notions. He knew what must be done. Nicolette had fashioned interesting shapes. But in her naiveté and inexperience, she'd neglected important elements of shimmer and loftiness. He must spend more time with the dear girl to help with her with these refinements. He knew what sold hats.

On the settee lay a pink ostrich plume. Yes. A perfect start. Midas lunged upon the worktable as Gus set about enhancing the curious hats, ornamenting them, certain Nicolette would be pleased when she opened the boxes.

Chapter Three

Nicole stood before her dressing bureau staring at herself in the small, blackened mirror hanging on the wall. She wanted Luc Chatillon to see her at her best today. But viewing the murky reflection, she felt disheartened. Perched on her head was Sarah's taffeta bonnet, covered in tattered silk flowers, with strings of beads dangling about her face. In the mirror she could see Aimée watching from the bed with a dubious expression.

"I can't wear this," Nicole sighed.

Aimée shrugged. "It's not so terrible."

"Oh Aimée, here I am, finally showing my hats, and not one of my own." She jerked free the ribbon tied in a big drooping bow under her chin. "It was sweet of Sarah to lend it to me. But how can I deliver a hat to a real lady wearing this? It would ruin everything. And I won't wear my yellowing linen cap. I'd rather go bareheaded."

Aimée came behind her and made adjustments as best she could. "I don't understand why you've not made yourself a hat."

Nicole watched her efforts in the tiny cracked mirror. But no matter how Aimée tried, the bonnet sagged upon her head like a lifeless, overgrown bird. "I would love to. But fabrics are expensive. I've only got Gus's scraps to work with for hats that must be sold. Perhaps if I sell some, I can."

"I see. The cobbler has no shoes. The hatmaker no hat?" Aimée smiled and removed the bonnet. "But look at yourself," she said, pulling aside Nicole's wheat-blond hair so that her large green eyes and angled cheeks reflected back. "*Bien sur*. Such a face. You do not need to cover up."

Nicole gazed at her cloudy reflection. She'd always been told she was pretty. But staring at the woman in the mirror, she saw only the lack of a hat.

"Aimée, if I learned anything at Legros, it's that looks aren't enough. You've got your Jacques. But a woman alone needs her own income. Her own security. Otherwise we're at the mercy of the world."

"And you believe this *Madame* Chatillon can promise you such security? This mother of your handsome man? This rich man, who speaks of America and Boston and so much adventure? Remember, *ma mie*, you don't know him. Or these people. You mustn't expect too much. The wealthy are different than us commoners."

Nicole turned to her with a gentle smile. "There's nothing common about you, my darling Aimée." She traced a finger along Aimée's cherubic face. "You are the most wonderful, extraordinary person I know."

Aimée shrugged. "Eh, *bien*. I think we both are." Her eyes twinkled. "But you're right, Nicole. You can't wear *Madame* Baston's ugly bonnet. It looks like a ruffled-up hen ready to lay an egg." They burst out laughing. "Stop at my apartment on your way to this great *Madame* Chatillon. You can wear my shepherdess hat."

Nicole gave a quizzical look. "I've not seen it."

"Jacques took it as payment for a chest he made for a sheep farmer."

She thought on it. Would a sheep herder's hat be suitable? "I'm not sure. What's it like?"

"It's like the song. You know, *Have you seen my little girl? She doesn't wear a bonnet, She's got a monstrous flip-flop hat with cherry ribbons on it.*"

They laughed again. "You never could sing, Aimée."

"Maybe not, but you must see my shepherdess hat."

"Does it have cherry ribbons?"

"You'll simply have to wait and see."

Arm in arm, they merrily made their way downstairs to the waiting hatboxes.

***

The white January sun offered a hint of warmth, though not enough to keep a young woman wearing a thin cloak from shivering. Unable to afford even the oldest, smelliest of public coaches, Nicole made her way along the narrow avenues of her neighborhood where the streets were cobbled up to the doorsteps, without walkways, so that she dodged carts and horseback riders. Wearing Aimée's wide-brimmed hat, which indeed was topped with cherry ribbons, she wound through a maze of passageways and boulevards all leading in a web-like circle that met at the Seine.

All around the city, clocks sounded each hour on the hour, and now, when Nicole heard the chimes strike two, she quickened her pace. She must not be late. She had to go all the way to the outer precincts to reach Faubourg Saint-Antoine, a place she'd never been. She chastised herself for starting so late and, feeling the pressure of time, quickened her pace.

She knew she had to be close when she found herself walking along rows of immaculate cobbled streets winding through expansive, parklike parcels of land teeming with trees and dotted with ponds. So, this was where the bourgeoisie lived.

Setting down the hatboxes, she took *Madame* Chatillon's note from her pocket. *Rue de Vangonne*. Gus had told her it was near the cathedral. She looked about. Shaking out her numb fingers, she took up the boxes and headed toward the cathedral spires.

The Chatillon mansion stood behind an iron fence in the middle of a field. Two bubbling fountains framed the entrance, and stables spread around back. The iron-gray limestone chateau rose three stories, its façade broken by tall windows on each floor and a steep roof of slate topped with eight-pointed iron Huguenot crosses. It was grander than she'd imagined.

Nicole had always associated large buildings with the institution of Legros, and even now she experienced a moment of dread. Could she really bring herself to march into this majestic estate? She was suddenly afraid. But only for a moment. Taking a deep breath, she lifted her head and walked through the open gates, gates wide enough to allow carriages to enter. Should she go to the servants' entrance? She wasn't sure. She'd received an invitation. She might make a fool of herself, even embarrass Luc, if she arrived at the back.

At the main door, she thudded the knocker. If she had thoughts, they fled as quickly as they came. She imagined Luc answering. No, there would be servants. After a moment, the door was opened by a porter dwarfed in a cavernous foyer. He wore pea green livery, his skinny legs encased in immaculate white stockings, his exquisite coat cuffs shimmering with silver brocade.

The man shrewdly eyed her thin cloak, then her straw hat. He sniffed with distaste. "Yes?"

"I am Nicole Vogel, assistant to Gustave Baston, milliner. *Madame* Chatillon has requested a showing of hats from our establishment." She set down the hatboxes and searched in her pocket, finally pulling out the invitation.

Giving the card a cursory glance, he seemed unimpressed. "I shall ask if *madame* will see you." He paused with authority. "Though you must go around to the back, to the domestic entrance. Knock and someone will usher you in."

The clock in a small antechamber at the rear of the chateau struck three when Nicole took a chair by the wall. The hands had moved close to four before a different servant, wearing the same green livery, appeared and, taking the hatboxes, ordered Nicole to follow along. Walking behind him, up a back staircase, Nicole grew more and more unsure. Where was Luc? He must not have been told of her arrival. Why else would she sit for an hour? Had she misunderstood the note? Following the servant, hatboxes dangling at his sides, she stared ahead at the corridor that seemed to stretch forever before them. No, she reasoned. It couldn't be a mistake. Luc had arranged the showing. She was sure the note said three. He *must* be with his mother right now, wanting to make a proper introduction. Maybe they'd been called to something important.

The porter stopped before a closed door and, turning to her, addressed a point over the top of her head. "*Madame* has only a moment for you." He tapped at the door. Nicole could not take her eyes off the spot he'd knocked. How could she do this? But there was no turning back now.

"*Entre.*"

The servant pushed the door open and stepped aside. At once Nicole saw that Luc was not in the room. There were two women, a middle-aged lady of refinement seated on a sofa and a younger woman standing by the window, her abundant ebony hair piled high in curls and twists.

As Nicole entered, her senses were bombarded with the sights and scents of a lady's salon. Pale gray watered silk covered the walls. Miniatures and tiny clocks were perched on the tables, along with bottles of perfume and vases of flowers. As she drew closer to the women, the older lady turned in greeting. She looked exquisite in a lavender *robe à la lévite* that loosely floated to the floor. Her eyes rested on Nicole's wide-brimmed straw hat.

"Ah, the milliner's girl," she said. "I am *Madame* Chatillon. This is *Mademoiselle* Georgette Fontenay."

Nicole curtsied. "*Madame*, I am most honored."

"Morane, do bring the hats," called *Madame* Chatillon. As the servant set the hatboxes on a large table in the middle of the room, Nicole searched the side doors in anticipation, thinking that any moment Luc would open the door and join them. And who was this fetching lady, *Mademoiselle* Fontenay? A family friend? A cousin? The woman was wrapped in a mink neck scarf, despite the warmth of the fire. Nicole felt an odd chill as the woman raised a darkly penciled eyebrow at her .

Madame Chatillon motioned for Nicole to draw closer. "Let me say I was most surprised that my son brought your establishment to my attention. I have never found Luc to be interested in fashion, particularly my own, so I could only imagine *you* are the interest he is advancing." She picked up her teacup, which was nestled in a tiny saucer, and took a sip.

Listening with a polite smile, Nicole saw from the corner of her eye the dark-haired *Mademoiselle* Fontenay was approaching the hatboxes on the table.

"But hearing the name Gustave Baston brought back an old memory," *Madame* Chatillon went on. "I mentioned *Monsieur* Baston to the great *Madame* Duffand, and she remembered the man from years past and wondered whatever had happened to him."

Nicole watched as *Mademoiselle* Fontenay stood at the table, unfurling Gus's neatly tied black ribbon. The woman lifted the lid and stared inside.

Madame Chatillon took another sip of tea. "Yes, as I recall, Gustave Baston had a reputation as milliner for the court of the old king. He was once on his way to becoming one of the great milliners of Paris." She set the cup and saucer on the table beside her and smiled at Nicole. "It took some time to find you, *Mademoiselle* Vogel."

Nicole's attention flew to *Madame* Chatillon. Her? *She* had found Gus's shop? Not her son Luc?

Madame Chatillon folded her hands expectantly onto her lap. "I have such great hopes to make a find, you know, have my friends pounding at my door for the milliner's name."

A high-pitched half laugh sounded from across the room, drawing a gasp from *Madame* Chatillon. Alarmed, Nicole turned to see that the dark-haired woman had opened the second hatbox and was looking at its contents.

"*Madame*," Georgette said with amusement. "I am afraid this girl has not come from our sort of establishment. These hats are not satisfactory."

Nicole struggled to keep her expression solicitous. Whatever was the woman saying? The hats were perfection. "Is something wrong?" she asked, coming to see for herself.

"I'm not sure you would understand how wrong," Georgette said, replacing the lid with a wrinkle of her nose.

"But I must see them," *Madame* Chatillon insisted, waving for them to be brought to her. "Dear girl. Show me."

A small smile crossed Georgette's lips as she sank onto a settee and lifted her satin slippers to a footstool. "Why not, then? Show *Madame* Chatillon what you have to offer." She narrowed her eyes at Nicole.

Nicole took a moment to lift the lid. When it came off, her heart sank. She pulled out what had been her beautiful hat, Boston. Gus had ruined it. He'd wrapped it in cheap netting with multicolored flowers stuck onto the brim and smothered it in feathers, too small, too many. It was all wrong. She flung it back into its box and pulled open the second. She could only stare. There, sprouting out of the hatband, was a wispy pink fluff. The ostrich feather. Her eyes closed.

Georgette's lips curled. "*Madame*, if you wear those...things your friends will not stop talking, but behind your back, I'm afraid."

"A moment, please," Nicole heard herself say. "I'd like to show you something, *madame*." Her tone was conciliatory, but firm, and addressed as much to the dark-haired woman as *Madame* Chatillon.

"Not another hat." Georgette laughed.

From somewhere—somewhere deep—came a resolve, so that Nicole began to remove the notions. Her fingers were nimble and sure. As the assorted notions came flying off, her beloved creation Boston began to re-emerge.

"See, look at these lines, *Madame*," she said. "Please, allow me to try it on you. Once you see the shape of the hat..." Nicole helped *Madame* Chatillon rise to her feet, and placed the hat on her coiffed hair, repositioned it, fastened it with pins, then stepped back. "There. Take a look," she said.

Madame Chatillon stepped before a gilded mirror hanging over the fireplace and stared at herself.

"You will have the most outstanding chapeau in Paris," Nicole said. "Don't you agree?"

"Hmmm. It *is* different like this," *Madame* Chatillon mused, turning her head back and forth to admire herself. "I've never seen a chapeau quite like it."

Nicole watched her closely, looking from the mirror image to the woman herself. How could she not find the hat striking, with that exquisite brim framing her face in a most attractive way?

Georgette's smile faded. "*Madame*," she insisted. "You *cannot* wear that. It looks like a man's hat. It is simply not right. For refinement, you must go to eminent names, not these street corner hatters."

"Please, if you'll wait." Nicole tilted the brim so that it dipped charmingly over *Madame* Chatillon's right eye. "There. Look now. See how it reveals the curve of your lovely face, *madame*?"

"Why, yes. I see. Truly, Georgette, don't you think this is lovely?"

"No, I do not. I think these hats are peculiar. Everyone will think so. This milliner girl has made a mess and taken your time." Georgette approached and unceremoniously removed the hat.

As she did, *Madame* Chatillon murmured to Nicole. "You should go. How unfortunate for you, *mademoiselle*. The hats are simply not right for us. After all, they are for Georgette's wedding, and the bride should be happy."

Nicole sank to the carpet on her knees and stuffed her hats into the boxes. What a mean, hateful lady, this Georgette Fontenay. She was getting married? What unlucky man would have to live with such a horrid woman? Gathering up the ribbons and notions and feathers from the floor, she stuffed them inside. Her ears were ringing. She felt she might stumble as she came before the settee, and with a half curtsy managed an almost inaudible *merci* and slipped out the door.

She walked along the corridor in a daze. She wanted out of this place. Ahead, a staircase cascaded downward like a graceful shell. The main one. The one she should have been escorted up by Luc Chatillon. But he didn't even know she was here. What a fool she'd been.

And then, halfway to the bottom, her foot hesitated on the step. Someone stood below. She almost dropped the hats.

It was Luc.

Chapter Four

Luc was completely caught off guard. Here in his home stood the stunning revolutionary beauty from the café carrying a hatbox in each hand. It took an instant to pull his thoughts together to connect the chain of events that could have brought her here. His passing comment to his mother about the talented hatmaker from Baston Millinery, followed closely by the realization that somehow his mother had taken matters into her own hands and found the young woman.

Nicole was her name. He'd forgotten the last, then it came. *Vogel. Yes.*

And now she stood before him in his home. What a stunning creature she was, with incredible eyes—pale green—and luscious full lips.

"*Mademoiselle* Vogel?"

Clearly she was angry. She gripped the hatboxes she carried and, without a word, brushed past him. Luc reached out and caught her wrist.

"Wait."

"Let me go." Her words came out like a command.

Surprised at her tone, Luc released his hold. "Tell me, what has happened?"

Nicole cast him an accusative glare. "*Madame* Chatillon requested a showing of hats. I thought *you'd* invited me. I was mistaken. Now please, I want to leave this place."

Luc looked beyond her, up to the corridor where Georgette had smugly disappeared this morning *"to plan our wedding"* as she'd flippantly announced when passing him on the steps. She'd had no idea he'd written to her father this morning. A letter that would change everything. Though he'd already told Georgette his intentions, he should have guessed she would fight him.

"Georgette," he muttered. "What did the lady say to you?"

"The *lady* told me to leave," Nicole replied in a cold tone. "If you'll step aside, I plan to do just that."

"I don't blame you for wanting out of this household," he said, his eyes again searching the upper echelons of the stairway for any sign of Georgette. Though, in most cases one would hear her before seeing her. "Here, please, let me help."

He gently took Nicole's arm, ignoring her flinch, and escorted her with her two hatboxes down to the bottom of the stairway. "I truly am sorry," he said. "Let me make amends. Allow me to carry your hats to my cabriolet and take you home."

Despite his gentle appeal, Nicole pulled away. "I don't need your help."

Luc could feel her anger as she brushed past him and hurried across the foyer. He raised his eyebrows. This was more serious than he'd thought. Something unpleasant had happened. Georgette must have been on the attack. *Merde.* Lately he'd been picking up the pieces of Georgette's tantrums and schemes.

Quickly at Nicole's side, Luc assessed her lovely face, framed by a wide-brimmed hat, but she ignored him in her determination to reach the door. He kept in step, admiring her profile as she stared ahead. She was as stunning as that night he'd been captivated by her in the café, the way she'd smiled sweetly at the server; how she savored the coffee, her lips lingering on the cup. *Mon Dieu.* It had been the most sensual thing he'd ever seen. He'd scarcely been able to keep from gawking at her. When she'd sat beside him, he'd had to stare at the damned table to keep from making a fool of himself. And now in the light of day, he realized she was strong and able to carry herself with dignity, even after an attack from Georgette.

"Will you please open the door? My hands are full."

He obliged, then rushed after her as she took off down the front steps. "I did mention you to my mother, *Mademoiselle* Vogel," Luc explained. "I meant no harm. I blame myself for any injustice you've received here. Say you'll forgive me. Allow me to escort you home."

Nicole stopped. "That's kind of you, but I can find my own way."

"I must insist. It's the least I can do."

"I can walk home," she insisted.

Before she could protest, Luc grabbed the hatboxes and strode across the driveway. "There's a cabriolet right here."

"What are you doing?"

"You can't possibly carry these boxes all the way. It's cold and getting dark. You must allow me to make amends for my family by driving you back."

She stopped and stared at the cabriolet. He could see she was thinking.

***

As the cabriolet sped along the street, Nicole arranged the hatboxes at her feet, feeling both angry and disappointed as she tried to retie the bows like Gus had done so skillfully. It took a few moments before she noticed Luc was watching her. She did not look away but held his gaze. He reached over and pulled a lap fur across her knees.

"Are you cold?" he asked. "I can stop and raise the top."

"No," she replied, perhaps too sharply. After all, he was being polite. "I'm fine," she added more softly. As he looked ahead at the roadway, she chanced glances at him. He seemed sincere in his apology. His appeal was undeniable, though no sooner had that thought come to her than Aimée's words rang in her ears, *Remember, the wealthy are different than commoners.* Aimée was right. She would not subject herself to any of them.

She stared out at the passing streets, well aware that Luc's shoulder touched hers in the closeness of the carriage. Odd, she thought. His touch felt warm, but not welcoming. She could feel his privilege all the way through the expensive fabric of his finely tailored jacket. She took a deep breath, looked around. Here she sat in a beautiful, fast-moving cabriolet pulled by a plumed, high-stepping horse. She'd often imagined herself riding in such a cab, wondering how such speed would feel. Now she knew. It wasn't what she'd imagined. The ride was jarring and bumpy and windy, so much so she had to keep her hand on Aimée's hat to keep it from blowing away.

This morning she'd allowed herself to dream. To hope. Now she felt hollow, without direction. She closed her eyes. She'd believed she could actually walk into a household like the Chatillon mansion, wearing Aimée's shepherdess's hat, and turn the Paris fashion world on its heels. She rubbed her eyes with her forefingers. What a fool.

The cabriolet passed a bonfire burning in one of the many wire cages built for the hordes of peasants that roamed Paris at twilight. Their eerie forms huddling close for warmth looked like phantoms. Nicole shuddered, overwhelmed by the contrast of this destitution against the sumptuous world she'd left mere minutes ago.

"Is this the right avenue?" Luc asked, bringing her back to the moment.

She glanced about. "Yes," she said. "I'll tell you when to turn."

She thought it odd that soon he would know where and how she lived. The narrow street, littered with manure and broken-down tumbrils. The shop, with its crooked shutters on broken hinges and one missing on the upstairs window. Not that any of it mattered. She'd never see him again. She didn't want to. Everything was ruined.

Growing uncomfortable in the silence, Nicole chanced a glance at him. He stared ahead at the road. In his shadowy profile, she could make out his freshly shaven jaw. Curls of black hair touched his ears. She looked down at her hands, wishing today had been different. It might have been. She was sure *Madame* Chatillon had liked the hat.

"I'd like you to know something," she said, breaking the quiet. "Your mother was quite kind."

Luc gave her what she took to be a grateful smile. "I'm glad of it," he said. "I've always known her to be sympathetic. When I mentioned the millinery to her, and you, I had no idea she'd actually reach out to see your work."

"Why did you tell her about me, then?"

Luc shifted his weight. Nicole thought he looked uncomfortable. Had she asked a personal question? Maybe he wasn't accustomed to explaining his actions. Or sharing his thoughts.

"Perhaps I was bored with my life," he said suddenly. "Maybe I wanted to do something good."

She never would have expected such an answer. It startled her out of her own misery. "Bored? With *your* life? But you have everything. An incredible home. Why, you must have so many wonderful friends, I'm sure. With balls and suppers and servants. Your travels. And your ideas…they could never be boring. You inspired me the other night. And many of the others, I'm sure."

Flicking the reins, Luc urged the horse faster. "The truth is, I wanted to see you again, Nicole."

Taken aback with this confession, Nicole eased against the cushion. A confusing rush of feelings quickened her breath. "But I thought you'd planned to join us next week. I expected to see you then."

"Honestly, Nicole, I hoped to see you alone. Without your friend. You ask my thoughts about why I told my mother about Baston Millinery? I'd hoped she'd express interest, and I'd pick you up with your hats, and bring you to meet her. I don't know. It wasn't thought out. In truth I'd mentioned it to her in passing. I had no idea she'd actually send for you."

Nicole listened, and yet, what could she say? Besides, she was almost home. "There, just ahead," she said. "My street."

Luc steered the cab around the corner. As he slowed the horse, Nicole watched his gaze roam along the ramshackle buildings. "Right there," she said, pointing.

Luc pulled the cabriolet to a halt. The shop was shuttered and dark. He jumped out and ran around to open her door. Taking the hatboxes, he escorted her to the doorstep.

Gus had left out the lock-string for her. She jerked it several times, fumbling to open the heavy latch. A dog barked in the distance. A few drops of rain began to fall in splotches, darkening her cloak.

As her shaking fingers worked with the key, she felt Luc's presence behind her. He came closer and startled her by taking the key lock-string and gently unlatching the bolt. He pushed the door wide, and Nicole slipped inside. Once in the shelter of the hat shop, she turned back. Was that pity on his face? Or kindness and understanding?

"Thank you for your help," she said softly. "What happened was not because of you, Luc. Someday I shall make a name for myself. But I'll do it by myself. And…I only trust a few dear friends."

She tried to close the door, but Luc caught it. "Wait, Nicole. I hope to be a friend. If you'll allow me." A gentle smile spread across his face.

The sincerity in his expectant half-smile filled her with a comfort, a sense that everything could work out. What would it be like to have such a friend? "But how can that be with such differences between us?"

"Differences? I see. So, *Mademoiselle* Vogel," he said, his dark eyes twinkling in humor. "Do you think a parvenue like myself might be pompous? A flaunting braggart who looks down his nose on the less fortunate?" He grinned, lifting his chin in mock arrogance.

Warming to his mirth, she had to laugh. "That will be for you to prove."

He shrugged. "My grandmother taught me not to be haughty." He leaned closer and murmured, "When I was a boy. And that was because she loved me."

They stood on the threshold, him outside and her within.

She tried to imagine him as a boy. At last she said, "Good night, Luc."

He tipped his hat and released the door.

She closed it softly and leaned her weight against the panels. She listened as his steps echoed on the street, and the cabriolet door slammed shut. Finally the horse pranced away. In the silence of the empty downstairs she pulled off her hat.

"Nicole, is that you?" Sarah called from the kitchen upstairs.

"Yes," Nicole said. "I'll be right up."

For a moment longer, she absently ran her fingers along the ribbons streaming down from the hat, savoring the memory of Luc Chatillon's smiling face.

***

That evening, running late, Luc entered the downstairs salon where the family gathered before dinner. He whistled a song he could not have named if asked. Something from his childhood, a happy tune that always came to mind when his mood was high. Like now. Yes, he was happy, purely thinking about—

His whistling came to an abrupt halt. What was this? His mother sat on the sofa, twisting a kerchief in her hands. His father, standing at the fireplace, looked up from the pocket watch in his palm. Luc glanced away from his reprimanding face and took in the rest of the room. What was this? A pirates' parley? On the settee languished Georgette, caressing her fluffy lap poodle with those exceedingly long and bejeweled fingers. Her nervous little first mate of a mother, Helaine Fontenay, perched on the cushion beside her. Leading this expedition, Gilles Fontenay paced the deck. He looked the part of a picaroon, his black wig curled and crimped, a tiny black *mouche* pasted on his rouged cheek, and a scarlet satin jacket flaring around his hips. All he needed was a scabbard. The fortune he'd amassed in manufacturing cloth was as well-known as his reputation for excess in drinking and gambling. Not to mention the rumors that he speculated on risky ventures. Here was the family his father chose for him to marry into.

So, they'd mutinied? What else could he expect from his putting his foot down about the marriage? With a deep breath, he resumed whistling and entered as if coming upon a pleasant soiree. Without a word, his father pulled a letter from his pocket and thrust it out, demanding, "How *dare* you write this?"

Luc didn't have to read the paper being shaken at him to recognize the letter he'd sent to Gilles Fontenay this morning. It had produced a quicker impact than he'd imagined. He should have guessed as much. Georgette must have read it the moment she arrived home and rushed her reinforcements here. He'd need a drink or two to face them.

Luc bent and kissed his mother on each cheek. "What's this?" he murmured into her ear, taking her nervous hands between his as he looked into her eyes.

"Oh Luc. How could you?" she uttered in a heartbroken whisper.

In that moment he realized there was no escape. This would hurt her. He wished he could have avoided that. Squaring his shoulders, he stood to face them. Damn but if Georgette didn't look pleased now that she had him cornered with her father leading the attack.

"I demand an accounting of your letter," Gilles Fontenay bellowed. "You dare insult my daughter? Why, I should take it to a duel. And I would, too, if it wouldn't land me in prison." This last remark drew a frightened gasp from Helaine Fontenay.

Ignoring him, Luc approached his father, took the letter, and gave a cursory glance to the words he'd painstakingly written this morning. Victor Chatillon snatched it back. "It's disgraceful. We'll be the scandal of Paris."

"I doubt that," Luc said, looking over at Georgette. "No one need know any of this. Unless the lady in question wants to make it public."

Georgette twisted her lips in a frown. "Your accusations are a figment of your own imaginings, darling. I've always known you to be jealous of me. But there is no foundation for your suspicions. Do you realize how you'll sully my name if you persist in this folly? How can you hate me so?"

"It's time to step up to manhood," Gilles Fontenay bellowed, drawing up to his full height, a head shorter than Luc. "You have no right to break off this engagement," he protested, vigorously shaking his finger. "If you persist, there will be dire consequences."

Luc had not fully taken in the threat when his father joined in the assault. "And without consulting your family. Can you not see how you've distressed your mother?"

"And my wife," Fontenay added, his flabby cheeks growing as crimson as his jacket.

While they piled on their tirade, Luc crossed to the sideboard and filled a glass with port. Here in this very room were the unhappy marriages he'd been raised to accept as the realities of life. His mother, if she'd admit it to herself, wanted more. His father had long ago lost any belief in love. He shuddered to imagine what marriage looked like in the Fontenay household. Downing his drink in one quick toss, he turned to face them. "Then let's end it now," he said, his words directed at Georgette. "I'm only surprised this has been allowed to go on so long."

It seemed Victor Chatillon's frustration had come to a head. "You will listen to me, Luc. All your life you've been headstrong. It's time to become a man. Your recklessness—first taking off to America like you did, then England—" Luc rubbed the back of his neck, letting his father's rant run its course. "Luc, I've never worried about your reputation with the ladies, but by God, this one is expecting a child. Your child. *My* grandchild. And the young woman has been your fiancée for months. What has gotten into you? Why, our families have done business since before you were born."

"I am not marrying Georgette Fontenay," Luc said in a calm but forceful voice. He addressed Georgette. "And she knows the reason rests with her." Luc paused, letting his words settle with a meaning shared only between the two of them. She knew the truth, and she understood his message.

He turned from her and addressed the group. "You speak of duty? Responsibility? Only duty prompted me to this engagement in the first place. I had no particular desire for marriage, but my family wanted an alliance with the Fontenay fortune."

"Then what has changed?" his mother beseeched. Gabriele rose, her gown falling about her in a rustle of silk as she approached him. "Is it that you've learned Georgette is with child? We will simply rush the wedding date. The banns can be posted at once."

Victor joined them. "But to tell the woman there will be no marriage? Why would you behave in such a manner?"

"Because it is not my child Georgette carries."

Gabriele gasped. Victor's face grew slack. Gilles Fontenay's mouth dropped. His wife put her gloved hand to her lips. They all stared at him, each trying to digest what Luc had said. Georgette looked away, her body rigid.

Gilles Fontenay, his face and ears now red as his jacket, was the first to react. "This is an outrage," he bellowed. "You lie to avoid responsibility."

Luc's hand tightened on his glass. The man was an unbearable hypocrite. "Responsibility prompted my engagement to your daughter in the first place. My family wanted the alliance, and she seemed as good a choice as any presented to me. And if Georgette hadn't been so careless as to get herself with child while I was away, I would have carried out my agreement."

"But you are the father," Georgette pleaded, her eyes filling with tears. "How could you consider anything else?"

Oh yes. She could convince them. Those crocodile tears were quite realistic. He had never fully appreciated Georgette's capacity to deceive. And this was a superb performance: the pitiful innocence on her face, the convincing tremor in her voice. She had them in the palm of her hand.

"Oh, my darling." Georgette sobbed into a kerchief. "I've been faithful all the while you were away. I waited, giving you time, for…" She paused, appealing to her audience, "I don't know for what. I still don't know why he had to leave me. And now, you write that horrid letter. I don't think I can live through this."

It was all too much for Gilles Fontenay. "Luc Chatillon, I'll see that you acknowledge this child and marry my daughter if it's the last thing I do."

Luc scanned the collection of faces with a sudden, fierce conviction before his stare landed squarely on Georgette. "I'm afraid, dear Georgette, neither you nor any other person will tell me whom I shall wed." With one last look at the assemblage, as if daring any of them to challenge this, he slammed his glass upon the sideboard. "I left France in October. It's now March. By my count, the child should be five months along. Yet look at Georgette, the size of her waist."

The statement quieted the room. It was Helaine Fontenay who broke the silence. "You cannot tell about these things, Luc. I've seen many dainty women who carry a child with the same finesse as my daughter." She sniffed into her kerchief, obviously pleased with herself at having navigated this small obstacle.

Luc scoffed at her reasoning. "*Madame*, in the spirit of trusting what you say, if the child is born by the second week of June, I shall wed your daughter. You have my word on that. But if the birth comes later, I cannot have sired your grandchild. One need only count on one's fingers."

Madame Fontenay's eyes widened at the logic of his statement. Flustered, she appealed to Georgette for a rebuttal. None came. Georgette sat quietly, stroking her poodle, her stare fixed on Luc.

"So," Luc said, glancing from her stony stare to the others. "Do we all agree?"

The room fell quiet except for the clock ticking.

"Very well," Luc went on. "Preserve your marriage plans if you wish, Georgette. Though it would be wise to keep your condition discreet. Closet yourself with your mother if you must. Plan a wedding for June. Until then, the letter stands."

Chapter Five

All week, Nicole had anticipated Tuesday night. She held tightly onto Antoine's arm as they walked through the dark, icy streets toward *La Fenêtre*. Bertrand Le Mansec would be inside, perhaps with Luc Chatillon, which Nicole found both exciting *and* a bit awkward being that she was with Antoine. Since the ride in Luc's cabriolet, the week had dragged along, though thankfully Gus and Sarah had left her to her musings, probably worried that she was disappointed about the hats. She was, and she wasn't. Somehow, her confidence had grown. After all, hadn't *Madame* Chatillon liked "Boston"? She would have taken the hat had it not been for the bride-to-be, that dreadful *Mademoiselle* Georgette Fontenay.

Antoine ushered Nicole into the bright and lively café. Her pulse quickened as she searched the room for Luc. The tables were filled with loud and wildly gesturing men, their guffaws and conversations filling the air in a boisterous din. Her heart sank. He wasn't here. But he *said* he'd come. She'd been so sure. She'd thought about him all week, his funny smile that made her laugh, the way he'd leaned close and said, *I'd like to be your friend.* The memory sent a surprising tingle up her spine.

"There's Le Mansec," Antoine said. "By the rear door."

Nicole flashed a nervous smile. "Yes, I see."

Placing his hand on the small of her back, Antoine guided her along, past an old, matted dog that lay asleep near the fireplace. With each step, her heart fluttered. Had Luc come with Bertrand? Was he, like before, hidden in a shadowy corner? As she came closer and surveyed the men surrounding Bertrand Le Mansec, her spirits fell. No Luc.

Bertrand, looking dapper with his clipped beard and tailored red wool jacket buttoned snugly around his slim chest, was holding court over a group of working-class militants. Nicole knew most of the men from previous meetings, though even on the street she'd recognize them by their red-and-white striped trousers. They were burly, with calloused hands and dangerous eyes.

"*Salut*, Antoine, *Mademoiselle* Nicole," Bertrand exclaimed. "We've been waiting."

Grinning with confidence, Antoine grabbed a handful of his newspapers from the linen sack hanging on his shoulder. "Take a look at the latest edition," he said, distributing them around the table.

"*Ahem*," exclaimed Bertrand, clearing his throat and holding up a paper to read the headline aloud: "*Il Faut Avoir Coeur a l'ouvrage.*" He looked questioningly up at Antoine. "You must have *heart* for the work?" He shrugged. "And what work is that?"

"The work of building a nation," said Antoine, pulling a chair out for Nicole. He swung his leg over his chair and scooted beside her. "It won't be easy," he implored the men, now curiously inspecting the newsprint. "A nation that is above a king," Antoine explained. "Above the church. One that gives rights to everyone."

"And these ideas have caused quite a stir in the countryside," came a voice from behind. Nicole recognized it at once. With a catch in her breath, she turned to face Luc.

Peeling off his gloves and coat, he made his way around the table, brushing by her, his muskiness drifting past. It was the same scent she remembered in the cabriolet, and now it overtook her with—*something* that made her light-headed.

"Excellent, Chatillon," said Antoine. "We need all the help we can get."

Luc took a seat across from her. "Good evening, *mademoiselle*," he said, inclining his head. She didn't know what to do with her eyes, her hands. The proprietor of *La Fenêtre* created a welcome distraction by arriving with a bottle of wine and a stack of glasses.

As the glasses were filled and handed round, Antoine scraped back his chair and stood. "Let us toast the nation of France," he proclaimed.

"*Liberté, Egalité, Fraternité,*" one of the men at the table began chanting until others joined in with their glasses lifted, pounding tables, shouting in unison, "*Liberté, Egalité, Fraternité.*"

In the commotion, Luc raised his glass as if in a private acknowledgment of Nicole. She felt the room grow warm. Her cheeks warmed, too. Unwinding her scarf, she lay it across her lap. Did he see her nervousness? Toying with her cup, she felt foolish.

Bertrand poured more wine, and when Antoine resumed his seat, from under the table Nicole sought out his hand and squeezed it in allegiance. Surprised, Antoine looked over at her, then pressed her hand in return. She smiled tenderly at him. Antoine knew her. Protected her. Yes. She and Antoine, orphans both, belonged together. His and her life, and the life of France, crisscrossed at the heart of revolutionary ideas.

Bertrand had downed his glass of wine and was pouring another. "Of course, we all agree on equal taxes for all. Even the clergy should pay. But let's be clear," he expounded, lighting a cheroot. "Ideas too far reaching are doomed to fail."

"And you say equality is too far reaching?" asked Antoine.

Bertrand scoffed. "Well, the idea that we abolish the monarchy *is* too lawless for my blood. It's taxes that are destroying us. We need reform, not anarchy."

Antoine flared up. "To live by rules that some Frenchmen are nobles, and that priests are appointed by God, while the remainder of us are commoners, is not a natural law. It's a man-made law to keep the commoners oppressed."

Bertrand leaned back and coolly inclined his head toward Luc. "Speak up, Chatillon. Tell us your enlightened thoughts on this matter. It seems you more than anyone here stands to lose much if the monarchy topples."

Nicole looked to Luc, curious about his reaction. He appeared unruffled, with that detached smile, though she wondered if others saw the deliberation with which his eyes held Bertrand's.

"I'm of a mind to agree with Antoine," Luc said. "As Voltaire so aptly observed, 'Man is born free, but he is everywhere in chains.'"

Bertrand set his glass on the table with a thud. "I'm surprised you listen to such provocation. Mustn't bite the hand that feeds you, Chatillon."

Nicole thought Bertrand Le Mansec rude. But it was Luc's expression that captured her attention. The placid coldness of his mouth. His brown glittering eyes half lowered as if in an inward debate. She recognized the moment he decided not to take the bait. He gave Bertrand a half smile and shrugged.

"I've never held to the notion that self-serving beliefs hold much truth," he said.

Nicole sat staring at him, wondering if he was completely truthful. Could a man of wealth—gained solely at the favor of the Throne—possibly desire such radical change? If only she had the courage to ask him.

"All beliefs are self-serving," countered Bertrand.

A few men laughed.

"What beliefs do you suppose I hold?" Luc said. "That the social order you protect will one day benefit everyone, with enough work, enough diligence? You're wrong. It benefits only those who created it. My family's fortune is but one breath away from the displeasure of the king."

Bertrand chewed on his cheroot, watching Luc from lowered brows.

"And yet, your family *does* benefit from the Crown," challenged Nicole. She realized her unexpected statement startled everyone. All the men around the table were looking at her with surprise. Though it was only Luc she addressed. As she did so, her heart thudded in her throat. Still, she held his stare. "Why would you wish to diminish your advantage?" she pressed.

He remained silent a moment, studying her with what felt like penetrating curiosity. Then he too leaned his arms on the table, drew himself closer, and gazed directly into her eyes. "Because, *mademoiselle*, it's the right thing to do."

Nicole could not look away. She felt herself being drawn toward him as the world about them dissolved into darkness. She knew he felt it too. Then Antoine's voice broke the spell. She blinked. Looked about. The moment had been shared only by her and Luc. Antoine was speaking his own piece. "Well said, Chatillon. We must look to America. They have given the world a nation that endows its citizens with a written contract. A Bill of Rights."

"Ha," exclaimed a red-haired a man from the next table, obviously drunk, and maybe even looking to challenge what he'd overheard. He stood, legs wide, a cup of wine in hand. "Don't look to the Americans for equality. *Sacre*. They hold slaves. Where's your rights of man in that?"

An uproar surged from the table, with men talking over one another. Nicole felt Antoine growing tense beside her. She knew that look, when he tightened his lips. He was ready to explode.

Bertrand lifted his hand to quiet the chatter. "What say you, Luc?"

Nicole looked nervously at Antoine for his reaction. His eyes had grown large, intense.

Luc folded his arms across his chest. "Irrespective of the ideals of justice," he answered. "Americans are struggling with equal rights for all. Only landowners can vote. Not Africans. Not women."

"*C'est vrai,*" agreed Antoine with a pound of his fist on the table. "We fight for a nation where all men *and* women are born free and equal." He turned his accusing eyes on the red-haired man. "Which means France must free all those enslaved in the colonies we unjustly hold."

Bertrand let out a laugh. "*Allons, hut.* And in this free-for-all, shall your next suggestion be that women receive the same wages as men?"

"Why not?" Luc said.

Bertrand gave an irritable exhale of smoke. "You must be intent on bankrupting this country," he quipped.

"Already the aristocrats have done that, and without our help," interjected Antoine, clumsily taking to his feet. With a vein at his temple throbbing, he leaned against the table and stared around. "Who is not with us is against us," he said darkly. Nicole placed her hand on his arm to calm him, but he jerked it away. "The nobles don't care if our children scrounge in the streets, starving like dogs. By doing nothing, we are no better."

Bertrand took a slow sip of his wine. "On that point, Antoine, I won't argue," he said, flicking ashes on the floor. "And yet we need rules and order. Leaders. A chain of command."

Nicole sensed that Bertrand enjoyed unsettling Antoine, as though all of this were a game.

Luc seemed to have come to the same conclusion. "Le Mansec, if there are not torturers, we need no dungeons."

"Riddles suit you, Luc," quipped Bertrand. "We could talk all night in puzzles."

Several of the men laughed and clinked glasses. The mood shifted. A few men stood to leave. Others spoke quietly to one another. Nicole tugged on Antoine's sleeve for him to sit back down. Her heart was pounding, and she could see he was perspiring.

Antoine pulled free of her and twisted around to grab the sack from the back of his chair. "I'm going to pass these out," he muttered. Shoving the chair aside with his knee, he headed to the next table and sat with the group, his voice becoming loud and animated. Nicole flushed, finding herself alone. She'd said her piece to Luc, and hoped Antoine had been proud of her. That he would sit for a moment or two and say something about her courage. She should have known he would be carried away in his own passion. It was no surprise that he'd left her alone. When his mind filled with nationalistic fury, he became blind to her.

With the table broken into several conversations, Nicole sat, thinking. Her own racing pulse was still in her throat. Luc and Bertrand were talking intimately, though she wasn't listening. She felt light-headed from the talk and heat. The fireplace and cigars had filled the room with smoke.

"Nicole?"

She looked up.

"Would you care for more coffee?" Luc asked.

"Oh, no, I've had enough." She made an attempt at a smile. "I'm quite enjoying eavesdropping on everyone."

She thought she saw concern on his face, then decided she was only fooling herself. It must be pity. She'd challenged his wealth publicly. Is that what had prompted his remark about working women? Guilt? No doubt he guessed she earned little as an apprentice, and even less than a man would have. Yet what did he really know about such things? He'd lived his entire life in luxury. He'd never experienced anything close to what she had. Abandonment. The loss of everything. The humiliation. Such deep degradation to her core. But it was even more than that. The cruelty. Every night she'd prayed for *Madame* Colère to leave her be. Or for God to tell her how to keep from making the directress so angry.

Feeling a bit dizzy, she closed her eyes. She didn't like to think about *Madame* Colère. Her entire body filled with that unpleasant, prickly feeling that took her to the place where she could not fight, in a deep part of her mind ruled by memory. *The closet. At the end of the corridor.* All at once she was there, surrounded by blackness. She couldn't see her hands. She felt them reaching out for the walls, frantically searching for the doorknob. Touching, fumbling. Something large and flowing and unseen engulfed her. Her arms flailed, catching onto the strangling cloak. *Someone help me. Oh, please... anyone.* Her fists pounded, fighting off *Madame* Colère's cloak smothering her, its heavy wool reeking of jasmine.

Unable to breathe, she opened her eyes to the noisy, smoky café. Her chest struggled against a heavy weight. There was no air. She had to get out. Out of the hot stuffy room filled with men's voices and Luc across from her.

She stood suddenly, her scarf falling from her lap. It tangled in her feet as she tried to free herself from the table. Kicking it away, she nearly tripped. She was suffocating. She couldn't swallow. She had to leave. Now.

"Nicole."

As she pushed through the crowd, she knew it was Luc who'd called her name. The door opened before her, and a pair of laughing men entered, pulling off their caps. She shoved past them into the cold night. Drinking in lungsful of icy air, she hugged her arms around herself. *Breathe. Breathe.*

"Yes, that's right, breathe deeply, Nicole."

Luc stood at her side. He'd brought her scarf and draped it over her shoulders, keeping his arm wrapped around her. Slowly, the wintry air sobered her, clearing her mind. She pulled away from his embrace, her thoughts now clear enough to realize her humiliation was complete. He'd seen her secret shame.

"Are you all right, Nicole?"

"I'm fine," she said, pulling her scarf over her hair.

"Are you sure? If you'd like I can—"

"No. I was overheated. I should go find Antoine."

He said nothing, only gazed at her.

All around him she saw tiny snowflakes had begun drifting down from the night sky, landing on his broad shoulders and glistening in his dark hair.

"Are you in love with him?" he asked. The question took her by complete surprise. "With Antoine."

She looked away. "He... You see it's that I..."

He guided her face to look back at him. Her breathing stopped as he touched his finger to her lips. Leaning close, he drew the finger down and raised her chin so that she could not avoid his eyes. "*Mon Dieu*, Nicole. You're an extraordinary woman." And then he brought his lips to hers.

As though her body had a mind of its own, she found herself kissing him back, wrapping her arms around his solid shoulders. His mouth slanted across hers, softly, airily, thrilling her down to her toes. Moments ago she'd been lost. Now she was found.

Realizing the snow had begun to fall faster, Nicole pulled away. Her eyes locked on his as he guided her beneath an overhang on the side of the building. Under its protection, she wanted to bury herself inside his coat, against the warmth and strength of his body. Instead she whispered, "I really must go."

"Let me take you home."

"I can't. Antoine will be looking for me."

"Forget him." He pulled her close to kiss her again.

Just as she reached up to meet his lips, she caught herself. What was she doing? This was wrong. She pulled away and ran through the falling snow to the café door. She yanked it open, then stopped. Inside was Antoine, lost in the revolution, engaged in animated discussion. She turned back and searched for Luc. The snow had blanketed the street in a layer of white.

And Luc had disappeared into the night.

Chapter Six

Gray morning light crept into Georgette Fontenay's bed chamber, illuminating the four-poster bed where her naked body lay entwined with that of a large, muscular man. She gave a quick gasp as he rolled over onto his back and pulled her atop him. She moaned, as her mother had instructed her. *Always make little sounds, my dear, like pleasurable gasps. It will endear you to them.* The *them* referred to any man of position and wealth who might be the golden goose that would save the Fontenay fortune. The problem was that Éric Royer was poor as a church mouse.

"Move," he groaned. "Faster." She obliged, forcing out a few more gasps. She may not have the instinct for lovemaking, but love him she did. Simply being naked with Éric warmed her with the desire to be his wife, to have his children. Only he could make her feel, could soften her heart.

Éric twisted onto his side and rolled over, pulling her beneath him, lifting her buttocks as he thrust hard.

"Easy," she moaned. "You know I like it gentle."

With a throaty chuckle he lay his weight on her. "Like this?" He rubbed his torso up and down her body, grinning down at her, his slow thrusts deep and deliberate to please her, so that she could hold on to his shoulders, marveling at being one with him. During sex, he was the most vulnerable. It was the only time she felt power over him.

"I love you," she whispered, trying to catch his gaze, but his eyes were now closed. She shifted her stare to the chandelier. "Éric, tell me you love me," she murmured, roused by his warm breath on her neck. His hands gripped her, moving her against his need. "Éric, tell me." His body tensed as he pounded, faster and faster, until he arched his head up, his face knotted into a red grimace. Georgette held on to him as though he were the saving raft in her sinking life.

Spent, he pulled himself free and flopped onto his back beside her, his arms flung out, his breathing ragged. Georgette let out a sigh, luxuriating in the glow where his body had covered hers, warming her abdomen, warming his child, the child he had yet to know about. She'd need to find exactly the right time to tell him.

She turned to look at him. His eyes were closed, his face serene. Perching on her elbow, she watched him a moment, then, biting her lip, played with the hair on his chest.

"I wish you'd tell me you love me. Why do I have to ask?" She plucked a hair close to his nipple.

"Ow." He turned his head away. "Stop it, Gette."

"You make love to me then ignore me?" Annoyed, she grabbed his jaw tightly so that his large blue eyes opened and peered into her face. He was impossibly handsome, with those thick blond eyelashes, those tanned arms covered in curly blond hair. God, she adored him.

"Why won't you tell me you love me like you used to?"

"Because you're a greedy, demanding woman. Once I say it, you'll not stop until you get my promise to sell you my soul. You will not own me, Gette. No matter how much money you have." With a grimace, he rolled out of bed. "*Sacre bleu*, woman. You're relentless."

Frustrated, she blushed and looked away.

He stood and looked down upon her. She liked how his eyes moved over her voluptuous body curled on the sheets. "We both know where this will end," he said. "Not with marriage. We are afternoon lovers. Period. You can stop any time you want, Gette. So don't press me. You won't like me if you do."

"But maybe it doesn't have to end. Maybe there can be another way."

"That's so much horse crap, and you know it."

She sat up, her bottom lip stuck out like she did when trying to get her way. "You don't have to be so rude. I can't help it if Papa won't let us marry."

"Marry? Ha. He'd have an attack if he even thought I'd looked at you. I'm not sure what he'd say if he knew *you* had chased *me*."

Georgette bristled. "Why are you being so mean?" she muttered. She saw it worked.

He softened, then winked. "I'm not angry, Gette. I do have to leave before the entire household is up, though. Don't you think I'd rather lounge with you by the fire than rush out into the snow to work?"

"But you do love me?"

"*Ah-ah*, no demands." He wagged his finger. She smiled at his charming grin.

"Besides, I don't even know what love is." Her smile faded. He could be so slippery.

Pulling her knees up to her breasts, she wrapped her slender arms about her legs and gave him her most enticing pout. "Love is what you feel for me in moments like this," she purred. He gave a low *humph* and grabbed his britches from the floor where they'd been doffed with haste less than an hour before. As he crossed to a mirror, she watched the reflection of his angular face, his curly blond hair, his baby blue eyes. God, how she loved him.

"Do you need cash?" she asked.

"Since you ask, yes," he said, turning and walking back to sit on the edge of the bed.

"How much?"

He pulled on his knee-high boots, caked with mud from the stables. "Five *sous* should do."

She propped herself up against the pillows, flinging her long black hair behind her shoulders. "And while I'm at it, shall I ask Papa to give you a raise?" she asked, opening the bedside table drawer. "Heaven knows, I can't imagine how you survive on what you get." It was a deliberately cruel thing to say. But he deserved it for that remark about not knowing what love was.

Éric stiffened and looked away.

"Do you want your money?" Georgette taunted, holding out her arm, her fist tight. Bending his knee on the mattress, he reached for her hand. She playfully pulled it back. "First tell me you love me."

Éric grabbed her arm and pried open her fingers to reveal the gold coins in her palm. He smiled into her mocking face, then wrapped her fingers back around the coins, pressing them so hard that she winced. "No," he announced. Letting go, he stood up from the bed.

"Éric," Georgette called with a laugh. "I was teasing."

He pulled his cloak about his shoulders. "Forget it, Gette."

"Oh, don't be asinine. Here, take the coins," she insisted as he walked to the door and opened it. "Éric. Stop. It's five *Louis d'or*."

Tilting his head out, he surveyed the corridor.

"No. Wait." Georgette jumped from bed and scampered naked across the rug. She pulled him back inside, kissing his shoulders, turning him toward her. "Forgive me," she whispered. "It was a silly thing to do."

He pushed her away. "And insulting."

"I promise not to do it again." She shoved the money toward him.

"If you ever do, it will be the last time." One by one he took up the five gold pieces off her palm. "I'm tired of your games, Gette. Up to now, this agreement has been working for both of us. You are very beautiful. And you've always been available to me. I've always known that. Since I was hired at your father's stables, you've followed me around, putting me on a pedestal like some sort of god, your eyes shining whenever I broke a horse." He pocketed the money. "At first, I admit, it was flattering." He bent so close that she pulled back from him. His blue eyes were narrowed and angry. "But in these past weeks you've changed. You've become more demanding than ever. Stop it. I mean it, Gette. If you want to keep me risking my neck coming up to your room with your mother and father sleeping down the hall."

His face relaxed into a crooked grin, revealing strong white teeth. "Truth be told, if we did get caught, I'd miss you like mad, *ma chère*." He looked about the room, cozy with a flickering fire. "And all this." With a quick kiss on the top of her head, he stepped out.

She hoped these words were true. But there was always something about Éric that kept her from being sure. Maybe that's why she said these things. And she was always sorry afterward.

***

Nicole rose from her tousled bed, pulled on her shawl, and tiptoed barefoot to the window, opening the shutters to greet the day. She was met with a glorious sight. The rooftops were covered in snow.

She lightly touched her lips. It *had* happened. The kiss last night. She felt astonishingly alive. More alive than she ever had. And happy. As though something bright had erupted from a dark spot deep in her heart, and in its place was this delirious feeling of joy. Something beyond her own will.

She went about her morning toilet, washing up and laying out her clothes, her one working skirt and blouse and corset she'd been wearing for four years, since she was sixteen. Last night Antoine had walked her home, recounting in detail what he'd said to each man at each table. And how he'd liked Luc Chatillon's ideas—though he wasn't sure someone from such wealth could be a trusted ally. Antoine had said, *We need to be careful. The man could be playing us.*

Tying her heavy hair back with a ribbon, Nicole frowned. Was the revolution talk a game to Luc? Nothing more than an escape from ennui? He *had* told her he'd grown bored with his life. She remembered the gentle strength of his arms as he held her. She couldn't bear the thought that she was only an amusement for him. And, oh God, the more she thought about it, the more she realized how she'd made a fool of herself last night. She'd stumbled out of the café like a helpless child.

Shivering, as much from her thoughts as from the cold, she pulled her nightgown off over her head and tossed it on her bed, then quickly grabbed her chemise and stepped into it, hastily buttoning up the front. She jerked her arms into her full-sleeved blouse. Luc might have thought she *wanted* him to follow. And so he'd kissed her—and she'd kissed him back. What must he think? What should she do?

She sat and pulled on her black stockings, then her flat leather shoes. No matter how she felt—this surge of happiness—hope was futile. Luc was from a different world. One she could never belong to. Her heart sank. There was only one answer. She would never be alone with him again. With each layer of clothing, the dark green broadcloth skirt, the faded black corset laced snugly over her ample bosom, her thoughts went over her course of action. If they ever did accidently meet at *La Fenêtre*, she'd ignore him. In fact, it occurred to her she no longer wanted to go to the café. She didn't belong there. She'd continue to help Antoine paste up his posters—but then she'd return home.

Going to her dresser, she stopped. There on the top lay a dried flower from Aimée's bridal bouquet last spring. She picked it up and touched the faded rose petals. Aimée and Jacques had the love she dreamed of. He adored her, and she him. Slowly she placed the discolored rose on its spot. A sense of sadness filled her.

The kiss last night had been a mistake.

Closing her eyes, she willed herself to feel the kind of love for Antoine that Aimée felt for Jacques. She cared for Antoine. They shared a passion for justice. And she felt protected by him, even in the streets at night. Wasn't love about comfort? Antoine indeed brought comfort to her life. And familiarity. He was easy to be with.

Hastily she tied a yellowing lace fichu about her neck—but then her fingers stopped. How could she ever forget her kiss with Luc? When she was near him, she was consumed with something scary and thrilling—and, oddly, a feeling like she was exactly where she was supposed to be. When he'd gathered her in his arms, when he'd kissed her, she'd felt as if she'd come home.

Walking to the window, she looked out at the white scene. There was no getting over the truth, though, that Luc lived in a different world. Even if he really did support the Cause. Even if he was the dream she'd always hoped for. Even if he was the man who would take away the coldness inside. They could never be together.

She leaned her forehead against the cold pane of glass. What did she imagine? That he would marry her? No. There was only heartbreak with Luc Chatillon.

***

By Sunday, the snow had stopped, but the wind felt icy cold. After mass, Aimée joined her and the Bastons for supper, while Jacques left to deliver a writing bureau to a client. They'd gathered in the kitchen. Hanging over the hearth, a bubbling pot of fish stew steamed the windows. Nicole and Aimée sidestepped a meowing and underfoot Midas as they laid out bowls and spoons. Nicole was wondering whether to tell Aimée about the kiss, which as much as she'd tried, she couldn't get out of her mind. Aimée made up for Nicole's quiet with merry complaints about being so pregnant it was awkward to climb the steps into the kitchen, and how at home Jacques had to put on her shoes for her. Even as they sat at the table, with Sarah saying grace and Midas purring over a fish head in the corner, Nicole remained in her deep inward study.

Sarah filled the bowls with ladles of steaming broth chock-full of anchovies and cod. Then she heaped toasted bread on everyone's plates, giving Aimée an extra slice. "Eat," she commanded. "You're feeding two, remember."

"*Madame* Baston, you shall make my baby fat." Despite her protest, Aimée buttered her bread extra thick. "Nicole," she said, munching heartily, "you look pale today. Is something wrong—" Aimée turned her head toward the door. "Was that the bell?" she said, her eyes bright. "It must be Jacques returning early."

Gus clasped her arm to stop her from jumping up. "Stay put. I'll let your husband in."

When Gus reappeared in the kitchen, alone, he held up a letter. "It's from *Monsieur* Chatillon," he announced as solemnly as if it had come from King Louis XVI.

Nicole almost dropped her spoon.

"*Madame* Chatillon's husband?" Sarah exclaimed.

"No, no." Gus shook his head. "It says here it's the son, Luc Chatillon."

"Luc Chatillon?" Aimée scooted her chair back and limped in her light-footed way to join Gus and look at the letter. "Nicole, this is wonderful news," she said. "*Monsieur* Chatillon has found a buyer for your hats."

Aimée's words seemed to come from out of nowhere, making no sense to Nicole. The very notion of Luc sending a letter about her hats stunned her.

Gus read aloud: "*Monsieur Baston, I have arranged for your assistant, Mademoiselle Nicole Vogel, to bring a sample of no fewer than six hats from your establishment to be presented to M. Hervé Marchand, purveyor of Maison de Coutour, a shop located in the Palais Royal. M. Marchand has promoted trade between France and America since the Treaty of Amity and Commerce as a supplier of hats, shoes, shawls, ribbons, and other accessories for the American market.*" Gus's eyes scanned along for a line or two, then he continued: "*If M. Marchand finds the hats acceptable, he offers to purchase all six, with orders for more to come.*"

Aimée's face lit up. "But what luck, *Monsieur* Baston." She glanced at Nicole with a half-smile of cautious encouragement.

Gus shrugged, considering the turn of events. "I know of this treaty," he mused. "Any citizen of France is given favored status to sell goods to America. There have been fortunes made. And lost."

"When does he want to see them?" Sarah asked.

Gus ran his finger down the letter. "Oh here, we have two weeks. *Monsieur* Chatillon will pick up *Mademoiselle* Vogel and the hats, to deliver them to his country estate where they will be met by *Monsieur* Marchand as well as *Monsieur* Le Mansec." Gus looked up. "Who is *Monsieur* Le Mansec?"

Nicole rubbed her temples. "A friend of *Monsieur* Chatillon."

"Two weeks," Gus muttered, taking his pipe from his pocket. "We'll never produce six hats in such a short time."

Nicole had enough time to collect her thoughts, enough to know she would not do this. What they didn't know was that Luc Chatillon was toying with her life. "You're right," she said, seizing on his hesitation. "We cannot possibly meet this order."

Gus lit his pipe, taking his time. "Perhaps, though, we can," he mused.

Nicole frowned. What was Gus thinking? They were—what had Georgette Fontenay said?—*street corner hatters*. No one would take her seriously. Or Gus.

"We start with the two that you brought to *Madame* Chatillon." Gus was calculating.

Nicole frantically detected everyone's agreement. Were they seriously considering this?

"I've been able to save up a bit since you came," Sarah said, pulling out a step stool and hefting herself up for a tin on the top shelf. "We can use it for textiles." She stepped down and held it out to Nicole. "Of your choosing, my dear."

Gus grunted in agreement. "Take it, Nicolette. Christophe-Philippe Oberkampf's factory produces the best. I'll take you to choose what you like. This is your order."

"This *Monsieur* Chatillon," Sarah said, placing the tin in Nicole's hands. "He's a good man. He wants to make right his mother turning you away like she did, Nicole."

Nicole held Sarah's prized tin close to her body. She wondered if it were true. Was giving her hats another chance due to guilt about his mother? Or did he want to see her again? Either way, part of her felt unnerved. Part of her felt excited. She slowly sat at the table and drew her finger down the letter.

Gus leaned back in his chair as mentally he estimated how they would complete the order. Aimée held her hands prayerlike to her lips, as though she were holding back her true thoughts. Sarah took back the tin and began searching through it, her lips moving as silently she counted the golden sous.

Nicole thought they were the most wonderful people in the world. How could she disappoint them? She glanced at the letter. *A sample of no fewer than six hats from your establishment.*

She rubbed her eyes. Hadn't she just promised herself never to see Luc Chatillon again? But they didn't know that. The idea of seeing a country estate, and showing her hats to a buyer of the stature of *Monsieur* Marchand...

It was so difficult to know what to do. Antoine would be unhappy. But she could explain she wasn't alone with Luc. Bertrand would be there. And this was business. Business that could change all their lives. How could she turn down such an opportunity?

Midas sat in the corner, licking his paws. "So, what do we think, Midas?" she asked him with a smile. "It seems you're the only one with a clear head in all this." The cat looked up and gave a low meow, followed by a yawn.

Nicole sighed. "Oh yes, your majesty, I think I agree." Filling with a sense of excitement, she looked about the room. "We should get started. We've a lot of work ahead."

Chapter Seven

Two weeks later, a sleek two-horse jewel-box of a carriage, with the Chatillon coat of arms displayed on each side, stood outside the hat shop. With four hatboxes strapped atop, and two tucked inside, the driver held open the door. Nicole clasped Luc's hand as he assisted her up the steps. In wonderment she took in the satin-tufted ceiling and the embroidered silk walls, each displaying one of the four seasons. She closed her eyes. She didn't belong here. She should climb back out and go to the shop and tell them all it was a mistake: the hats, being with Luc, all of this.

But it was too late. He had climbed inside, his stature taking up most of the cabin as he sat on the opposite seat and stretched his legs. She scooted aside to give him room. When he'd arrived, she'd said nothing as he politely told Gus he'd bring her back before dusk. She'd inwardly groaned, wishing Gus had stopped her—and wondering if she should have told Aimée about the kiss.

But she hadn't. And now she was alone with a man she barely knew. Going to his country chateau. A man she had kissed.

"I'm afraid it's going to be a cold journey," Luc said. He reached for a lap fur on the overhead rack and placed it across her knees. She flushed, aware that her cloak offered little protection from the March air.

"Thank you," she said. Her gaze strayed from her thin cloak to Luc's thick double-breasted overcoat that reached his knee-high boots, unlike the wide-cuffed formal jacket she'd seen him wear. As he fussed with one of the hatboxes on the floor, she noticed his jaw was covered in the faintest dark stubble, as though he'd outfitted himself in a rush this morning—that, or he hadn't bothered with refinement today.

Settling back, he removed his tricorn hat, revealing slicked-back hair tied at the neck. "My country attire," he offered, noting her assessment. "A much welcome freedom."

"I wouldn't know," she replied. "I've never been outside Paris." He kept his eyes on her. She could only imagine what he was thinking. Her stomach lurched. Was he remembering the way he held her outside the café? The way she responded to him? Would he say anything? Should she?

"Then I shall delight in showing you the real beauty of France," he said. As he leaned closer to adjust the lap fur, the faint musk about his clothing sent her blood thudding to her head. She looked away, out to the street, anywhere but at Luc. Still, she could feel his presence. This was a mistake. She never should have let anyone talk her into it.

After exchanging a few pleasantries, they rode in an awkward silence. Nicole kept her focus on the streets they sped through, though her thoughts lingered on the man sitting across from her. She could feel him watching her. The driver snapped his whip, faster and faster, and as they traveled into a district she had never seen, she broke the silence, slowly asking Luc questions: What was that building, how far were they from the shop? Luc pointed out the magnificent *Hotel de Ville* with its ornate clock tower, and farther out, the grim Bastille looming against a gray sky. Nicole shuddered. "I've heard they torture prisoners," she said. "Even nobles who are enemies of Louis."

"No one knows its secrets," Luc said. "They've been hidden since the monarchy began."

They approached the city gates, the carriage wheels spinning past the guards without slowing. Once the coach sped outside the walls, the cobbled avenue gave way to a much-used hardpack roadway, filled with the commerce of hay carts and farmers' tumbrels coming into the city. But as they traveled out farther, the traffic thinned until they were alone in countryside that spread in foggy mists along distant fields. Enthralled, Nicole leaned out, into the brisk wind. "It's breathtaking."

"I always breathe more freely when I'm away from Paris," Luc mused.

Curious, Nicole glanced at him. "But you have everything in Paris," she said, sitting back in her seat to study him. "Wealth. Luxury. Everything."

"And the truth is, I don't care for any of it, Nicole. I sometimes wonder if my life would have been happier being brought up in the provinces tending goats." His face darkened. "I think I would have preferred it."

"I assure you," Nicole said, "changing places would not be pleasant. There is no joy in being poor—neither in the provinces nor in Paris."

He shifted in his seat and changed the subject. "Were you raised in Paris? Does your family live nearby?"

Nicole had wondered when he would ask about her family. Her lips twitched at the question—was she *raised* in Paris? The word assumed a mother giving nighttime hugs and sitting on a papa's knee before a fire. Being raised with care and concern. Yes, she'd been *raised* in Paris—*like one raises stray barn kittens, or sheep.* She lifted her chin in what *Madame* Colère would have called her defiant spirit. The woman had tried to break it for years.

"I spent my childhood in Legros. A boarding school in Paris. Not in a nice section of the city, so you've probably never seen it."

"An orphanage?" he said, surprised. "I had no idea. Then, you have no family?"

"No," Nicole said, withholding an impulse to say more.

"You—lost your parents? Both?"

She stared at the embroidered wall behind him, a scene of spring blossoms and applewood branches. "Yes. When I was little girl." She wasn't about to explain her dreams about a mother and father that sometimes seemed like memories. She'd had them since she was a child. She took a deep breath, then flashed an insincere smile. "I have no memory of my parents."

"It must have been difficult," he said, visibly regretting he'd brought up her pain.

"Actually, I learned much in those years," Nicole said coolly. "The lessons of life not taught from books. The main lesson being that family and security are a blessing. Don't ever think you would want a life other than the one you've had, Luc."

"And yet, I've seen a better way of life," he murmured, leaning his elbow on the armrest and staring out the window.

Nicole watched him, her eyes narrowing. His disdain for the ways of the wealthy seemed real. There was a hidden depth to Luc. Something withheld. She'd seen it in his eyes that first night in the café. "You speak of America," she said softly. "But do you believe our people can bring about such change?"

Luc turned to her. "Isn't that the purpose of your café meetings and pasting posters around Paris? To overthrow the king and replace him with—what? What do you hope will happen, Nicole?"

"That's the problem. No one really knows. Everyone has an idea about the Cause, I suppose. We all hope to lower taxes. We demand equality. We want the king to protect his subjects." She met his eyes. "But I don't know if I believe in abolishing the monarchy." His eyebrows lifted with what she took to be curiosity. "What I mean, Luc, is that it's always been a part of our lives. Like the Church. There's beauty and tradition and pageantry. I think it would be sad to lose all that." She blushed, surprised that she'd told him these thoughts she'd shared with no one else. "I'm sorry," she said, looking away in discomfort. "It sounds so trivial."

"Not to my thinking," Luc said. "I think what you say is important. It should be part of the discussion. Have you told this to Antoine?"

Nicole shook her head. "No. You don't understand."

"Perhaps I do. More than you know. Is that why you're with Antoine? Putting your life in danger—because you think his ideas are more important than yours?"

She shook her head. "Not at all. I do agree with Antoine about so much. He's filled with such passion. The monarchy has become callous, even cruel, to its subjects."

"And yet?"

"And yet I don't believe nobles are the only ones who can be cruel." Her gaze flashed about Luc's face. "I've seen cruelty. It's in the nature of the person. Even if we could overthrow the Throne, how do we know the new power won't be even more merciless?"

The carriage wheels began to jerk and careen over a bumpy stretch of road so that Nicole clutched the armrest. Seeing the sky thickening with dark clouds, she remembered the hatboxes strapped atop the carriage. "Luc, why is this meeting being held in your country chateau? I had no idea it was this far out."

"It's only an hour drive. Marchand already had plans to be our guest in the country. It seemed a convenient way to introduce him to you." He stopped. "To be honest, Nicole, I asked Marchand to come. But I didn't want you to have to return to the house where…you'd been treated so poorly. This is my attempt to make amends for what happened."

She mulled over his words. "I see. I meet *Monsieur* Marchand, perhaps he even buys the hats…and your conscience is clear?"

"Something like that." He gave her an imploring smile.

"That's all very well. But what if he doesn't like my hats?"

"My mother confided to me they were lovely—and my mother is a woman of rare taste."

The carriage at last slowed and turned off the road onto a lane that ran alongside a narrow brook, its surface reflecting silvery clouds. The wheels crunched along the gravel lane lined with willow trees, their barren branches trailing to the ground.

"We call it *Les Saules*," Luc said. "I was born here."

"The Willows," Nicole marveled, taking in the sight.

"In my youth I took many a fall out of those trees." Luc smiled in remembrance. "I've always been akin to them. Not only their beauty, but their *esprit vital*."

"A tree? Has spirit?"

He gave a chuckle. "You've lived too long in the city. As a boy I took my lessons from the trees. Willows are the last to lose their leaves in autumn. But the first to leaf in spring. They taught me about the nature of things. How a thing can't be rushed. It must wait until the right time has come." As Nicole listened, she studied with fresh eyes what before she'd seen as lifeless trees.

"And there," Luc said pointing, "is my home."

Ahead in the middle of a lavender field stood a two-story stone chateau with chimneys on each side pouring out plumes of smoke. At the rear were stables built around a courtyard, and nearby a cluster of out-buildings that, Nicole assumed, housed the stable hands and field workers. Several stable grooms led about what appeared to be magnificent racehorses.

Luc rapped for the driver. "Drop us off at the stables," he ordered. Even before they'd fully stopped, Luc jumped out, then opened the door to offer Nicole his hand.

"You raise thoroughbreds?" she asked.

"Some of the finest. And besides, there are goats and milk cows."

"I've never seen a cow," Nicole exclaimed.

"Well, then, it's time you do. They're some of the nicest creatures you'll meet."

Nicole couldn't help but laugh as he took her arm and guided her toward the arena. He seemed suddenly relaxed and happy, different than she'd ever seen him. He was making it impossible not to like him.

"I'd like you to see my last purchase. A stallion I found in England on my return from America. There. In the arena." He indicated a horse bucking up against the weight of a young man with curly blond hair. The man's shirt was sweaty, his sleeves rolled up to reveal muscles that rippled as he jerked the reins. Dogs outside the fenced arena yelped and scratched to get inside, while a half dozen grooms watched from atop fence posts. The horse, wide-eyed and neighing, reared up with its forelegs dancing in the air, then plunged to the ground. The blond rider rolled with the motion again and again, so that Nicole's heart pumped in excitement. At last, the horse, dripping with foam, pranced about a few steps, circled, then with a final neigh, quieted and stood still with sides heaving.

At once they were joined by Raoul, the stable master, a small, leathery-faced man. "Master Luc. Just in time. Looks like Royer finally broke your stallion."

"Well done," Luc replied.

"Weren't easy, neither. But mark my words, you'll earn a fortune on this one, sir."

Éric Royer dismounted, drying his neck with a towel. He grabbed the reins and led the horse to Luc. "High-spirited," Éric said with a grin, patting the horse now shivering with energy and tossing its head. "But a winner."

"This is Nicole Vogel," Luc said, drawing her forward.

Nicole nodded. "*Bonjour*. That was magnificent to watch."

Éric gave a half bow. "*Merci*."

"Nicole, this is Éric Royer. You're right in your assessment. He's the best trainer in four provinces—we use him for special horses."

Éric nodded. "Pleasure to meet you, *mademoiselle*." He turned to Luc. "I'll be leaving now. Raoul can manage from here."

"Éric is employed by *Monsieur* Fontenay in Paris," Luc explained to Nicole. She raised her brows at this bit of information, thinking it must be the same Fontenay family as the horrible Georgette Fontenay. This young man seemed too pleasant to work for such a household. She thought his eyes were perhaps the bluest she'd ever seen.

"Likewise, pleased to meet you," she said. She could hardly keep from staring at the stallion that stood a full two heads taller than she. "You're quite beautiful," she said to it, fascinated by the majestic creature. The horse neighed, bobbed its head, and stretched its nose closer. "Is it all right to touch him?"

Luc laughed. "It seems he wants you to."

Nicole reached out to stroke the horse's muzzle, then flinched as he nudged her hand with a whinny. "Oh," she exclaimed with a nervous laugh, pulling her hand away.

"The animal has taken to you," Luc said, drawing closer to the stallion. "Come, let me show you how—" He stopped. "Here. What's this? Have a look, Raoul. He seems to favor the right foreleg."

Raoul squatted on his haunches. "Gone and cut the shin, sir."

"Nothing a bit of salve won't heal," Éric said matter-of-factly. "I'll see to it before I leave. He'll remember the favor. Best to stay friends with this fellow."

Luc scrutinized the leg. "Can you stay longer and keep an eye on him?"

"I'll stay to the evening if need be," Éric said, gathering up the reins. "But I wouldn't worry. It's not deep."

"He's a superb animal," Nicole said, now comfortable enough to caress the horse's muzzle. She felt a few raindrops on her hand and glanced up, noting the darkened sky. "I think it's going to rain," she said.

"And soon," Luc agreed. "We should go inside." As more drops began to dampen her cloak, Nicole pulled her hood over her hair. "*Bonjour, Monsieur* Royer," she said, turning back to wave.

"Come along, Nicole," Luc urged. "I think we're in for a drenching."

As he escorted Nicole toward the chateau, a downpour descended on the meadows as far as the eye could see. Luc pulled Nicole with him under a tree for protection, but after a moment, murmured, "Doesn't look like it's stopping soon. We'll have to run. Can you make it?"

Nicole smiled. "I've been in the rain before, Luc."

"Not a country rain, I'd wager. Here goes," he said, rushing out with his head ducked.

Nicole lifted her gown and rushed alongside him, dodging puddles, keeping up with his long strides, when suddenly the heavens broke open and a deluge surged down. "Take my hand," he called out. She did, and together they sprinted across the open field.

With her hood fallen back and rain drenching her hair and face, a wild sense of freedom swept through her. She began to laugh. Never had rain smelled sweeter. Her cloak and gown were soaked, but she didn't care—

Suddenly she stumbled. Before she could right herself, Luc had caught her. She felt herself swept up into his arms, and he whisked her along. Clasping her hands about his neck, she held on tightly as he rushed up the back steps and set her on her feet. Gasping and shaking herself off, Nicole looked up at him, then burst out laughing. Luc's tricorn hat was full to the brim and dripping water down his face.

"You're soaked," she giggled.

"And you, *mademoiselle*, look like a wet puppy," he said, pushing back a strand of her hair. Her smile faded as she gazed into his glittering brown eyes. She remembered the thrill of their closeness, the night he'd kissed her. She held her breath, wondering, hoping he would again—

But Luc turned away and opened the back-entrance door. "Come in. You need to dry and warm yourself," he said, apparently unaware that a moment between them had passed.

Chapter Eight

Their entrance brought a stout woman from the kitchen, carrying a mixing bowl on her hip and a spoon in her hand. "Oh, Master Luc I thought it might be you," she said, then looked to Nicole. "And I guess you'd be the milliner girl. Look at you both. Half drowned."

"May I present the house matron, *Madame* Lamont," said Luc, removing Nicole's cloak. "And this is *Mademoiselle* Nicole Vogel." The two women's eyes met in mutual assessment. This robust matron with husky arms reminded Nicole of *Madame* Baston, a woman who oversaw the entire household from the four walls of the kitchen. Nicole couldn't tell if the woman had Sarah's warmth. She seemed sweet, but moved about with an air of formality.

"*Madame* Lamont, would you find something dry for *mademoiselle?*"

The woman took the dripping cloak by her fingertips. "Clothing, sir?"

"Perhaps something of my grandmother's."

Madame Lamont hung the cloak on a hook. "I'll do my best, Master Luc." She surveyed Nicole. "You're tall like *Grand'mère* Françoise. Hm. There must be something." She turned and respectfully dipped her head to Luc, indicating that she'd manage fine. "I'll put Colleen on it at once."

"Good," Luc said. "And we'll take our luncheon in the library, before the fire. Will *Monsieur* Marchand be joining us?"

"No, Master Luc. The gentleman took his meal early. Tea and pastries was all he wanted. Hardly ate a bite at that. He's resting in his chambers." She leaned forward and whispered confidentially, "The man says riding in carriages gets him a bit sick in his middle. But *Monsieur* Bertrand will be down shortly."

Luc nodded. "Very well. Then, you can show *Mademoiselle* Nicole to the fire in the library." He turned to Nicole. "If you'll excuse me, I'll change out of these damp clothes and be down shortly."

Nicole watched him disappear up a back stairway. She shivered, suddenly realizing how wet and cold she was. She slowly took in the room: a pantry filled with jugs of olives, sacks of potatoes and turnips, and baskets spilling over with cabbages and carrots. Plucked ducks and skinned rabbits hung from the high ceiling. Dried herbs dangled from the rafters. She marveled at the tall shelves stacked with dusty bottles of wine, and cupboards brimming with cheese rounds and sacks of flour. It was exquisite. And yet, looking about, she couldn't help but think all this food would feed her whole neighborhood for weeks.

"Come with me," *Madame* Lamont said, returning.

Nicole followed, wondering what this woman thought of her—a girl clearly out of her station, having arrived dressed in a muslin skirt and cotton blouse, and a vest that was beginning to pull at the seams. And now Luc was asking this woman to find clothes for her.

As they passed through the center corridor of the chateau, Nicole could see open doors offering glimpses of shadowy, unlit salons filled with pine tables, desks, and fraying rugs.

Nicole preferred this rustic home to the gilt and polished marble of the Chatillon Paris mansion—with the house help here dressed in their own clothes, not like those liveried servants with their noses in the air. These rooms felt welcoming, with stone floors and beamed ceilings, a place to kick off muddy boots after a day outdoors. Still, even with its rustic simplicity, to Nicole this country house felt like a palace. There were iron chandeliers filled with more candles than she'd use in a year, and stacks of wood spilled half onto the floors beside blazing fires.

As she followed *Madame* Lamont into the library, Nicole's eyes lit with astonishment. *Books.* The walls were covered with shelves of them. She'd never seen more than three books together at one time. Here were hundreds. As *Madame* stoked the fire, Nicole pulled out a slim volume with a worn spine. Opening it, she discovered a collection of poetry. The inscription told her it was a gift to Luc on his nineteenth birthday from his grandmother: *Avec tout mon amour, Grand'mère Françoise.* Nicole slid the book back and withdrew several more, discovering Luc's name and his notes inside many of them. There was a sweet honesty in his thoughts jotted along the margins. She stopped at one entry and read, *As Grand'mère says, don't put on airs.* Nicole had to laugh to herself, remembering their conversation about that very thing when he'd first brought her back to the shop.

Curious as to what prompted his observation, Nicole read the poem next to it: *To a Louse, On Seeing One on a Lady's Bonnet at Church*:

> *To see ourselves as others see us.*
> *It would from many a blunder free us,*
> *And foolish notion:*
> *What airs in dress and gait would leave us...*

Nicole laughed out loud. So, perhaps Luc *did* find the world of wealth ostentatious. Had he learned those sentiments here, in this very room?

"*Mademoiselle?*" *Madame* Lamont interrupted. Nicole flushed with embarrassment to see *Madame* Lamont standing at the doorway. Awkwardly, she slipped back the book. "If it would please you, *Mademoiselle* Vogel, Colleen will take you upstairs to help you change into a dry garment." A fresh-faced chambermaid, her hair wrapped with a yellow scarf, approached with a quick curtsy. "*Bonjour, mademoiselle.*"

Nicole stared at the maid, at a loss. She was to have someone help her dress? No. She couldn't. "Thank you," she demurred. "I can manage myself."

"Oh, but it would be no trouble, *mademoiselle*," replied Colleen.

"Actually, I'm quite fine," Nicole insisted. "I only need, perhaps, a mirror? To fix my hair?"

"Colleen," snapped *Madame* Lamont. "Show *Mademoiselle* Vogel to the entry hall glass."

"Oh yes, at once," said Colleen with an eager smile. "Come with me, *mademoiselle*."

Unaccustomed to being looked after, and a bit self-conscious, Nicole followed Colleen to the main entry, where the maid stopped and motioned her closer. Nicole found herself looking into a full-length mirror. She'd never before seen her entire image, how tall she was, how long her legs. But it was her wet, stringy hair that horrified her. It had never looked worse. She began to fuss with the wild strands curling down to her shoulders, trying to imagine meeting *Monsieur* Marchand looking like this.

"Perhaps *mademoiselle* would like to follow me upstairs?" Colleen timidly offered. "I am quite good at brushing. And maybe you'd like to refresh? *Monsieur* Luc wishes this."

Luc wanted it? Maybe expected it? It seemed she had little choice. She couldn't offer up her hats in this condition. And now that she had come so far, she was determined to sell them. "Very well—" she turned her head to the maid "—I'm sorry, is it Colleen?"

"Oh, but everyone calls me Coco," she said, motioning Nicole up the staircase. "Everyone except *Madame* Lamont, you know. She likes it all so formal. Do it this way, do it that way. She cares only about making *Monsieur* Luc happy when he comes." She stopped and added softly, "I think *Monsieur* is like the son she never had." She affirmed her feelings with a significant nod.

Nicole had to smile. "And is that often?" she asked. "That he comes here?"

Coco gave a little shrug. "Not so much lately. But he used to, you know. When the *grand'mère*, *Madame* Françoise, was with us."

Upstairs, Coco led Nicole to a bedchamber. Nicole took in her surroundings with wonder. Slowly she walked around, trailing her hand on the bureau, then across a table. An absence haunted the room, a pervasive yet faint perfume lingering. A pile of blankets was folded at the bottom of the four-poster bed. New tall candles flickered in the chandelier, lit no more than half an hour before. The fire was fresh, with no ashes from the night. She turned about, studying the faded turquoise walls dotted with delicate Oriental watercolors of drooping willow trees.

She noticed a deep rose-colored gown spread across the back of a much-used sofa with blue satin cushions hollowed by someone who had passed many hours on it. A pair of matching rose-colored slippers had been placed on the floor. Was she to wear these beautiful things?

Coco urged her to sit at a gold-leaf dressing table. "Oh, *Monsieur* Luc, he came storming in," Coco chatted while brushing out Nicole's hair. "Never have I seen him so demanding, ordering me to hurry, hurry, and inspecting the gowns, choosing one himself." Coco giggled, speaking with her mouth full of hairpins. "You are so lucky, *mademoiselle*. All the young ladies are so much in love with

Monsieur Luc, you know. And never has he brought a lady guest here like this. We are all so excited. I think *Monsieur* cares about you so much."

Nicole forced a quick smile that faded at once. Others noticed Luc's attentions to her. The thought made her inexplicably nervous. "Luc is extremely kind," Nicole said. "I'm so grateful for all he's done." She was going to say more, but stopped. After all, the maid's expression spoke volumes more. She bit her lip, remembering being carried in his arms in the open for anyone to see, how she felt she belonged there.

A white clock painted with a spray of pink roses chimed. "We're late," Coco gasped, startling Nicole from her thoughts. "*Madame* Lamont said lunch is served at one, and you're not even dressed. Come along, we've no time to waste."

***

Waiting in the library, Luc moodily sat with his elbow resting on the arm of the chair, his chin against his hand, staring out the window. Across the room Bertrand was seated at a card table, playing solitaire. Luc welcomed the quiet, broken only by Bertrand shuffling cards, then the soft rhythmic thudding as he laid them one by one on the table.

Luc was surprised at how much coming to *Les Saules* had unsettled him. It was the first time he'd been here since the scene with his father last summer, the day Luc had threatened to take up residence in the countryside and never return to Paris. He frowned, remembering the argument. He'd been angry and announced he was leaving for America. His frown deepened, thinking about the words they'd both said in the heat of anger. Maybe he'd handled it all badly. But what in blazes else could he have done? He set aside a book opened on his lap and stood from the chair. It seemed his every action was misunderstood by his father. Especially now. There was the situation with Georgette. The demands for marriage. Maybe it *was* time to leave Paris and live here. Hadn't a break with his father been brewing for years? And then, *Grand'mère's* death had been the final doom. Split them asunder. He recalled the hurt. A young boy's hurt. But that pain had hardened him, he now realized. Maybe he should thank *Grand'mère* Françoise for toughening him to life.

Luc walked to the glass door looking out to a stone patio. His eyes went to the gray field of winter lavender plants spreading around the chateau. It all started here. His love for the country. For *Les Saules*. His hours of roaming this countryside. Watching the fields change with the seasons. He remembered one summer sitting under the tree, the one outside the patio wall there, sketching a pastel of the lavenders blooming in a flourish of purple. Later, his father had refused to even look at it. Luc set his jaw. Turning his back to the window, he pivoted around to view his library. He adored this room, all these books. He pictured in his mind *Grand'mère* Françoise taking a volume from the shelf and sitting with him to read one of the great thinkers, instilling in him the ideals of justice and nationhood. And then, his father had entered, irritated, demanding he join him in the stables.

Bertrand groaned out a huff of frustration. "Damned game," he uttered, throwing down his cards. "Why even bother with this misery? It's impossible to win." He arched his back with a deep stretch. "Gad. I find I'm ready for a bit of champagne." He looked toward Luc. "To celebrate the little hatter selling her wares."

"Mind yourself," Luc said sternly, "Be the cordial charmer you are, or you'll be put to bed with no supper."

"My, my," Bertrand said, crossing his leg and swinging it slowly. "I had no idea the subject was so delicate." His brow lowered. "What is this all about, Luc? Why this girl? Why me?"

Luc walked over to a sideboard and lifted a bottle of champagne from an ornate pewter bucket. "Unfortunately, you're the one person I have in common with Nicole," he said as he untwisted the cork. "I'd like you to help her feel welcome, Bertrand. I'm sure this venture is stressful to her," he added with a grimace, working the cork. "A friendly face will be a comfort." The cork shot up as a bubby foam ran out, spilling over Luc's hands.

Bertrand abruptly stood and looked at the closed entry doors. "Speaking of which, I believe I hear the lady's approach. And you needn't worry, my dear Luc. I promise I shall be a good boy." He smiled archly, handing Luc a towel. "Dry your hands. I'll get the glasses."

Luc replaced the bottle in the bucket. What *was* he hoping for from all this? And why here of all places? Why *Les Saules*? Behind him the clock struck one. He walked slowly to the center of the room and stared at the door. It simply felt right. Something in him wanted Nicole here.

**

Nicole followed Coco along the corridor, quickly approaching the full-length mirror, shooting it a fleeting glimpse as she passed. Was that lady *her*? Or orphaned Nicole Vogel trying to be a lady? She tightened her fingers about a folded fan clasped to her wrist. Was this the way real ladies felt, ensconced in metal hoops and yards of gauzy petticoats giving form to a rose-colored open gown that shimmered with her every step? It had taken an accomplishment of balance to negotiate the stairs in high-heeled slippers, all the while so tightly laced into the gown that breathing became a conscious effort.

At the library doors Coco paused. She flashed an expectant smile at Nicole then quickly rapped.

"Enter." It was Luc's voice.

Nicole smoothed her hair. Was this foolhardy? Did Luc really believe she could fit into his world?

As if reading her reticence, Coco winked in encouragement. "You are so lovely, *Mademoiselle* Nicole. Never have I seen such beauty."

"Thank you, Coco," Nicole said. "For everything." With a deep inhale she stared straight ahead. Colette opened one door, then the other, as if presenting her finest creation.

Nicole stepped across the threshold.

She thrilled at the way Luc appreciatively took in each detail of her transformation as she made her slow way toward him. Colette had swept up her hair to reveal what the maid had complimented as her long, slender neck. Nicole saw how his gaze followed the line of the gown, the way it fell off her shoulders then tapered off into gauzy lace sleeves. As she stopped before him, he took her hand and murmured, "You look stunning."

Her heart leapt. She mirrored back to him his gaze of admiration. Luc looked the consummate country gentleman, handsomely dressed in tight buckskin breeches and a close-fitting black jacket, his boots reaching his knees.

Bertrand Le Mansec approached, holding two glasses effervescing with champagne. "What say, eh?" he hailed, looking Nicole up and down. "Is this the same Nicole Vogel I met in Paris? Antoine's girl? No one has seen you in the café for ages. What a surprise to find you here at *Les Saules*." He handed her a champagne glass. "And with Chatillon. Selling hats."

"Good afternoon, Bertrand," she said, giving him a cool, inquiring look to hold back a sudden feeling of unease. Had he insinuated that her being here was improper? And perhaps that he'd say something to Antoine?

Bertrand lifted his glass in a toast. "To a most intriguing venture. Luc, I never imagined you to have an interest in ladies' *chapeaux*. Perhaps you have plans to invest with Marchand?"

"This is Nicole's venture," Luc said. "I'm following my mother's lead. She saw the hats and suggested Marchand."

Taking a sip of champagne, Nicole turned away, wishing she were alone with Luc. Being here at *Les Saules* had given her such a sense of joy. She wondered if Luc had wanted her to love it as he did. She hoped so. Walking to the window, she absently opened the fan dangling at her wrist and briskly cooled her face. This champagne. It was marvelous. The bubbles were a delightful surprise. She looked out the window but thought of Bertrand's words. He'd been implying she belonged elsewhere: in Paris. With Antoine. Fighting for the Cause. She took another sip of champagne. Perhaps he was right. Maybe true happiness wasn't possible for her. Especially in Luc's world.

Turning around and looking over at Bertrand, she saw a half smile curled his lips. His insinuating eyes narrowed. As if this were a masquerade she played.

She snapped her fan shut. And yet, she thought against her best efforts not to, perhaps it *was*.

Chapter Nine

After being shown from the library into the main salon by a male servant, Nicole stood before the fireplace, looking up at the portrait of a beautiful dark-haired woman with a soft smile and strong features. She saw Luc in that face. Was this *Grand'mère* Françoise, who'd given Luc books and whose gown she now wore? The woman whose presence lingered in the bedchamber? Nicole felt herself drawn into the deep brown eyes, kind and penetrating, almost welcoming her. Yes. She felt a connection with this woman. She couldn't explain it. But somehow, Nicole felt as if she knew her. Knew her spirit. Strong and capable. Yet refined and kind. The connection spread into her body, a feeling of gentleness and compassion. *I wish I'd known you*, she thought. *I wish I'd had someone like you in my life.*

"Aha. The hats," Bertrand announced.

Nicole closed her eyes. If only Luc had not left her alone with Bertrand. She turned toward him as he bent to take a closer look at six black-and-white striped hatboxes lined along the floor. He picked up one and gave it a shake, as if speculating on the contents.

"So, this is your little *pièce de résistance*?" He set it down. With his hands behind his back he walked along the line of hatboxes, inspecting the bows like a lieutenant his troops.

Was Bertrand this flippant with everyone—or did he merely not like her? Perhaps he felt she was betraying Antoine, his friend. Or maybe he didn't approve of her relationship with a man of Luc's station. During their lovely luncheon in the library, his constant insinuations that she was foisting herself onto this family had grown tiresome—to the point that Luc had told Bertrand to be quiet. Bertrand had responded with a witty quip that made them all laugh. It had been funny, but still, she found him offensive. She'd never considered the question before, but now wondered how Bertrand was connected to the Chatillon family. *Madame* Lamont had treated him like a trusted family friend. Clearly he knew *Les Saules* well. He'd led her along the corridor after Luc excused himself to accompany *Monsieur* Marchand downstairs.

It was most curious. Bertrand didn't appear to be a man of wealth. But in some ways, he did. He had the table manners of a man of high status. He knew the wines being served. She'd never thought to ask Antoine how he had met Bertrand. And how Bertrand fit into the Cause. He certainly seemed intent on a rebellion against the monarchy. And yet he upheld class distinctions. Who was he? Before an answer could make its way into her thoughts, Luc entered, escorting a man of small, erect stature, dressed in a long black frock coat and a black wig, twirling a cane before him. Her mouth went dry. It was *Monsieur* Marchand.

He approached with measured steps. Stopping, he placed both hands on the ivory grip atop his cane, seemingly used more for effect than need. "Good afternoon," he announced.

Luc's reassuring eyes met Nicole's. "*Monsieur* Marchand, may I present *Mademoiselle* Nicole Vogel, the milliner."

"Good afternoon," Marchand announced.

Nicole nodded. Luc had told her to say nothing upon the introduction. Merely smile and nod. Marchand gave her a quick assessment.

"Well, *Mademoiselle* Vogel, are you to show me these hats *Monsieur* Chatillon has been telling me about?"

Luc leaned forward and offered his hand. Nicole felt his fingers on her elbow give a reassuring squeeze as he helped her rise. She managed a small smile. "Of course. I'm most honored to do so." As she walked across the room, it was not her own nervousness she thought about, but the fear of disappointing Gus and Sarah. She wasn't sorry she'd come today—any humiliation she'd receive, even if Luc witnessed it, was worth the risk. She'd learned how to withstand humiliation. No, this anxiety was not for herself. It was for the Bastons. Their weeks of hard work. Scrimping on food to buy more material. Burning candles late into the night as they sewed. Gus exhausted.

Trust yourself, she thought. *They are beautiful hats. If Marchand doesn't like them, it's his mistake.*

The room hushed as she removed the lid from the first box, hesitated, then seized with an impulse, turned to face him. "Before I show you the hats, I'd like to tell you about them. I've been inspired by *Monsieur* Chatillon's trip to America. The hats are named after cities there."

She glanced quickly at Luc to see if he had a recollection of mentioning Boston to her. She couldn't tell, only that he smiled as if he found it a brilliant concept.

Marchand raised his chin. "Very well. What is the name of this one?"

"Boston," she announced, lifting the hat out of the box. She held up her creation of blue wool with scalloped silk sweeping around the wide brim, the restrained and delicate cluster of silk flowers featuring a single, floating quail feather.

Marchand stared, unblinking. "I see. And the next one."

You can do this, she thought. *If you make a mistake, simply laugh.*

"This is New York," she said, holding up a black wool hat with a sleek brim featuring three white egret feathers surrounding a pale pink bow. *Monsieur* Marchand studied the hat a moment, then nodded and said, "Next."

With each hatbox she opened, Nicole grew more anxious about his unreadable reaction. Yet she believed in her work. She prayed that he would, too.

After viewing "Philadelphia," *Monsieur* Marchand sat a moment. He at last rose and held out his hands, bringing them together in slow applause. "Marvelous."

Nicole gave a long exhale of relief. She had no words. She felt she might cry. Or laugh. He liked the hats.

"Excellent," Luc said. "Then you'll take them, Marchand?"

"I will."

"How many?" Luc questioned.

"Why, all of them of course. And more. We must have a contract drawn up at once."

Nicole watched as Luc took over the negotiations. He stood at her side, arranging the details. When they'd reached an agreement, he looked at her for approval, and in a daze she nodded, *yes*. Luc formally bowed to *Monsieur* Marchand.

"Then, it is agreed." He turned to her. "Nicole, if you'd like I can have my solicitors draw up papers."

She couldn't stop beaming as she kept nodding, relieved to have his expertise. "Thank you, Luc."

"And payment?" Luc asked *Monsieur* Marchand. "What do you have in mind?"

Marchand withdrew from his breast pocket a banknote. "I'm prepared today to get our venture started," he said. "Along with an advance for twenty more hats."

In a haze of excitement, Nicole sat listening to the terms, with Luc speaking up for her, negotiating, so that in the end *Monsieur* Marchand handed her the hefty banknote payable to *Monsieur* Baston, with the order for twenty more hats, the first ten to be delivered to the *Maison de Coutour* establishment in two months and the last, three months later. With the banknote in her hands, Nicole mentally calculated how she and Gus would do this, thinking about where to buy materials, excited yet somewhat overwhelmed at the thought of creating so many new hats in such a short time.

***

As Luc finalized the terms with Marchand, he was interrupted by three long-haired hounds running past the window outside, yapping and sprinting toward an approaching carriage that rattled along the drive. Even from this distance he recognized Georgette Fontenay's buff-colored cab, a gift from her indulgent father. He felt a deep frustration. Even anger. It was the worst possible timing. He drew close to Bertrand and pulled him aside.

"Why is Georgette here?" he asked darkly. "Did you invite her?"

"Not I," Bertrand said, glancing at Nicole, who was in conversation with *Monsieur* Marchand. "But I must say, it looks to be entertaining."

Irritated by Bertrand's glibness, Luc excused himself from the group and made his way out, his strides along the corridor measured, his thoughts irate, as he threw open the entry door and marched along to meet the carriage rolling to a stop.

"Luc. *Bonjour*," Georgette called, leaning out the window, her dark hair prettily coiffed under a fluffy bonnet.

"Why are you here?" he demanded, putting a boot on the step and leaning into the window.

"What a sour welcome," Georgette said, her smile fading to a pout. "And here I've made this awful trip merely to see you."

"How did you know I was here? Did Bertrand tell you to come?"

"Of course not, silly. Oh, don't be angry, Luc." She reached out to touch his whiskery jaw, but he pulled back. She shrugged. "I've come to fetch Éric. Papa's favorite mare is foaling early and it's not going well. And besides, I'd heard from your mother that Bertrand was here today. I haven't seen him in ages. So, I took it upon myself to come." She leaned out and fluttered her lashes with deliberation. "You see, my darling, the truth is, I miss you terribly."

Luc wasn't amused. He leaned in until his face loomed but inches from hers. "We both know why you came. Must you insist upon this? You make an awkward situation worse."

Her gaze darted around his face. "Is that what I am? An awkward situation?"

"You are a beautiful woman who should be addressing the father of her child."

Her nostrils flared in a sudden fit of temper. "I am doing precisely that. Now, are you going to open the door for me, or shall I have to climb through the window?" She didn't wait for his answer but pulled open the door, and head held high, moved past Luc into the house. He sighed and followed her hurried clatter of high heels as she rushed along the corridor.

"Georgette, do not make a scene," he said. "One you will regret."

She didn't respond, but burst into the room, looking imperiously about as if she were the lady of the house. Luc clenched his teeth as he saw Nicole look up with alarm.

"Why, it *is* you," Georgette exclaimed. "What's this about?"

Luc drew up beside Georgette. "I must ask you to—"

"Is it true?" Georgette exclaimed, eying the black-and-white striped hatboxes. She pushed Luc aside and turned a suspicious gaze to *Monsieur* Marchand. "Are you actually *buying* those hats?"

"I am, *mademoiselle*. Is there a concern?"

"You cannot be serious," she exclaimed, flustered. "They're hideous. I've seen them."

"Obviously you've not seen the hats *Mademoiselle* Vogel has presented to me. Either that, or you have questionable taste. Anyone who knows fashion would recognize they are exquisite, *mademoiselle*."

Georgette's face grew red. "Why, how dare you?"

"If you'll excuse me, everyone, my business is done here," *Monsieur* Marchand said coolly, rising. "*Mademoiselle* Vogel, will you be staying on for dinner?"

Nicole's cheeks flamed. "No, I'm returning to Paris."

"Then I should like to suggest we ride together. Would that suit you?"

"It suits me perfectly."

"Nicole," Luc said, coming to her. "Don't leave like this. I told *Monsieur* Baston I would bring you—"

"Gus won't mind. You've got guests. I prefer it this way."

Luc thought she sounded more outraged than dismissive. What a mess. Another Georgette disaster.

Marchand picked up his cane. "I look forward to meeting *Monsieur* Baston. I shall take leave within the half hour, *mademoiselle*. The carriage will be waiting." Bowing to the room, he made his way out, tapping his cane all the way.

Georgette stormed across the room and stopped directly in front of Nicole. "Are you sleeping with Luc?" she asked, her mouth hard and demanding. "Is that what this is about?"

"That's enough, Georgette," Luc warned.

"No," she insisted, turning to address both Luc and Bertrand. "I want to know why this woman is here." She raised an arched brow. "I made it quite clear to your mother, Luc, that this woman's merchandise is not wanted. How dare you go behind my back like this." She pinched her lips together angrily, her piercing eyes flashing about their faces.

Luc took her by the forearm and walked her to the door. He leaned close to her and murmured, "Either you will go with Bertrand to the library to compose yourself, or I shall ask you to leave this house."

"Me?" she exclaimed, pulling away, aghast. "You would ask *me* to remove myself? Not her? Never mind, I'm leaving. With Éric."

"Wait, Georgette," Bertrand said, coming to her aid. He tried to take her hand, but she flung it away.

"Don't bother following me. I'll find Éric myself." She squared her shoulders, comporting herself with dignity as she turned to address Nicole. "Don't think you can so easily dig your way into this family. Wait until I tell *Madame* Chatillon what you've been up to. She'll take care of you." She huffed out, slamming the door.

"Egad," Bertrand exclaimed. "That was rude. Even for Georgette."

Filled with frustration and anger, Luc came to Nicole. He saw the hurt. The look of devastation in her eyes. He wanted to take her into his arms. Instead, he said softly, "I am so very sorry. It was a mistake. She wasn't supposed to be here."

"I don't understand," Nicole said, turning away from him. "Why does she hate me?"

Bertrand gave a half laugh. "Georgette? She's jealous of everyone and everything. I'm afraid, Nicole, you and Marchand did something few can do." Nicole gave him a questioning look. "You've put Georgette Fontenay in her place."

"That means little to me. Excuse me, I'm getting out of these clothes." Nicole brushed past Luc and out the doors.

Luc turned back to Bertrand, stewing in silence. "What the hell was that about? Don't deny you didn't put Georgette up to this."

"I didn't, I swear." Bertrand laughed. "But I'm so pleased I was here to see it." He went to the sideboard and poured himself a drink.

"How am I supposed to fix this?"

"That, my dear Luc, is your problem. Come. Have a drink with me. You know women are never worth it."

When Nicole returned, having changed back into her own clothes, Luc thought she looked as beautiful in her plain dress as the flouncy gown. If possible, perhaps even more lovely. He tried to take her arm, but she pulled away.

"Nicole, please accept my sincerest apology," he said, keeping up with her strides toward the entry. "Don't leave this way. Today was a triumph for you."

"Was it?" she replied, staring ahead.

"I give my word that woman will never again speak to you in such a manner."

Nicole nodded curtly. Her face was flushed, her bearing tense. "This Georgette," she asked, still staring ahead. "Who is she to you? How do you know her?"

How did he know Georgette? God. How could he explain his entire life? The pressure to be who he was not, no less in a mere few words? It would take unraveling the pressure of having to fit into the mold of an entire class of men.

"Our families are old friends," he said simply. "You should know Georgette was not invited here." He winced at the half-truth. As his fiancée, she was always welcomed into his family's homes.

"Then why did she come? Is she so intimate she calls upon you anytime?"

They were almost to the doorway. "She came here for the man you met earlier outside the arena who broke my stallion. Éric Royer. He's *Monsieur* Fontenay's head groomsman. Georgette came for him. Her father's favorite mare is foaling."

He knew in his heart it was a lie, but could she understand the truth if he told her? How his life was drowning in convention and tradition? No, he already knew the answer. She couldn't. She'd not understand his wish to have been born a sheepherder. Maybe not believe it.

Nicole stepped through the door out onto the gravel. "Do you like this woman?"

Luc hesitated. "She's a woman of privilege, set in her ways."

The rain had stopped, with a few last drops falling from the leaves. *Monsieur* Marchand's driver was securing the hatboxes atop his carriage.

She said, looking at him at last, "Thank you for today. For the change it will make to the Bastons' lives, and mine."

In spite of her words, Luc could see she was hurt and pulling away from him. He wanted to reach out and hold her and tell her how proud he was, and how sorry at the same time. But he had no excuse. Georgette had ruined everything.

"Forgive me?" he said.

The driver hopped down and, seeing her, rushed to the door and opened it.

"There's nothing to forgive." She lifted her hand to the driver, stepped up inside, and settled in beside Marchand.

As the door shut, Luc came close, hoping she'd look at him one last time. But she stared straight ahead as the carriage lurched away.

Chapter Ten

Luc was late finding his way to *Taverne Anglaise*. Of course, his father would choose the *au courant* restaurant of the day, a place where wealth could be flaunted. This was foolish, to keep up the pretense that life was normal, to ignore the unrest in Paris. "It's good to be seen," his father had said. Which was even odder. The nobility were doing the exact opposite, disappearing behind their wall of privilege like ostriches with their heads in the sand. Rarely did a nobleman's coach appear on the streets. Not with so many bands of disgruntled peasants milling about. Congregating. Conspiring. The rebellion was getting serious.

Today he was to play the obedient rich heir to please his parents.

The *maître d'hôtel*, a man with precision to his walk, escorted him to the table. Luc bent down and kissed his mother's fragrant cheek. "I'm sorry to be late."

"We took the privilege of ordering," said his father as Luc was seated. A server, wearing a red coat with gold brocade, draped a napkin across Luc's knee and poured a glass of Bordeaux. Luc took a long draught.

On cue, a second server ladled consommé into thin white bowls, placing each with precision before the guests.

Luc was more interested in the wine. He drained his glass and signaled for another, ignoring his mother's soft gray eyes appealing for him to slow down.

"What kept you?" demanded Victor Chatillon. "A particularly engrossing engagement with artisans and radicals?"

Gabriele gave a small laugh, as though her husband had spoken a witticism. Luc knew the tactic, an attempt to reduce the tension between him and his father. It never worked.

"Luc, your father ordered a lovely *Lapin à la moutarde*."

"I'm sure, *ma mère*." He turned to his father. "You're not too far off, sir, about the artisans and radicals—most of whom I met at that university you sent me to. We spend our hours getting drunk and arguing about Montaigne and the American experiment. You should join us sometime."

Victor took a slow sip of wine, then set his glass aside. "I don't have the *time*. Someone must keep you in means to while away your hours with such important endeavors."

"Please, Victor." Gabriele placed her bejeweled hand on her husband's arm. "Let's have a nice meal together." She turned to Luc. "Have you heard they're opening the Tuileries Gardens at the end of the week? You know with spring coming I look forward to the flowers, the concerts, the promenades."

Victor lowered his brows and sipped his consommé.

Luc welcomed his mother's patter. It allowed him to be the good son who showed up for the twice-monthly restaurant obligation. After the consommé was cleared, the waiters returned with *foie gras* and brioche, followed by braised hare with artichokes *à la Barigoule*.

"Luc, dear, what do you think?" his mother was saying. "The Tuileries Gardens? What a pleasant outing after this dreadful winter." She sniffed gently into her handkerchief. "I'm ready for color and warmth, aren't you, dear?"

Victor had been quietly eating, keeping his eyes on his food, and yet his anger was deafening. Luc could feel it from across the table. He knew the signs that his father was chomping to say something. He'd been cold and distant since the meeting with the Fontenays. And now he was going to use this dinner to force the issue, to convince him to marry Georgette. To merge fortunes with the Fontenays. It wouldn't make a scintilla of difference. The marriage wasn't happening.

"Luc, we have not resolved this. You say you will not marry Georgette Fontenay. And do you think you have final say in such a decision?"

"Victor, please," coaxed Gabriele. "Must we argue?"

"We have a contract with the Fontenay family," Victor went on, leaning across the table. "What are you thinking here? To dishonor it? And so dishonor your mother? Forget me and what it will cost my reputation. But do you plan to publicly humiliate that young woman?"

"Victor, please," whispered Gabriele. "Please."

Luc stared vacantly across the room. He thought about his father's estrangement from his own mother and wondered if families were doomed to repeat the past.

"Well, have you nothing to say?"

Luc turned his head and stared into his father's eyes. "Do you honestly desire to give your inheritance to a child who is not your own blood?"

"Marriage is not what you want it to be," said Victor coldly. "Marriage is a convention. It protects our society. And our women."

"So does the office of sanitation. My God. Haven't you left out something important? Love? That two people love one another before joining in marriage for life?"

"There it is, isn't it? More nonsense. Love? Is that your magic potent for marriage? Do you think I had that liberty?"

His mother looked down at her food.

Luc's brow lowered. His father always hurt her. This respectable husband, generous to his wife, even kind. But there was no love. His wife was a *convention*? He was sick of these ideas.

"This is about a child, Luc. *Your* child, damnit. How can you walk away from this responsibility?"

"Sir, let's get this out. Right now. It's not so much the innocent child. Don't think I haven't concerned myself with that. It's the woman who carries him—she lies and schemes to get her way. And she's desperate not to give birth to a bastard. Is this the woman you wish me to share my life with?"

Gabriele gasped. "Luc, you cannot say such things."

"What? That I'm not the father of the child? That's not news."

"You, Luc, are naïve," Victor said. "You go about with your head in the clouds thinking there is something more than what is right before you. But this tiger you fight is pure imagination. You will marry Georgette. Her child will be your child. You will have other children. You will do all this, Luc, because it's the way it is."

"There you're wrong. I will *not* do things merely because they've always been done that way." He hated this. Wanted to walk away, go back to America. "Damn your conventions," he said lowly. "In case you've not noticed, things are changing. Your rules, your conventions, they only serve tyrants. But how much longer?"

"I will not sit here and listen to such insolence," Victor shouted, pounding the table. A group of nearby diners glanced over. Luc raised his chin, holding back his anger as his father leaned his elbow on the table and pointed his finger at him. "You will marry Georgette Fontenay," he commanded in a low, strained voice. "I will not hear another word on the matter." He stood, whipping his napkin from his lap. "If you have anything to say beyond that, I'll be at the club. Don't wait up, Gabriele."

In the wake of his father's leaving, Luc took a long drink—then stopped, seeing the sadness on his mother's lovely face. He reached across the table and took her hand. They sat in silence while the waiters removed the mostly uneaten main course, then went about filling their coffee cups.

"I'm sorry, *ma mère*," Luc said when they were alone. "You must trust me. Believe in me. I will not marry Georgette."

She withdrew her hand from his. Her face was composed, emotionless. It almost frightened him that she could cover her feelings so well.

"You know," Gabriele said softly, pouring cream into her coffee. "Life is not as black and white as you think." She brought her cup to her lips, then paused and set it down into the saucer. "You are a man, my dear. You can do as you please. You can marry and still have—" She gave him a gentle smile. "Well, a certain freedom." She held his eyes for a moment, then looked down at her coffee. She took up her spoon and stirred, lost in thought.

He filled with tenderness for her. He loved this woman so much. What was she saying to him? That he would be afforded the same freedom her own husband enjoyed? He frowned. Her beloved husband was probably on his way this very moment to that *freedom*. He wondered if she'd ever felt passionate love for her husband...or for any man.

"I am quite aware of that standard," Luc replied. "It's part of the *marriage convention* Father speaks of. But it's not what I want from life."

"What *do* you want?" she asked, putting down her spoon.

The question took him aback. He wasn't sure he could answer.

His mother gave him a long, hard look. "Luc, this wouldn't have anything to do with that beautiful milliner, would it?"

He'd not expected that observation from her. It caught him completely off guard. "Why would you say that?" he asked, plucking a brandied plum from a candy dish and popping it in his mouth.

She shrugged. "I was simply wondering. She certainly is an attractive young woman—in a unique and charming way. I believe she is talented. Her hats are unlike anything I've seen. She has..." Gabriele paused, seeking the right word. Finding it, she looked at her son. "...she has vision."

He could hardly believe the words came from her mouth. He wanted to hug her. She was always sympathetic toward anything he wanted. Yes, she had to maneuver about her husband, but he knew at that moment that she wanted his happiness. He adored her for that. "Yes, she does have vision. I agree."

"But, my dear, please think about the...gray areas. Do not rush toward anything, or away from anything. Stay even. Take your time. Be careful."

Luc knew then that he *would* hug her. He rose and approached, and to her surprise and delight drew her up into his arms, leaned close, and whispered, "And now, my beautiful mother, let me escort you home."

***

Antoine was busy cleaning up the last of his inking by the light of an oil lamp. Nicole sat in a corner illuminated by the dim light of a candle stub. She may as well have been in the dark as she stared unseeing at the open pamphlet in her lap. Months ago while cleaning in the back room of the shop she'd found a stack of forgotten pamphlets and church missives, dog-eared and dusty. They'd been a treasure trove for her to read whenever she waited for Antoine to finish up. But tonight she couldn't focus on the words.

Her mind's eye played over and over the scene of being in Luc's arms, with the rain pouring down on them. They'd given in to the deluge, powerless to stop the force of nature—in the very way she couldn't stop her thoughts about Luc. Try as she might, it was impossible.

Antoine rose and stretched. She looked up. Something about the fatigue on his face as he arched his back moved her. He was such a good man. He labored countless hours each day, inking and pressing Jules Tout's etched copper plates.

He caught her look. "Read to me, Nicole."

The request surprised her. He'd never asked before. "Now?"

"Yes, as I finish up here."

She glanced down at the pamphlet. "It's Voltaire."

"Really?" he said. "What a surprise that Tout would have subversive ideas in his shop. His words are everywhere on posters. What is it?"

"A poem. Maybe there's more to *Monsieur* Tout than you know."

He grinned. "Maybe. What's the poem about?"

"He's writing about gardens," she said, "but not those you'd find in a park." She stopped, suddenly remembering *Les Saules*. The wild birds, and the meadows. Riding with Luc—

Antoine interrupted her thoughts. "It seems odd to write a political satire about gardens."

She looked back down. "He's writing about the formal ones that are precise and clipped and full of symmetry."

"Like the gardens of Versailles," Antoine said, coming closer. "Have you seen them? I went once. Nothing feels natural."

"I've never been. Is it beautiful?"

"It's pompous. And vain. The people of France will no longer tolerate this flaunting of wealth."

"That's what Voltaire writes. Nature does not grow in lines and squares. It takes wealth to create that."

"Read me a line."

She looked down.

The spacious forest suits my mind,
Where nature wanders unconfined...

She looked up. "Nature is free. It belongs to everyone." She continued, slower, more thoughtfully:

The world with ancient fables tire,
I new and striking truths admire.

Wiping his hands on a rag, Antoine murmured, "Ah, see. He's saying time to abandon the fable of a monarchy. With all its artificial beauty, beauty and art owned by a few. It's a call to revolution. And now the time has come. Hurry, Nicole. Let's get these posters up." Turning, he knocked over a tray of typesetting tools and sent them clattering to the floor. "*Merde*."

As he bent to gather them, she reread the lines. *The spacious forest ... nature unconfined.* She'd felt it that day. That day in the rain. It brought out something...wild, dark, and unknown. A chasm had opened within—frightening yet exciting. When Luc carried her through the storm, she'd never felt freer. Happier. And now, being *here*, she felt—oh God. She did not want to be here, in Paris, in this shop.

"Antoine, I can't go tonight. I—I don't feel well."

Antoine stood, holding the box of typeset. "What's wrong, Nicole?"

"It's just—can we do this tomorrow night?"

"Don't worry. I'll go out myself. Let's get you home."

Nicole stood and slipped her cloak over her shoulders. Her *new* black cloak. She'd never owned such a fine piece of clothing. It had been the first thing she'd purchased after handing the bankcheck to the Bastons. Gus and Sarah had insisted she buy something to replace her threadbare cape.

Antoine shouldered his canvas bag, grabbed the basket filled with glue and brushes, and ushered her out the door—when he noticed it.

"What's this?" he said, his fingers gliding over the edge of wool cloak, lined in red silk.

"It's new," she said, her pulse quickening. Why did she feel guilty? She had the right to sell her hats. "A surprise."

"A surprise?" said Antoine.

"Yes. I've been excited to tell you. Gus and I have a buyer for our hats. *Monsieur* Marchand. A prominent merchant. He believes they're going to be the next new thing in Paris. And he wants to export them to America."

"Is that so? And how is it that this buyer discovered Gus's shop?"

For an instant, her mind went blank. "That's what's so wonderful." She didn't like the elevated tone in her voice. "Luc Chatillon's mother heard of Baston Millinery and asked Luc if I'd show some hats."

"I see," said Antoine. "That's rather convenient, that the man who couldn't keep his eyes off you would arrange a way to see you again."

Her face flushed. "Antoine," she pressed. "It's not what you think. *Monsieur* Marchand was so certain of the quality of the hats that he outright bought all six for twenty-five *livres*."

Antoine's face grew stone cold. "That's a lot of money," he said. "Enough to purchase something else he wants?"

Nicole froze. Had he suggested she would *sell* herself? "Oh, Antoine," she said, turning to make her way to the shop door. She placed her hand on the knob and looked back. "I can't believe you'd say such a thing."

Antoine dropped his sack and came to her, reaching for her arm. "Nicole, wait. That was rude. Unforgivable. It wasn't meant to hurt you. It's only that everyone knows you've been selling hats. The Bastons. Chatillon. God knows who else. But not *me*."

Nicole wanted to leave. She couldn't bear the truth of his words. She felt exhausted, like she could sleep three days straight. "I'm leaving."

"Wait. I only say these awful things because I love you." He reached out and held her face in his palms. Nicole strained to get free. But he pulled her closer and pressed his lips to hers. She closed her eyes. For a confused moment, her mind envisioned Luc kissing her. She reached her arms around him, feeling for Luc's broad chest and powerful arms—

Antoine pulled back. "Nicole, I think we should marry."

Her eyes flashed open to see Antoine staring at her. "Marry?" Her mind searched for a response but found none. "I—I need to think—there's Gus and—well, we'll have to ask him."

"I take that as a yes," Antoine said, smiling. "Let me take you home. Tomorrow I'll speak with *Monsieur* Baston."

"There's so much happening," she said, groping for words. "Wait until the order is finished. Will you do that?"

Antoine pulled her close. "Of course, my dear Nicole. And no more nights out for a while. You don't look well. I'm getting worried about you."

***

That night as she lay in bed, a shaft of moonlight fell across Nicole's eyes. What was happening to her? She must get hold of herself. Antoine wanted to marry her. She'd been living in a dream these past weeks. What did she think, that a man of Luc's station would wed a hatmaker? People like her worked for the Chatillon family, didn't marry into it. Hadn't she learned that lesson at *Les Saules*?

And now, she had so much. The success of her hats. Gus and Sarah. And a best friend who would be having a child soon. She would be an aunt. Her life had become more than she'd ever hoped for. She would give back to the people who had given so much to her. And she had Antoine, a good man who understood her world. Their betrothal was fitting. Yes. It made sense for them to be together. She could only ever be Luc Chatillon's plaything. She would never again be so foolish.

She rolled onto her back and looked up at the shadowy ceiling, thinking about their last moment together. She knew in her heart Luc had been sorry. He'd written to Gus on the pretense of asking about the hat orders, though she knew he was trying to make amends. But it didn't matter. It hadn't been his fault. He couldn't help his family's friends. Georgette Fontenay hadn't been invited. And yet, it was good the woman arrived when she had. It gave her another peek into the Chatillon family. She'd *never* fit into that world. Luc's world.

Tomorrow she would write Luc a short letter of thank you, because that's what one must do when someone has been helpful and kind. She would need to find a way to convey her clarity about their relationship being business, only business. She imagined herself sitting at the kitchen table with paper, pen, and ink. *Cher Luc…* No, no. Only formal language could create the proper tone of distance. *Monsieur Chatillon.* Yes. That was how she would begin. The letter would be short, to the point. She would thank him for all he'd done—for her and the Bastons.

Growing tired, she closed her eyes, her thoughts drifting. And then she was again at *Les Saules*, in the rain. He was carrying her in his arms, saying how she looked like a drowned puppy, and they'd laughed, and she'd felt so safe and happy. And she'd felt the butterflies within when he'd touched her—and now they were here again, just thinking about him.

Chapter Eleven

M. Chatillon,

We write to thank you for your inquiry about the contract between Baston Millinery and Maison du Couture. We thank you for all you have done to further the reputation of Baston Millinery, and we will endeavor to satisfy our agreement with Monsieur Marchand, and in doing so honor your trust in our establishment. If you have further questions, please contact your solicitors who oversee the arrangement for complete details.

Sincerely,
M. Baston & Mlle. Vogel

Luc crumpled the letter in his hand. He resumed pacing the length of the library, a vacuous chamber off the foyer—used rarely, with few books, the fireplace never lit. He'd always found it cold and austere. More an appendage to his father's great chateau, a showcase. Like so much of his father's world.

Luc expelled a deep breath. A heaviness pervaded his thinking, a sense of being lost. What Nicole's letter *didn't* say spoke volumes of her pain. Her suffering affected him more than he would have thought possible. He closed the library door, turned around, and leaned his weight against it. He'd let Nicole down. She had put her trust in him. Actually accompanied him to the country—her first time outside Paris—to meet a powerful man. *Sacre.* Few *men* he knew would show such courage.

He stared across the room. He should have ordered Georgette's carriage around the minute she'd arrived. What had he been thinking? He'd opened the carriage door. Pandora's box. If only—

Slowly he walked across the floor to the elegant desk and smoothed out the crumpled letter. All these weeks he'd not been able to think of anything but Nicole. She hadn't answered his letter. Until today. Only this. This—*farewell.*

The thought of never seeing her again left him cold and empty. He rubbed his temples. What was happening? He couldn't think. Eat. Sleep.

My God.

Was he falling in love?

He pushed the thought aside. Whatever this was, the need to see her again was too compelling to ignore. Sitting at the desk, he pulled out a sheet of stationery from the drawer. He began: *Ma très chère Nicole—*

He stared across the room out the window. A yellow bird flew low then swooped out of sight. He crumpled the nearly pristine page and threw it to the floor and drew out a fresh piece. This would be from his heart.

Chère Mademoiselle Nicole,

I deeply enjoyed our time together in the country. You appeared to appreciate, as I do, the land where I spent much of my childhood. With spring upon us, the meadows are bursting with flowers and ripe to explore on horseback. I invite you to spend a day with me at Les Saules. I have much to explain, and much to ask forgiveness for. Please give me that chance. This Sunday at 9 a.m. a coach will come to fetch you. If you choose not to take it, I will know you do not wish to see me, and I will not trouble you again. But I only hope that you will.

Cordially, Luc Chatillon

***

The sun was setting on the Seine as Nicole and Aimée finished with their laundry, then stripped down to their chemises and navigated the river steps down to the muddy bank. Aimée looked more and more pregnant each week, yet she nimbly slid into the water and paddled herself to the pilings and grabbed hold of one of the many thick, waterlogged ropes dangling along the dock.

Nicole eased in beside her. The water felt refreshing on this warm April evening. For days now she'd been utterly confused. She'd read Luc's letter over and over. In truth she knew what he wanted. She knew he was attracted to her, that he wanted to make love to her. What a mistake it would be to go back to *Les Saules*. She'd come to understand how she could be little more than his passing amusement. And yet, she couldn't get the invitation from her mind.

Making out Aimée's smiling face in the torchlight, Nicole felt glad to be with her for the first time in weeks. She needed her. Needed the solidity of this world of family and friends. She loved the wonderful change happening in the shop. She did appreciate how much Luc had helped their lives. And she was coming to accept his words that day: *Georgette was not invited.* It wasn't his fault that Georgette Fontenay was a family friend—even if she was a horrid person. But none of that was her concern. Her life was here. With her family. Antoine. And Aimée.

Dear God, Aimée. She couldn't shut her out any longer. She deserved better than this. "I'm glad you joined me tonight."

Leaning back and floating buoyantly, Aimée said, "Ah, I feel like a sparrow, not a fat turkey waddling about."

"But such an adorable fat turkey," Nicole teased.

Aimée giggled and pulled herself closer to Nicole. "Isn't this wonderful? Not only the water. The night. You can feel spring, can't you?"

Nicole nodded, lying back in the water and looking up to the dark sky. She let go of the rope and floated on her back in silence for a moment, watching the stars come to life. She could not go with him. She could not. Still, why did she want to?

Aimée splashed water in her face so that Nicole rose up, laughing. "What?"

"Don't keep me in suspense, Nicole. Tell me what you want to tell me. Why you really wanted to come here tonight. I know how all these weeks you've been acting so pleased—with the hat orders, and your shop so busy. But, Nicole, I know you. Something is wrong. What troubles you? Is it still this rich man in your thoughts?"

Treading water, Nicole stared at Aimée's expectant face. She had made up her mind to tell her. Grabbing the rope, she pulled herself alongside Aimée. "Something did happen with Luc. But not that day. It was a while ago."

Aimée was instantly alert. "When?"

"In February. It happened outside *La Fenêtre*. Well…we kissed."

"You kissed him?" Aimée exclaimed so loudly that Nicole shushed her. "But does Antoine know this?"

"No. Of course not." Nicole flushed. "He can't know. I would never hurt him."

"Oh, Nicole, how could you? Antoine is kind and loyal. He loves you so much."

Nicole ran her hand through the water. "Antoine asked me to marry him."

Aimée gasped in surprise, so that she almost choked and had to spit out a mouthful of water. "But this is wonderful, Nicole," she sputtered.

Nicole let go of the rope and plunged underwater. Her thoughts grew loud in her head in the cold, alien space. She had been foolish to kiss Luc. But never would she let Antoine know. She'd already paid the price, thinking she would find happiness outside her world. What had *Madame* Colére said? *You make yourself special.* Absurd, thinking she could really—

She surfaced with a gasp for air. Wiping water from her eyes, she found Aimée watching her. She swam closer to her.

"The kiss was a mistake," Nicole said. "It never should have happened."

Aimée groused her agreement. "I told you to stay away from this rich man."

They floated in silence.

"Nicole, why didn't you tell me about Antoine's proposal?"

"Oh, I can't say, Aimée. I'm not sure."

"You do not want to marry him?"

"I... I'm not sure."

"But how can this be? You've got your business. There is no reason to stay with the Bastons. You and Antoine can be wed. You can start a family."

"There's something else," Nicole said, her voice sounding flat in her ears. "Luc has invited me to return to *Les Saules*. On Sunday, a coach is to pick me up."

Aimée shook her head, pulled herself close, and grabbed onto Nicole's wet shoulder. "No. You *cannot* do this. Antoine wants to marry you." Nicole could not meet her eyes. "Nicole, what are you thinking? That you will go there so you might kiss some more this handsome, rich man whose magnificent life you can share for a few moments before he tosses you away? Nicole, he's dangerous."

Aimée's words felt like a slap. But, she deserved it. She *had* wronged Antoine, the man who loved her. He was the reality of her life. Luc was a fantasy—the one to ride in on a white charger and take her into a sunset where her nightmares of *Madame* Colére's anger and lost parents faded. "Luc is nothing like that," she said softly. "He's truly a kind man. But it doesn't matter. I won't be going anywhere with him. And now, I think it's time we go home." She released the rope and swam toward the shore.

As they walked with their baskets of clean laundry, Nicole admitted to herself she'd never be able to make Aimée understand the real Luc. How she'd felt so *alive* that day in the country. She'd seen his books. His world. Without even trying, Luc had revealed something of himself to her, something warm and tender. And yet...the sting of Aimée's words held truth. Her friend was trying to protect her. She and Luc *were* from different worlds, and nothing could change that. Aimée was right. Antoine was the one. No more steeping herself in a dreamland that could only end in heartbreak.

"Don't worry, my friend," she said when they came to Aimée's street. "And thank you, dear one, for helping me see this clearly. I will never see Luc Chatillon again."

***

When Sunday morning came, Nicole stayed in bed, complaining of a headache. Before leaving for church, Sarah brought in a mug of oxtail broth.

"I knew this would happen with your nonstop work," Sarah said, placing her palm on Nicole's forehead. "No fever. Still, I'm staying here with you."

"No," Nicole murmured. "Really. I'm fine."

"We'll be late," Gus called from downstairs.

"Please, go with him," Nicole insisted. "I need to rest this morning."

"You're sure? I can stay and make you—"

"I promise. Now hurry before Gus decides to skip mass altogether."

That thought got Sarah out the door, her heavy footsteps clunking downstairs. Nicole could hear her all the way, and the Bastons' bickering followed them out of the shop.

The minute the door clicked shut, she rose from bed. It wasn't really a fib she'd told Sarah. She wasn't ill, but she wasn't feeling herself. She needed some time alone. Pulling Luc's letter from her nightstand drawer, she reread it for the millionth time. Slowly, thoughtfully, she tucked it back into the drawer. Was he really coming here today?

She paced barefoot, back and forth, her mind whirling. *You are not of Luc Chatillon's status*, she told herself. *You never can be.* She paused at her wardrobe. Maybe, though, she should dress. Of course. Not that she would be leaving the shop. Still, she should dress.

She absolutely could not go with him. What would it lead to? Still, she might step out and say hello. She selected her freshly washed stockings, sat and pulled on one, then looked vacantly across the room. She closed her eyes, remembering *Les Saules*. Being in the carriage as it passed by the open fields. Her eyes flashed open. To ride through those fields on *horseback*? She yanked up the other stocking.

She chose her thick gray skirt. It only reached her ankles, she noted, as she twirled about and admired how it swayed prettily. Oh, and her white blouse. She grabbed it from a hook. She paused in her buttoning and returned to the nightstand and read the letter again. *I have much to explain, and much to ask forgiveness for. Please give me that chance.*

Not that it mattered, she thought, shutting the letter firmly away in the drawer. There could be nothing more between them. Luc had helped her. Helped the Bastons. That was enough.

She grabbed her boots, thinking it was good she'd cleaned them last night. Perched on the edge of the bed, she pulled them on and laced them. Why were her fingers trembling? She was being silly. She was not going with Luc.

Still, maybe she should go downstairs. To see if a carriage really did arrive. She washed her face and splashed rose water on the nape of her neck, remembering the words she'd memorized: *The meadows. Horseback. I invite you. I won't trouble you again.*

She looked in the mirror. "And why shouldn't I go for an afternoon in the country?" she asked her image as she pinned up her hair. "He's been kind. He's a friend."

At the kitchen table, she wrote a note to Gus and Sarah, explaining she felt much better and had gone to visit Aimée. Downstairs, she crossed the shop to stand at the window, shuttered for Sunday. Midas leapt up to the settee beside her. In the semidarkness Nicole stroked his fur. "Oh, don't worry," she murmured. "I'm not really going. I'll only look out when I hear the carriage. In fact, who's to say there'll even be a carriage? This is all so silly. I'll go to Aimée and tell her everything. How I've been foolish. And that I will marry Antoine."

Midas's tail flicked.

As the church bells began chiming the hour, the clomping of hooves and the rattle of coach wheels rumbled to a stop at the front of the shop. Nudging Midas aside, Nicole stood to peek out from the window shade. There it was, the same coach that had picked her up before, the same driver dressed in green livery staring straight ahead. Her heart thumped against her ribs. Was Luc inside? Waiting?

The minutes ticked by. Midas jumped onto the back of the settee and stretched his legs toward her for attention. Her gaze could not move from the coach. She saw no movement inside. Was Luc there waiting? She closed her eyes. She almost felt faint. *What can I do? I can't simply ignore him.*

She opened her eyes to see the driver had lifted the reins and snapped them against the horses. Disheartened, she watched as the carriage lurched forward. *They're leaving.* She stared, unable to breathe as the carriage pulled into the street.

She paused, then rushed to the door and flung it open. "Wait," she called, running outside. The carriage rumbled along. "Don't go," she called. But the carriage was picking up speed.

She ran into the street, waving her arm to the driver. "*Attendre.*"

And then the horses were slowing and the wheels rolling to a stop. Breathing heavily, she stood there, her arms dangling at her sides, feeling foolish, afraid and unsure as the coach door opened.

Out stepped Luc. Her breath caught. He was smiling luminously. Even from this distance she could see the happiness in his eyes.

"Nicole, you're here," he said, doffing his tricorn hat and bowing at the waist. "Come. Your coach awaits."

Chapter Twelve

Nicole felt herself floating in a dream. The dream of sitting across from Luc Chatillon in his beautiful carriage. He looked so handsome, wearing a gray linen jacket with a white shirt tied in a loose bow at the throat. His dark hair was secured at the nape of his neck. She could tell he'd been outdoors since she'd seen him last. His skin had taken on a golden hue. She didn't think he had ever looked more attractive to her. And how polite he'd been. He'd left her to her thoughts, to accustom herself to being alone with him. He'd made their being together feel natural. And yet—there were flashes of Gus and Sarah finding her note on the table, and she felt sad that she'd lied to them. But had it really been a lie? Had she really known she was coming today? And even if she had known deep inside, and she was now on this adventure, was it really so wrong, when it felt so…wonderful?

In silence, the city passed by in a blur, until Luc began to fill the cabin with his soothing voice, pointing out the Tuileries Gardens, telling her how he'd gone there with his mother a few days before. They'd sat on a park bench, watching people promenade in their pastel spring fashions. Luc had smiled when he repeated his mother's words, that Parisians were *like butterflies emerging from cocoons*. Nicole could see the beautiful image in her mind's eye. Clearly, Luc adored his mother. *A man who loves his mother is a man who loves his wife*, Aimée once said.

A wistful feeling surged through her, of missing the mother she never knew. Well, she had a family now. She let her sadness float away, out the window, over the trees. No gloomy thoughts. Not today.

A sweep of green hills appeared. Her heart leapt. The countryside. It was as beautiful as she remembered. She could hardly believe she was here—with Luc.

Beside her, Luc's voice came soft and low, telling her about the afternoon he'd planned for them. The horses. A ride in the meadow. All at once, from out of nowhere she wanted to throw herself into his arms. Turning her head to look at him, she imagined her lips on his. A flutter swirled in her chest. She wanted to touch his temple. To trace her finger along his jaw. The flutter became a somersault.

As Luc spoke about horse riding, she turned back and watched the green fields and meadows passing by. She took in his words, her pulse fluttering at the sound of his voice and at the thought of being on a horse.

Or so she imagined, until worries about Sarah and Gus began to creep in. Had they gotten the note by now? Had Aimée come for an unexpected visit? Would they worry about her? It had been silly to mention Aimée. She should have—

The carriage slowed as the horses made the turn onto a gravel drive. Nicole sat taller, realizing they were rumbling through the gates of *Les Saules*.

"Ah, see there," Luc said, putting his hat aside and leaning closer to the window. "They never disappoint."

Nicole's breath caught. The willow trees had come alive, as Luc had promised they would, with spring-green branches trailing to the ground.

She realized he too was taking it all in. In the silence she felt an invisible thread linking them in a shared awe of the nature outside the coach windows. A sudden and overwhelming surge of joy filled her. She was almost light-headed. This was happiness. The happiness she'd dreamed of years ago. And the moment she felt herself release to it, something—a voice, an old warning—came to her: *What you seek is a delusion. A trick of the mind.* She clinched her fingers into fists in her lap. *I'll not listen. I'm here. With Luc.*

"I wanted to share this all with you," Luc said. "Les Saules is most magnificent in spring."

Ahead, the honey-stone chateau appeared, a fairy tale castle covered with wisteria vines. The carriage passed round to the back, toward the stables, then rolled to a stop. Luc jumped out and ran around to her side to assist her down, his hand lingering on hers even after she was firmly on the ground. She looked up into the full sunlight to see his deep brown eyes hooded with ridiculously thick black eyelashes. Those eyes seemed to read her every thought. Her desire to be here with him. And deeper. Her longing for him to hold her, to kiss her with urgency and passion.

Instead, he turned as Raoul, the leathery-faced stable master, rushed forward, three hounds at his heels. "Morning, Master Luc. Lovely day."

"It is, isn't it," Luc said, looking up at the brilliant sky. "Do you recall my friend Nicole Vogel? She's never ridden a horse."

"Well, we'll fix that," he said with a smile. He bobbed his head toward her. "*Mademoiselle*, for you." He held out a pink rose. "Welcome to *Les Saules*."

Taken aback, Nicole accepted the rose, wondering if this man had actually picked it himself. "Thank you, Raoul." She lifted it to her nose, and with a smile at him, tucked it in her waistband.

Raoul swept his hand toward two horses tied in the shade. "Got the ones you asked for all readied, Master Luc."

"They're beautiful," Nicole said, drawing closer. Up to this moment she'd not given much thought to riding a horse. But now, seeing the huge animal, she wasn't sure. "Do you really think I can manage horses like these?"

"Horses have a sense about people," Luc said. "They can read a person's character. You'll be a natural."

"It's an instinct," Raoul added. "These animals straight away can sense cruelty in a stranger. They back off every time." He took a stub of carrot from his pocket and held it out to Nicole. "Take this, *mademoiselle*. You'll make easy friends. We approach horses from the front," he instructed, guiding her forward.

"Hold it flat on your palm," Luc directed. "Hera, look what we have for you," he said to the golden brown horse, smartly outfitted with a sidesaddle. Hera stretched her neck and muzzled the prize, her whiskers tickling Nicole's palm. Nicole smiled, amused at the comical way the horse daintily took up the carrot and began chomping. Finished, the horse nudged Nicole's arm for more.

"Hera, you're a sweet girl," Nicole said, rubbing the mare's jowl.

"That's why we chose her for you," Luc said, adjusting his saddle.

"And you'll ride *him*?" Nicole's eyes indicated the magnificent stallion.

"Yes. Apollo."

"Do you name all your horses for Greek gods?" She smiled, thinking it told her much about him. Or were these his father's horses?

"Only the best ones," he said with a grin. "You're not afraid?"

"Not to ride Hera." She patted the beautiful horse's sleek neck. "But I'd think twice about Apollo."

"Smart choice," Raoul said.

She laughed, and Luc joined in.

"Nicole, you'll be fine," he said.

"I'm not afraid." And truly, she wasn't. She was excited.

Raoul fetched a wooden stair step and helped Nicole onto her saddle. She wondered what the stable hand thought of her, off for a ride with the master of the estate. Perhaps he'd seen all types of women come and go in Luc's life. Yet, touching the rosebud at her waist, she sensed a kindness, a generosity, in the man.

"All set," Raoul said, slapping the horse's thigh. "With Master Luc out ahead, there'll be no worry."

Luc swung up into his saddle and urged the muscular Apollo alongside her. Hera's head bobbed toward the stallion.

"I think she likes Apollo," Nicole said with a laugh.

"She does. She'll follow him anywhere. Just click the reins. Hera will know what to do." With that, Luc jabbed Apollo's flanks and trotted off.

Nicole felt Hera shift beneath her and suddenly she was bouncing in the saddle, holding on, and just as Luc had said, drawing beside Apollo. What had Luc said in the carriage? *Trust the horse. Sit tall. Look forward.*

It was true. This felt unreal being transported through such breathtaking land, Luc at her side. She felt like a mythical goddess as she was carried away from the stables, out to flower-filled meadows. As though Hera had wings.

"I understand something better now," she said, once Luc had slowed to a walk. "Something you said earlier, Luc."

Luc looked to her. "And what is that, Nicole?"

"How you're at peace in the country. That you feel free here." A smile filled her face. "I feel free here, too. Maybe for the first time in my life."

"I'm glad," Luc responded.

They approached a grove of trees alongside a brook. That was when Nicole noticed a table veiled behind a curtain of willow branches.

"What's this?" she exclaimed.

"A surprise." Luc picked up the pace, and Hera trotted after him. Ducking through willow branches, Nicole saw the table draped with white linen and covered with bell-shaped glasses, *couverture de plats*. A bucket of wine. Two crystal wineglasses.

"Our meal," Luc announced. He jumped from his horse then came and reached up for her so that she dropped into his arms. Her breath caught with his nearness. But before she could think, he'd let her go and turned to bring the horses to tie them to a limb. As he did so, she walked about. Luc had arranged all this? It gave her an odd feeling to think she'd been at the center of planning by the staff here. Probably *Madame* Lamont? Coco?

She ran her hands over the rough bark of a tree trunk, thinking how Luc said the trees had spirits. Looking about, she believed it. Everything here was alive, from the grasses edging up through the ground to the bees flitting in the flowers. She took the rosebud from her waist and smelled its sweet perfume. "Raoul is a kind man," she said as Luc approached her.

"He's salt of the earth," Luc said, tossing his tricorn on a blanket that had been spread beneath the tree. "He's taught me much about being a man."

As they sat, Luc filled their glasses. They toasted to the day and dined on cheeses and hunks of bread, nuts and dried fruits. Nicole wondered at Luc's statement about Raoul teaching him about manhood. *Not his father?*

Luc watched her. "*Gather ye rosebuds while ye may,*" he recited, refilling their glasses. "Come, join me." He pointed out the blanket spread under the tree.

"*Old Time is still a-flying,*" she added with a smile, feeling warm and bold with wine as she stood.

He laughed and guided her to the blanket. She sat, curling her legs beneath her.

"Poetry? You surprise me, Nicole."

She shrugged. "A kind nun was in my life, for a short time, in my schooling at Legros. I wondered why she'd become a nun. She was so young and lively. I'd always imagined she'd lost a lover."

Luc leaned back on his elbow and stretched out his legs before him. "A lover?" He smiled and took a sip of his wine. "Go on. You intrigue me."

Nicole had thought her first time alone with Luc would center around him telling her about his exciting world. And she'd brought up *lovers*? She might as well have told him outright the direction of her thoughts. "What I mean," she said, flushing, "is that Sister Anna loved romantic poetry. She believed we should live life before our youth fades away." She plucked a petal. "Like this rose. Look. It's already wilting."

Luc glanced at the rose in her hand, then back up to her eyes. "So, Nicole Vogel, should we seize the day?" He sat up and leaned so close to her she could smell his familiar musky scent. "Time's a-flying."

Her heart began beating faster. She wondered what he might do if she told him her fantasies. Of him taking her into his arms. Asking her to marry him. Living here at *Les Saules* and raising a dozen children. "I think my being here today answers that question."

Luc's smile faded. Solemnly, he reached out and removed her wide-brimmed straw hat and set it aside. "Nicole, when I got your letter, I was afraid you never wanted to see me again."

She looked hesitantly into his eyes. "Maybe I didn't."

"And yet you're here."

"You don't know how close I came to *not* coming, Luc."

He frowned. "Nicole, I once told you I wanted to be your friend. That's not completely true. I'll be your friend if that's all you wish to offer. But I will not lie. I do want more." He moved closer.

She didn't look away. She'd made her choice the moment she'd opened the door of the shop. The instant she'd called for the coach to stop. She'd chosen this.

"Luc, I don't want to be only friends, either."

He reached out and covered her hands with his. "Then, may I kiss you?"

The floating feeling returned. She absently crushed the rosebud in her hand as she felt herself nodding, yes. *Oh yes.* He slipped his hands to the back of her neck and gently drew her closer. She leaned into the fullness of his mouth. He responded, kissing her harder, moving closer and closer and guiding her body down onto the blanket.

Ohhh, the feel of his lips. The warmth of his body. She draped her arms about his neck, loving the way his mouth moved across hers, soft and moist, tickling, thrilling. Being with him like this, his breaths coming harder—

He broke away, leaving her gasping. She stared into his eyes. He held her face between his hands, then lowered them down to her shoulders. "Nicole, *belle femme*, will you let me make love to you?"

If she said yes, her life would change forever. She could never marry Antoine. She would become Luc's lover. Deep in her heart, she knew marriage with him was impossible. His family would never accept her. But did that matter? If she said yes, she would be part of his life. She would feel his body with hers. If she said no, he would pull away, take her to the carriage, back to—back to what? No. She belonged here. With him.

He was waiting for her answer.

"Yes," she whispered, stunned that the word escaped her lips.

He reached out and caressed her face, then kissed her softly, running his hands through her hair. Sitting back, he began unbuttoning his shirt. Oh God, oh God, she should say *stop*. But stopping was not what she wanted. He peeled off his shirt, revealing his powerful arms and chest. Her breath caught as he fumbled with the buttons of his trousers.

"You're an incredible woman, Nicole Vogel," he murmured, bending on his knee. "I want to know everything about you."

He leaned to her, kissing her again and again, helping her remove her boots and stockings, lifting her blouse over her head, and her chemise, until her breasts were bared to him.

She felt a delicious rightness in being here, with him, in the open air. He ran his fingers along her breasts, his eyes on hers. He lowered his lips to touch his tongue on her nipples, tracing them, lingering, opening his mouth to her fullness—then with his breathing growing urgent, he pulled up her skirt and grasped her hips. What had been gentle, unhurried caresses shifted, became intense as he raised his body atop hers, hovering above her on strong arms, then gently settling onto her.

The hardness of his body thrilled her. She wanted him closer, closer and closer. He obliged, shifting himself nearer and then, with the fullness of his passion, entered her. She gasped in surprise. Pain and pleasure burst through her body. As she gripped his back, he held her close, rocking into her, his movements building in power and rhythm as slowly her desire overcame the natural pain.

"Oh Luc," she breathed.

"Nicole," he growled into her ear, his cheek rough against hers as he lost himself in his own emotions.

And then she was engulfed in a white light, an intense flood of pleasure pulsing through her body, past her mind and into her soul.

Chapter Thirteen

When Nicole awakened, Luc was tracing his fingers along her arm. Her body filled with adoration for the man who'd been the first to make love to her.

"You've slept," he said.

"Mmm."

He kissed her wrist and said, "If I could stop time right now, I would stay with you here forever."

Did he mean it? Or were these mere words? "Alas, we can't."

"So true. It's time to go."

In silence they took to their horses, and as they galloped across the flower-filled field, Nicole savored the warm horse beneath her. Had these hours with Luc really happened? It hardly seemed real. He'd seemed so loving, not taking his eyes from her. My God, how she wanted him. She could not deny it. She would stay with him forever if he asked.

"I have something else planned," Luc said. "Would you like to bathe before returning home?"

"Bathe?" she laughed. "Where?"

He smiled. "In the *chateau*. We can have a light supper afterwards. Please say you'll stay longer, Nicole."

She bit her lip. Should she? Already Gus and Sarah would be worried. But everything had changed. "Yes," she said with a smile. "I'd love it."

At the stables they gave up the horses and Luc escorted her inside. She wondered who would greet them. *Madame* Lamont? *Gather ye rosebuds*, she repeated to herself, but as Luc ushered her inside, her thoughts stopped.

It was indeed *Madame* Lamont who met them. By the look on the woman's face, Nicole could only imagine their disheveled clothes and hair, their flushed cheeks.

"Master Luc, *Mademoiselle*. You look like children in from play."

"We enjoyed the luncheon," he said. "Afterward we spent the afternoon riding through the countryside." Nicole felt herself blush under *Madame* Lamont's regard. She was sure the woman knew there was more than that.

"*Mademoiselle* Nicole will need to freshen," Luc said.

"I'll have Coco draw a bath. And you, Master Luc, there's a fresh change upstairs in your room."

Luc made no comment, just winked at Nicole as *Madame* Lamont turned her back on them and waddled toward the door. "We'll have a light supper of cold chicken," she called over her shoulder. "You both must be starved."

***

With Coco's help, Nicole undressed and lowered herself into the fragrant water. The maid lit a cluster of candles on a nearby table. Yesterday she would have been shy about undressing in front of a near stranger. But now, somehow, it seemed natural.

"Looks like you and Master Luc had a day of it," Coco chatted away. "When you finish, you can dry with this"—she indicated a towel that looked large enough to cover the entire body—"and then call me, *mademoiselle*, and I will help you dress." With that, she left the room.

Nicole ran her fingers through the silky water of the huge copper tub set up opposite a bed draped in satin. She liked Coco. She might even be a friend. Aimée would love her. And today, how welcome she had made her feel. And cared for.

Next to the tub, a marble table held bottles filled with who-knew-what potions. She eased her head back. Gardenias floated on the surface, grazing her breasts and toes. *Where was Luc?* she wondered, and that very thought lit up her body. She ran her hands down her sides, caressing her thighs. She had never wanted so much to feel a man's touch as she did at that moment, as though something inside would burst through her skin. How could she want him again, so soon? But the day was passing. She must return home.

The thought of her real world in Paris flooded her with a sense of urgency. "Coco," she called out. She heard a rap on the door.

"Yes, please come in," she called.

"Are you certain?" Luc's voice drifted to her.

Yearning swept through her. "Yes," Nicole said.

Luc stepped inside. In the golden candlelight, he walked toward her, his robe unbuttoned, his chest covered in a matting of hair. Standing before her, he dropped the robe so she had full scope of his magnificent body. Her gaze lifted to his face, so handsome with that square jaw and his dark hair slicked back.

He lowered himself into the tub, sloshing water and flowers over the sides so that he faced her. He lifted her right foot and massaged it, then the other. A current flowed from his fingers right up through her legs, fanning out through the rest of her body. He continued the massage up her calves. No one had ever touched her this way. She felt faint and closed her eyes, luxuriating in his touch. When she opened them, she found him staring at her with a penetrating gaze. Then he shifted his body over hers, and for the second time that day, their bodies melded in pure pleasure.

"Let it happen with me," he murmured against her ear. "My dear, sweet Nicole."

"I'm so happy I came here today, my love," she whispered. "I wanted to be with you, but I was afraid."

"Nicole, *ma amour.*" He kissed her eyelids, the tip of her nose, the hollow of her throat. "You never have to be afraid of anything ever again."

***

Taking her seat in the carriage, Nicole was grateful for everything. For this incredible day. For Luc. It was all so easy, even natural to be with him. And now it had come to an end.

"Are you certain you want to go back alone, Nicole?" Luc said, leaning into the window and taking her hand. "Are you all right?"

She smiled, holding his gaze. "Yes, really, everything is perfect. I need—some time alone, Luc. To think, before—" She caught herself before saying *I need to face everyone.*

He seemed to understand. Lifting her wrist to his lips, he lightly kissed it. "I'll call on you soon." He stepped back and directed the driver to leave.

As the carriage jolted forward, Nicole watched Luc disappear in a glare of sun. She leaned against the wall of the carriage, wrapped in her cloak. She felt satiated. Content. A knowing smile played on her lips as the magical hours played over in her mind. She could not have imagined a more perfect afternoon.

She looked out the coach window at the countryside, reflecting on the day, then laughed out loud. *My God.* To make love outdoors? To gallop on a horse? Oh, how Raoul had greeted them with nonchalance, even if he had guessed the source of her and Luc's conspiring smiles—it didn't seem to matter to him.

Nicole quietly watched a line of geese flying low across the dimming sky. And then, unbidden, came the dark voice deep in her mind. *But do not fool yourself. There can be no marriage.*

The floorboards rattled over a rough patch of road so that she held on to the armrest. She rubbed her temples. Dear God. What was she thinking? This was impossible.

And then came the dark voice again, *You will be hurt one day.*

Her lips hardened. Well, didn't she already know about hurt? She pulled her cloak to her throat. It was getting chilly. And late. Her eyes searched the darkening clouds. By now Gus and Sarah would be sitting down for supper.

She stared out the window, unblinking. She could not deny that the hat shop was her world. She didn't belong at *Les Saules*. Today would mean nothing to Luc. *Nothing.* It was only a day for him. He had his father, and his mother whom he'd taken to the Tuileries. Luc could never leave them, his home and society—not for her. Even if he did love her. And even if he did, even if he married her, and left his past, all of them, behind—there would come a day he would begrudge the loss.

No. There would be no marriage.

The dark voice came. *If you see him again, there will be losses. Great ones. No marriage. No children.*

A hard coldness crept into her musings. Or possibly there would be children. *With no father.* And what of their feelings of abandonment? She shook her head at the thought. Luc would never abandon a child. He would provide for her. She'd have a lovely apartment. He would visit her and their children. He would, of course, wed someone of his station, someone proper, a pretty young woman who had the approval of his parents. He would have a family of his own.

Her stomach tightened thinking about it. Could she live such a life? Would Aimée abandon her if she knew what she'd done today? Would Luc, one day, tire of her?

And yet, there was one truth that no one, not even *Madame* Colére, could destroy. She *had* been loved in her life. She'd had a mother. A father. They had loved her, wholly and completely. At least that was what the memories deep in her heart told her. Yes, Luc may leave her one day. But he loved her now, didn't he? She would risk his abandonment. Yes, so she could live, even if only for a while, in love. And if she had his children, they would never want for a mother's care, a mother's love.

She closed her eyes. *Trust, Nicole. Trust your heart.*

***

The coach slowed at the city gates. Nicole had been pensively staring out at the darkening sky for some time. Now back in the city, a brilliant orange and purple sunset filled the horizon. She was exhausted. What would she tell Gus and Sarah? The truth? That she'd ruined her life with a man who could never marry her? Oh, but she couldn't hurt them like that. Perhaps she might pull Aimée into it? Ask her to lie for her? The thought was abhorrent. She needed to think. Reaching up, she pounded her fist on the coach wall for the driver to stop.

"*Mademoiselle?*" he asked, appearing at the door window.

"I'd like to get out."

"Ma'am? Not here. It won't be safe."

"I'll be fine," she said, opening the door herself. The driver, his brow knotted in a dubious expression, helped her down. "At lease let me follow behind you, *mademoiselle*."

"No." She smiled. "I know my way through Paris."

"But it will be dark soon. Master Luc would not be happy if—"

"I know my way, even in the dark. You can tell your Master Luc that, if he asks. He'll understand. Though you needn't say anything."

Nicole walked along the narrow streets. A wagon full of squealing pigs passed by. Ahead two men were fighting outside a tavern and she quickly crossed the street. What was she doing here?

Only certain women were out like this. A woman selling wood was packing up her last few unsold pieces. The woman gave her a thoughtful look, one she knew meant the area was dangerous. For her to be careful. *Ha.* She'd not been careful all day. In fact, now that she thought about it, she had not been careful at all. They'd made love. What might happen?

Suddenly frightened, she walked faster, not from the dangers on the street, but from a terrifying thought. *What if? Could she be?* Lost in her thoughts, she somehow drifted through the streets in a kind of half-dream state, making a plan. She would say she'd spent the day in Tuileries Garden. She'd watched the ladies in their new spring fashions. She'd gone to *Maison de Couture* to check her hats. She couldn't tell the truth.

At the door of Baston Millinery, it may have been her hands that opened the latch and her feet that stepped inside, but her mind still lingered beneath the willow trees, on the blanket, in Luc's arms.

The smell of cooking cabbage wafted down from the kitchen. With a deep breath she began to climb the stairs. Midas met her halfway, mewing.

"Hello, Your Majesty," she said, reaching down to pat his back.

"Nicole."

She looked up. It took her a moment to realize Antoine was standing at the top of the stairs.

"Where have you been?" he called with a smile.

Antoine? *Why was he here?*

She slowly came up to the landing, reaching out as he took her hand. He pulled her into an enthusiastic embrace. She stiffened against him, her thoughts confused. What was happening?

"Come," he said, taking her hand and pulling her along. "We've been waiting."

Entering the kitchen, she was met with heat and candlelight and Gus and Sarah seated at the table. If Antoine took his arm away, she might collapse.

"Such good news," boomed Gus, rising to embrace her.

"We're so happy, my dear," enthused Sarah, coming to her and kissing her cheek

Nicole frowned. And then the dreadful reality dawned on her. She knew the words that would come before Antoine spoke them.

He grabbed her hand and turned her around to look into his eyes. "My darling Nicole. *Monsieur* Baston has given us permission to marry."

PART TWO

Betrayal

Chapter Fourteen

"You're engaged," Aunt Charlotte gushed. At the fire grate of her well-kept kitchen, she poured piping hot water into a teapot. "Oh, my darlings, I've been waiting for this news."

Antoine was stacking logs in the wood box. Nicole sat at the table, toying with her empty teacup.

"My dears, I'll help you prepare the wedding. Along with *Madame* Baston, course."

"It's not to be anything special," Antoine said, dusting his hands. "A civil ceremony."

"What?" Aunt Charlotte exclaimed, carrying the teapot to the table. In middle age, Charlotte Durand's once-narrow face had rounded into a double chin, though she still had the porcelain complexion of a young maid. At all times she wore a muslin cap atop her upswept hair, crowned with a large blue bow. Her dresses, the two she owned, were well-mended broadcloth, the lace-edged sleeves spotless white.

She filled Nicole's teacup. "Is this what you want, my dear? A civil ceremony?"

What Nicole wanted was to leave this room, this house, this city—and run away to a place where she could be free. A meadow of flowers. A fragrant bathtub, with Luc's glistening body merging with hers.

She toyed with her cup, avoiding their eyes. "Well, I always dreamed of—" She pictured herself in a shimmering green gown, the color of willow leaves in spring, her hair laced with irises and daffodils. She dared for a moment to imagine Luc standing there, while she walked toward him.

"There will be no church wedding for us," Antoine declared. "The clergy is corrupt."

"Now, Antoine," Aunt Charlotte said. "Think of what your mother would have wanted."

"Mother is dead," Antoine said, his face souring, his habit at the mention of her. "Where were the clergy with all their wealth when she was starving? Eh? *Not* marrying in the church honors her."

The bedroom door burst open, and a skinny blond boy emerged holding before him a long, narrow stick, thrusting it forward like a fencing sword. "*En garde,*" Sebaste shouted.

With a grin, Antoine grabbed a spoon from the table. "*En garde.*" He jabbed his spoon again and again as they sparred noisily around the table.

"Oh my, what Musketeers," Aunt Charlotte exclaimed, clapping her hands.

Nicole's spirits lifted. She loved these sweet moments between the brothers. Their mother had died giving birth to Sebaste. She'd already lost two babies: one at age four months, one stillborn. Antoine said her malnourished body was too weak to withstand childbearing. He blamed everyone for it, including his father, Charles Durant, Aunt Charlotte's brother. He'd disappeared before Sebaste was born.

Aunt Charlotte whispered into Nicole's ear, "Antoine could hold Sebaste in his palm when he was born. It's a miracle such a tiny infant survived. And now look at him. Antoine raised him into this fine boy." She sat back and took a sip of tea. "Antoine will be a wonderful father."

Nicole nodded. Watching their roughhousing, she believed that to be true. It was one of the qualities that endeared Antoine to her. He hadn't had a father and yet he had taken so well to that role with Sebaste. Thinking about it, she wondered about Luc. What kind of father would he—

Her stomach clenched at the thought. How long had it been since *Les Saules*? Two weeks, to the day. She'd been waiting, and her monthly should have come by now. Could she be with child? *Dear God…*

"Argh, I'm dead." Antoine dramatically fell, the spoon clattering across the kitchen floor as he sprawled out.

Sebaste tossed his long blond bangs from his eyes and planted one foot on Antoine's chest. "I win," he cried out, raising the stick aloft in triumph. "I am undefeated." Then, melting into giggles, he threw his tiny body on top of his brother's. They wrestled until Antoine popped up, holding Sebaste upside down by the ankles. The boy's face grew red while he laughed and laughed as Antoine swung him back and forth like a pendulum.

"Now, don't make him ill," chided Aunt Charlotte. Nicole was struck by the woman's patience with such roughhousing in her sparkling kitchen. She liked Aunt Charlotte very much. There was a common sense to her, an everyday wisdom that balanced Antoine's tendencies to view the world from one spot on the spectrum.

Antoine righted his laughing brother on his feet. Sebaste ran up to Nicole and threw his arms around her. "I'm so happy you're marrying Antoine," he enthused. "Antoine says you'll be my mother *and* my sister."

Nicole drew him onto her lap and brushed back his hair. "I will always be in your life," she vowed.

"Will you live with us?" he asked.

"Why, of course she will," answered Antoine jovially, plopping down in a chair at the table. "And she'll work with us in the print shop."

Nicole went pale. "Antoine, what are you saying? We've not talked about this."

"It only makes sense," he said with a shrug. "After we marry, you can quit that bourgeoise business of selling hats to the wealthy."

"But it's what I do," she protested. "What about money?"

"We won't need your money."

"But why? I can help with the household. Even help Aunt Charlotte." Nicole frowned. "And Gus? I can't simply leave him."

"Gus owns the business, not you. With you helping in the print shop, we'll increase our output. It's meaningful, honest work."

"Why, there's no shame in making hats," said Aunt Charlotte, pouring tea for Antoine. "All people need hats."

"The wealthy need nothing," Antoine said. Pushing aside the teacup, he stood from his chair and walked to the window. He looked out, his back on them. "And that's who Marchand sells to."

"But, my dear," persisted Aunt Charlotte, "the print shop income is barely enough now. It may not support your family as well. Think about when you have children. Nicole can make hats while staying at home with the babies."

"Babies?" repeated Antoine, turning around to face them. "We will *not* bring children into this world of rebellion and poverty."

The room fell silent. Nicole noticed a shadow pass over Aunt Charlotte's face. Perhaps the woman was thinking about her own empty nursery. Bringing Sebaste and Antoine into her home had been the greatest joy of her life, she'd often said.

Aunt Charlotte gathered herself together in dignity as she stood to pick up the empty teapot and teacups. "Don't be so rash, dear. The future will change. Everything changes. Children bring great happiness to life."

"Happiness is a fairy tale," said Antoine. "Our revolution is real."

***

As Nicole walked through the shuffle and clatter of Rue St. Vincent, the whole world felt as upside down as Sebaste dangling in Antoine's grip. Antoine's words about having no children echoed in her mind. She pressed her hand to her abdomen. Children. Of course, she'd fantasized about being a mother, but the truth was, having a family seemed an idea that belonged to others, not her. She wasn't sure she even understood what family *meant*. But what if, after her lovemaking with Luc—

At the thought of Luc part of her felt elated. But then there was a part that felt uncertain. Where was he? What was he doing this very moment? Was he thinking about her? It had been weeks.

I will call on you soon.

Those last words to her had been a buoy, keeping her from drowning in doubt. And yet, not even a note. *Soon,* he'd said. She'd clung to that vague hope. A dim memory came to her, something he'd said on their way back to the stables at *Les Saules*. This was foaling season. It was possible he was helping his father. If only she could talk with him.

No matter what, though, it was becoming clearer and clearer she could not marry Antoine. She *did* love him, but as a friend. She'd always admired his passion for justice, and he was so pure—and yet, he was changing. Over the last months, he'd become consumed with the Cause. It was all he talked about. And, oddly, and more troubling, since their engagement he'd grown colder, not more loving. Thinking regrettably of everyone's happiness about the

124

engagement—Gus and Sarah, Aunt Charlotte and Sebaste—she knew she'd have to speak to Antoine soon.

A deep, rusty voice startled her out of her thoughts. "*Mademoiselle.*" Nicole turned to see a toothless woman huddled on a stool, a ragged wad of a bonnet hanging around what must have once been a sweet, heart-shaped face, now distorted into a walnut shell of hardness. The woman held out a pink peony. "For you." The woman's eyes squinted against the sunlight. "Only a *sous*. For an old woman."

Nicole's mouth went dry. In her haze of repulsion and pity, a clarity surfaced in her mind. Antoine would not stop her from her work. No one would. She would have her own money. No matter who she wed. She would not become this tragic woman—or worse. She reached into her little purse, pulled out a coin, and placed it on the woman's palm.

Even if somehow she could marry Luc, she would follow her dream of making hats.

***

"Oh, perfection." Aimée smiled from her pillow as she took the pink peony from Nicole and buried her nose in its petals. "Ahhh. How many days since I've left this bed? Sweet of you to bring the outside to me."

Jacques stooped to get through the bedchamber doorway, proudly displaying a garden pot he'd filled with greenery. He arranged the flower into it and set it on the bedside table. "Very nice of you, Nicole," he said, taking Aimée's hand into his calloused one. "Aimée likes flowers."

Nicole acknowledged him with a nod. "What did the midwife say?"

Jacques drew his burly arms across his chest. "That our babe is excited about coming into the world." He lowered his brow, casting Aimée a chastising look. "And that my wife should be in bed until the little one calms down. We've got to make sure she does that."

Nicole brightly smiled, but inwardly was worried. Aimée looked pale and fragile. She glanced up at Jacques to see if he, too, shared her concern. But the only emotion on his face was adoration as he bent over Aimée and pushed strands of hair away from her cheeks. "Isn't that right, my little bird?"

"You worry too much," she murmured, clearly pleased with his attention and care.

In the intimacy that passed between the married couple, Nicole suddenly felt like an intruder. She thought theirs was a true love story. Aimée had once confided to her that Jacques feared he'd never find love. Nicole delighted in the story of their courtship. Jacques had been almost twenty-five on the day he'd delivered a cabinet to Legros. He said he'd caught sight of a petite girl with white hair falling about her shoulders, and later confessed to Aimée he believed he'd seen an angel. For weeks he came back, ingratiating himself to *Madame* Colére in any way he could, somehow always finding himself in a room with Aimée. They'd fallen in love. It took some doing and plenty of bribes, but he'd convinced *Madame* Colére to allow Aimée to marry him.

And now Nicole adored him for his gentleness with her dear friend. She watched as he placed a quick peck on Aimée's cheek. Standing tall, like a giant in the low-ceilinged room, he reached for his cap on the bedpost. "Thank you for being here, Nicole." She noted the formal reserve in his voice, his custom when addressing her—though now she wondered if there wasn't a tone of reprimand there also. As he buttoned his jacket, she looked away. Yes. She could almost feel his rebuke for her absence. She'd been involved in her own world. Her own wants. Her own needs.

"I'm only sorry I didn't come sooner," she said, vowing at that moment to change. "Until Aimée's baby is safely in her arms, I'll come visit as much as I can."

Jacques inclined his head. "That would be good. She needs you." He pulled his cap onto a thatch of blue-black hair, and with a wink at Aimée and a nod to Nicole, he ducked out the door.

Nicole watched him disappear into the next room. Jacques had always been a bit distant with her. Aimée said he was shy. But Nicole believed Jacques sensed she was different than Aimée. Oh, he thought she was a good person, she was sure, but perhaps— unsettled? A restless spirit? And she had to admit he was right. Aimée wanted nothing more than to be with Jacques, to make a home for him, which she'd done with very little. Aimée's love for her husband could be seen in the basket of washed red apples on the kitchen table, the embroidered floral pillowcases on the bed, the way she dried flowers—as she would this pink peony—and hung them from the rafters of her kitchen. Aimée had created a home with Jacques, a beautiful place to raise a child together. Nicole wondered if maybe Jacques was right. Maybe there *was* something restless about her spirit.

"How do you feel?" she asked, coming to Aimée's side and taking her hand.

"Tired," Aimée admitted. "And I wish this was over. I know I shouldn't say so because it's best to go nine months, but I'm so ready to have this baby."

"It's almost your time," she said, easing beside her on the mattress edge.

"Nicole, I'm so happy that you and Antoine are betrothed," Aimée said, clasping her hands, the sincere smile glowing from her blue eyes. "When is the wedding? Have you made plans?"

"No. Not really." She wanted to tell Aimée that she wouldn't marry Antoine, and yet she didn't want to disappoint her either. Like now. With Aimée's eager smile, waiting to hear all the details of a wedding that would never happen. It struck her that she'd stayed away precisely to avoid this conversation.

"Nicole, you haven't made *any* plans? About a dress? A date to post banns?"

"It's—I'm not sure."

"You don't have to wait for the baby to come—" Aimée suddenly pulled her hand away, her body wrenching in pain.

"Aimée, what's wrong?" she asked, alarmed.

Aimée took in a deep breath. "Oh, this—" She grimaced, grabbing her pregnant belly and moaning.

Nicole squeezed her hand. "What should I do? Call for the midwife?"

As the pain subsided Aimée's face grew peaceful. "No, no," she whispered, calming. "She's already told me a few are natural. It's...like the monthly." Aimée looked up with a teasing smile. "Well, maybe a little worse—" She closed her eyes as another wave came. She rolled her head on the pillow.

Feeling paralyzed, Nicole watched helplessly. After a moment, Aimée's eyes fluttered open. Her breathing was soft, and she gave a faint smile. "And then it passes."

Nicole was filled with an overwhelming relief. Embracing her dearest friend, she whispered against the pillow, "I will be here for you, I promise."

Aimée shook her head. "Of course," she said, her eyes fluttering shut. Nicole stroked Aimée's forehead for a few silent moments until she opened her eyes.. "Nicole, let's talk about something happy. You are engaged to Antoine. Have you told—everyone?" She raised her brows in a question. "Does Luc Chatillon know?"

Nicole had not expected the question. She began to fuss with straightening the blanket.

"I see," said Aimée. "And so, there was more kissing—that day in the countryside?"

Nicole was at a loss for words. Could she admit to her friend, or to anyone, everything about that day? It felt private and personal. Between Luc and her. To speak out loud the joy and spontaneity of her and Luc's lovemaking would change everything. Spoil the purity of it.

"We rode horses," she began quietly. "It's so beautiful there, Aimée. I wish you could see it."

"And that's all you did, ride horses?" Aimée's face twisted in a sudden spasm of pain. She moaned, then, struggling to breathe, gasped, "Another one, Nicole. I think they're coming more often."

Hurrying to a bowl on the dresser, Nicole brought back a damp washcloth and smoothed it over Aimée's forehead. "What can I do?"

Aimée grabbed her hand and squeezed hard, clinching her eyes shut, then slowly let go as she eased her head against the pillow. "Tell me more," she whispered. "About the countryside."

"Yes, Aimée. Let me tell you everything."

She pulled up a chair and sat, rubbing Aimée's hand as she described the sweeping meadows and fragrant flowers against the blue sky, the spring willows reflected on the pond water. She talked about riding a horse—making Aimée smile—telling her how much easier it had been than she'd imagined. But only, she was sure, because she sat atop the wonderful and gentle Hera. She added that Luc had been kind and generous—and though she wanted to say more, to tell her about the joy of being with Luc, and that she could never marry Antoine—Aimée's eyes had closed and her breathing softened in sleep.

Nicole sat there, relieved that Aimée was not in pain. And disappointed. She hadn't told her everything. She longed to. But not now. She rose and paced the floor. She was all alone in this.

Chapter Fifteen

All week Nicole forced herself to present a smiling face to the world. She was busy with the hat orders, working dawn to dusk in the shop with Gus. She had yet to tell Antoine she could not marry him. She was not sure if she would tell him *why*. That she had made love to Luc. Or maybe she would tell him she wouldn't marry anyone. Marriage did not fit her career. One thing she knew. Whatever she did choose to tell him, she had to do so soon. She vowed to do so, the first time they were alone.

However, her thoughts were not only on Antoine. Or the hats. Her every waking moment was consumed with Luc, wondering why he hadn't called on her, wondering if she'd ever see him again. But as the days passed, her beautiful memories were fading. The dark thoughts were growing, leaving her in self-doubt. *You're too naïve. You've mistaken his actions for something more.*

As the days dragged, the darkness grew. She could scarcely concentrate on work. Several times Gus corrected a careless stitch. She didn't care. Her monthly came at last—and while she had been relieved, she also felt a loss. The idea of carrying Luc's child had become a warm companion, her reminder of their day together. And now, that was gone, too. While her fingers stitched hats, she played in her mind again and again each word they'd shared, each action, searching for anything she'd said or done to turn him away. There was nothing. It had ended perfectly.

Then with her work done, in the dark of night, lying awake staring at the ceiling, the chastising voice would come. *He gave no promises You let yourself believe because you wanted to believe.*

And finally one day she awoke, tired of it all. She would put Luc from her thoughts. She came down the stairs into the shop feeling free. Feeling lighter. She was strong. She'd been abandoned before, by people more important in her life than Luc Chatillon. She would not think about him.

Reminding herself of what mattered most, she saw Aimée as often as she could, bringing flowers and helping her friend pass time in her bed confinement. They never talked about the day with Luc, though Nicole knew Aimée probably wondered. Still, she never asked. Instead, Aimée chatted about names for the baby, how she longed to get out of bed, and about the upcoming wedding. When would it be? Had she ideas for her wedding dress? Where would they live? Would they bring Sebaste to live with them? Nicole found each of Aimée's questions a challenge. She didn't want to lie to her. And yet, she couldn't tell her. She kept putting off going to the print shop to see Antoine. It would mean telling him. She was afraid. Confused.

And even with her decision not to think about Luc, the voice inside her head still tormented her. *You were nothing but another conquest for him—a rich and powerful and gorgeous man.* She pinched her wrist, reminding herself of her decision to stop thinking about him. It wasn't easy.

The time had come to tell Antoine. He was coming for supper. But no sooner had he entered the shop than he began his excited discussion of the trouble in Paris. He showed no interest in the hats being made downstairs. Upstairs at the dinner table, he was swept away with the intoxication of the latest news. Nicole tried to focus on what he was saying—that the king had requested lists of his subjects' grievances to be drawn up and presented for deliberation at the States Meeting to take place in May. Many subjects of the king felt their needs would be met. There would be more grain. More equality. Lower taxes. When Gus said this sounded wonderful, Antoine assured him that the king would never give in to their demands. Gus nodded and slurped his soup. Sarah dropped scraps to the floor for a begging, mewling Midas.

Later, Nicole let Antoine out at the door, knowing she could not tell him about Luc. Not now. Not like this. Oh God. She was so alone.

She grew sad. Depressed. All her life she'd dreamed of designing and selling hats—and now her dream had come true. Gus took her with him to buy fabrics and taught her how to barter with the manufacturers, where to go for the best notions. And now she had the luxury of buying special things for herself. While at *Monsieur* Marchand's shop, she purchased a new pair of slippers, not walking shoes, but pretty calf-skin slippers with an inch-high heel. She also bought a silk blanket for little Jac, the name Aimée and Jacques decided upon, so certain were they that she carried a boy.

After giving the blanket to them, Nicole left their apartment. She walked along the street, thinking how happy they'd been with the gift. They had little money. And she had the money and success she'd always dreamed about. And yet she was sad. The dark voice had won. Luc did not love her.

Her eyes were dry. If only she could cry. But try as she might, there were no tears.

***

Luc clicked the reins on his cabriolet, the sporty one-horse carriage he enjoyed. It moved lightning fast through the streets. Part of the speed came from its design, a small, lightweight frame, with room for two. Perhaps that was why he brought it today. He could be alone with Nicole. No driver. Just the two of them. Not that he was sure how to approach arriving at the hat shop, or if she'd be there. He should have sent a note beforehand. But everything had happened at once: the breeding of Apollo, the foaling of five mares all within a week. Still, he should have sent a message.

He honestly wasn't clear in his mind why he hadn't. Since that day at *Les Saules,* Nicole had never left his thoughts. Though in truth, thinking of her was always accompanied with some guilt. He'd not fully considered the consequences of bringing her to *Les Saules.* It had been a rash action, perhaps foolhardy, and if—even now—he used his best sense, he would turn the cabriolet around and return home. He *would* send her a note. A note to tell her how lovely she was, and how he was happy to have been able to help her career. How she was fresh air in his stale life.

He stared ahead unhappily. Despite what happened, they both knew in their hearts there could be nothing more than that day between them. He guided the horse around a corner without thought, as if his body alone guided his actions.

Nothing more between them? He should say that *nothing* meant no marriage. In a deep moral sense, he knew that's what a woman like Nicole would expect. He had taken her virginity. She was—he slapped the reins faster—she was an innocent in many ways. She knew nothing of his society, the permissive mores of both men and women, how staunchly they protected their status, which meant keeping at all costs a barrier between themselves and the "others" of the Third Estate. The *commoners*. Like Nicole. Those in his world were not noble blood, but they were fiercely determined to keep their distinction as *special people.*

Could he expect Nicole to easily step into his world? Even if she were strong enough, what about his family? His mother? It would be unfair to her as well...to face her society circles with a son who'd married a working woman, a trade union laborer. And he *knew* what his father would say. He might forbid Nicole to step into their home. No, not *might. Would.*

And yet, even with such misgivings, Luc's thoughts lightened as he saw the hat shop ahead. Oh God, how he wanted to see her.

What rules were written saying he could not be with her? *Marry* her, even, if he chose? After all, his mother had married a man of modest means, a man far below her own father's wishes for his treasured daughter.

Luc pulled the reins on the horse, bringing his cab to a stop before the shop. Yes, Nicole was poor. He jumped out. She was also delightful and beautiful. He straightened his jacket. She had a gift for wonderment and spontaneity. She brought light into his life. Today was today. Tomorrow was an illusion. He walked to the shop door.

He wanted to see her now.

***

Pushing aside the hat she was stitching, Nicole looked up with a start. She'd heard the carriage stop outside. Throwing aside her work, she ran to look through the window. Her somersaulting heart left her breathless.

Luc. He'd come. Her feet somehow got her to the door. *Calm yourself,* she said. Taking a deep breath, she smoothed her hair, her skirt, then, standing tall, pulled open the latch. And there he stood.

Happiness overflowed her thoughts, her senses, so that she had to lean against the door for support. "Luc, *bonjour*," she said, with a cordial smile. "Have you come for more hats? We've just finished one. We're naming it Concord. I think you'll like it."

She waited as his gaze roamed over her hair. She was so happy she'd washed it yesterday. It would be shimmering in the morning sunlight.

"*Bonjour*, Nicole. I should have sent a messenger."

"No, no," she said. "I can only imagine your hectic life. Mine has been occupied with all our orders." She stood rigid, reluctant to ask him in, not wanting to have to explain his presence to Gus or Sarah. "Gus is out," she said, rather lamely.

He nodded, looking past her into the empty shop. "Might you be able take the morning for yourself?" he asked respectfully, meeting her eyes. "To join me for a ride? It's a beautiful day. Perhaps I can make up for my bad manners by showing you the gardens at the *Bois de Boulogne*. It's quite beautiful."

Nicole bit her lip. *Wanting* was never the problem. But how? She couldn't leave without a reason. "I—well—" A welcome thought came. "I have a basket of woolen caps *Madame* Baston knitted for the church. She asked me to deliver them. Perhaps you can take me? It's not far. Only a few blocks. Afterwards we can see the gardens."

"I'd enjoy that," Luc said. "Shall we ride?"

Nicole laughed, looking out at the sleek cabriolet. "In that?"

"Why not?" He smiled.

"I would love it," she said. "Wait." She rushed to gather the wicker basket, covered with a shawl and tied by Sarah's fastidious hand with a thick red ribbon. She pulled her cloak off the hook and joined Luc outside in the sunlight.

"Let me take it," Luc offered, drawing the basket from her arm. He brought her to the carriage, secured the basket behind the seat, then helped her inside.

"Nicole," he said, closing the door firmly and leaning against it to look into her face. "It's unforgivable that I didn't call sooner."

She put her hand over his and leaned closer. "Don't, Luc," she murmured. "You're here. That's all that matters."

***

Entering the small parish, they both grew hushed and reverent. It was empty, with light streaming in from overhead stained glass. Nicole pulled up her shawl to cover her hair, and Luc removed his hat. It was a narrow church with rush-bottom chairs. Their footsteps were muffled on the worn-stone aisle as they approached the simple altar. In a small side chapel stood a multi-tiered iron stand filled with flickering prayer candles.

Luc drew her to it. "I promised my grandmother I'd light a votive for her whenever I'm in church." He handed Nicole the basket. "I'm afraid I haven't lit many."

"I do like these rituals of the church," Nicole said, watching him put a gold *sol* in the collection plate. "But I've never lit a votive. Not for my parents. Not for anyone."

He took a long taper to one and bowed his head, making the sign of the cross. Nicole stood back, moved by his reverence.

"Were you close to your grandmother?" she asked as Luc stepped back with his final sign of the cross.

"*Grand'mère* was a delightful woman," he said, taking the basket from her. "She was my father's mother. Françoise Rainier Chatillon. She insisted I call her Françoise, not *Grand'mère*. She told me her name meant *free one*. And she *was* a free spirit. You might have felt that spirit at her chateau."

"*Les Saules* was hers? Not your father's?"

The question seemed to surprise him. His face darkened before he answered. "Yes. She owned *Les Saules*. I thought I'd told you. My visits to the country were to see her."

Nicole drew closer. "I found *Les Saules* quite unlike your Paris mansion. Truthfully, it seemed to belong to another family."

"In a way it did. One I felt more akin to."

"And those years as a boy in the countryside, you were with your *grand'mère*?"

Luc stared at the flickering prayer candle. It seemed as if his thoughts were far away. "Yes," he murmured. "Françoise was very important in my life. She had a kind soul."

Coming out from the sacristy was a gray-haired priest. He stopped upon seeing them. Nicole nudged Luc. A smile spread across his face as he stepped down from the altar and approached them.

"Nicole, welcome," he said, holding out his arms for the basket.

"*Bonjour,* Father Poitier." She gave a brief curtsy. "Here are *Madame* Baston's caps," she said as Luc handed them over.

"Ah, so many for our children. Tell *Madame* she will be in my prayers tonight."

"This is *Monsieur* Luc Chatillon," Nicole added. "A friend."

She felt a sense of pride as Father Poitier turned to look up at Luc. She went on to explain how Luc had helped the Baston millinery, with no reward for himself. Father Poitier shook his head that he understood. As he looked from her to Luc, Nicole felt a warm belonging. A rightness in being here. She wondered if Luc felt it, too.

"And so, now," Father Poitier said, setting the hat basket aside. "What are you two young ones planning to do on such a day as this?"

"I hope to take *Mademoiselle* Vogel to see another side of Paris, the *Bois de Boulogne*."

"Ah, the woods of Boulogne," Father Poitier said, raising his brows in delight. "Today is a good day to see the lake. It should be filled with geese and swans. Come along. I have something for you." He brought them to the entry, stopping before the breadbasket left out for the poor. He shook the last of the crumbs into a handkerchief. "Take this," he said, handing it over to Luc. "You can feed our feathered friends. Geese are wonderful creatures. And the swans. They mate for life, you know. Like a man and woman's sacred covenant with God."

Nicole felt her heart warm as Luc and the priest appraised one another. "I understand, Father," he said. He dropped several *sols* in the basket.

Taking her and Luc by the arm, Father Poitier led them out down the steps.

"You have my blessings," he said, patting Nicole's hand. She lowered her head in quiet gratitude. And then she heard him say, "You both have my blessings."

Chapter Sixteen

As the cabriolet sped through the streets, Luc pondered the priest's words. They struck at a moral compass he'd put in place when he'd been no more than fifteen. A compass that for some time had been pointing far from true north. Perhaps the priest guessed as much. Reluctantly, Luc acknowledged a truth about himself. His actions with Nicole had been careless, perhaps reckless, while she had been brave—and good-hearted. His grandmother's voice came to him. *Do not wrong a good heart. There are few of them.* Ah, Françoise. *She* had been his moral standard. In these years without her, he'd drifted. He had no doubt that if she were still alive, he would not have become the feckless spirit who'd been drunkenly seduced into Georgette's bedchamber.

God, if only Françoise were here to help him through this Georgette nightmare. At least Francoise had been spared this scandal. If only she'd been able to meet Nicole. If she had, he knew Françoise would say that Nicole deserved to know about Georgette. She deserved to know every detail of his betrothal to a woman his parents were demanding he marry. She deserved to know about Georgette's claims about the child. And if it *were* his child, he thought bitterly, she needed to know that, too. But on his life, he *knew* there was no possibility of that—

"Luc? How far out are the woods?"

Coming to himself, Luc turned his eyes from the road and took in Nicole's watchful stare. At that moment he felt an unexpected tenderness for her. He wanted to gather her in his arms and forget the wreckage of his family. She deserved to know everything, before this went further.

"Nicole," he began, then stopped, feeling suddenly empty, as if he were about to fall into a pit. "Sometimes we find our lives entangled—in ways that are not easily solved."

She did not reply, not with words, but with the spirit draining from her face.

"Do you suggest I entangle your life in some way?"

"You?" Luc repeated, surprised that she'd so misunderstood. "No. No. This has nothing to do with you. Nothing." He struggled to unravel his thoughts, to explain something he didn't fully understand himself. And then, with a swift surety, he knew. Yes. It had *everything* to do with Nicole.

"Perhaps it *is* you," he said in a contemplative murmur. He reached to take her hand from her lap and pull it to his lips in a kiss. "Perhaps you *are* the entanglement, my darling Nicole." He held her hand against his jaw. A bolt of understanding struck him. This incredible woman was his true north. His attraction for her went beyond her beauty. She was the pure heart he'd searched for. Let his family rage against his decision. He would stand against an army to have Nicole at his side. So…this was love. This wild abandon. This willingness to challenge anything and everything that could get in the way. This willingness to let go…

He put his arm around her, drawing her close. "And yet, Nicole, what a delightful, enjoyable quandary you are."

In an instant decision to say yes to her, his heart reached out to hers, and he knew she knew it had. The smile on her face. The radiance from her eyes. God, he loved this woman. And she loved him. Without words, they both said *yes* to one another.

With a teasing look of consternation, she raised one eyebrow. "Quandary, am I?"

"That may be the wrong word," he said with a grin. "Perhaps I should say *shipwreck*?"

Nicole withdrew her hand and playfully crossed her arms before her. "A shipwreck."

He rubbed his jaw in mock contemplation. "Yes. A complete disaster in my life."

Her eyes narrowed, then a tiny smile touched her lips. "You hardly flatter me, Luc Chatillon. If that's your intention."

"My dear Nicole, little do you realize how much I do flatter you. Yes, you are my shipwreck. *And* my sea change."

***

"I wanted you to see the wilderness that exists in Paris," Luc said as their carriage arrived at the *Bois de Boulogne*, a vast forested acreage of land at the edge of the city. He explained it was the vestiges of the old king's hunting grounds. Once closed to the public, King Louis had opened the land for everyone to enjoy—an attempt, many believed, to reach out to his subjects.

"I love it," Nicole exclaimed, looking around. "Even more than your Tuileries, I believe."

"Somehow, I guessed that would be so." He took her arm. "And I agree."

They made their way along a gravel path, enjoying the antics of bluebirds, woodpeckers, squirrels. Now and then Luc would point out a deer, and with the sighting of each new creature, Nicole expressed delight with smiles and gasps. "I never realized Paris was so untamed," she exclaimed.

They neared a lake, surrounded by shrubbery, and in the middle a small island green with trees swaying in the breeze. The sound of quacking geese filled the air. "There," Luc said, pointing out a flock on the water's edge. "Father Poitier's geese."

Scores of gobbling, babbling geese frantically squabbled with one another for tufts of grass. Nicole laughed. "And they look hungry."

"I'm sure they're always hungry." Luc took Nicole's hand and led her off the path onto a weedy, soggy slope. Carefully they made their way down to the edge of the lake. A dozen or more geese, honking at the intrusion, took off in all directions. Nicole turned and, at the sight of Luc's expensive, polished boots covered in mud, burst out laughing.

Luc's eyes narrowed, but his mouth held a smile. "Careful," he teased, steadying himself on the slope, "we've yet to climb back up. And you, *ma chérie*, have the disadvantage of a gown."

"A gown may be a disadvantage to *you, Monsieur* Chatillon." She threw out a handful of crumbs into the murky water. "But *I've* had a lifetime of experience, thank you." A hoard of honking geese, tails waving, descended, followed by strutting ducks and, finally, a graceful line of swans.

Together Luc and Nicole tossed out breadcrumbs until they were surrounded by waterfowl squabbling at their feet. "I think it's time to go," Luc said, emptying the handkerchief into the breeze and, hand in hand, they made their way up the slippery embankment.

"*Mademoiselle* Vogel," Luc said, once on the pathway, turning his head to her with a charming grin. "I do protest at how you abused me in front of the waterfowl by insulting my manhood, conjuring images of me dressed in a gown."

Nicole pressed her lips together, holding back a giggle. "And yet," she countered, her voice growing seductive, "there is no danger of your manhood being in question."

He grew serious. He traced her chin with the back of his hand. Nicole closed her eyes as he did so. The moment lengthened until finally he stepped back. Nicole's eyes opened as he tucked his hands in his waistcoat.

Luc shook out his handkerchief and tucked it inside his jacket. "Come along, *ma chérie*, before I take complete loss of my senses." Pulling her along, he called, "There's something else." He pointed ahead. "See that?" The top of a towering roof appeared beyond the trees. "It's the Chateau de Madrid, an abandoned castle."

"A castle? Why was it abandoned?"

"The old king's daughter lived there until she died."

"Louis XV?"

"Yes. My university friends and I used to dare one another to stay the night there." He scratched his jaw. "Rumor is, it's haunted."

Nicole laughed, holding on to his arm. "How delightful. You must show me."

"You're not afraid?" he taunted.

"Of ghosts? Never."

He chuckled. "Somehow I didn't think so. Follow me."

They strolled arm in arm until the castle emerged from behind the trees. "It's quite massive," Nicole marveled. She urged Luc faster until the path opened onto a square surrounding a dry fountain filled with debris. Behind it loomed a six-story stone castle. Even in daylight it looked dark and forlorn, a fortress with enormous round towers and gothic windows and smokeless chimneys rising into the sky.

"It's dreadful," Nicole exclaimed with glee.

"Wait until you go inside."

"Do you think we can?"

He shrugged. "There are no locks. No guards. We'll probably come across others prowling about with the same idea. Shall we?"

"Only if you promise a ghost."

"I'll do my best to conjure one."

They entered through double doors and stumbled about in semidarkness until Luc felt his way to a window and pulled open a shutter. Nicole followed, laughing with the thrill of it all. She marveled at the painted ceiling with cherubs floating in a fresco of clouds. "It's magnificent. The art. The craftsmanship."

Luc crossed his arms, looking about the filthy room. "Yes. You help me see this in a new way. The ruins of a royal palace."

As they made their way across broken tiles littering the floor, Nicole was intrigued by the thought that a princess had once lived here. She imagined the lavish splendor now buried under decades of ruination.

They came upon a marble staircase leading up into the shadowy recesses above. The second-floor windows were flung half open so that sparrows had flown in and made nests in the rafters. They passed through the ramshackle rooms littered with upside-down tables and overturned chairs. Entering a long room with windows at the end, Nicole unexpectedly shivered. It was as if she'd passed through a cold spot. Something flashed by outside the door.

And then, unbidden, a white-hot sense of dread blazed through her body. She stopped, recognizing the feeling. The same dread she'd felt in the café when she'd first met Luc. But it couldn't happen now. *Not again, not in front of Luc.* She stared about apprehensively, taking in the ugly crumbling plaster. Scorch marks from a fire had blackened patches of the wall. She looked up at the high ceilings, about the tall windows glaring with sunlight, yet letting in no brightness. She looked down to the wide plank floors scabbed with years of wear. Dizziness overtook her.

She was back in Legros. Her chest felt heavy. *No, stop, stop, this is only your imagination...* But she knew even as she tried to calm herself that nothing could prevent it once it started. Nothing could stop this icy feeling and the voice in her head hissing: *Leave. Now.* In terror she stared at the walls. They were closing in.

Luc was looking at her, somehow she knew, but she couldn't focus on him.

"Nicole. What's happening? Are you frightened of the dark? Let me open a window."

Before he could move, Nicole rushed to the shuttered window and frantically shook it to open it. She had to escape. To get out.

Luc came behind and pulled her to him. "What's happening?"

She stood rocking back and forth against his chest, her breathing collapsing on her.

Luc drew back. "What is it, Nicole? What's inside you doing this? It's like the night you rushed from the café."

"Please," she gasped. "Take me out. Now."

He drew her close. "Nicole. Don't run from it."

She pushed away from him and made her way to another open window and leaned out, taking deep breaths.

"Nicole." Luc stood directly behind her, smoothing her hair. "Breathe. Deeply. In. Out." His voice was kind but insistent. Feeling herself calming, she nodded that she was better. He leaned close to her ear. "What's happening inside you? Let me help."

With her heart racing, she stood tall and stared out at the bright sky white with clouds. The vise on her chest loosened. She leaned on Luc, feeling the tightness release its hold on her throat. His arms were so warm. She could breathe.

"You asked if I'm frightened?" she said quietly. "I *have* been, in my life. True fright. Something here reminded me of Legros, the orphanage."

He held her tighter. "I've not asked you about it. Tell me. Let me take your pain. Free yourself."

Free herself? she thought. Was that possible? Dully she pulled away and walked to the window and looked out. "You wake up in the morning—itching, scratching your arms and hands. They're covered in welts. You pull back the blanket—" She swayed, almost losing her balance. "They're everywhere. Bedbugs crawling on your body."

Luc came to her and wrapped his arms about her in a hard embrace. "My dearest, sweet Nicole. I'm so sorry." He buried his lips in her hair.

"These memories overcome me sometimes. I can't—"

He was kissing her eyelids, stroking her hair. "I would do anything," he whispered against her ear, "to make this go away.

You're haunted, my love. More haunted than this palace. You live with memories that are dead *and* alive—both at once."

She put her hand on his chest to steady herself against the panic again overtaking her. *No. No. Breathe. Listen to Luc. Stay calm.* But the upheaval was building again.

"Something happened to you? Tell me, Nicole."

A darkness spread through her like poison. She saw the face in her mind. "It was her," she whispered. "She is the one who did it."

"Who, Nicole?"

"*Madame* Colére." She nearly choked on the name.

Luc tightened his arms around her. "You're safe, Nicole. Tell me."

"That night. Her hands were cold, pulling my hair…"

Nicole felt herself drawn into memories she'd forgotten. And there was Luc, listening. She softly told him, reliving it all, feeling the cold floor on her bare feet, *Madame*'s fist yanking her hair by the roots and holding out a handful—

"Cut here," Madame demanded.

Aimée's whole body trembled.

"Do. As. I. Say."

"Do it," whispered Nicole.

"Shut up," ordered the directress. "Now, cut."

Aimée's tiny fingers pressed the scissors.

"It's like a horse's tail," Madame complained. "Try harder."

Aimée pressed until her fingers were white, managing to snip a few strands until Madame snatched the scissors. "Give them to me." Like a mad seamstress, Madame chopped and chopped, the wild scissors catching skin and causing Nicole to cry out. Tears flowed down Aimée's face as she sobbed over and over, "Stop, stop."

Nicole wanted to cry with Aimée, to cry for Aimée, to cry for herself, but her eyes were dry as stone. Something hardened inside with each hank of hair dropping to the floor. She would never cry. Never in her life.

Madame pushed her so that she stumbled back and fell onto her own hair strewn about like piles of corn silk.

"Now get in bed until tomorrow's bell," she ordered. "No breakfast for either of you. Stay and clean up this hair. And don't burn it. I don't want the stench."

As the door slammed shut, Aimée knelt beside her and begged forgiveness. Nicole rubbed the bristly stubs sticking out from her head. Aimée kept sobbing.

"It's not your fault," Nicole soothed, stroking her little twin's hair.

Nicole felt strong arms about her, pulling her closer. "It's not your fault, Aimée," she whispered again and again.

"It's over, my love."

She wasn't sure how much time had passed. The sun was setting through the widows when she opened her eyes. Seeing Luc's loving gaze, feeling his deep embrace, something broke open.

Suddenly, for the first time, she was crying.

"You're free from it now," Luc whispered in a warm, soothing murmur. "It's over. You're free."

She repeated the words. *It's over. You're free.*

She didn't know how to stop the tears, or why they were pouring, only that she needed to empty herself, let them come, even though they felt like they'd never end.

Chapter Seventeen

Standing before the full mirror in her boudoir, Georgette grimaced as Pierre de Fleury fussed with adjustments on her wedding gown, a cream and ivory open-front petticoat with a long train. De Fleury held his pince-nez to his eyes to examine the boning that fortified a triangle-shaped stomacher he'd designed to cover the bodice front. It was exquisite, with over two hundred pearls sewn into a floral pattern.

"Stop," Georgette ordered. *Monsieur* de Fleury looked up, startled, and stepped back. "I simply cannot—" she cried, snapping threads loose as she yanked off the stomacher. "I refuse to be a fat bride." She pulled a silk pillow from beneath her corset and tossed it to the floor.

"Now, Georgette," Helaine Fontenay said from the side of the room. "You will not look fat. You're pleasantly *enceinte*."

Georgette cupped her hands around the slight rise of her belly. She hated losing her figure—and being an expectant bride. For Luc to make her wait was cruel. "I don't need a pillow to look pregnant," she complained. "I am."

"Ah, but not enough," came a comment from the corner of the room, where Bertrand Le Mansec leaned against an armoire, sipping champagne.

As Pierre de Fleury unfastened the bodice stays at her back, Georgette yanked her arms from the tight sleeves, dripping with lace, and stepped out of the gown. Clad in a chemise and underskirt, she brushed past the tailor and slipped into her gauze wrapper. Glaring at Bertrand, she plopped on the sofa, gathering her poodle into her arms.

"Bertrand, why are you even here?"

"Georgette, dear," *Madame* Fontenay scolded. "I asked Bertie to come."

"Why?" she demanded.

"I'm here to be a supportive brother for my sister's wedding," Bertrand said casually. From a platter of chocolate-drizzled profiteroles, he lifted a pastry oozing with whipped cream and took a bite.

"Make that my bastard *half*-brother," she corrected.

"Oh my, seems someone's had her cup of venom today," Bertrand retorted, wiping cream from his beard with a napkin.

Madame Fontenay glanced over her shoulder toward the tailor, who was scrutinizing the bodice with his measuring tape. "Oh, *Monsieur* de Fleury," she called airily, "we're done for today. Would you return tomorrow?"

"Certainly, *Madame*," he said, tucking his pince-nez in his vest pocket. "I do have a few adjustments before our next fitting. I'll leave the petticoat, but this bodice? Perhaps it needs a more…generous cut?"

Madame Fontenay lowered her eyes with a smile. "You understand perfectly."

"Very good, *Madame*." Tucking the bodice into tissue, he popped on his hat, bowed, and made a hasty exit.

As soon as the door closed, Madame Fontenay turned, her face filled with displeasure. "Both of you," she admonished. "Must you make a public spectacle of this wedding? And you, Georgette, how rude to announce to the world your father's—dalliances."

"Which ones?" Georgette scoffed. "Having an illegitimate son or gambling away our money?"

Bertrand's face paled. Georgette gloated at him, knowing he disliked her when she was like this. What he called her superior attitude. He turned his back on her and filled another glass with champagne. "I vote for a bigger pillow," he said.

"Yes," *Madame* Fontenay agreed. "We need to assure the timing is beyond doubt."

"Ah, Helaine—*ma belle mère,*" said Bertrand, bringing her the champagne glass and sitting on the sofa so that their shoulders touched. "Always the cool head in the family. One would think that *you* were my mother."

Madame Fontenay patted his hand with affection. "Oh, Bertie, I adore you as if you were my son."

"*Bon sang*," Georgette swore under her breath. Tossing aside her poodle, she crossed the room back to the full-length mirror. "Luc agreed to marry me. He cannot simply now refuse."

"Yes," Bertrand quipped, "you do need the Chatillon cash, dear sister, since Papa's little gambling habit is getting quite serious. However else would you support your lifestyle?"

"Or yours?" Georgette snapped, turning to him.

His unsmiling eyes locked on hers as he sipped champagne.

"I've been thinking, Georgette dear," *Madame* Fontenay mused, "if you want to be the slim bride you were born to be, perhaps I could arrange—" she shrugged "—an intervention?" She reached for a cherry on the side table and plopped it into her champagne glass. "If Luc won't marry you because he's not the father, then perhaps the problem can go away. These things do happen. In a week or two, have a tearful scene with Luc about the loss of your *enfant*. Between your little sobs and sniffles, tell him you can make another child once you're wed. Tell him his offspring means everything to you."

"I love this family," Bertrand chortled, lifting *Madame* Fontenay's hand and kissing it lightly. "How clever you are, Helaine."

Turning back to the mirror, Georgette fell into thought. *Destroy Éric's child?* She'd heard of special herbs used for such a reason. Jumping off chairs. Inserting implements. She shuddered. No. She wouldn't. Once she found a way to tell Éric, he would swear his everlasting devotion to her and his child. If only Luc would marry her. She could have everything: wealth, status, heirs—and love, Éric's love. Luc was such an idiot not to see he could have the same.

She twisted from side to side and examined her figure from all angles. There was only one answer. "I believe I shall proudly display the Chatillon heir at the wedding. But, yes, I'll need a larger pillow."

"Ah, now that's my girl," said Bertrand. Setting aside his champagne glass, he brought the platter of profiteroles to her. "Have one, darling, to fatten your love child." He inclined his head to hers.

Scrunching up her nose at him, Georgette lowered her eyes to the cream puffs. She selected the largest one. As much as Bertrand irritated her, she did admire how cleverly he'd endeared himself to her mother and wormed his way into their father's affections. Sometimes even she succumbed to his charms.

"I am going to have this baby," she declared, holding the profiterole to her lips then taking a big bite. "And I'm going to be a very fat, very happy bride."

***

Luc had skipped dinner. He wanted to be alone. Exhausted, his thoughts on Nicole, he prepared for bed. He'd asked her to face her fears, and when she had—so bravely—she'd found release from her unseen wounds, her shame. Perhaps he'd always sensed it, the shadow hidden below her smile, yet lingering in her eyes when she quietly walked across a room. He pulled off his boots and dropped them to the floor. On the way back to her home, she'd been quiet and fragile, but happier somehow. Or...content. As if she'd been freed. And she had opened to him so warmly, so deeply, to his good-bye kiss. He had never felt a woman respond to him that way...

Now that he thought about it, from the beginning it was not only Nicole's sensuality but her mystery that drew him to her, from the night at the café when she'd hurried out. He'd gone to her because he'd recognized her pain. Her hidden suffering. *Her aloneness.* He slowly unbuttoned his shirt and hung it on the bedpost. Yes, he understood Nicole because he lived with his own shame. The shame of never being what his father wanted. And hadn't it only gotten worse after Francoise's death? He'd been made into a thief. A thief and a traitor—to the man he'd craved acceptance from with his entire being. His father.

Luc walked in his stockings to the fireplace and gripped the mantel as he stared into the flames. And now, his sense of honor was being attacked. He was being made to feel guilty about rejecting marriage with Georgette. He'd agreed to the damn marriage in the first place merely to *please* his father. He should have known. Nothing about his son would please Victor Chatillon. His father knew Georgette's child was not his. And still he insisted on this marriage. No matter what, the son was expected to do what his father demanded.

Luc dropped to the chair and unbuttoned his dark wool breeches. No, he could never live with himself if he married Georgette. The marriage would not happen. No matter what.

Luc sat, staring at the wall. This wasn't right. None of it. It was his life to live. Tomorrow he would announce to his parents his intentions. He would wed Nicole. If his family, his friends, chose to turn from him, so be it. It was time to lead with his heart.

A rap sounded on the door, and his valet entered, announcing that *Monsieur* and *Madame* Fontenay had unexpectedly arrived with their daughter Georgette. Luc cursed under his breath. Not tonight. Maybe he could slip out. Or refuse to join?

Thinking about it, he drew in a deep breath. No. His time to face the darkness was here. He wouldn't try to escape. He would face them all.

When he walked to the main salon, Luc paused at the doorway to face the assemblage. Georgette sat between the two mothers. Beautiful Georgette, her black hair swept up and fastened with diamond-tipped pins. She wore a gown of purple luster... His face paled. Pure, white fear paralyzed him. No, no, no. This was not possible. He'd just seen her. And yet there was no denying the obvious.

Georgette was well along with child.

Somehow he entered the room. Somehow he gave his cordialities to everyone. *Monsieur* Fontenay. His father. The ladies. He spoke with practiced finesse, while his thoughts tangled into a knot. When *was* the last time he'd seen Georgette? Not that long ago. A few weeks at most. My God, she'd looked nothing like this. But he could not question his eyes. She sat beside his mother, her hands atop her belly, looking nearly ready to deliver the child. Almost dizzy, he crossed to the sideboard to fill a brandy glass. What date was it? May twenty-eighth, twenty-ninth? If she gave birth next month, which looked likely, it might be his after all. *His? His child.* He turned to her as she drew closer to him. He looked down to her swollen gown. A cloying sickness filled him. What had he done?

Georgette placed her cool hand atop his. "Darling Luc, Papa has given us the most wonderful surprise. A wedding voyage. A honeymoon in Venice." She glanced around the room. "Perhaps we can all go together."

Luc downed his brandy and poured another, buying time. Georgette expectantly waited for his answer. His vacant focus took in the faces in the room, meeting his father's glare peering out from under dark, unhappy eyebrows, while Gilles Fontenay's face was pinned into an absurd little grin. Luc rubbed his mouth and his jaw, then ran his fingers through his hair. This couldn't be happening. His dear mother was smiling nervously, nodding at him ever so slightly. She knew what he was feeling. And there, Helaine Fontenay sniffing into a lace handkerchief. A frail woman, she seemed incapable of having borne such a vivacious daughter. But now she sat there with the confidence of a mother-in-law, her smile saying, *I told you so.*

"I so want to journey to Italy," Georgette cooed beside him. "Say we will, Luc, dear. We will be so happy, like we were, if only you would get over your jealousy. In your heart surely you know I've never betrayed you."

Luc's father snapped his pocket watch shut. "By God, if I were young, I would never be able to resist a face like that."

Monsieur Fontenay puffed up. "I don't easily sit by and watch my daughter beg," he exclaimed. "I'll send you two anywhere in the damned world you want to go if that would settle matters. If you choose to have us along, fine. Whatever you want, Luc, is yours."

Luc felt the trap closing in.

"Mother," he said, "surely you—"

"My dear," Gabriele said, "you know how I feel about this marriage."

Luc poured himself more brandy. When he turned back to the group, he could not stop staring at the bulge of Georgette's gown as she sauntered up to him.

"Oh, yes, wouldn't it be lovely in Venice?" Georgette urged.

Luc felt himself drowning. "Or Verona, perhaps," he quipped. "Now there's a city for tragic lovers."

Georgette pressed her hand to his. "My love—"

Luc cut her off. "If you all will excuse me, I have…a newborn foal in the stables that needs attention. *Monsieur* Fontenay. *Madame.* A pleasure. Georgette, *adieu.*" He turned his back on her to leave.

But she had not yet given up. "Please, Luc. Must you leave—"

Luc kissed his mother's hand, his look telling her not to press further.

"Careful out on the streets this late," she murmured. "It's close to curfew." He smiled tightly at her but said nothing. As he exited the room, he heard his father bark his name. He slammed the door on him. Hurrying to the back of the chateau, he grabbed his cape from the cloak room and flung it around his shoulders. Welcoming the night air, he strode to the stables. He could not think.

The smells of straw and horses wafted through the stalls as he walked along the aisle. Lifting his lamp, he found himself looking into the shining eyes of the foal hugging its mother's side. Healthy. As he thought. He gave them a reassuring cluck then continued walking to the end of the stable until he reached a gray stallion with flowing white mane and tail.

"Ares," he whispered, opening the stall door. The horse's head bobbed at his name, then neighed, stomping his front hoof.

The movements awoke Pepe, a boy of eleven paid to sleep on a nearby cot and run for help in case of fire. Rubbing his astonished eyes, the boy was quick to join Luc as he saddled one of the stallions.

"Sir," Pepe called out. "Do you need help, sir?"

"Go back to sleep. And a *sol* for you to say nothing about this."

"A *sol*. Sir, I wouldn't, sir." Pepe caught the tossed coin, and Luc galloped out into the cloying darkness.

***

It was almost midnight when Luc arrived outside the hat shop, bathed in moonlight. He dismounted and looked up to what he guessed to be Nicole's room. The entire shop was dark. He thought to toss a pebble against the window. But he might wake the Bastons. And what an absurd notion anyway, whisking Nicole away into the night. A deep misgiving gripped him. Georgette was carrying his child? God. It hadn't seemed possible before. And yet tonight, she looked so far along... The reality of it ran through his veins like ice water.

He sharply reined his horse around and rode away from the shop, back along the route he'd come. Suddenly he wanted to get very, very drunk. Three brandies had barely touched him. He wanted to forget the image of Georgette round-bellied with child. He wanted to wipe out the memory of carrying Nicole in his arms in the rain. Laughing with her at the duck pond. He wanted to forget her tears and anguish when she'd told him about the orphanage. To never again think of her lips on his. She was a beautiful, kind, wonderful—

Luc clicked the horse faster. The thought of living out his life without Nicole was too impossible to bear. How could he be with anyone else? How could this have happened? He needed help to pass this dreadful night. Leave it to Philippe Montpellier. Maybe he'd be with a woman. A woman with a painted mouth and nothing to say.

***

Philippe Montpellier was indeed in his lavish Paris apartment with a lady caller, a beauty with a heart-shaped face and flowing chestnut hair. Any trace of lip color had long ago been smeared upon her wineglass or on Philippe's lips. The laces of her bodice were loosened so that her lush breasts spilled forth.

The porter knocked: Two short raps. A pause. Then two more.

At the sound of the signal, Lulu squealed as if a mouse had run over her slippers. Pulling her skirt over her dimpled knees, she fumbled with the laces on her gown.

"Damn," Philippe muttered, pulling his thatch of copper-colored hair into a queue. "Who can be here at this hour?"

Lulu pouted. "Philippe, I'll lose my mood." Philippe leaned over the soiled dishes, the remains of their late supper, and spooned up a heap of caviar and fed it into her mouth.

"I'm sure you'll get it back," he said with a wink and turned as she wiped her chin with the hem of her satin gown. "Be a love and go to the boudoir and anticipate my—entry. I shall join you soon."

Moving into the salon with a discreet adjustment of his cuffs, Philippe opened the door. He paused upon seeing Luc Chatillon. With a broad smile, Philippe rushed forward, giving him a warm embrace. "Chatillon. You wolf. What in hell are you doing out this late? Is the moon full?"

Luc came in and slumped into a chair. "I hope you have a good bourbon."

"Ah, you've come to the right place." Walking to the cabinet, Philippe studied him. "It's been weeks since I've seen you, Luc. The word is since your escape to the American colonies you've changed. I hear from Bertrand your time has been taken by some ravishing beauty who makes hats."

"Don't bother with a glass, Philippe. I mean to get goddamn drunk."

Philippe reached in the back of the cabinet for a full decanter of his finest. "You could sit here and get drunk by yourself," he said, handing over the bourbon. "But I can think of things more entertaining."

Luc pulled the stopper and took a hearty drink. "Such as?"

Philippe indicated the boudoir with his eyes. Luc took another gulp. "Someone I know?"

"Louise-Marie."

Luc tugged off his boots. "Lulu? I thought she was in Austria or some such place."

"She got bored with German lovers, it seems." Philippe accepted the decanter from Luc and held it to his lips in a long draw. "What say? Would you like to watch our little sport? The night has only begun. You know Lulu wouldn't mind."

He silently watched as Luc stared miserably across the room. This was odd. He poured himself a drink from a crystal decanter.

"Or perhaps you would like a private little ravishing of Lulu yourself," he suggested, bringing over the decanter.

Luc took it. "I tell you what." He stood, steadying himself. "Tonight, I'm in the mood for both."

***

A city clock chimed three in the morning as Luc galloped away from Philippe Montpellier's apartment. Ares's hooves echoed along the vacant streets. Luc's head swarmed with unwanted thoughts. He had never felt more miserable. Damn, what happened to the forgetful bliss of intoxication? Bourbon and sex had always been his staples to block out unwelcome truths. But not this time. Maybe he'd never be able to—

A shout in the dark startled him.

"*Vous arrêtez.* You there. Stop in the name of the King."

"*Merde,*" Luc muttered under his breath. He pulled Ares to a halt. In a matter of seconds four uniformed *Guet* surrounded him on horseback, lanterns glaring.

"Announce yourself. What business brings you out?"

Luc ran his palm across his jaw, hoping the shadows hid his rumpled, bourbon-soaked state. "My name is Luc Chatillon, son of Chatillon, Master of the Royal Livery Stable."

This bit of information seemed to settle the officers. The policeman in front lifted his pointy chin in respect. "You know the curfew laws, Master Chatillon?"

Luc nodded. "We've just had a foaling, highly anticipated by Count Montpellier. I brought the news to his son."

"A thoroughbred for the king's stables?"

"A beautiful gray Andalusian Cross," Luc said. "We're outcrossing the Oriental and European breeds. They're powerful, and fast."

"So, it seems you've been celebrating," the policeman observed with a grin.

"Maybe too much." Luc grimaced, regretting the entire night, maybe his entire life. He only wanted to get home and fall into bed, to blot out everything with sleep.

The men laughed at Luc's remark.

"Well, off with you. Nothing good can come from being on the streets at night. There are more and more gangs every day."

Luc nodded his understanding.

"Give congratulations to *Monsieur* Chatillon. Let's hope you've a winner."

"Yes. A winner." Luc reined Ares who cantered into the night, back toward the Chatillon estate. With each mile he felt worse and worse, like a man on the way to his own execution.

Chapter Eighteen

Sarah shuffled down the stairs, holding in one hand the teakettle wrapped in a towel and a tin of biscuits fresh from the oven in the other. "Come along, cat," she said.

Following the scent, Midas scampered down to the small table set up before the fireplace and leapt upon Nicole's lap. Sarah placed the biscuits near Gus and poured tea for three from the steaming kettle.

"Gus was just speaking about *Madame* Duffand," Nicole said to her, feeding Midas a pinch of biscuit. "The lady has ordered a hat, did you know? Gus says she was a client years ago."

Sarah hung the kettle from a hook on the fire grate. "Yes indeed," she said, coming back and sitting heavily in her chair. "Gus was once on his way to becoming one of the great milliners of Paris. As a young man he'd gained a reputation with several fine families, even the wife of a chevalier. His designs were worn to the opera and in some of the most fashionable salons."

"But then," Nicole puzzled, "what happened?"

Gus sat, silent, intent on stirring his tea.

Sarah placed a biscuit on her plate. "It started when the old king died. Even in death Louis XV robbed his subjects. Every milliner and dressmaker in Paris made mourning clothes for the old swine's funeral. How did the song go? *Tremble you thieves / Take flight, you whores. / For you have lost your father."* Sarah gave a sarcastic *humph.* "They sang that in the streets when he died."

"Yes, I think I remember," Nicole said, frowning. "It sounds familiar. I don't know, something vague."

"Probably you sang it, too. Everyone did."

Nicole shrugged. "Yes. Perhaps."

Sarah buttered her biscuit. "Gus had been commissioned an order of black velvet caps for the royal livery cavalcade. Over two hundred, there were. We put everything we had into it, every last *sous*, and notes, too. We worked day and night, along with Rosalie."

At the mention of this daughter, Rosalie, Nicole glanced about the shop. There was no trace of the mysterious daughter anywhere, not even upstairs in her room, which used to be Rosalie's, she knew.

"The caps were delivered on time," Gus said, staring into his teacup. "They wore them in the procession, directly behind the coffin."

"We watched," Sarah said softly. "The three of us. It was the proudest day of our lives."

"So," Nicole said with some confusion, "you *did* get the commission finished in time."

"Oh, we did," Sarah said with uncharacteristic bitterness. "But payment was another thing. The funeral cost more than anyone counted on. By the time it came to paying us bottom merchants, there was nothing left. Later, new taxes were levied, but we never saw one *livre*. We spent years paying off our debts. That's why we were finally able to hire you, Nicole."

Nicole shook her head with disbelief. "But surely you can petition the throne for payment."

"I think not," Sarah said, stacking the empty cups and saucers. "The new king and queen had their own obligations, what with Marie Antoinette's gowns and jewels." She gathered up the dishes. "Who would care a fig for an aging milliner? No. It's over. We only want to finish our life with some bit of security."

Gus stood, scraping the chair. "It's all in the past. Let's get to work, Nicolette."

***

That evening Nicole was exhausted as she climbed the stairs, plopped on her bed, and stared up at the ceiling. They'd finished four hats today. Her fingers were stinging from pinpricks and tight thimbles, and her eyes burned from the close work in the dim candlelight, especially black thread on black cloth. But this order was close to complete.

Hearing a knock on her door, she called out, "Yes?"

Sarah peeked in. "Am I disturbing you, my dear?"

"Not at all. Come in." Nicole sat up, dangling her feet over the side of the bed.

Sarah stood at the door with her hands clasped before her. She was dressed in nightclothes, a baggy linen sack gown with long sleeves and a scarf tied behind her ears. Nicole noted that Sarah did not indulge in frills, even in sleep.

"Nicole, you must be very special for Gus to say such good things about your work."

"Oh? I—I didn't know." She took it in. "He likes my sewing?"

"He says you're talented. You'll never hear it from him, though. Gus is like that. I sometimes think…he drove Rosalie away. She was never good with a needle and thread, not that Gus didn't try to show her, but she's a big girl, like me, with bulky hands. We're built for hard work. The two couldn't stay in the shop together."

"Tell me more about her. Is she married?"

"To a fisherman. She lives in Le Havre." Sarah paused, studying her reddened fingers. "It wasn't that Gus didn't love her. He has a hard time showing his feelings. After everything that happened, he became—" She stared across the room. "He wasn't always like he is now. When Gus was young, he was forever laughing with his jokes. We had so many people coming here, Nicole, and celebrations of saints days and anniversaries—" She compressed her lips, composing herself.

"And…do you ever see her—Rosalie?"

Sarah's eyes lit up. "Once. She came for a week with our granddaughter. But it's so far away—" Sarah took a deep breath, studying the floor. "Let's see. Sylvie was five then. Such a pretty little thing. I guess it's been over ten years now."

"And you've never written?"

"Oh no. That's not something I do. And Gus, well, he's a proud man." She looked over her shoulder toward the kitchen. "That pesky cat needs to be let out." She looked back. "And you need your rest, my dear. You're almost finished with the order?"

"Hopefully tomorrow. It's hard to believe, but we did it."

Sarah turned to the door. "I knew you would," she said, her hand on the doorknob. "Nicole, I want you to know, dear, you've brought much to our lives. And now, you've found a good man in Antoine, with marriage and children of your own soon. They will be like grandchildren to us. You've made our lives full." She gave a rare smile. "Good night, my child." She exited and softly shut the door.

Nicole stared after her. She finally rose and dressed for bed. She tried not to think of the trace of happiness in Sarah's voice. How could she tell the dear woman she would not marry Antoine? And yet, an equal voice in her mind pleaded, *they can't ask you to marry someone you do not love.* She knelt beside her bed in despair, remembering Gus's arthritic hands this afternoon as he showed her a stitch. And the way Sarah's eyes had spoken a depth of longing when she talked about her daughter.

She lowered her forehead to her clasped hands. "Help me. Help me find the way."

***

The next morning, Nicole awoke with the words from Sarah's song in her thoughts:

Tremble you thieves
Take flight, you whores.
For you have lost your father.

That song. Where had she heard it? Last night it had haunted in a familiar dream. She was running to her father standing atop the steps. It was always the same: all around bells were clanging. Everyone was dressed in black.

Nicole sat up, her eyes wide. Could it have been the king's funeral—people shouting and rushing and pushing. And then came...a sudden memory of a doll lying on the ground by her feet. She felt her throat tighten. The doll made her sad. And that song, *for you have lost your father*—

She clenched her eyes shut. Something else. She pressed her fingers to her temples, trying to remember...

She gave up. It was a blank.

***

After breakfast, Antoine dropped by the shop, excited about a rumor that an important man in the Cause, Camille Desmoulins, was to speak today at the Palais Royale.

"Nicole. You've got to see him. They say no one can move a crowd like Desmoulins. He's become an enemy of the crown, he's so good."

Nicole set down her needle. This was her chance. To be alone with Antoine. It was perfect. He'd been so involved with the Cause he'd not even mentioned it since that first night. Maybe he'd even forgotten. She would be casual. *Antoine, I've decided I'm not going to marry. I'm going to become a hatmaker.* Yes. He would understand. Perhaps at the *Palais Royale* she could take him to see her hats at *Monsieur* Marchand's shop. Antoine would understand. She felt happy, ready for this misunderstanding to end.

Though as they walked through in the heart of the city, Nicole grew increasingly uneasy. But it had nothing to do with her engagement to Antoine. Normally at this time of year the streets teemed with farmers' wagons bringing to market potatoes and beets, rhubarb and carrots. Where were they? Also missing were the grocers and bakers with wares displayed on tables outside their shops. How could she not have noticed? Her mind had been so involved with Luc and hats and Aimée. And now she was bewildered to find the streets vacated, except for mobs of men standing about street corners, sinister enough that even Antoine crossed the streets to avoid them. They passed a shop, then another, with the same sign: SHUT FOR GOOD.

"What's happening?" she asked.

"This has been going on for a while, Nicole. You've been too busy at the shop to see it." His sarcastic tone felt like a voice of conscience. "There are no supplies," he explained. "How do you bake bread without flour?"

They passed a wood-domed circular building, *Les Halles du Blé*—the Corn Market—the central marketplace of Paris. "Look," Antoine said grimly, pointing it out, "where is the grain, the corn? This building is the stomach of Paris. It's empty."

Nicole felt a trill of alarm. "I didn't realize things had become so bleak."

"The government hides it," Antoine said. "Just like they're trying to hide the strength of the rebellion."

Ahead a patrol of soldiers marched, keeping step, bayonets over their shoulders. Never had Nicole seen such a military presence, not in daytime. It was difficult to believe the changes in the city, and how quickly they'd happened. Or had she not been looking, she wondered with shame.

In contrast to the empty streets, the Palais Royale was rife with throngs of visitors. The vast building and grounds that had once been a spectacular palace, after years of abandonment, had been remodeled to become a thriving center of commerce: public coffee rooms, taverns, restaurants, and exclusive shops, all built around a central square.

"Perhaps we could find Marchand's shop?" Nicole wondered aloud.

Antoine cast her a look. "Hats? At a time like this?"

She flushed.

At the end of a long colonnade they arrived at the courtyard, filled with a crowd of noisy bystanders. Antoine found them a small table near the entrance of a coffee shop. He ordered for Nicole but refused anything himself. She'd never had coffee outdoors. Antoine draped his arm on the back of his chair and turned to look behind. Nicole took in the square filled with people booing and loudly whistling. A young man stood on a chair, trying to capture the crowd's attention. She sipped her coffee, her eyes following along wherever Antoine watched. The group's boos became so loud that the young man gave up and stepped down, to a burst of applause, though as soon as he did, another man pushed through the crowd. "There he is," said Antoine, sitting up straight. "Camille Desmoulins."

Amidst the audience cheers, the young man lunged upon the chair and raised his hand for silence.

Fascinated, Nicole set her cup in its saucer. The man's face was soft and pale, probably from a life indoors. His mud-colored coat was much too warm for the weather. But there was something about him that fascinated her. His bearing. The way he perched upon the chair looking larger than life.

"Citizens," he called out in a rich, deep voice. Nicole leaned her elbows on the table, her attention rapt.

"All of you, members of the Third Estate," he continued, "or, as the aristocracy call us, commoners." A reply of hoots and boos arose. He raised his hand to silence them. "But those self-proclaimed nobles will have a different name for us soon. They shall call us the New Nation." The crowd erupted in a roar.

Desmoulins lifted his arm for silence, which was slow to come. "The moment is at hand," he pronounced in his deep voice. "We *commoners* are being forced to accept a meeting of the Estates General, as the *only* way to present our grievances to the king. Why? We are the majority. We should decide. And yet the king and church with a two-thirds vote have told us we must accept this meeting." Boos rang out, and Desmoulins had to speak over them. "We, ninety-five percent of the people of France, have a one-third vote." The crowd flared up in protest, one that grew to the point that Desmoulins had to raise both hands and call for silence.

"We refuse His Majesty's proposal," he shouted. "There is real hope for a citizens National Assembly to meet instead. *Our* assembly, separate from the nobles, separate from the clergy. We will *force* the First and Second Estates to listen to us. We will break the back of the tyranny of the Throne and the Church."

Nicole just at that moment saw passing along the periphery of the courtyard, slowly making his way to their table, Bertrand Le Mansec. She touched Antoine's arm, and motioned for him to look.

Antoine turned as Bertrand arrived.

"Le Mansec," exclaimed Antoine in genuine surprise. "What luck to find you here."

With a grin, Bertrand pulled out a chair, turned it backwards, and sat. "I *thought* it was you sitting here, Durand," he said in a jovial voice. He gave Nicole a brief glance, though she saw in his eyes an accusation of her having been with Luc. She looked away. Was he going to mention the hats at *Les Saules*? And Luc? She looked back to see, but Bertrand seemed altogether disinterested as he called for coffee.

Antoine put his arm about Nicole's shoulders. "You remember my fiancée, Nicole Vogel?"

At the word "fiancée," Bertrand stared at her an instant before he cockily tilted his cap. "Of course, I remember Nicole." He smiled. She reluctantly returned it. Why did this man annoy her? "Who could forget such a face?" he added, then folded his arms across his chest and turned toward the speaker. "I came to hear Camille. What do you think of him?"

"The man is the best journalist in Paris," said Antoine. "And as good a speaker. We must try to meet him."

"Quite possibly we can. I'll try to flag down the man. But my, what a devil he is. Look at the size of the crowd he's drawing."

They quieted as Desmoulins spoke. Nicole listened with fascination.

"If we, the Third Estate, the common man, *if* we stand together, what can we not accomplish? Look at America. It was the common people there who threw aside a parliament that taxed them without a vote. Why, then, should the people of France not demand the same?"

A thunderous applause broke out. Antoine jumped up and cheered, applauding heartily. Bertrand slowly clapped his hands over his head. Nicole felt herself caught up in the excitement, and felt the old thrill of being on the streets pasting up posters.

But then, in the midst of the celebration, she slowly became aware of the thud of galloping horses arriving at the back of the courtyard. She looked in the direction, and amid screams, a squadron of the King's dragoons wearing their green jackets and leopard fur turbans burst into the crowd. Camille Desmoulins shouted out, "Do not be afraid, citizens."

The dragoons galloped head-on, muskets out, bayonets fixed, knocking down men and women until they were surrounding Desmoulins. "Stop in the name of the king," the first dragoon ordered.

"I have every right to speak here."

The dragoon pointed his musket directly at Desmoulins. He raised the hammer. "Camille Desmoulins, you are under arrest for sedition. Step down." A young woman cried out and tried to break through. The dragoon turned his musket toward her. "Keep back." People began pushing. Antoine stood and grabbed Nicole's arm and pulled her up from her chair. A sudden loud report rang out, nearly deafening her, followed by screams and cries.

"Come, follow me," Bertrand said in a quiet, authoritative manner. Antoine took her hand and followed him along the corridor jammed with people now trying to escape. Nicole felt herself jostled about, elbows in her back, boots stepping on her shoes. She passed a man slumped unconscious on the ground. A woman screamed and tripped over him. People pushed and ran in all directions.

Bertrand found an empty shop, the door ajar, and pulled them inside. He shut the entry and bolted it. The three of them stood at the window, watching the riot.

Nicole leaned against Antoine's side. "The guard struck that poor woman. I saw blood."

"At least Desmoulins was not shot," Antoine said in relief, craning his head to see the speaker now surrounded by dragoons.

"There will be more violence before the meeting of the Estates General next month," Bertrand said. "Unless it can be stopped by men who still have their wits about them."

"It won't stop," Antoine said. "It's only beginning. This is what we've been waiting for."

"No, not like this, Antoine," Nicole whispered. "This is horrible."

Bertrand craned his head to see the arrest of Desmoulins better. "More troops are arriving, Antoine. There will be more arrests. Take Nicole from here at once. I'll see you tonight at *La Fenêtre*."

Chapter Nineteen

Walking away from the arrests, Bertrand strolled away from the courtyard and up a wide staircase leading to an upper colonnade. It was quiet. He took a deep breath, free from the turmoil raging below. He pulled a cheroot from his pocket, stood still as he lit it, tossed the match aside, and continued on. A smile playing on his lips, he exhaled a puff of smoke. Did the fool Antoine Durand have *any* idea that his fiancée had spent a day with Luc Chatillon? It was intriguing. Durand might be useful in this challenge to get Chatillon to marry Georgette.

How could he get Durand to help persuade him?

Bertrand chuckled softly. What pleasure he'd take in watching Luc get saddled with another man's bastard. *Oh, and for fun, after the wedding, tell Luc everything, when it's too late. The bastard child will inherit the family fortune and carry on the Chatillon name. And then Luc will see how it feels to have your life ruined by asinine, archaic laws.*

At the end of the colonnade, Bertrand came to an elegant restaurant. He'd not been here before. Yes. Quite lovely. The glass doors stood open, and several tables topped with linen cloths and vases of flowers spilled out onto the walkway. Bertrand spotted Philippe Montpellier at a table near the back, barely visible behind potted trees. He took a last puff on his cheroot and tossed the stub to the floor, then made his way over. "You missed quite a spectacle."

"Desmoulins was there?"

"As I said he'd be," Bertrand said, seating himself. "And the dragoons made a show of it, too. This arrest will be quite the feather in your hat."

"Not for myself," Philippe quipped, leaning forward and pouring Bertrand a glass of wine. "My father. The Count will be most pleased." Philippe snapped his fingers for a server. "There will be a hefty bonus for your mother in all this, Bertrand. Dear Élisabeth is a lovely woman. The most loyal of our staff. Father's words. Though I most heartily agree."

The waiter arrived and placed a *carte du jour* on the table. "Not for me," Philippe said, waving it aside. "Go ahead, Bertrand. Whatever you want. You've earned it."

"Champagne," he told the order, pushing the menu aside. "And I have another piece of information."

Philippe looked sidelong at him. "What tell? Whatever helps the Count helps you, Bertrand. And our dear Élisabeth. You see how we all gain?"

Bertrand leaned his elbows forward on the table. "It's about Luc Chatillon."

Philippe raised a brow. "Luc?"

"He's involved with a woman."

Philippe snickered. "And *that* is news?"

"She was here today, during the riot. She's part of the group I've been telling you about. Up to now they've been harmless. Wandering the streets at night pasting up posters. But one of them, a hot head, Antoine Durand, works in a print shop. Owned by Jules Tout. The owner is unaware that Durand uses his press to print a seditious newspaper. The last edition called for a boycott on the Royal Customs meat levy."

Philippe nodded. "And how does this affect Luc?"

"Durand was here today…with his fiancée. She is the woman involved with Chatillon."

"Do say."

"I saw her several weeks back at the Chatillon country estate. I'm not happy to admit this, but it's becoming impossible to deny…Luc may be in collusion with them." Bertrand lifted his wineglass and took a sip. "Would you like me to find out more?" He set the glass aside.

Philippe's face darkened. "I'm quite fond of Luc. He was just with me and Lulu." He stroked his chin. "But you must find out about this fiancée. What is the woman's name?"

"Nicole Vogel. She's a milliner."

Philippe stared at the slice of blue sky visible from their table. "I want to know everything about the woman. Where she lives. With whom. Her parents. Everything." Philippe scooted his chair back and rose to his feet. "And I want to know how Luc is tangled in this group of rebels. As soon as possible."

Bertrand rose and gave a bow of his head. "I shall do my best. And Philippe, please tell my mother I will see her soon."

With a nod, Philippe grabbed his cane and hat and hurried off along the colonnade.

Bertrand eased back down to his chair. Sipping wine, he studied the *carte du jour*. "The lamb looks interesting," he murmured to himself.

***

It was a long, miserable walk back to the hat shop. Nicole's legs were trembling as images of the uproar flashed through her mind. All the way Antoine had been going over each detail of Camille Desmoulin's speech, surprising her, as if he'd not been affected by the violence. She dumbly stared at her feet, watching one step after the other, unable to rid herself of the sound of the woman's screams. And the deafening musket fire.

She thought back to the months last winter, pasting up posters with Antoine. Had it been pure adventure? She couldn't accept that idea. It *had* been more. It had been a stand against injustice. And again today, listening to Desmoulin's impassioned speech, she found herself drawn again into the Cause. And yet, had not the beginnings of change arrived? Louis *had* begun to give in to demands. He had agreed to hear a list of grievances. And now, time was needed for change. This was not the time to squelch all hopes of a peaceful change with violence.

She chanced a glance at Antoine. What troubled her most was how he'd become visibly aroused by the violence, not repelled. Even now, his body was alert, his words were eagerly expounding demands for the future.

When they at last arrived at the millinery shop, she took his arm. "Before we go in, Antoine, please don't say anything to Gus or Sarah about today."

"Why not? Those two are stronger than you think," he said with surety.

"And yet, they're gentle people. They would be worried about me."

"Very well," he replied with some irritation. "If you want to protect them, Nicole. But they'll sooner or later be part of this. All of Paris will be."

"Did it not trouble you," she asked pensively, "...the bloodshed?"

He pulled away. "I welcome it. Blood must flow to overthrow this monstrous monarchy. First it will be ours. Then *theirs*. Let them die. All of them. They've never cared for any of us."

A shiver of repulsion fought its way up her spine. My God, to hear these words from him terrified her. Something *had* changed in Antoine. She wasn't sure she even knew him any longer. "Antoine," she said, her words coming from a place of courage deep inside. "I need to talk to you about something, something important. About us."

A look of annoyance crossed his face. "Here?" he said, sounding vaguely annoyed. "Now? Whatever is it, Nicole?"

Nervous and unsure and sad and hopeful, she took his hand. "My dear Antoine. I care deeply about you, you know that. I admire your sense of justice. Your love of your family. I adore all that about you. But I must tell you, I am not ready to marry."

Antoine's body stiffened. A dark, cold wave of disbelief passed over his face. "What are you saying?"

"The Cause. I saw everything so clearly today...it's your passion, Antoine. I so admire you for that."

His disbelief changed. His face reddened with indignation. "What has that to do with you not being ready for marriage?" he asked, his eyes flashing about her face.

Nicole felt herself on the precipice. Was this a mistake to tell him now? Were his passions too high after what they'd just seen? But she knew there would never be a good time. No, as hard as it was, she knew she must do it, and she must tell him the truth. "My darling, I've come to understand that I cannot marry you. I do love you, Antoine, but when I search my heart, I realize...it's with the deep and undying love of a sister."

He looked up over her head, his gaze fixed at a faraway spot. She saw how she was hurting him, and she so wanted to stop that hurt, wanted him to understand, to offer back his brotherly love to her for the rest of her life. She wanted to offer him the pure, undying devotion of a sister. But she could tell by the way he stood rigid and unyielding that she was about to lose him.

"Forgive me, Antoine. But I know this freedom will allow you to follow your conviction to change the destiny of France." She took his arm, wishing he'd say something. "I pledge to stand by your side in that struggle. Tell me you understand."

Antoine said nothing as his eyes met hers. In the street a mule-drawn tumbril passed by, its huge wooden wheels making a great racket. Nicole stood helplessly, wanting Antoine to say something. To tell her he understood, that he too cared about her with a tender devotion. Still, he stared at her, his lips twitching as he took in the full meaning of her words.

"Is this about Luc Chatillon?" he asked flatly.

Her breathing quickened. How did he know? He *couldn't* know.

"Why…why would you say that?"

"Do you deny it? Ever since you met him, you've changed, Nicole. You're not the same. Why, I almost think you've been to bed with the man. Have you?"

Stunned, she shook her head in denial. He was right about Luc. But also, he wasn't. No matter what had happened with Luc, she could not force herself to love Antoine as a husband. "Antoine, I— I—"

"Yes, I see. You've become the man's whore? A rich man who doesn't care anything about you beyond a night's entertainment. Ah, your pretentions, Nicole Vogel. You turn *me* away, the man who has offered you marriage, brought you into my family, into the Cause. *He* uses women. Everyone knows that." An ugly smirk crossed his lips. "I'm staggered at your commonness. To think I put you on a pedestal. What a fool I've been." He brushed off her hand and walked away, arms rigidly at his sides, his strides long and hard.

"Antoine," Nicole called, feeling tears of shame and sadness fill her eyes. "Please, wait, don't go like this—"

Without looking back, he turned the corner.

She stared at the spot where he'd disappeared. He was one of only a handful of people who had been kind to her in her life. She stood there a long while, feeling a tumult of emotions: sadness, rejection, and yet, finally, relief. She wiped away the tears. She had done it. And if she was very honest, the sense of relief grew stronger and changed into resolve. It had had to be done. It was over.

Nicole found the shop was empty. She could hear Gus and Sarah's conversational buzz drifting down from the kitchen. She crossed toward the stairway, dreading having to tell them—when something from the corner of her eye made her stop mid-step. There on the table had been propped an envelope for her to see.

She slowly walked over to look closer, lifted it and read on the front: *Mademoiselle Nicole Vogel.* Luc's handwriting. She tore open the flap, pulled out a letter and read:

My dearest Nicole,

You are in my every thought, ma chérie. My father is sending me to England to buy several horses. I won't be gone more than two weeks. Know in your heart I adore you and will impatiently wait to see you again. When I do, allow me to take you to the finest restaurant in Paris. I have something very important to discuss with you. I shall send a messenger with details as soon as possible. Until then, my every moment will be filled with thoughts of you.

With all my love, Luc

Chapter Twenty

The gown was stunning, a midnight blue brocade with silver threads woven through that glittered like stars in an evening sky. The petticoat canopied over clouds of crinoline underskirts which undulated gracefully. Nicole turned slowly for Sarah, who sat on the floor wide-legged, pinning up the hem.

"As for jewels," Sarah mumbled, pins in her mouth, "let the ugly ladies wear their diamonds and emeralds. With a face like yours, Nicole, you'll be the gem."

Gus sat grumpily at the worktable stitching the brim on a hat. "I think this is risky business," he muttered. "Selling hats to the wealthy is one thing. Cavorting with them is another. Our worlds don't mix."

Sarah peeked around the gown at Gus. "Are we suddenly so rich we can turn away clients? Hasn't *Monsieur* Chatillon brought new life to the shop?"

"You listen to me, Nicolette," Gus persisted. "I do like this Luc Chatillon. He seems a good man. But those people have their own rules. They feed off commoners like us."

Nicole flushed. Gus had been unhappy about the dinner invitation from the moment she'd told them. Of course, his concern was understandable. He'd behaved like a father would, *if* she'd had a father. And yet, how could she tell Gus she loved Luc? She couldn't imagine he'd ever understand any of it...how free she felt with Luc, or why she'd told him about her inner demons from Legros and how he'd helped her overcome them. Maybe that's why she hadn't yet told them about Antoine.

"There are bad people and good people everywhere," she said gently, "regardless of their wealth."

"Did you hear that, Gus?" Sarah said indignantly. "Nicole's got a good head. And if she thinks Luc Chatillon is an honorable man, I agree."

Gus harrumphed and, pushing aside his work, rose from his chair and stood, his back hunched from work. "Well, don't come to me later and say I didn't tell you so. I'm going to bed."

"Oh, don't mind him," Sarah said after Gus had climbed the stairs. "He's just tired. Besides," she said with a sudden sparkle in her eyes, "I'm glad he's gone. I have something for you. Wait." She struggled to stand, so that Nicole took her elbow to assist her up.

"For you," Sarah said, pulling a small black velvet box from her voluminous apron pocket.

Nicole had a moment of surprise. "Oh Sarah, you needn't. You've already done so much, helping me make this gown—"

"Hogwash," said Sarah. "Take it, my dear."

Nicole lifted the lid. Nestled on a bed of white silk lay a bracelet unlike anything she'd ever seen. The intricate gold cuff featured a flower at the center with leaves and vines woven through, all molded into one wide cuff.

"It's astonishing," she whispered in awe. "But—how?"

"A duke used it to pay his bill. A long time ago."

"You've kept it all these years?" Nicole marveled, unable to take her eyes from such an extraordinary object.

"Many times I thought to sell it," Sarah said. "I sold the others. A rope of pearls. A silver tiara. But I hoped one day to give this to my daughter." She grasped Nicole's hand and slipped the bracelet onto her wrist. "I want you to have it, my dear."

Nicole twisted the cuff, feeling the cool, heavy gold caressing her skin. "Oh Sarah, I cannot—"

"Don't argue. Now, let me get you out of this gown so we can finish the hem. It's going to take us all night."

Nicole tried to catch Sarah's eye, but the woman's attention stayed fixed on unfastening her bodice. She looked down at the astounding gift on her wrist. Never had anyone given her anything like this. But it was not only the bracelet that brought a catch to her throat—but the suggestion that she was like a daughter. A daughter. So, this was what it felt like to have a mother. *Someone who understands you. Someone who knows your inner thoughts.* In a flush of intuition she realized at that moment that Sarah knew the truth about Luc. And she knew about Antoine. And she understood. Sarah knew the dinner was not about business. What Sarah didn't say said everything.

Slipping on a robe, Nicole gathered up the lavish gown in her arms and carried it to the table where Sarah sat threading her needle. "I'll start on this side," Sarah said, "and meet you in the middle. Together, we can finish."

Nodding, Nicole threw the huge gown on the tabletop and pulled up a chair. Sitting opposite Sarah, she threaded her needle. In the quiet, with Sarah lowly humming as she stitched, Nicole grew sure Sarah knew why Antoine had disappeared from their lives. Sarah was wise. Gus once broached the subject, but Sarah had hushed him. The subject was never mentioned again.

Nicole loved Sarah for this kindness; still, it had been awkward, no one saying anything. For so long she'd tried to please everyone. She'd hoped to grow into love with Antoine—not a passionate love, not what Aimée had, a true marriage of love...but a marriage that pleased everyone. And over the years she would have drifted into a life of...settling. That is, if she hadn't met Luc.

The thing is, she'd fallen in love. With someone forbidden, someone Aimée had told her she should not love, someone Gus had never trusted completely. In all her doubt the only person who seemed to understand was Sarah. Like a mother would understand a daughter's heart.

Nicole looked up from her stitching. Sarah's face in the lamp light looked tired, her lips pinched as she concentrated on the hem. Nicole looked back to her stitching. And yet Sarah would be devastated about her and Luc making love. She felt so caught. She would do anything to be with Luc, but could she see him again, live with him outside of marriage? Could she, even if it hurt the people she loved? She looked up again. Sarah was rubbing her fatigued eyes. Nicole's heart sank. She wanted so badly not to hurt them. But deep down, she knew if Luc wanted her, she would go to him, even if it meant upsetting these two wonderful people—and her best friend.

***

Luc hadn't gone to England merely to buy horses. He'd also gone to stay with his mother's brother, Lord Lindley, at Fernsby House, his uncle's country manor. He needed to get away from Paris. To think. He needed two weeks away from his family and Georgette and all the wedding madness. He needed time and the country to bring clarity to his thoughts. Drinking and whoring with Philippe surely had not. The memory of that night still left him nearly nauseous with self-disgust. And it had offered no real escape.

All during the voyage to England, all through the afternoons riding with his uncle across the English countryside, during all that time he was unable to think of anything but Nicole. And the possibility that Georgette carried his child. No, not the possibility. The likelihood. Each night he would lie awake, thinking about it. *Sacre.* He'd been so sure the child wasn't his. He'd clung to an alcohol-clouded memory of that night with Georgette. It should never have happened. It was a foolish, drunken party last September. And even then, even as he was in her room that night, even with the fog of whiskey clouding his memory of being there, he still to this day clearly remembered his surprise. He was not Georgette's first.

He'd left for America several weeks later. If the child wasn't born soon, he was not the father. And yet, who was? It was a mystery.

But he had to face facts. Maybe he'd believed what he wanted to be the case. Maybe Georgette was not lying. The truth was, he'd been careless. Life had its own plans. And now life demanded payment.

Very well. If he was to be a father, he vowed to be a good one, and a kind husband to Georgette. Never would he forego such responsibility. His child would never feel the abandonment he had from his own father. How well he knew a father need not have to physically leave the house to forsake a child. There are many kinds of abandonment.

In a slow reckoning of what he must do, Luc welcomed his long walks along the roads outside his uncle's manor. He had moments when he clearly heard the no-nonsense voice of Françoise mixing with the wind in the trees, telling him, *Face consequences. Be a man.*

And always, in all these thoughts, when he opened his eyes after sleepless nights—in his heart, at the center, was Nicole. He needed her at his side. It was a plea he sent to her each night, across the English countryside, over the water, to Paris, to her room in the hat shop. *I can't do this without you.*

Even now. Sitting in the carriage and watching the city streets of Paris pass by, Luc realized he'd never known a woman like Nicole. She was no pampered butterfly. Or high-born *chienne* who expected the world to fall at her feet. She was sensual and forthright, strong yet soft. She'd never been coddled. Perhaps those were the qualities in her he loved so deeply. She made him a better man.

And tonight, he would tell her everything. There may be a child. His child. He told himself withholding was not a lie. Just not tonight. Maybe he was afraid. Maybe he'd never felt real fear before. Maybe he wanted to have these precious hours. Maybe their last.

He took a deep intake of air. No. He must tell her. He'd risk losing her, his one hope for happiness in life, his everything. But he'd tell her. He might not be able to offer the marriage they both wanted. But it would be the marriage he could offer, a wedding of souls. He would give her *Les Saules*. If, God willing, they had children, she would be his wife of the heart. As well, he would tell Georgette this truth: she would be the family of his duty.

***

Strains of violins and laughter wafted through the evening air. Luc took Nicole's arm and led her into the reception room. He watched her take it all in. "Luc," she said in wonderment. "It's like stepping into the pages of an old storybook. See there." She smiled, pointing out a group with her fan. "The ladies. I've never seen such tall wigs. And their panniers. They're amazing. They must protrude a foot out on each side. How do they even walk?"

Luc was amused. "Everyone gets out of their way."

She pointed at another group. "And gentlemen with rouged cheeks."

"Yes," he said with a smile. "A fashion I've never quite taken to."

She laughed. "Don't start."

Luc watched Nicole take it all in. He'd never felt happier. His burdens had disappeared the moment he'd seen her coming down the stairs of the hat shop. He'd been unable to take his eyes from her. Her golden hair was pulled atop her head and secured with a black plume that swept down to her jaw. A black velvet ribbon encircled her throat. She'd drawn before him, her statuesque height showing off a gown unlike any he'd seen. It seemed to float about her like a dark glittering cloud. At that moment he felt so sure. Yes. So sure they could navigate this storm. So sure they could be together.

They passed a group that turned to watch as they passed. Luc lifted her hand and kissed her wrist. "You'll have to forgive them all if they stare, Nicole, but you look incredible. You *are* incredible. Heart-stopping."

"Do you really think I'll fit in? Will they think I don't belong here?"

"You belong with me, Nicole." He kissed her fingertips. "And remember, there are no nobility here. Only very old, very bored, very rich commoners. Trying to act like nobles. Come, let me introduce you. These are the people who will make you rich."

Taking Nicole's hand, and filled with a desire to introduce the world to the most wonderful and talented woman he'd ever met, he guided her to the group she'd pointed out. "Good evening, *Monsieur* and *Madame* Dubois," he said, nodding to a lady drenched in pearls, and to her paunch-bellied husband. "*Monsieur* and *Madame* Lamoureux," he added, turning to the other couple.

As Nicole graciously smiled at them all, the men adjusted their spectacles for a better look at the newcomer. The women took in Nicole's simply cut blue gown with its narrow waist and crinoline-bouffant petticoat.

"Let me introduce *Mademoiselle* Nicole Vogel," Luc said with pride. "She is apprentice to the milliner Gustave Baston. *Mademoiselle* Vogel is the designer of *Monsieur* Hervé Marchand's latest line of *chapeaux* being sold in America."

Madame Lamoureux clasped Nicole's hand. "Why, my dear, everyone is talking about your hats. And *Monsieur* Baston. All week I have intended to send someone to take an order."

With a polite inclination of her head, Nicole raised her folded fan and touched it to her jaw. "Thank you, *madame*. We shall look forward to, perhaps, arranging a showing of hats for you?"

Madame Dubois elbowed her way forward. "Oh, my dear, I have seen your marvelous hats at Marchand's. They're quite wonderful—*au currant*. I, too, shall send someone by."

Nicole looked from one woman to another. "We look forward to that," she said with a smile, fanning herself.

Luc had never felt prouder of anyone. Nicole could navigate through a sea of sharks. He formally bowed to the group. "We must take our leave."

"Oh, and Luc, do give my regards to your mother," *Madame* Dubois said sweetly.

"I shall," Luc said. Smiling at Nicole, he took her arm and drew her along with him into the crowd. "Exactly as I thought. You dazzled them," he murmured in her ear. "Are you still worried?"

"Only a little terrified," she teased.

Luc bent his head close, unable to hold back his pride and admiration. "I've arranged a private room for us upstairs," he murmured. "To have you to myself."

"It sounds scandalous, *monsieur*," Nicole said, snapping shut her fan.

"Ah, my little *coquette*, if only we *could* scandalize them," Luc said with a mock frown. "Unfortunately, these people are quite jaded. They don't easily scandalize."

With a laugh Nicole took a deep breath, and Luc took her arm and carried along toward the sweeping staircase. "Perhaps tonight we'll change their minds," she teased.

"Why, *Mademoiselle* Vogel," he said, loving her play. "You surprise me."

"Why, *Monsieur* Chatillon," she said, bringing the tip of her fan coyly to her face. "*You* surprise *me*."

He threw back his head and laughed outright. "Oh, do not fret, my dear, I plan to do precisely that."

Chapter Twenty-One

Upstairs, the *maître d'hotel* swept open the door to reveal an amber-lit room with dozens of candles flickering in candelabras, a table set with flowers, a glowing fireplace, and a divan draped in a silver fox coverlet. Nicole at once realized the room was a hideaway from the excitement and clamor of the public dining downstairs. She also gathered from the wide, soft sofa in the corner, half hidden in shadows, that Luc had every intention of making love to her tonight. The thought was shockingly exciting. Quite sophisticated, she thought as they stepped inside, a deep shiver of anticipation running through her body.

"You are happy with this, Nicole?" asked Luc.

"Oh, yes." She shook her head, *very much so*. Before tonight, her life seemed a haze of unknowing. Now, in this golden room above the gaiety and commotion below, with Luc at her side, she felt complete.

For the next two hours, Nicole delighted in being pampered by a troupe of four servers. Appearing with plates of pâté, consommé, and roasted venison, they entered and exited with miraculous judgment and efficiency as they served and cleared each dish so that Nicole all but forgot she was not alone with Luc. Although everything was delicious, she had little interest in the food, only in what had happened in the time they'd been apart. She related the frightening day at Palais Royal, to which Luc frowned the entire time. Then, she brought a gentle smile to his face as she described the hats she was making, and about her friend Aimée's child due any day. She told him the story of the gold bracelet she wore, and about the Bastons' daughter Rosalie. She asked him questions about England—what was it like? What new horses did he acquire?

Luc explained his visit to his uncle's manor, relating the weather in England, the stables, the food. Nicole looked into his brown eyes.

While he shared openly about his trip, she felt there was something he was withholding, Something she didn't understand.

"Tell me a memory from your childhood," Nicole said, hoping to draw him out. "Your very best one."

"Hm…" he mused, setting aside his fork. "Well—" He paused, seemingly disarmed by the question. Finally he said, "I was quite young. Perhaps four or five at most. I spent a lot of time with my father in the stables, watching his skill in handling horses. It fascinated me as much as the animals themselves." Luc looked down at his plate in thought. "I had begged for months to ride—" He looked up at Nicole with a hint of merriment on his lips. "And finally, my father took me up in the saddle with him."

"And then what happened?" Nicole encouraged softly.

"I was encircled in my father's arms, galloping across a meadow. It was like—I'd been transported into a fable, flying on Pegasus. It felt as though we were soaring over the trees. And all at once, my father put the reins in my hands." Luc inhaled deeply, as if reliving the moment, before his gaze found Nicole's. "It was my first riding lesson."

Nicole had heard Luc speak little about his father. This memory seemed tender and a little sad. And haunted by a feeling of loss. She'd first intuited some sort of tension at *Les Saules*. She took a sudden deep breath. *Dear God.* She hoped it was not because of *her*.

She looked at him over her wineglass, filling with such love that she wanted to go to his side and wrap her arms about him.

"Now, it's your turn to tell me a happy story of your childhood," Luc said, and then caught himself. "I'm sorry, I—"

"No, it's fine," Nicole assured him, leaning her forearms on the table. After all, he'd been so honest—yes, she would tell him. "My memories about my childhood before Legros are dim. And few." She reached out for his hand. He leaned forward and clasped it. "I believe I remember my mother, her arms around me. I felt safe. But it's only the briefest image, and then—then there's nothing."

"I hope you feel safe with me."

"I do, Luc. For the first time in a very long time. When I was a child, I believed that those who love you leave you. It was something that kept me awake at night. But now, with you, I trust from my heart."

Luc sat quietly, caressing the stem of his wineglass. "I hope you remember those words."

Nicole shook her head in wonder. "I always will."

"Nicole, please know that no matter what comes, I'm here with you. I care nothing for who knows. Those people downstairs. Others. I don't care if they see us together."

"Yes, Luc, I realize that. And I—I should tell you...I think Sarah has guessed about us. I believe she approves. And I hope...I'm sure, Gus will come around. I also want to tell you, I no longer see Antoine—"

They were interrupted by the server arriving with the last course—a platter of figs surrounded by creamy dabs of Roquefort.

"That will be all tonight," Luc said in dismissal. "We'll let ourselves out."

With a nod, the man left, latching the door behind.

"Ah, the cheese of kings," Luc said as he took a sample of the tangy cheese. He smiled, holding up a plush fig. "And the fruit of love." He rose from his chair and knelt beside Nicole. "It tastes of desire," he said gently, biting the fig in half, chewing slowly, holding the other half out to her. Nicole opened her mouth so that he could place it on her tongue. As she chewed the fruity softness, Luc reached out and caressed her lips.

"Do you taste it the way I do?" he asked.

"I believe so," Nicole said, running her tongue along her lips.

Drawing closer, Luc pulled her from her chair into his arms and kissed her gently, then fully. He freed the plume securing her hair then drew it down her cheek, down to her throat, as an avalanche of wheat-colored locks tumbled around her face. Dropping the feather, he ran his hands through her silky tresses.

"Such incredible hair," he whispered. He lifted her into his arms. "Let me taste your love. Will you?"

His muscles, and the heat of his body against hers, caused Nicole's heart to quiver. She felt dizzy and warm. "Yes," she said, clasping her arms about his neck and burying her face in the crook of his neck.

Carrying her to the divan, Luc lowered her onto the fur. Freed from his arms, she lay back. "Do with me as you will," she said with a bright, immodest smile. "I am yours."

Kneeling before her, Luc removed one of her slippers, then the other. He slowly rolled down her silk stocking, kissing her thigh, her knee, her ankle—tossing the stocking over his shoulder, and then removing the other. Nicole arched her head against the divan and closed her eyes as he caressed her ankles, and up the sides of her legs, beneath her chemise.

"Is this all right?" he breathed, and now it was his tongue trailing along her inner thigh.

"Yes," she whispered, his tongue moving higher and higher and then—she gasped— touching her womanly, glistening warmth.

"Oh, yes," she breathed, her hands now in his hair, bringing him closer.

She felt his mouth and tongue, first gentle, then firm, so that she moaned and moved with him. Never had she imagined such intimacy could be possible. The idea that it was Luc's mouth upon her stirred her as much as the shudders of pulsing pleasure.

"You are my only love," he murmured, pulling himself up, drawing his muscular body atop her, entering her gently. His eyes met hers. "You are the wife of my heart."

Her breath caught in a sob. "Oh, Luc. Never will there be anyone but you."

As she felt his body find her rhythm, rocking again and again to her moans, she pressed her lips to his. He ran his hands through her hair. Wave after wave of pleasure throbbed through her body. This lovemaking was theirs and theirs alone. She felt the world disappear. And now, with his avowal of love, this was a sacred act. She was no longer alone. "Oh Luc," she whispered, losing herself in a white light of ecstasy.

A final low moan escaped Luc's mouth and he collapsed atop her. With a deep breath, he rolled to his side, his strong arms pulling her to him. They lay entwined. She burrowed into his warmth, feeling his heart thudding against hers.

"I love you," he whispered, his lips at her neck.

"And I, you," she whispered back, tears blurring her eyes.

And then he was kissing her again, moving his body into hers, slowly and tenderly making love to her once more.

***

Afterward, lying next to Nicole, Luc wanted time to stop, for the two of them to exist in another world with no one else. Forever. He longed to be her harbor, to protect her. Give her everything she deserved. And yet, what he must tell her—

"Nicole," he murmured, nuzzling his lips into her neck. "Are you happy, *ma chérie?*"

She traced her fingers along his jaw. "I'm wonderful."

"I know you received a special gift today, from *Madame* Baston," he said softly. "I hope you can enjoy another."

"What do you mean?" she murmured dreamily.

He rose and comported himself. With a quick kiss on her temple, he went to a chair and rummaged in the inner pocket of his frock coat. He returned to her and held out his hand. "Come. Sit, my love." She grew serious with his new mood and sat up, draping the sheet about her shoulders. "Nicole, this is for you. It belonged to Françoise." He held out a small ring box.

She stared at it.

"Take it, my darling. It's for you."

She opened the box to reveal a gold ring, inset with a tiny heart of rubies. Her lips began to tremble.

"Françoise's last wish was that I give this ring to the woman I love."

Nicole stared at the heirloom.

"I can't," she said, snapping the lid shut. "It's not for me. It's meant for the woman you marry."

Startled at her reaction, Luc frowned. "I don't recall Françoise ever having said that."

Nicole placed the box in his hands. "But you can't deny it's what she would have wanted."

"*Grand-mère* was a wise woman." He reopened the box and took out the ring. "She probably wanted me to love the woman I wed."

"But not someone like me," Nicole said, sitting straight and putting her feet on the floor. "An orphan. With no parents. I'm a working woman. Poor by your standards, Luc. Your family will expect you to marry into wealth."

"You know that means nothing. If we could only—"

"Luc, more than anything in the world I would want to take Francois's ring this moment and put it on my finger and never take it off. But I know what this is about. You said it, 'You are the wife of my heart.'"

"Yes. It was my declaration of my love for you."

"But not a proposal. I understand that, Luc. Being here tonight, like this, is one thing. A separate part of your world. I'm prepared for such a life. I'm prepared to face my friends. And my little family at the hat shop. But do you really think your family will so easily let you throw away your life? Stand back and allow you to marry someone like me?"

She boldly stared at him, her eyes dry and unblinking. He could see the courage it took her to come to these terms. She was telling him she was willing to be with him. Without marriage? She was willing to give him everything. All she wanted was his love.

And suddenly he realized, that wasn't enough. She deserved more—for *him* to give *her* everything, too. Love should include marriage. A real marriage. He had to be as brave as she was.

"Nicole, *amour*. Let me confess—if life were as I wished it, if I'd met you last summer, everything this moment would be simple. I don't care about any of the things you say, your place in the world, that you were an orphan. It only makes me admire and love you more. What my family says doesn't matter. It hasn't for a long time." He took her hands into his and brought them up between them. "But I *didn't* meet you last summer. And because of that, there are complications. God knows I wish I could easily make you my wife. I believe there may be, but it will take time."

Nicole's breathing stopped. "You want to marry me?"

"Yes," he insisted. "It's what I *want*. But I know the kind of man you'd want to marry. The kind of man you may think I am right now. The kind of man I want to become. If I am to be that man, you must trust me."

"Luc, I'm confused. I've told you I trust you."

"Will you still say that, I wonder, will you still trust me and love me when you know everything?"

"What are you saying, Luc?"

He held up the ring. "Nicole. If I possibly could, I would wed you…tomorrow, happily." He slipped the ring on her finger, lifted her hand and kissed the ring, kissed her palm, kissed her fingertips. "But there are, complications that I must untangle," he said, covering his fingers about hers, enfolding the ring in her fist. "There were indiscretions—"

Her calm and direct stare stopped him. He couldn't say it, not now, not here in this room where they'd shared such intimacy. He rose from the sofa. His shook his head, wanting a clarity to come. What was he thinking? He couldn't tell her yet. He had to wait for the child to be born, to be absolutely sure. The one thing he knew in all this, Georgette had not been a virgin last summer. Hadn't he, from the moment she'd told him about her condition, hadn't he even then wondered about the real father? He'd ask around, learn more. And if he was right, he'd expose them both. Damn if his father objected. Damn if he disinherited him. His father would have his say, anyway, when Luc refused to show for the wedding Georgette insisted on planning. He *must* find out the truth, first. No matter what, he would sweep Nicole away from all this mess.

"I need a few days, Nicole. Truly. You must promise to trust me."

"I do," she whispered.

He drew her close and whispered into her ear. "At some point I will ask you to remember those words. But now, please know, Nicole, this ring on your finger is a token of my undying devotion."

***

Nicole was in a state of half-dread, half-ecstasy as they exited the room and walked down the narrow staircase. Luc wanted to marry her. It seemed impossible. Yet, she knew something troubled him. Something grave. *His father.* She was sure of it. He would disinherit Luc. He might even disown him. What could she do? Could she ask him about it? And could he really, as he said, *sort it out* in only a few days?

A deep fear chilled her. She twisted the ring around her finger. It was Luc's promise encircling her soul. Yes. She would trust him. Always.

"Luc Chatillon?"

Nicole looked up. A red-haired woman had stopped them. She felt Luc beside her tense, then pull her closer.

"Lady Boucher," he said in what she thought to be a steely voice. Who was this woman?

"Ah, I thought it was you I saw earlier, Luc, with this delightful creature."

Nicole watched as Lady Boucher slowly fanned her narrow, white-powdered face. She felt herself almost undressed as the woman's deeply charcoaled eyes assessed her. "So *you* are the milliner girl—making a name for yourself, it seems." The woman's dark red lips lifted into an unpleasant smile. "Yes, I've heard of you."

"Lady Boucher," Luc said curtly. "If you'll excuse us. We're late."

"Ah but, Luc, you naughty boy. Where are you going so quickly? To see your darling Georgette Fontenay?"

Nicole felt the blood drain from her face.

"You know, Luc, I spent the afternoon with Georgette a few days ago," Lady Boucher went on, and as she did, Nicole felt the room grow warm. "I helped her plan for next week. A garden wedding, La Jardin Cuisiniere. What a lovely place to get married, Georgette has such exquisite taste. So much less common than this outmoded relic here, don't you think? I cannot wait to see you as a groom, Luc. You handsome cad. You'll be spectacular."

The moment closed around Nicole in a black cloak, choking her, numbing her. Her eyes closed. She felt herself sway against Luc, and felt his arm holding her up. She heard Luc brusquely say, "We must be off, *madame*."

With her eyes closed Nicole felt him half guide, half pull her through the reception room. When she did open her eyes, she was assaulted with the chaos of mirrors and chandeliers. Violins and conversations shrieked in her ears. And then they were outside in the cool evening air and Luc was draping his arm about her shoulders and turning her to look at him.

"The woman is a fool—"

"Georgette Fontenay is your betrothed?" Nicole asked, knowing his answer didn't matter. She already knew. She suddenly felt physically ill.

"Come into the carriage," Luc urged her. "Let me take you home."

Nicole felt she might collapse. "You're getting *married* next week?" she whispered. The sidewalk tilted. The street and buildings blurred into a whirl around her. "All this time," she whispered, clasping her throat, "you've been engaged?"

"It's not what it seems."

"And you asked me to *trust* you?" Nicole let out a half laugh, fighting back a hysteria threatening to break free. "Now I understand why the woman hated me so much. She knew—"

"You don't understand. Georgette's going to have a child—"

Nicole's eyes flashed wide. She lost her balance so that Luc reached out to steady her.

"Don't touch me," she ordered, jerking away from him. She could not think. Could not piece together real and not real.

"She claims I am father of the child. And it may be that I am—"

"You made love to Georgette Fontenay?" Nicole demanded. But as soon as the words were out, she didn't want the answer.

"Last summer—the timing—I'm sure it's wrong."

No. No, Luc, don't say this. She stood stock-still, seeing before her a stranger, one that moments before had been the heartbeat of her life. She could not catch her breath. She had to get the ring off her finger. Yanking it off, she raised her arm to throw it into the bushes, then caught herself. *No. No. She couldn't. Not the ring of Françoise.* From deep inside, she somehow found the wherewithal to hand it over to Luc.

"Gus is right," she said, her mind suddenly empty.

"Nicole, please, listen to me. The duty my family insists upon, I will not—"

"You rich use us, like cats playing with mice."

"It's not what you think. I can fix this."

"And you, Luc, you're no different." She had to get away, and turned to leave, but he grabbed her arm.

"Don't leave like this, Nicole—"

"Let. Me. Go." She wanted to pound her fists against his chest. Slap him. Again and again and again—

But she couldn't. She wouldn't. Never would she let him bring her to that. She stood looking at him, struggling to find in all her anger and confusion a place of calm. "I ask one last thing of you, Luc Chatillon. That you do not follow me. That you never try to see me again." She did not for a moment believe she'd ever want to. "And that you—oh." She steadied herself, stood tall. With clear-eyed dignity, she looked at him and added, "Nothing more. Only that I pity you."

She turned and walked into the dark street.

Chapter Twenty-Two

In the darkness of the chapel, Nicole knelt before the Blessed Virgin. In desperation, she clasped her hands in prayer and looked up. But unable to bear the statue's tender gaze, she buried her face in her hands. Her breaths were deep, her heart pounding from walking so quickly past a dark alleyway filled with a group of shouting men. She'd kept her eyes on the church spires. And now the nave's stale, musty air pulled her into a place of pure despair. *Oh God, oh God. How did this happen?* These past months, she'd opened her heart to love, to life, and she'd shut doors on past wounds...

Holy mother, she prayed, *please hear me. Please give me strength—*

It was no use. There was no light. Only darkness. Everything that she'd believed true about Luc, about her life, was a lie.

He was engaged. He was to be married—to a woman carrying his child. His family must hate her, must think her a harlot. She covered her trembling lips. *Oh God. The hats.* All those people tonight. They knew. What must they really think? She had ruined everything not only for herself—but for Gus and Sarah.

She must protect them. From her mistakes. *Hail Mary full of grace...*

She'd not been naïve enough to think Luc had not been with women...but *Georgette Fontenay?* Luc had kissed that woman's cruel lips, had touched her body, *had been with her* in the same way he'd made love to her tonight. Feeling sick, she squeezed her eyes tighter, trying to obliterate the image.

Blessed art thou amongst women...

"My child. You are troubled."

Startled, Nicole looked up. An old priest stood beside her, his hair a corona of white, his face creased by the years. "You've come to share your burden," he said softly. As he knelt beside her, a world of understanding filled his tired eyes. "Let me help."

Nicole struggled to compose herself. His kindness released a floodgate of emotion. Tears spilled down her cheeks. "Someone has betrayed me, Father. Someone I loved...deeply."

The priest nodded that he suspected as much. "And yet," he said, "the only real betrayals *are* by those we love."

Biting her lip to hold back an avalanche of sobs, Nicole turned again to the statue. "So much has been taken from me," she said, her voice catching. "My mother and father. This man I love...loved...he was someone I wanted to spend—forever with. My life is over."

She searched his face for understanding. What must he think? Her impressive gown, her disheveled hair. What must he think?

He calmly nodded. "This man. Does he have...other commitments?"

Closing her eyes in anguish, Nicole shook her head. "Yes. He is engaged...to be married."

"And you discovered this tonight."

She could hardly swallow, much less speak. She closed her eyes and lowered her head in shame.

"And he promised you marriage?"

Nicole touched her finger where Luc had put his grandmother's ring. "He lied, Father. I know that now. I've been so foolish. So vain."

The priest smiled gently. "And you, such a lovely young woman whose life is over, are there no other young men who can win your love?"

She looked up to the serene statue that gazed upon her. "There is another," she murmured. "He's a good and steadfast man."

"And yet?"

No easy answer came. "I do love him. But not with my whole heart."

It was an impassioned admission, and the priest did not attempt to respond at once. He lay his hand over hers. "And yet, love can grow, my child," he said. "You say he is a good man."

"He is that. And noble," Nicole added with an inkling of pride. "He struggles daily against the injustices of the monarchy. At first, I admired him, his cause, to end poverty and oppression." She clinched her fingers in agitation. "But now—it troubles me."

"And why is that, my child?"

"There may be violence ahead, Father. I fear it's already begun. A man was wounded. I saw blood on his face, and he was left on the ground, trampled, maybe dead. Can I be sure this is God's will?"

The priest squeezed her hand in assurance. "If this man you speak of stands against injustice, my child, he is doing God's will. Trust this is so."

Hearing truth in the words, Nicole felt ashamed of her doubts. Antoine had always believed in her. And yet, she had misled him, then abandoned him—betrayed him, as Luc had her. The self-reflection struck her to the core. She condemned Luc for his unfaithfulness, but had she not deceived Antoine? Antoine had been steadfast and true.

"I too have been unkind," Nicole said softly. "I have wronged someone."

Rising, the priest touched her shoulder. "Tomorrow you will see everything anew. You should go to your home, child. Curfew is almost upon us."

"Wait," Nicole pleaded. "Father, please, hear my confession."

In the darkness of the confessional, Nicole poured out the vanity of her goals, the selfishness of her actions, the lies she'd convinced herself to be true. Her murmurs floated along the deserted church aisle, moonlight streaming through the stained-glass windows, shadows shrouding the statues standing frozen and listening to her sins. In the tight box of the confessional, Nicole clutched her hands in prayer, pleading for absolution.

***

Nicole hoped Antoine would be finishing up for the night when she rapped at the print shop door. He pulled it open and stared at her, not uttering a word.

"I must speak with you, Antoine," Nicole entreated.

Glancing suspiciously about the street both left to right, Antoine ushered her inside. Silent, he returned to his worktable. He lifted several boxes and thudded them down on the floor.

"Antoine—"

"Why have you come?"

Nicole drew close behind him. "To tell you I've been wrong," she admitted. "Everything you warned me about the bourgeois world, it's all true."

Antoine backed away from her, his face growing stony as he began stacking newspapers. "Is this about Chatillon?" he asked coldly. "Has he thrown you out? You let him buy that gown you're wearing, then he treats you like a common whore? Why would you expect anything other?"

Nicole closed her eyes for a moment, letting his words settle. "I'm not proud of my behavior these past months. I'm sincere in asking your forgiveness, Antoine. I've even taken confession tonight."

He smirked. "People think their offences can be wiped clean by magic. Real life is harder than that, Nicole."

She rubbed her temples miserably. He had every right to hurt her. Humiliate her. She deserved his anger. "I know I've wronged you. And, honestly, Antoine, it's your honor and integrity that make me most ashamed. Tonight I realized my own deceit. But what pains me most is that I've not been honest with myself—not about who I am, or where I belong."

Antoine stopped fiddling at his worktable and stood still, turning to watch her, as though trying to gauge her sincerity. Nicole fingered the gold bracelet that Sarah had given her in what now seemed a lifetime ago. Touching it, she could feel the trust Sarah had placed in her. And Gus. She belonged to those people. Luc's world of servants and carriages and restaurants was a fantasy. Even selling hats in La Maison de Couture was vanity. Hadn't Antoine tried to warn her? And Gus as well. How could she have been such a fool? And what about Aimée, telling her that the rich are different than commoners. How could she have ignored them all?

"Antoine—" She lowered her head in shame and anguish. "Please forgive me."

After a long moment, Antoine reached out and drew her into his arms, pulling her close. A shattering relief engulfed her. She wept in relief of his acceptance.

"I've always loved you, Nicole," Antoine whispered, pushing aside the unruly waves of hair from her face. His lips found her mouth.

Nicole leaned against him, feeling his scalding lips on hers. She remembered the feel of Luc's airy kisses brushing her lips in warmth, and all at once she felt ill and pulled away.

Antoine released his embrace and held her at arm's distance, looking into her eyes. "And you vow never to see Luc Chatillon again?"

Nicole stood thinking about the question. *Never see Luc again?* A wild revolt rushed through her. As quickly came an avalanche of self-reproach—*Luc lied from the beginning*— What did it matter? She felt dead anyway. There was nothing but repentance and remorse.

"I swear," she whispered. "I will never see him again."

With the words spoken, a dull acceptance of her future seeped into her mind: marriage to Antoine. Working with him in the print shop. Living with Aunt Charlotte and Sebaste. This was for the best. She could grow to love Antoine. Hadn't the priest told her so? She must at least try.

"We need never speak of this again," Antione said with finality. "All that matters is that you've come to your senses. And none too soon. Wait until you hear." His eyes filled with an intense light. "Today deputies of the rebellion declared the Third Estate is dead. There is a new political body, the Commons, to represent the nation of France. It's what Desmoulins called for. Do you understand what this means, Nicole? We are on the brink of revolution."

It took a moment for his words to break into her thoughts. Nicole shook her head for clarity. "What are you saying?"

"The First and Second Estates no longer have power. Here, look at tonight's press." Antoine handed her the paper.

The headlines stunned her. *King Agrees to Constitutional Monarchy.*

Her eyes fled down the column. "I can't believe it," she uttered, then read aloud: *"The king has agreed to abandon absolute power and follow the rules of a constitution."*

"A constitution that *our* deputies will write." Antoine beamed. "But don't be fooled by the nobles saying they agree. They won't roll over and play dead. We must push forward and demand the entire aristocracy be abolished."

Nicole clutched the newspaper, hardly believing it. "But, Antoine, we've won."

"As long as a king sits on the French Throne, our liberty rests in his power."

Nicole dropped to a chair, overcome by all the events of the day. "I don't know. I can't think."

"It's time you rejoin the Cause. Tonight, you can help me bind up bundles. We must get the word out." Antoine rummaged through his newspapers.

"Tonight?" she repeated. No. Too much had happened. She needed time to think. "I'm exhausted, Antoine. I cannot possibly."

He glanced up from his papers. "You must. By dawn Paris will know the people have weakened the monarchy. And now," he grinned, holding up a newspaper, "we will topple it. Hurry, we don't have much time. You'll find a spindle of twine in the backroom."

In its own way, Antoine's passion for justice felt like a reassuring friend. Nicole rose and walked to the backroom. *Yes. A routine is good. Life with Antoine will be calm even in the face of anarchy. Order even in chaos.*

Still, her fingers trembled as she lit a candle. Nothing felt real. The restaurant. Luc. Their lovemaking. His…wedding? Could it be possible? *Next week.* She picked her way through the jumbled boxes scattered about, holding the candle aloft as she searched for twine. Her heart felt sluggish. Was it even beating? She had to focus. Twine. The king had succumbed. It was the sign of a new future. It would be a good life with Antoine, a life that would save her from her own fancies and cravings and infatuations.

Suddenly a flurry of shouts exploded as the shop's front door crashed open against the wall. A deep voice called out: "Antoine Durand. You are under arrest by order of the king."

Confused, Nicole turned toward the sound. The reality struck her like a blow. She snuffed out the candle, her breath stuttering in her lungs. She edged to the door, opened it a crack more, and peered out. Antoine was surrounded by five or six of the king's militia, unmistakable in their blue coats with red breeches and white leggings.

"What's happening?" Antoine cried in a panicked voice. "You've mistaken me."

"Do not claim innocence for your crimes," said the lieutenant-general, a menacing man who was glancing through newspapers littered on the tabletop. "It will not serve you. We have what we need right here. And we will find everything else." He turned to the guards and barked, "Search the premises. Letters. Seditious writings. Notes, names, anything."

Nicole covered her mouth with her hand to keep from crying out. The guards rifled through pamphlets stacked on the counter. Several boxes of freshly printed newspapers had been shoved under a table. Two guards hauled them out and began searching through.

"Show us your weapons," the lieutenant-general commanded.

"I have none. You've mistaken who I am."

A guard yanked open the drawers of a desk, emptying the contents on the floor. Another rummaged through the shelves, pulling printing blocks onto the floor, cans of ink, scattering sheets of paper. In the pandemonium, a guard brought a stack of papers from the desk to his superior. "They belong to the owner. Jules Tout."

The lieutenant-general leafed through the papers. "Where is this proprietor?"

Antoine stumbled toward the lieutenant-general. "*Monsieur* Tout knows nothing of any of this, I swear. The newspapers are my work."

"Enough," the lieutenant-general ordered. He glanced around the room, and as his eyes passed by the door, Nicole drew back. "Are there others on the premises?"

Oh God, she thought. She looked desperately about. There in the corner was a wardrobe. She quickly crossed over and climbed inside, hiding behind the cloaks. No sooner had she pulled the door shut, in the dark, than the memory came to her. *Madame Colére's closet.* She struggled to calm her racing pulse.

The sound of the guards storming into the backroom frightened her.

"She's not part of this," Antoine entreated, following them into the room.

Terrified, she could hear boxes being thrown over, chairs knocked down. Her body stiffened. Certain they would find her.

"Look," a guard called. "The window is open. She must have escaped."

"Outside. Hurry. Follow her."

Nicole's breathing was ragged as a flurry of boots ran, some toward the window to climb out, some back out the door to the shop.

She clung onto a cloak, her brow damp with perspiration as another guard entered the room, slowly and methodically. It was the voice of the lieutenant-general who demanded, "Her name. Who is she?"

"She has nothing to do with this," Antoine said. "You can put me on your wheel, I will never give her name."

"Take him. And find the woman."

She heard the shuffle of boots disappearing. From the next room Antoine asked, "Am I to have my coat?" Her heart broke with the small bit of dignity he had left. There was a racket of movement, then the door slammed shut.

She waited. The shop grew quieter by the moment. She slumped down into the corner of the wardrobe and clasped her arms about her knees. The childhood memory that had once haunted her now seemed small. It floated away. She knew real danger now. Never again would she fear the past.

Something more terrifying lay ahead.

Chapter Twenty-Three

Bertrand lounged with his arm draped on the back of his chair, half-listening to the carousers. He was bored. And slightly drunk. Already the celebration of the king's concession to representatives of the National Assembly had begun. In *La Fenêtre*, all the regular customers as well as fresh, excited faces had been gathering for hours, shouting and debating, waving newspapers and pamphlets telling of the news. Some of the men sang drunkenly, their arms slung around one another's shoulders. The mustachioed owner and his wife hurried about plunking down glasses of wine on the tables and mopping up spills as if unaware of anything but their profits.

"Louis is running like a chased chicken," announced a man with a craggy face sitting at a crowded table. He lifted his wine and took a long drink, set it down, and wiped his mouth. "Saying it's for *our* safety that the commons can sit with the clergy and nobility." The words were met with derision and laughter from the others around the table.

"Here, listen to this from Desmoulins." The man next to him read from a newspaper. "*We accept nothing as the concession of power. We secure all ourselves. Rights will not be given by the king but taken by the people.*" He looked up with a grin. "Fair reward for Louis. He wouldn't meet us halfway."

"We were ready to negotiate."

"And now we take nothing from him. We demand for ourselves."

Bertrand vacuously watched the owner approach and refill glasses. He should stay a bit longer, he thought. After all, it was part of his plan. Be seen celebrating. Later, others would remember.

"No self-proclaimed king or anyone will dictate my rights," declared a young, dark-eyed man, slamming his fist on the table. "It's not a gift. It's mine to take." The proclamation was met with a round of cheers.

Bertrand let out a deep breath. He was sick of it. The same words spoken over and over. He sipped his wine, wondering if by now he could leave for home...when, to his astonishment, he saw entering through the café door the milliner Nicole Vogel. She stood there uncertainly, her wild eyes sweeping the room. He sat up tall, taking in her disheveled state, her unruly hair, her beautiful face pale and haggard. What in hell had happened?

Shoving back his chair, Bertrand stood and made his way through the ruckus to join her.

"Bertrand," Nicole exclaimed. She clasped his arm to steady herself. "Thank God you're here," she said. "Please, Bertrand. I must speak to you. Something terrible has happened."

"Shh, shh," Bertrand murmured into her ear. "Come, let's sit." Taking her elbow, he guided her through the room. He suspiciously took in the luxurious gown she wore and the fabulous gold bracelet on her wrist. What was all this? A gift from Chatillon? Had something happened to him? "Whatever are you doing out alone on a night like this?" he asked, seating her at a secluded table in the corner. "It's dangerous. Paris is going mad—"

"Antoine has been arrested," she said. "It was terrifying. There were a half dozen guards, bayonets pointed at Antoine, surrounding him."

Bertrand was taken aback, surprised she'd witnessed the arrest. He clasped her hand in a show of sympathy. "Calm yourself, Nicole. You're safe. Have some wine."

She shook her head. Placing her elbows on the table, she rubbed her temples. "I can't believe it. Poor Antoine. He was so brave."

Bertrand pulled a cheroot from his pocket. He wondered what she was doing with him. What had happened to Chatillon? "And to think, you were there, Nicole. *Sacre.* How frightening for you. You must tell me everything. Did the guards say anything?" He struck a match, gazing at her with his best sympathetic expression.

Lacing together her fingers, Nicole inhaled a trembling breath. "They burst in with no warning, shouting that Antoine was under arrest. They searched the shop and asked for his weapons." She lowered her head into her hands. "It was terrifying."

Bertrand stoically puffed at the cigar. He'd not anticipated this scenario. *Merde.* She'd witnessed the whole thing. "And the officers," he asked, "they said nothing about the charges? Who brought them against Antoine? Were any names given?"

"Nothing." She tried to remember. "Oh, I don't know. I don't really remember." She looked up. Her eyes were red. Her face drawn. "I was hidden in the back room. I escaped through the window."

In spite of his self-concern, Bertrand couldn't help but admire the woman's grit. How astonishing that she'd managed to escape the guards...and by climbing out a window at that.

"Bertrand, where will they take him?" she asked. He believed she actually cared for the poor devil.

He flicked ashes on the floor. The key was not to say too much. "It's difficult to know. Probably a local jail," he said evasively. "Though perhaps even prison. And yet, who can truly know. For a political prisoner?" He frowned, taking a puff. "Maybe even the Bastille." He blew smoke toward the ceiling.

"Oh no," Nicole moaned. Frantic, she stood up. "I've got to find him."

Bertrand stubbed out the cheroot on a saucer. "Wait, Nicole. That's impossible. You must let me take you home." He slowly rose and took her arm and gently pulled her to his side. "You look about to collapse. Let me help you. There's nothing you can do tonight."

"Bertrand, please, we must try—" Nicole pleaded. "Antoine once told me your mother serves in the household of a count in Versailles. Is there any hope she can help us find Antoine?"

Stiffening, Bertrand drew his hand away from her arm. "Well, it's possible," he said elusively. He leaned close, lowering his voice. "Don't say anything more. You cannot tell who may be a spy here. My cabriolet is outside." He threw a *sous* on the table and grabbed his cloak. The idea that she might become a problem for him was growing in his thoughts. "We can do nothing tonight. What's important now is to get you home. It's dangerous to be on the streets." He leaned closer and murmured, "And you should know, because of your association with Antoine, you too may be in danger."

***

Settled next to Bertrand in his rig, Nicole could hardly breathe. She could not imagine what was happening to Antoine at this very moment. And if Bertrand was correct—the guards might be looking for her. As the cabriolet sped round the corner, they were nearly waylaid by a bonfire burning in the middle of the street, surrounded by a hoard of drunken revelers openly defying curfew. With a low curse, Bertrand swerved to avoid them.

"Viva la France," one of the men shouted as the cabriolet passed.

"Liberté, égalité, fraternité," another yelled, running toward them, his fist raised.

"Idiots," Bertrand said, urging the horse faster away from the throng. "By dawn every household in Paris will know about the king's concession. Antoine risked his life for nothing. Newspapers weren't needed. This news can't be kept from the people."

Lowering her head in despair, Nicole stared at her folded hands. "I don't understand how the authorities knew about him," she puzzled. "He was always so careful. And his press was so small compared to others. How did this happen?"

Bertrand whipped the horse faster. "Have you seen Chatillon lately?"

The question was so unexpected that Nicole looked up from her lap and stared at the street ahead, trying to keep a calm face. Why did he bring up Luc? What did Luc have to do with Antoine's arrest?

"Why do you ask?"

"I've been thinking," Bertrand went on, lashing the horse even harder, "it was Luc who told me about Antoine's newspapers. The other day he dropped by my apartment and showed one to me. He said Antoine should be careful or he might get himself arrested. I thought it odd. Luc had been away to England, and this was the first time I'd seen him since he returned. I wondered why he was so interested in Antoine's press."

Nicole's thoughts swirled as she tried to keep up with Bertrand's meaning. Luc had one of Antoine's newspapers? She sat staring ahead, confused. Was Bertrand accusing Luc of betrayal? But Luc believed in the Cause. In liberty. Freedom.

Bertrand turned his head and stared at her with calm deliberation. Nicole felt a sudden shiver looking into his eyes. She drew back.

"You should know this," he said. "There are rumors that Luc has been gathering information for the Crown."

His words were like a blow. She had to grasp the door handle to steady herself.

"I hadn't wanted to believe it, at first," Bertrand went on. "But it does make sense. Luc's father is Equerry for the royal household. And being that Luc's devotion to his father is absolute, his coming to *La Fenêtre* may well have been to gather information about Antoine." Bertrand shrugged. "After all, Antoine's a printer. He may have been identified putting up posters. They wanted to know more about him."

Nicole focused on the passing streetlamps, trying to breathe. It was impossible to believe. None of this could be true.

"And if you think about it, Nicole, remember that night Luc took the pamphlets from you? He'd said he would put them up in the countryside. At the time I thought it odd. Very unlike Luc."

Her head roared. *No. No.* Impossible. And yet, the Chatillon wealth *was* made at the favor of the throne. She thought back to the restaurant. Remembering Luc's betrayal made her physically ill. He had lied about so much. And with no shame. His grandmother's ring. His protestation of love...and marriage. Such an utter fool she'd been. Could it really be that all this time he'd been using her to get information about Antoine? No. It made no sense. There was the day at *Les Saules*. It couldn't have been a lie. Her mind raced back over the past months. Luc never once asked questions about Antoine. Of course, Luc knew about pasting up the posters but—

Pressing her fingertips to her temples, she sorted through jumbled images in her mind. Had she ever mentioned the newspaper?

"As you know," Bertrand confided, leaning his head closer to her, "Luc finds you quite attractive. He likes beautiful women. It only makes sense he'd want to remove Antoine. More than once Luc suggested...forgive my saying this, I am reluctant to, but Luc has several times talked of...his plan to seduce you away from Antoine."

The cabriolet walls closed in around her. She had to get out.

"These wealthy men, that's how they are," Bertrand went on. "A wife *and* a lover."

Hearing the word *wife*, Nicole stared at Bertrand. "You know about his wedding?"

"Dear Nicole," he said softly. "*Everyone* knows. And, of course, Georgette knows about you—" Nicole shut her eyes. The entire world seemed to teeter beneath her.

A hand shook her shoulder.

Blinking, she opened her eyes and saw Bertrand watching her. "Nicole, are you all right?"

Her stomach clenched. She was going to be sick. Of course, they all knew. Everyone knew but her. What a fool she'd been. And yet, breathing deeply, she felt something else in Bertrand's voice— perhaps a note of triumph in telling her this?

"Nicole?"

"I'm fine."

Bertrand leaned so close their shoulders touched. "Georgette is a sophisticate," he said. "Long ago she accepted Luc's transgressions. She knows Luc is cut from the same cloth as his father. Everyone knows the Chatillon reputation with women."

As the cabriolet turned onto her street, Nicole's gripped the door handle. Her eyes fixed on a spot several blocks ahead. She could not shut out Bertrand's voice.

"I've not wanted to tell you this before. After all, Luc has been a friend."

The last block was taking as long as the entire ride.

"But so is Antoine a friend," Bertrand went on. "Though I never thought Luc would actually betray him like this. Then again, Luc can deceive. I know. He's left a trail—"

"Stop."

Startled, Bertrand glanced at her.

"Stop the carriage. Now."

Frowning, he pulled the reins hard. The moment the wheels rolled to a halt Nicole jerked the handle open. "Don't get out," she said, and gathering up her voluminous gown, she climbed out.

She turned to look back. "I'd like to walk the rest of the way."

Bertrand sat shrouded in the shadows so she could not see his face. "I shall see what I can learn about Antoine," he said. "I'll call on you tomorrow."

"*Merci,*" was all she could say.

She turned from him and stumbled along, hearing the whip crack and the horse clomp away.

Chapter Twenty-Four

Stopping before the shop, Nicole braced herself. The lamps were lit. Were Sarah and Gus up waiting for her? She wanted to cry. She couldn't explain everything that had happened. Not tonight. With a deep inhale she reached for the lock-string, but before she could unlatch it, the door swung wide open and there stood Jacques Guerin, filling the frame. Nicole froze for an instant. This made no sense. Her confusion grew as Sarah and Gus rushed up behind him.

"Nicole," Jacques said in his deep voice. "It's Aimée. She's in labor. There are...problems."

Nicole stared at him without moving, unable to think. She had to hold on to the door to take it all in.

Sarah took Nicole's arm and pulled her inside. "Oh, my dear, we've been so worried. Why has *Monsieur* Chatillon kept you out this late? And look at you—"

"Oh Aimée," Nicole whispered. "I'm coming."

As she disengaged from Sarah and rushed up the stairs, Jacques called out, "It's been over fourteen hours."

Already pulling off ties, she ran into her room, Sarah following, helping her undress. The gown, the shoes, the bracelet, all were thrown onto the bed. The two women said nothing to one another as Nicole dressed in her skirt and blouse.

"God be with you," Sarah said at last, her gentle eyes filled with understanding. "Be safe, Nicole. It's dangerous out tonight."

Nicole stared at her, unable to speak, then rushed from the bedroom and back down the stairs two treads at a time. At the bottom, Gus held open the door. "Give Aimée our love," he said.

Nicole nodded blindly.

Jacques guided her across the street and helped her climb into his donkey-drawn cart, half hidden beneath a tree. She'd been so involved with her own life she'd not even noticed it earlier. Once more she'd failed her best friend.

"Is the midwife with her?" she asked.

"*Madame* Miraleu's been there all along," Jacques said in his deep somber voice. "The baby was on course. Until a few hours ago." His voice broke.

His fear frightened her more than anything. Nicole held her head in disbelief as she tried to take it in, the idea that Aimée might— *Oh dear God.* She could *not* lose Aimée. Why was this happening? She reached over and clasped Jacques' bear-like hand. He did not pull away.

"She will be fine," Nicole said. "You mustn't worry. And the baby." Her words sounded so insincere. So weak.

Jacques wrapped his thick fingers around hers. Nicole thought she heard a sound from him. She would not look. Her body jostled and bumped with each rotation of the huge wheels. She no longer had strength to question anything. She must endure, not question. Luc's lies. His grandmother's ring. His engagement to Georgette. And then, the horror of Antoine's arrest. Luc's betrayal of the Cause. She could endure it all.

A wave of despair swept through her. *Just please, please don't take Aimée.* Her eyes filled with tears. She squeezed Jacques's large hand.

Her eyes fixed into a blank stare. There was nothing left inside her. Nothing but a hard resolve. It congealed deep within, a heaviness around her heart. A resolution in her core. Aimée would not die. She would not let it happen.

***

"Something is wrong with the baby." Nicole heard Aimée's weak voice before they opened the door. A moan of agony followed, and Nicole's breath hitched as they rushed inside.

She saw, standing at the dresser, a strong woman with sure movements. It would be Angélique Miraleu, the midwife. She was washing her hands in sudsy hot water. Aimée said the woman had told her she did it in spite of Parisian doctors' claims that a caregiver of good morals could not infect a patient.

Angélique dried her hands and came to Aimée's side with barely a glance at Nicole or Jacques. "The baby is fine," she soothingly assured her. Angélique was almost as tall as Jacques, and together the two seemed to fill the low-ceilinged room. The woman's heavy-lidded eyes uneasily met Jacques's then turned to her for an intense moment before glancing away.

What had that look meant? It frightened her.

Jacques came to the bedside and gently took Aimée's hand. "Someone is here to see you, my little bird." He stepped back as Nicole approached.

Aimée's sunken eyes fluttered open. "You came," she whispered, reaching out for her hand.

Nicole knelt and, taking Aimée's hand, kissed her fingertips. "Dearest Aimée," she whispered, pulling her palm against her cheek. "I didn't know. I would have come sooner."

Aimée moistened her parched lips. "I think little Jacques has been waiting for you." Her face knotted in pain so that she lifted her head from the pillow and gave out a long wail.

Squeezing her hand, Nicole whispered, "Be strong, dearest sister."

The pain passed as quickly, and Aimée sank into her pillow. "Strong," she murmured. "Like we were at Legros."

"Yes. We helped each other, remember? And now you have Jacques. And Gus and Sarah send their love." Aimée nodded and closed her eyes. Nicole slowly stood. Aimée looked so frail and tiny in the bed that she wanted to pull her into her arms, ask forgiveness for all the months she'd overlooked what mattered, her true friends, her real family.

"And now, Aimée," Nicole said with feigned merriment, smoothing back her hair, "little Jacques is on his way."

Suddenly Aimée gripped the bedpost and let out a long, agonized moan, one that grew into a wail. Alarmed, Nicole stepped back as Angélique sprang to life. She approached the bedside, lifted the blanket and began touching and pressing Aimée's belly. "It's happening. Your baby is coming, *Madame* Guerin." To Jacques, she ordered, "*Monsieur* Guerin, more towels. Hot and clean."

He jumped in alarm, so overwhelmed he had to steady himself against the wall before rushing across the room.

"What can I do?" Nicole implored. She wanted to cry. But she must not. She must be strong for Aimée, who had quieted at last, closing her eyes in exhaustion.

"Nothing for now," said Angélique, rubbing Aimée's huge belly, assessing her condition.

Jacques brought the towels. Angélique gathered them into her arms, and with a head motion signaled for Jacques and Nicole to come to the corner of the room.

"I've seen this before," Angélique speculated. "I believe it's a nuchal cord."

Jacques's face sagged with pure fear. "What does it mean?"

"The umbilical cord gets twisted around the baby's neck. It can complicate the birth."

"But the baby will be all right?" Jacques beseeched, turning white. "And Aimée?"

"It will take all three of us. Everyone, wash hands. *Monsieur* Guerin, roll up your sleeves. *Mademoiselle*, tie back your hair."

A quiet tension ran through the room while they prepared. With efficiency the midwife went about her ministrations. As Nicole returned to the bedside, it seemed Aimée's groans were intensifying. Her skin had taken on an odd sheen, her face covered in perspiration. This had gone on too long. It was almost three in the morning. The baby was unable to be born. It was at that moment Nicole realized they were losing her.

Jacques drew beside Aimée and clutched her hand. "Be brave, my beautiful wife."

But Aimée didn't seem to hear. "Help me," she cried with bloodcurdling urgency.

"We must get this baby out," declared Angélique gravely. "*Madame* Guerin, push. Now."

"I can't," Aimée whimpered. "I—"

Jacques tenderly swept locks of white hair from her face. "I know you can, my beloved."

"Aimée," Nicole said, determined to help. "You must think of your baby. Think of Jacques. Be strong, my sister. We need you to be strong."

She gripped Aimée's hand. Her eyes motioned for Jacques to grip the other. The time had come. "Push, Aimée," she urged her. "Hard. Now."

An animal moan erupted from Aimée's throat.

"Yes, it's coming," Angélique encouraged. Nicole watched through tears as the baby's head slick with dark hair emerged.

Please. Let it happen. Please. Aimée pushed and pushed, groaning and screeching as the midwife drew out the baby.

Nicole stared at the tiny new life. She felt so relieved, so overcome, she thought she would collapse.

"A boy," Angélique pronounced.

"A boy?" Jacques cried. "A boy, Aimée."

"Wait," said Angélique.

Nicole's own gasp of joy caught in her throat at the midwife's tone. And then she, too, she saw the infant's neck entwined with a thick gray umbilical cord.

Angélique barked for her to bring a blanket. She rushed to the dresser and brought it back, then stood staring down at the unbreathing child.

"Nicole, what's happening?" Aimée cried.

"It's nothing." She clasped Aimée's hand. "He's fine." Her heart pounded while Angélique struggled to unwind the cord from the infant's throat. Once uncoiled, she cut it. Nicole came forward with the blanket. Angélique wrapped it about the baby and massaged his tiny back. No sound. His lips were turning blue.

Jacques's rigid body loomed over the baby. "What's happening to my son?"

Groggy, Aimée lifted her head. "My baby?" she whispered with alarm. "Let me have my baby."

Angélique continued to massage the infant's back. "Come, come, *mon petit fils*," she coaxed. Still, no cry. Angélique grasped him by ankles, held him up and gave him an expert smack on the bottom.

Finally, Little Jac took his first breath and let out a wail of protest. The blueish tint faded to white then blossomed into pink as his lungs erupted in an ear-piercing screech.

Jacques wiped his eyes with his huge palms. Aimée gave a quiet sob of relief. Nicole leaned against the wall. She glanced up to the heavens with a silent *merci*.

Cleaned and swaddled, Jac was brought to his mother. Nicole was moved at how the little exhausted mother, hardly able to hold open her eyes, still found strength to embrace her son.

"Hello, my little man," Aimée whispered, taking her baby in to her arms.

Nicole had never seen such a look of joy as that on Aimée's face. It brought tears to her eyes, and Jacques's, even the stalwart Angélique's.

Jacques sat on the mattress edge and drew his family into a protective embrace. "My son," he said, pecking the fragile forehead, then, with a tender smile, he kissed Aimée's cheek. "My two angels."

"Nicole," Aimée called. "Come see your nephew."

Nicole pulled herself up from the wall that had been supporting her, for who knew how long, and joined them.

"Say hello to your Aunt Nicole," Aimée whispered, offering her the baby. Gingerly taking the bundle, as if this were the most precious object in the world, Nicole drew the warmth to her bosom. She was awed at the baby's perfection, his pursed lips and azure eyes. She filled with the wonderment of life.

"Oh, Aimée," she said, tears spilling onto her cheeks. "I'm so happy for you." Her tears sprang from an ecstatic relief and joy. Aimée was now a mother. Her dearest friend's life was complete.

Yet, Nicole knew her tears flowed as much from a place of emptiness, knowing such happiness would never be hers.

***

In the fashionable *Faubourg Saint Germaine* neighborhood, Bertrand heard boisterous singing outside. Curious, he rose from the game of poker and went to the window. Pulling back the curtain, he stood stoically, witnessing men and women dancing in the streets. Philippe Montpellier joined him, a glass of champagne in hand.

"It looks as if Paris has gone mad," Philippe muttered. "This rebellion nonsense is getting serious. This must be about the new political body you told me about? The one Louis has allowed. The Commons."

"They're saying the common man will represent the nation of France. It will come to nothing. Still, I should go see. Would you care to come?"

Philippe stared out. "I think I'll stay in. This doesn't look good."

Bertrand gathered up his jacket. "I'll come by tomorrow to finish up."

"What's that?" said Philippe, still staring out.

"Our game. It's not like me, you know, to walk away from a winning hand."

"Don't bother. I'll go to Versailles tomorrow. To see my father."

Bertrand frowned. "You worry too much. This nonsense is what happens when hot-blooded young men take to the streets on warm nights. I'll come by tomorrow anyway."

Philippe said nothing as Bertrand pulled on his jacket. Outside, the sky glowed red from thick bonfire smoke covering the city. *Good God*, he thought. *It's like the entire city is on fire.* There was no use trying to get a coach.

He lit a cheroot and hurried down the street. Seeing a man running toward him, he called out. "What's happening?"

"It's the rebellion," the man yelled. "It's started."

Growing concerned, Bertrand made his way across town, hearing gunfire, watching fireworks exploding overhead. Bonfires roared on every street corner, with revelers drinking, calling out to him with the term he'd never heard before: "Citizen."

This truly was real, he thought, taking a puff of his cheroot. It was both exciting and at the same time a bit worrisome. Perhaps Philippe had been right to be concerned.

It was late when he arrived at the Fontenay household. He went to the back and knocked. No one answered. He opened the door and was greeted by the kitchen maid. "Where is everyone?" he asked.

"*Mademoiselle* is in her *boudoir*. *Monsieur* and *Madame* have shut themselves in their chambers. Everyone is so frightened, *Monsieur* Le Mansec. The servants have left. They're saying the people are revolting against the king. Is it true?"

"There's nothing to worry about. This is a lot of noise on a hot night."

He went up to Georgette's bedchamber and tapped on the door. "Enter," Georgette softly called.

He opened the door to find the room dark, with Georgette standing at the window watching silvery trails of fireworks. "It's rather exciting," he said with no apology for intruding so late.

"Is it serious?"

"I... I don't know what to think." He went to a side table and poured himself a brandy. "Do you want one?" he asked.

She turned. "Yes. I need it."

She joined him and sat in the darkened room, listening to the booms of fireworks and musket shots. He gave her a sidelong glance. He knew Georgette. Something was bothering her. Something other than the chaos happening in the street. His eyes narrowed, seeing her growing belly outlined in her sheer dressing gown. He looked up at her face, drawn and sad. He wondered about the father of her child. It was Éric, of course. Had she not told him? Were they in on this together? Maybe Éric liked the idea of standing back and watching Luc raise his child as his own. He took a long drink. Not that he would blame him.

He raised his half-empty glass. "Here's to the complete and utter failure of this rebellion."

Georgette said nothing. She twirled her fingertip around the rim of the glass. "Let us hope," she said. "But why haven't the police stopped all this?"

"Oh, they will. And after tonight, I think they'll once and for all squelch these radicals. They've gone too far."

"Mmmm," she said, setting her brandy glass aside. "Indeed."

***

Luc had not slept. In the Chatillon stables, he stood brushing Ares when he heard a strange distant roar. Curious, he put aside the curry comb and walked outside to see fireworks lighting up the skyline. He knew then. It had started. His nostrils flared at the understanding that life was now forever changed. He'd not seen it coming this quickly. And now that it had, where was Nicole at this moment? Was she awake, looking at the same sky?

"And so, Nicole," he murmured, "your Revolution is here."

Another overhead explosion brightened the blackness into a starburst of glittering lights, followed a second later with a low rumbling boom.

"Master Luc," Pepe called, pulling on his shirt and joining him. "What's happening?"

"Everything," Luc replied, his mind filled with that last memory of Nicole. How her eyes had been bright with tears. Tears of betrayal. His.

PART THREE
Justice

Chapter Twenty-Five

Near the center of Paris, on the River Seine, loomed the most despised symbol of the French Monarchy: *the Bastion de Saint-Antoine*, known simply as the Bastille. For hundreds of years Parisians lived in terror of secret arrests and torture within the medieval castle. Its ten-foot walls were impenetrable, surrounded by a moat, water swelling and ebbing with each rise and fall of the river.

The governor of the Bastille, Bernard-René de Launay, a tall, impeccably groomed civil servant of the king, lived in a flat of exquisite apartments within the prison castle. He'd neither ordered nor seen a torture. Unlike the old King Louis XV, his grandson Louis had no stomach for torture, or imprisoning enemies. His few prisoners were no longer the quality of those when he'd first arrived. In such heady days he'd housed the great Cardinal Rohan, awaiting trial for embezzling Marie Antoinette's diamond necklace. And the queen's fortune tellers, Count and Countess Cagliostro. Voltaire had been here. But that had all changed. And with the release of the Marquis de Sade a little over a week ago, the Bastille had seen the last of the great nobles.

De Launay now spent his days trying to justify keeping the crumbling fortress open. It had been slated for demolition and his best hope to remain governor of the albatross had been to promote it as a weaponry garrison.

He was worried. Two hundred and fifty barrels of gunpowder had newly arrived, and he received word that a group of deputies from the Paris counsel were coming to demand it. Drawing on his great coat, de Launay marched out and up the tower steps to the turret. Below in the square, he viewed what appeared to be a thousand men brandishing pikes and pitchforks, chanting, "Pow-der. Pow-der."

De Launay called an orderly. "Find the leaders of this seditious mob. And send word to the officers at the Invalides that we require auxiliary troops."

In less than an hour three representatives of the newly established National Assembly arrived, dressed in plain brown coats, adorned with leafy twigs stuck in their lapels and on the bands of their tricorn hats.

"Messieurs," de Launay greeted them from behind his desk, "how cleverly you identify yourselves in green. But as what? Surely not as rebels?"

"Green is our color as citizens of the nation of France, *Monsieur le Governor*," said the oldest of the revolutionary deputies, a mild-mannered man who held his hat to his chest and addressed the governor over the rim of his spectacles.

"I see," de Launay replied, leaning back in his chair, twirling his pen in his fingertips. "And what news does your *committee* bring for me?"

"You are instructed to remove your cannons from the towers."

"Astounding," de Launay said. "Why would I do such an extraordinary thing?"

"The citizens of Paris believe the cannons are a threat. And that an attack on them is imminent. To defend ourselves, you are asked to pull back your cannons."

"What you ask is treason," de Launay said with a polite smile. "My duty is to protect the Throne's gunpowder. I shall do exactly that."

The deputy was not impressed. "You must know, *Monsieur le Governor*, that over fifteen thousand men have joined the National Guard, men recruited from the streets, out of shops, off fishing boats, the citizens of Paris. The men that you of the First Estate have condescended to call the Third Estate, the bottom of society, have now thrown off the yoke of injustice."

De Launay's smile faded. "You think I will succumb to such treachery?" he exclaimed, throwing aside his pen. "And you should know, I have reinforcements on their way this moment. Tell your men to disperse unless you want bloodshed on your hands."

At that moment, storming through the door, a wild-eyed, whiskery man rushed to de Launay's desk. "We want your stockpile of guns, immediately. They belong to the people. All the gunpowder."

Startled, realizing the man had breached his guards, de Launay assessed the situation. "Sirs, you are aware that I cannot concede to such a proposition. I will relay your demands to His Majesty. When I have a reply from Versailles, I will send for you."

The following moments were filled with heated exchanges and threats until de Launay had his guards escort the men out. His hands shaking, he was pouring himself a full glass of sherry when his door burst open and his lieutenant rushed in unannounced. "*Monsieur le Governor*, troops from the Invalides have arrived, with cannons."

De Launay exhaled with relief. "At last. And if I give an order, will they fire on the crowd?"

The lieutenant stood frozen. "But the troops are on the side of the rebels. They're trying to break down our gates."

***

Midas scratched at the door. Nicole rose from her handiwork of mending socks to let him out. The sun felt good, and she closed her eyes, welcoming it on her face. She'd been cloistered for days, having failed all avenues to find Antoine. Bertrand had been no help. And after Antoine's arrest, she'd fully lost her spirit for the Cause. It had taken a turn, the lawlessness, shop windows being broken at night, public transport being disrupted—even the streetlamps were unlit. Everything seemed to be breaking down. Fear had gripped the city that the king was preparing a purge of anyone connected to the insurrection. If so, not only did Antoine face danger, she did as well. By association, the Bastons, and Aimée's family. Her activities begun in the name of justice now endangered the people she loved.

She opened her eyes and looked around. What was that? A dim sort of rumbling in the distance. She stood, listening. Something was happening. Something far away. She began to quickly walk toward the sound when a man turned the corner and ran past, waving his arms, shouting, "The Bastille. It's fallen. The army's joined us."

Nicole stared after him as he passed, shouting again and again the same words. It took a moment for the meaning to register. Then her eyes grew wide with the full magnitude of the news.

Hurrying inside, she grabbed her shawl. "The Bastille has fallen," she said breathlessly, rushing about to change from her house shoes.

"What?" Gus bellowed, pulling his pipe from his lips. "But such a thing isn't possible."

Sarah came ambling down the stairs. "What's happening? There's shouting outside."

"The Bastille," Nicole said. "They say the citizens have taken it." She pulled on her shawl. "Antoine surely is being released. I must find him."

Outside, the racket was deafening. The streets were crammed with people dancing, crying in joy, drinking. Nicole ran all the way, stopping now and then to catch her breath, her heart pounding, before she started off again. Everywhere on the route, people were shouting, "*Viva la Nation.*" Doors of houses and shops and cafés were swung open with people rushing in and out, hugging strangers. Children brandished wooden swords, fighting the imaginary King's Army.

"Is there room for me?" Nicole called to a farmer in a cart rumbling along the riverfront.

"Where are you going, *mademoiselle*?" he asked.

"The Bastille."

With a tilt of his hat, he reined his mule to a stop. "*Bien sûr.* I'd be honored, Citizen."

The driver slowly made his way through the streets until the crowd became so thick he couldn't move forward. Nicole thanked him and climbed down, walking the final mile. As she approached the Bastille, she stopped in shock. Her nostrils stung from the acrid smoke of cannons. Viewing the aftermath of battle, her anticipation of finding Antoine turned to pure horror. The courtyard was strewn with broken glass and smoldering debris, and bloodied bodies. Young men, old men, even women, all freshly dead, being sobbed over by their loved ones. Red-jacketed soldiers turned revolutionary soldiers were ceremoniously removing bodies, respectfully hoisting the fallen heroes onto carts.

Nicole lifted her gaze to take in the massive stone prison casting its shadow over the battleground. How would she find Antoine in so much chaos? Pulling her shawl closer, she approached the charred wooden drawbridge, still smoking. A revolutionary wearing a sprig of leaves in his tricorn hat held out a bayonet.

"No one is allowed inside."

"Oh, please, I'm looking for a friend, a prisoner."

"They've all been removed. What name?"

"Antoine Durand. I'm not sure, but he may have been brought here several weeks ago."

The revolutionary shook his head. "Not here. Seems there were only seven prisoners in the entire place. We took their names and released them hours ago. Your friend must be elsewhere."

Despondent, Nicole roamed the streets, torn between a sense of pride shared with her fellow Parisians and stunned at the cost of lives. She walked along, wondering where it would all lead. And where was Antoine? She'd always imagined him imprisoned in the Bastille, and while thankful he wasn't, a directionless, empty feeling consumed her. After hours of wandering, she realized she'd circled back to her own street.

Entering the shop, she encountered Sarah coming down the stairs to greet her, a strange look on her face. "Nicole," she said gravely. "Someone is here."

Nicole paused for an instant, then brushed past Sarah and fled up the staircase. There stood Antoine, leaning on a cane, his body skeletal, his face drawn and gray.

***

At midnight, Georgette slipped inside her *boudoir*. She fumbled for a candle, swearing under her breath as her foot bumped into the dresser. A strike of flint startled her, then a flash of light illuminated the darkness. She almost screamed seeing Luc standing there, holding up a candle.

"You," she fairly hissed. "Get out. Before I have you arrested."

"Sorry," he said with a wry smile. "It might be difficult procuring a policeman tonight."

"How did you get in?" she demanded.

"Easy. I simply walked in. It seems your father and mother were fast asleep. And the servants are no doubt celebrating other matters tonight." He drew closer. "So, you see, we're alone." The candle beneath his face cast dark shadows.

Georgette shuddered and looked away. "My servants are idiots," she muttered, fumbling to unbutton her cloak. "Do they really think this rebellion will help them?" She pulled off her cloak and turned to him. "Why are you here?"

Luc held up the candle to illuminate her very pregnant body. "I wanted to talk in private."

She flung the cloak at him. "*Foutre*. So you can gloat? You don't need to. You've already humiliated me."

He drew closer. "I wanted to tell you I'm sorry, Georgette." She cautiously studied him. "What I did was wrong," he went on. "I should never have allowed this wedding charade."

She scoffed and turned away. "We were engaged. It was to be a perfect wedding. All but one little detail. No groom."

Placing the candle on a table, Luc lowered onto the settee. "From the beginning I was clear I'd not be forced into marriage," he said. "If we look for fault, Georgette, we should search elsewhere."

Seeing him staring at her huge belly, Georgette bit her lip. "I'm ghastly tired," she grumbled, sinking beside him. "This day has been exhausting." She stared out at the nighttime sky, rosy with bonfires. "What do these people think they're doing, rebelling against the king?"

"Something honorable. Fighting injustice."

"Ahh, injustice," Georgette said, her voice ugly with sarcasm. "That's right. You're the one who went to America to see how the colonists were wronged by King George." She turned to him, impassioned. "The only injustice in my life is what you've done. Do you know how you humiliated me by refusing to marry me? I always believed sooner or later you'd want to please your father and mother. Now, everyone is laughing."

"Everyone except Éric."

Georgette's breath caught. "What do you mean?"

"Don't play. Not now. We're beyond games," he said calmly. "You and I both know what happened that night. We got drunk, and had sex. Once."

Alarmed at the truth of his words, Georgette pushed against his chest and tried to stand. He caught her hand. "You're a fool," she cried, struggling against him. "You should have married me. Our families wanted it." With all her might she shoved him and stood, but stumbled so that Luc stood to his feet and caught her. "We would have had a perfect life," she whimpered.

"Georgette, I'm not a fool. I knew that night that you'd been with someone else. It took me a while to discover it was Éric. I should have known. Anyone who's seen you with him would have to be blind not to know."

"Father guessed too," she murmured, leaning against Luc. "And now Éric's gone."

"Gone? Where?"

"After it was clear you could not have fathered my child, Father sent him away in a barrage of threats." She closed her eyes. Éric's chiseled face came to her. "I've not heard a word since then. Not even a note."

Luc lifted her chin so she was forced to look at him. "I'm so sorry, Georgette."

Her face filled with desperation. "Luc," she sobbed, throwing her arms about him and burying her face against his chest. "I know you once cared for me. Tell me you did love me." She drew back and appealed to him. "You *must* marry me. You must."

"Georgette."

She tried to pull him closer for a kiss.

Arching his head away, Luc lifted her into his arms and carried her to the bed. He lowered her onto the lavender coverlet, bending on his knee beside her. "Never should I have allowed the wedding planning to proceed," he said softly, smoothing her hair. "I know that now. It wasn't fair to you, or to the woman I love, Nicole Vogel."

"In *love*?" she gasped. "With the milliner? *You*?" She gave out a painful sigh. "Oh, *mon dieu,* Luc." She shook her head in disbelief. "I knew the girl was a diversion, but—" She looked up at him. "So, all this time, there *never* was hope? All these months. You had no intention of marrying me?"

"Only if I was the father. I never imagined you would carry things to the lengths you did. I thought the real father would step forward."

She scoffed. "As though that could happen. Éric knew Father would have him thrown in prison. Besides, Éric once said...he's not even sure he knows what love is." She felt unwanted tears. "If only Éric could have taken me away from all this. I'd have been happy."

She laid her head back on the pillow. "Luc, why didn't you tell me about your feelings for this woman before?"

He inhaled a deep breath. "I was angry at my father. For trying to control me. And I guess I didn't realize how much I did love Nicole. And that I was actually *in* love. But I know now. Nicole means more to me than my father's fortune. She's my entire life."

Georgette turned her head to look at him. "What fools we've been."

Luc took her hand to his lips and kissed her fingertips. "Do you want a boy or a girl?"

With fresh tears, Georgette shrugged. "Either. As long as it's healthy." She thought about the night she'd told Éric, how he'd grown quiet, and afterward how distant he'd become.

She sniffed and wiped away tears with her fingers. As she quieted, Luc smoothed her hair and said, "I remember you as a blossoming young woman. One of the most beautiful in Paris. The world awaited you. I was only one of many who admired you. Including Éric."

She began crying again, covering her face with her hands.

"Georgette, you should find him, tell him what you've told me. He's a good man."

"But how?"

"I will help look for him."

"It's useless. Father will never allow us to marry."

"Have faith, Georgette. Tell the truth. You'd be surprised what power lies in the truth. Remember your own mother. How she controlled you. How your father turned a blind eye to her meddling. If only they'd allowed you to live your life. Don't you see? We're the same, you and I. Both casualties of families trying to tell us who to love, who to marry. The young Georgette I knew never would have let them. Do you want the same for your child? Or do you want to be a loving mother, married to the man you love, giving your child the freedom you deserve?"

"I want all of that," she whispered. "Oh Luc. Can you ever forgive me for what I've done?"

"It's not you. It's our families. But I have a hunch that after what's happened in Paris today, everything will be different."

Chapter Twenty-Six

Nicole's honeyed lips hovered before Luc's. He yearned to reach out, to run his finger across her cheek, to swallow her kisses, to pull her body to his—but she stayed just out of reach, blurry behind a diaphanous veil.

His eyes flashed open to the sun streaming into his bedchamber. He was hot, his hair damp against the pillow. It took a moment for him to fully awaken, for clarity to come. But then, when it did, also came the regret. She was gone. He'd never see her again. The sense of loss and regret filled his body with a profound heaviness.

He threw his arm over his eyes. He was going mad. He could not stop his mind going over and over all he should have said to Nicole that night, all he should have done. Not that he hadn't tried to make up for it. He'd poured out everything in a letter, every last detail, and the truths of his heart. But she'd sent no reply. Had she even read it?

He turned in bed. Would he forever be plagued by the memories of that dreadful night? His grandmother's ring on Nicole's finger, Lady Boucher's malice, Nicole's running away. He'd followed her into a church. He ached to tell her there was no sin in their lovemaking. They'd united not only in body, but in mind and soul. He lay there, trying to fix in his brain on what he'd failed to do in person: confess everything to Nicole. Imagining what he should have said in the carriage. Or how he could have told her before dinner. Or ways he should have explained it all after their lovemaking.

Luc sat up against the pillows. The truth was, he'd been held back by fear. But now something had changed in him. Something deep and vast. Maybe the overthrow of the monarchy had broken him free of his own chains. No longer would he be held captive to his family or society. Up to this point, he'd lived life mindlessly, complaining about and yet accepting the culture and customs and habits of everyone around him. He'd been no better than Gilles Fontenay. Or his father. How foolishly he'd prided himself in being different. And yet, hadn't he sensed something was wrong for years, even as a child? He'd felt a different music at *Les Saules*, with Françoise. Maybe that's why he'd gone to America. Not to get away from Georgette, but to be free from his own captive life.

Throwing back the spread, he rose from bed. He had to see Nicole. Or at least try. He'd sent the letter over two weeks ago. She'd had time to make up her mind if she would forgive him. He could wait no longer. He must know.

Wrapping a brown satin robe over his nightshirt, Luc rang for his man, Symon, who at once appeared at the door, precise and prompt as always.

"My blue suit today," Luc stated.

Symon's sharp eyes, never missing a thing, fled over his master's disheveled hair. "Shall I prepare a wig, sir?"

"No," Luc replied, running his palm along his whiskery jaw. Wigs now seemed an affectation of a passing world. He thought about Nicole's natural beauty, how her unpowdered face and un-charcoaled eyes had captivated him from that first moment at *La Fenêtre*. No wig or face paint could outshine her dewy skin, her thick lashes, her pink lips. When they'd made love under the willows, and again that day in the bath, and then again in the restaurant, the naturalness of her skin and hair and pale eyes incited him with a tender passion he'd never known. She had a beauty that radiated from within.

Symon draped a linen about Luc's shoulders and smeared a soapy shaving brush over his jaw. Something about the practical intensity of Symon's precise strokes, the man's steadfastness even in the face of turmoil in Paris, caught Luc's attention. He ruminated on how little he knew about this man, even though Symon had been with the family for as long as he could remember.

Unaware of the scrutiny, Symon patted Luc's face with a steamy towel then prepared the wardrobe, helping Luc into a white shirt with ruffles at the neck, followed by dark blue britches.

"Where were you born, Symon?" Luc asked as Symon fastened a cravat about his neck.

"Pardon, sir?"

"Were you born in Paris?"

Symon secured Luc's cuff buttons. "Well, sir, no I was not. I come from Senlis." As Symon spoke, his ears reddened. Luc wondered if the man was embarrassed by the questioning, or perhaps captured by some memory of home.

Symon held out a velvet box holding an array of shoe buckles. Luc chose the dark brass and sat. "Senlis is a lovely village," he said, hoping to engage Symon further.

"Yes, indeed, sir." Symon bent to his knee to buckle Luc's shoes. With a sniff, he rose up with effortless finesse and strode to the rosewood armoire. Removing a dark blue waistcoat, he held it up in readiness. "Anything more, sir?"

Luc stood and slid his arms into the sleeves. "That will do," he said. Dressed, he crossed to the door, then paused. "Symon," he said, turning. "How long is it since you've been home?"

Symon's flawless posture settled a moment at the thought. But at once he resumed his rigid bearing. "I've not, sir. Not since I've arrived."

The answer astonished Luc. *Not once? Ever?* "Then perhaps it's time you do so," he said, ashamed he'd never thought of this before. "I'll arrange a visit, if you'd like. Would you?"

Symon stood somewhat confounded, before his head tilted in the briefest of nods. "I would like that very much, sir. Thank you, sir."

Nodding in return, Luc left him, wondering about the man's life before he'd come to Paris as a servant, and about the walls built between the classes, and how, as they were tumbling down, what that would mean for the life they all knew.

***

Bounding down the staircase, Luc considered sending ahead a note, alerting Nicole he was coming. But it seemed best to simply arrive at her doorstep. Throw himself at her mercy. Tell her everything.

With his mood hopeful, he found himself hungry for the first time in days as he entered the dining room. His mother and father were seated at opposite ends of the long table, half finished with their breakfast.

"Good morning, sir. Mother." He'd not taken a meal with them since the wedding fiasco ended a few weeks ago. He hadn't wanted to face them in the aftermath of Gilles Fontenay's noxious visits threatening legal action. Even now that Georgette's child clearly was not a Chatillon, his father remained cold and obstinate. More angry than humiliated.

Maybe it was time to make peace. Or try.

Luc helped himself to creamed egg and fruit compote from the sideboard. With a glance at both parents, he took his spot at the table. His mother's gaze encouraged him to be nice. His father kept at his food, eyes down.

As a server poured his coffee, Luc broke the silence. "I thought you should know I apologized to Georgette. For letting the wedding charade go on. And she made it clear I am not the father of her child. She now plans to marry the real father. It's what she's always wanted."

Victor Chatillon deliberately placed his knife on the edge of his plate. "You're being foolish," he scoffed. "Both you and Georgette. Paternity is always a question. How many heirs have been on the throne without a drop of royal blood? None of that matters. It's the principle of the thing." He set his jaw. "Be practical. There is strength in unity. And now with this instability in the country, families need strength."

Luc sipped his coffee, then set the cup in its saucer. "Father. I too intend to marry the woman I love."

His mother's silvery eyebrows lifted. A hint of a smile touched her lips as she gazed across at him. He knew that look. It told him she wanted him to be happy. She knew he'd been tormented about the wedding. Ever since the ceremony had been annulled by Georgette, his mother seemed relieved. "Of course, my dear," she said. "Love *should be* the basis of marriage. After all, marriage is a sacrament."

Victor yanked his napkin from his lap and whipped it onto the table. "Is everyone mad? Do you know what's happening in this country? To the Throne? Can we not come to our senses? Have you ever once, Luc, considered how I amassed the fortune that you've been so adeptly spending over the years? It certainly had nothing to do with my bloodlines. It's because I married into a family of means. As you will."

Not this again, thought Luc. The fact that *Grand'mère* Françoise had passed over her son, and bequeathed *Les Saules* to him, her *grandson*, had dealt a death blow to their father-son relationship. Luc remembered the pain of it, losing the hero-father of his youth, his best friend. As if the inheritance was *his* fault. He'd been as surprised as anyone. Over the years he'd tried to repair their split, even to deed back the property, but to no avail. The hurt ran deep. It was about his father's relationship with his own mother. Luc felt a profound sadness that always came with these thoughts. Françoise had no choice. She knew her son hated the countryside, detested being at *Les Saules*. Françoise was wise enough to know that her son would sell the beloved home before she turned once in the grave.

And she knew how much *he* loved it.

His father was still ranting. "Do you imagine I sauntered into Versailles to request the position as Royal Equerry? Ha! It was because your mother and I were married. Your *mother*, whose father served as Royal Stud Groom. Thanks to your mother's father, you've been able to live like you do. Even though he was dead before you were born. I secured my post through cunning, and, damn it, money. Love had nothing to do with it."

"Victor," Gabriele exclaimed. To Luc's surprise, her eyes were shining with hurtful tears. Or could it be anger?

Victor's face sobered. "Oh, my dear, I didn't mean—"

"You've said enough," she admonished, standing from her chair.

Victor went to her and, holding her by her shoulders, whispered into her ear. Luc watched his mother dab her eyes with a silk handkerchief. He couldn't catch the words from his father's muted murmurings, but noted how she calmed as he kissed her cheek. Seemingly placated, she turned and left.

"Now look what you did," Victor grumbled, taking his seat.

"What *I* did?" Luc scoffed. He darkly wondered if he could bear another minute in the same room as his father. They sat in silence, each picking at his food.

***

The day was hot, the streets all but empty. Only those with serious matters ventured out in the heat, mostly for fear of encountering the militants patrolling the city.

So, it was with some trepidation that Gus answered the knock. Opening the door, he stood there, startled to find Luc Chatillon. Words didn't come at once. It was difficult for him to know what to do. For surely Chatillon was not here for hats. He must want to see Nicolette. Yet Gus sensed how Nicolette felt.

"*Monsieur* Baston," Luc said, tipping his hat.

"*Monsieur* Chatillon," Gus replied. "If you've come for the order, it's not quite ready."

"I'm not here about business," Luc said. "I hoped to see *Mademoiselle* Vogel. I must speak with her."

"I don't think that's possible. She asked for no visitors." Gus saw a shift in the man, as if a light within suddenly went out. It even crossed Gus's mind that the gentleman looked broken-hearted. But that couldn't be. Men like him didn't fall in love.

"I want to apologize to her," Luc pursued, looking past Gus, surveying the shop. "And explain that things aren't what they seem."

Gus felt a spark of compassion. The man seemed sincere. Yet, although Gus knew little about this matter, he'd sensed enough to be against it from the start. "*Monsieur* Chatillon," Gus said, leaning closer to keep the words between the two of them. "Ever since your dinner, she's changed." He shrugged. "She reminds me of the young girl who first arrived here. She's quiet. Keeps to herself. Works too much. I don't like seeing her turn back into that wounded bird. It's none of my business, but if it has something to do with that night with you then I ask you to leave her be."

"Of course, I'd never—"

"I'm sorry," Gus interrupted, taking hold of the door to close it. "You should leave."

"But will you speak to her? Ask if she's read my letter and if she will agree to meet somewhere. Here. The park. Wherever she likes. At least allow me to explain to her."

"I'll talk with her. But you must know, Nicolette has a will of her own. I'll protect her in any way I can. That includes not upsetting her."

"Yes, yes, I understand." Luc took a step back, his gaze drifting behind Gus toward the stairs.

Luc thanked Gus and then retreated to his cabriolet. Taking the reins, he cast one last glance at the empty second-floor windows. Gus watched the magnificent white horse respond to the driver's flick of the reins, then he closed the door.

***

From behind her curtain at the upstairs window, Nicole watched Luc's cab roll away. She let the curtain drop. She'd heard every word. After pulling his unopened letter from beneath her pillow, she lit a candle. Then, her eyes filling with tears, she held the envelope over the twisting flame and watched it burn.

Chapter Twenty-Seven

Rounding the last turn, the jockeys whipped their horses headlong with manes and tails flying. Spectators rose to their feet in a roar of excitement as the pack thundered toward the final stretch, and then, in an explosion of cheers, the winner blazed across the finish line.

Philippe Montpellier wadded his ticket into his fist. "*Merde*," he muttered, tossing it to the ground and sinking to his chair next to Bertrand. Shaded by an umbrella, their small table held a bottle of Sancerre and two wineglasses.

"What do you expect?" asked Bertrand smugly. "Your *faire le champ* bets are impossible. How can one call win every combination on a particular horse?"

"*Bis, bis.* Don't reveal your peasantry," Philippe chided, pouring himself a glass of wine. "They are *wagers*, not bets, and it's not about money. One merely beats the odds."

Bertrand sulked, the offense at being called *peasant* ringing in his ears.

Philippe took a sip of wine, made a face and tossed it onto the grass. At once the server appeared at his side. "*Monsieur*, is there a concern?"

"Is this wine or horse piss?'

"*Monsieur*, would you care for another bottle?"

"Champagne. *Moët et Cie.* And ice the glasses. Damn. Do I have to tell you everything?" Philippe leaned against his chair and stretched his legs before him, crossed at the ankles. He studied the racing form. "*Putain d'idiots.*"

Bertrand glanced down at his racing schedule. "My, my," he mused, browsing through the upcoming races. "Such foul spirits today."

The server brought a bottle of champagne in an iced bucket. "*Monsieur*," he said, showing Philippe the label, "one of our best."

Philippe motioned for him to uncork it. In quiet he watched the twisting, popping, foaming, and pouring procedure. With the server gone, the two sat sipping their champagne, waiting for the next race.

Philippe stared across the grassy track. "Bertrand," he at last said. "Things are in a bit of a crump."

Bertrand looked up from the program. "What exactly does that mean?

"What's been happening in Paris. It's growing quite serious."

Bertrand took this in. "Things should settle soon. The king arrived in Paris last week. They say he was received warmly by the public. He even pinned the rebel's blue-and-red cockade over his white."

Philippe grunted. "Ah, yes. The new symbol of France. The Tricolor." He frowned, twirling his glass. "*Quel sacrilege*, covering the white cockade of the *ancient régime* with the rebel's colors. Louis is a fool to legitimize such lawlessness."

"Does he have a choice? He's wise to welcome it. The National Assembly have agreed his presence is important in the changes. They've given him the title Restorer of French liberty."

"You should know that same Assembly has abolished feudal rights and privileges. The seigneurial rights of the nobility are the basis of our income. Do you understand what that means?" Philippe marked a wager on the upcoming race. "The treasury has no funds." Scowling, he double checked his choices, muttering under his breath, "The problem is not that these rebels think they are capable of ruling a nation." He looked up with an insincere smile. "Rather that the nation they now rule is bankrupt."

Bertrand's eyes narrowed. "Surely you overstate—"

"I must tell you…without annuities, my father is bankrupt. Without our land dues and goods, how are we to support ourselves? The nobility are forbidden to venture into business. Or in any manner dirty our hands with factories or investments. We've had to stand back and watch commoners gain the wealth of this nation. You think nobles aren't capable of such? Of supporting ourselves? And now." He called a passing server. "Here," he ordered, handing over his marked wager. "Place this on the race six."

Bertrand looked off at the horizon, absorbing Philippe's words.

"And now we nobles must watch it all fall into chaos." Philippe removed his silk hat and scratched his wool wig at the temple.

"Damn. It's hot. I detest summer." He glanced at Bertrand. "I should tell you, my father had no alternative but to let Élisabeth go."

Startled, Bertrand knocked over his champagne glass, shattering it. "Let her go?" he uttered. "Where is she?"

Philippe shrugged. "Entire households are being lost. We've released all but a handful of attendants. Perhaps even as we speak, dear Élisabeth is making her way to Paris with a coach-load of our oldest, finest servants."

An attendant arrived at the table to mop up the broken glass. He dabbed Bertrand's soiled jacket. "Go away." Bertrand exploded. The befuddled attendant retreated.

"What can one do?" Philippe muttered. "We've loved Élisabeth as our own." He turned his head to view the horses lining up at the start. "I've picked a winner on this one. Let's see how it goes."

The pistol shot rang in the air and the horses charged ahead.

**

Sitting in a stuffy back corner at *La Fenêtre*, Nicole groomed a lock of hair away from Antoine's flushed cheek with the tenderness of a mother for a fevered child. She had once done the same with Luc, swept back a wave off his forehead, but that had been a lover's touch, filled with desire. For an instant she allowed an image of Luc's face to float before her, his eyes crinkled with laughter as he carried her in the rain, then catching herself, banished it. She could not dwell on the past. That was over. This was a new world.

"Antoine, I'm concerned about you," she said, touching his forehead with the back of her hand. "You feel warm."

He didn't reply, didn't seem interested in her care, merely kept reading his newspaper. Nicole noted the slight trembling of the paper. The quiver in his hands seemed to be getting worse. If only he would talk to her, let her help. Since his release from prison, a wall had grown between them. Antoine spoke little of his ordeal, and never to her, only a few times to Gus and Jacques, so that the horrors he'd endured came to her in overheard bits and pieces. And not once had he mentioned their engagement. It seemed his sole interest was the revolution. He read everything he could get his hands on about it: pamphlets, newspapers, essays.

"Where is Bertrand?" she mused as much to herself as to Antoine. She dreaded the meeting and wished Antoine had not agreed to it. Never would she forget how cruelly Bertrand had pronounced that Luc was a spy and a womanizer, the smirk on his lips, the insinuation in his eyes. As though he got pleasure from telling her the worst. She shivered, shaking off the memory of that horrible night. "It's not good for you to be in the café, Antoine," she said. "It's hot. And smoky. Why is Bertrand keeping us?"

As if on cue, Bertrand entered the café door, looking about and pulling off his riding gloves. Seeing him from across the room, Nicole clasped Antoine's arm, bracing herself. She truly did not like the man and worried about what he might say.

Antoine too had seen him and lifted his hand as Bertrand surveyed the packed café. Seeing them, Bertrand motioned hello. With a forced pleasant look on her face, Nicole watched his jaunty movements through the crowd.

"Bertrand," Antoine said in welcome, standing with the help of a cane. "You came."

"*Mon Dieu*, Antoine, of course I did. I've been anxious to see you." Bertrand touched Antoine's shoulder in comradery. "The news of your release has been a great relief to us all." A mutual look of respect passed between the two men before Bertrand turned to give Nicole a brief nod. "*Bonjour, Mademoiselle* Vogel."

"*Bonjour*," she replied without looking him in the eye.

"Antoine," Bertrand said, taking a chair and signaling for coffee, "you must tell me about the arrest. What a terror. Where were you taken?"

"They brought me to La Force."

"My God," Bertrand sympathized. "There are such stories of that place."

"You can see what they did to me." Lifting his trembling hands, Antoine gave a hollow smile. "They may have broken my body, but not my mind. Or my spirit."

Nicole pulled his hand into hers to quell the shaking. "I'd thought they'd imprisoned him in the Bastille," she said. "I went as soon as I'd heard it had fallen, but Antoine wasn't—"

"*La Force* was filled with revolutionaries," Antoine went on. "Men who questioned the arming against Paris by our own king."

Bertrand nodded gravely. "I've heard La Force uses torture."

Nicole bit her lip and looked down at her cup. Why bring this up? It only upset Antoine. Had Bertrand no sensitivity?

"All true," Antoine said, his face flushing red. "They tried to crack my bones on their rack." Carried away at the memory, he stared vaguely off. "The only thing that cracked open was the truth about our so-called French king and his armies. *They* are the enemies of the people."

"But, Antoine, if we try to completely abolish the monarchy," Nicole reasoned, "there will be more bloodshed. And who would rule?"

"The *Duc d' Orléans* is my choice," offered Bertrand. "He's been the force behind change. His opening the Palais Royale to anyone who wanted to speak gave a place for the Third Estate to unite."

"No," Antoine boomed, startling them both. "Orléans merely wants to become the new king. But France is done with kings. Done with *all* titles of nobility."

The fury on Antoine's face grieved Nicole. She could not undo what he'd been through, no matter how she tried. She reached again for his hand but he pulled away.

"I've been unable to identify my accuser," Antoine went on. "I searched for records at La Force. Nothing."

She turned to look at him. He'd not shared this with her. Never once. Why now? With Bertrand? It seemed he'd become a stranger, and that he...*resented* her. For what? His imprisonment? As though she were the one responsible.

Bertrand leaned his elbows on the table. "I've identified the informant," he murmured, leaning close in confidence. "You were set up by Luc Chatillon."

Nicole did not respond. She hated hearing this. It couldn't be true.

She glanced up to look at Antoine's face. He was now white, his lips compressed in rage.

"Chatillon?" he uttered. He straightened in his chair. "What proof have you?"

"I do not say this lightly," Bertrand said, folding his hands on the table. "At first I'd not been convinced. God knows I didn't want to believe it. But now, I'm sorry to say, Antoine, but there is no doubt that Luc is an agent of the Crown."

Nicole felt light-headed. She closed her eyes. It couldn't be.

"Why would Chatillon do this to me?"

"Isn't it obvious? For money. And power. The Chatillon family need both. Victor Chatillon is Equerry to the King. They paid him for his information. We now know hundreds of servants, even nobles, were rewarded to infiltrate the rebel forces. I've been told by Philippe Montpellier, son of Count Montpellier, that Luc was paid for any information he could provide."

Nicole rubbed her forehead, trying to take in these damning accusations. Luc was a traitor? Had he proposed marriage as part of his scheme? To gain her confidence?

Antoine thudded his fist on the table. "I knew it from the beginning. I've always been suspicious of Chatillon. We *all* should have known," he said with conviction, turning to Nicole. "Don't you agree?"

Nicole inhaled deeply. "It's devastating he would do such a thing," she said, unable to believe it fully. "Even if his father asked—"

"You were taken in by him," Antoine accused. "Why else would a wealthy man support our Cause? Certainly not only for a pretty face."

Humiliated, Nicole covered her lips with her fingertips.

Antoine scoffed. "It never made sense to me. Or to anyone else, either."

"It began with the fathers," Bertrand said. "Victor Chatillon plotted with Count Montpellier. They used their sons. Luc and Philippe are fast friends. Ask anyone. Their whoring and drinking are notorious." He glanced sideways at Nicole.

Reeling, Nicole half listened as Bertrand went on, word by word, accusation after accusation. She began to wonder if she were losing her sanity, for all around coffee was being served, people were laughing and arguing, a black and white dog plopping by the fireplace, all in a cold reality apart from her.

"You can imagine my own feeling of betrayal when I learned about Philippe and Luc," Bertrand was saying. He paused, taking a sip of coffee. "My mother is a servant in Montpellier's chateau. It was easy for the two of them to use me. She'd warned me." Bertrand toyed with his empty cup. "Philippe introduced me to Luc last summer, then when Luc returned from America, he asked to join me, here in this café." Bertrand turned over his cup with finality. "And now, it seems Philippe has had a change of heart. He's confessed it all. His father's annuity is cut off. At this point the nobility are like frightened hens, trying to ingratiate themselves with the new powers."

"To think, Luc Chatillon sent me to prison," Antoine murmured darkly.

"Do you remember that first night?" asked Bertrand. "How Luc took the posters from you, saying he would put them up?"

Nicole felt numb as Bertrand continued to lay out proof of Luc's guilt, until at last, no longer able to deny the awful truth, she broke into tears. "I'm so sorry, Antoine," she whispered under her sobs. "I was wrong. How can you forgive me?"

"I warned you, Nicole," Antoine said, standing up from his chair with the help of his cane. "See what your refusal to look at the truth has done to me? I never should have brought you into the Cause. This is not women's work. And now, I plan to see that Luc Chatillon pays for his treachery."

***

Bertrand whipped his horse, cursing under his breath as he maneuvered through the crowds milling in the streets. Fools, he thought. Mobs plotting more rebellion. He flat out believed the people had gone mad. Paris was being destroyed. City services had all but stopped. The municipal workers had joined the revolution, and now streets were stinking with horse manure and refuse. Streetlamps were unlit. Citizens were being robbed.

Though most troublesome were the scores of carts filled with exquisite furniture as nobles fled the city. Bertrand whipped harder. How could Paris be the same without the nobility? How could France. Before long, the high-born aristocrats would be genuflecting to gutter merchants and common businessmen. To anyone with money. Like the Chatillon family. Victor Chatillon was a skilled horse breeder. He'd be in demand regardless of who gained power.

Bertrand had a vivid image of dukes and lords flattering Luc, trying to pander off their daughters on him, of Luc's children carrying noble bloodlines. He'd always hated Luc. Born high on the wheel of fortune. He had it all. Looks. Women. The only son of a wealthy man.

What about *his* fair shake in life? With a slight twist of fate, his own father, Gilles Fontenay, could have been the most powerful textile manufacturer in France. Add to that, *he* was the sole Fontenay son. He should be the heir, not Georgette. If the buffoon Gilles Fontenay had acknowledged *him*, he could have stopped the man from squandering his fortune.

All because Gilles stood on worn-out thinking. Even the old Louis XIV had willed his illegitimate son the Throne. Over his own *blood* sons. If good enough for a king, why not the old fool Fontenay?

Bertrand reached into his pocket for a cheroot. He was out. Damn Philippe. Wasting a perfectly good bottle of Sancerre to buy champagne instead of cigars.

Bertrand whipped his horse to go faster, sending it careening and people dashing out of its path. His thoughts grew more bitter. Even now, his mother journeyed to Paris. She would come directly to his room. Maybe she'd already arrived. He stared ahead as he blindly passed through the streets. Without her help, he couldn't pay the rent, much less take on a larger place. His chest felt tight, and he had to struggle to breathe. Élisabeth must find placement in Paris. Some rich merchant would pay a pretty price to land a count's house servant, especially a lovely one. Élisabeth remained beautiful to this day.

Until then, he needed money. Philippe had paid him for information about Nicole Vogel's involvement with revolutionaries. But that was over.

His mind grew dark thinking about Nicole. He remembered her face in the café, the way she'd whitened like a sheet when he'd brought up her lover, Luc. He thought she might fall off her chair with his information about Luc and Philippe. Served her right, the bitch. She'd sabotaged his perfect scheme to get Luc married to Georgette.

In his investigations he had found little information about the woman. His one lead had been the Palais Royale shop, *La Maison de Couture.* Hervé Marchand had informed him that *Mademoiselle* Vogel's hats were selling well. The man had not known much about her, only that she'd been sent to the Baston Millinery as a ward of the Legros school for orphans.

Hm, Legros. An orphanage. Maybe a visit there would be worthwhile. Maybe find a few secrets from her past. Maybe ones Nicole Vogel would pay to keep hidden.

It was worth a try.

Chapter Twenty-Eight

Marthe Colére glanced at the clock. The man was late. As if she had nothing better to do than sit about waiting for him. This had better be worth her time. She was seated at her desk cutting strips of red, white, and blue silk. A tedious task, but needed in order to create the tricolor rosettes the revolutionaries wore as badges of rebellion. Especially now. With all the rumors that the government was insolvent, it was unclear how much longer the Crown could support Legros. In some way, she'd been bound to meet a man calling himself a deputy of the National Constituent Assembly. In a note written in opulent handwriting, the man had said he wanted to discuss a ward who had been in her care several years back, and he'd mysteriously added, *The meeting will be advantageous to your institution, and to you.*

Setting aside her scissors, she gave a low *humph*. The monarchy facing bankruptcy didn't surprise her. The Queen and her entourage were responsible for all of this. Their gowns. Their jewels. Frowning, carefully she laid out several strips of blue alongside the red. How could a country survive such scandalous squandering? The nobles taking milk baths. Their horses shod in silver while she raised hundreds of little beggars by scrimping and guarding against waste.

She began folding a strip of red, twisting and rolling it into a knot of ribbons, humming a song: "*You in your cockade, you're just an idiot, a fool.*" As a girl, she'd sung it, sneering at the nobles who thought they were better than the commoners, flouting their ribbons of white rosettes. Humph. Didn't they use a commode like everyone else? Push out babies between their legs? She twisted the last bit of red fabric into a pretty rosebud and began to stitch it atop a white rosette. Her lips inched upward. Behind the nobles' backs, people had called their little white rosettes *cockades*. Cock-of-the-walk fools. The gullible nobles adopted the name as a badge of honor. And now, these rebels wore tricolor cockades. The writing was on the wall. This new order would be unchanged from the last: different names, same cocky buffoons.

A rap sounded at the door. She paused in her work. "Enter."

A pink-cheeked ward with a cloud of curly black hair cracked open the door and peeked in. "*Madame* Directress," she said in a tiny voice. Her cheeks were gaunt and a darkness shadowed her eyes. "Someone is here to see you, *Madame*. A gentleman."

"Then don't just stand there. Let him in, and bring us tea."

"Yes, *Madame*." The girl pushed the door wide to reveal a young man. As he entered, *Madame* Colére found him unremarkable in looks, one of those men who flaunted a beard. His unkempt hair touched the collar of a modest coat. Oh, he had a certain style, she mused. But too much swagger to his walk. She hated his silly cap. Important men should wear hats, and be clean-shaven. Walk with an erect bearing, make calls in well-groomed wigs. So, this was the new world order.

"Come, have a seat." Her thick eyebrows arched in a question. "*Monsieur...?*"

"Bertrand Le Mansec." Removing his cap, Bertrand gave a slight bow. "Thank you for taking the time to see me, *Madame* Colére." He took the chair across from her, eyeing the pile of cockades on her desk.

"You're late," *Madame* Colére began, scrutinizing the man's face, priding herself with being able to read the character of the person at first meeting. He wanted something. The question was, how important was it to him? What could *she* get from the man?

"My sincerest apologies," Bertrand said. "There was an uproar in the streets, as there often is during these exciting times."

The dark-haired girl entered, carrying a tray set up with a silver tea service. It took all her strength to place it on *Madame* Colére's desk. She stood frozen in place, captivated by being in the presence of a stranger.

Bertrand pulled from his pocket a small piece of candy wrapped in pink tissue. Seeing the girl's eyes widen, he held it out. "Do you like sugared ginger?"

She turned to *Madame* Colére. "Oh, may I, *Madame*, please?" she beseeched.

Madame Colére crossed her arms and sat back with an irritable nod of consent. "Very well. Then get out."

Grabbing the candy and whispering to Bertrand "*merci*," the girl turned and ran to the door and shut it gently behind her.

"You shouldn't spoil them, *Monsieur* Le Mansec. They must learn their place. They're penniless beggars living off the crown." She poured tea. "Sugar?"

He nodded. "*Merci*. The sweet was to impress you, *Madame*," he said, accepting the teacup.

"Then you wasted your money. What do you want, *Monsieur* Le Mansec? I haven't much time. You said I might be able to help you with information about a ward I once had."

"Quite right," Bertrand said. "I've been investigating certain persons who may have plotted against our Cause. One of them was once a charge at Legros."

"Very well. What was the name?"

"Nicole Vogel. It is believed the young woman left here four or five years ago. She is now employed as a milliner with Gustave Baston. Do you recall such a ward?"

At the name, *Madame* Colére's eyes hardened. She'd never told anyone about the girl. A small trill of alarm sounded in her mind. What did this man know?

"Yes. I remember her," she said coolly. "The girl was defiant. I did my best with her, though she was arrogant and disruptive." She stirred her tea, thinking of Nicole. How could she forget? That thick rat's nest of hair. She could still feel the resistance as she'd cut it. Like cutting through a bale of hay. She set down her cup. "I arranged the ward's apprenticeship at the millinery. Never once has she thanked me for all I've done for her."

Bertrand flashed a sympathetic smile. "Knowing the woman now, I can believe all that you say."

Madame Colére noted the disdain in his voice. This visit was not about her treatment of Nicole Vogel. This was about the girl. She was in some sort of trouble. "*Monsieur* Le Mansec, why is it you're here, asking about Nicole Vogel?"

"We believe she orchestrated the arrest of her own fiancé. The man is a printer, Antoine Durand. All last Spring he put out newspapers for the Cause. *Mademoiselle* Vogel was in his printing office when the king's officers arrived and arrested him. Interestingly enough, *Mademoiselle* Vogel went free."

Madame Colére lifted her chin. It was as she thought. An investigation. Her chest puffed with indignation. "The girl has always been a liar. I believe she'd sell her own mother, if she had one."

Bertrand nodded. "You are quite perceptive, *Madame*. I believe the woman is as you describe. Now that her fiancé is freed from prison, she's saying she has no idea who informed the authorities. And many believe her. I hope her files can provide information for our leadership to shed light on the woman. If you can help us, *Madame*, it will benefit you greatly."

"Of course, I have the file," she said, growing imperious in bearing. "As I do for all my wards. I keep order, *Monsieur* Le Mansec. It is my duty."

"Excellent. Then, you can help me discover the truth about *Mademoiselle* Vogel?"

Madame Colére pushed herself up. Grimacing, she took a moment to straighten. "I think you will find the girl most interesting." Gripping the side of the desk, she made her way to the tall cabinet in the back of the room. In a minute of rifling through the middle drawer, she extracted a faded red leather folder, tied with string. Tucking it under her arm, she made her way back to her chair and sat, plopping the folder on the desk.

"You must remember this moment, *Monsieur* Le Mansec," she said gravely. "I am freely giving over documents that belong to the king's government. But I do so with the knowledge that what is in these files is of grave importance in the struggle of our people."

Bertrand sat taller. "Very well, *Madame*. I will remember."

"And I shall hold you to that." She pushed the folder across the desk to him.

Bertrand unwound the cord and lifted the leather flap to remove a pile of papers. *Madame* Colére sat back and watched as his facial expression altered from curiosity to confusion.

He looked up. "Am I reading right? She is *not* Nicole Vogel?"

"That's correct. Her name is Nicole Eugénie d'Ailly."

Bertrand referred back to the papers. "She is the great-great-granddaughter of Honore d'Albert, the Seigneur of Picquigny?"

Madame Colére's face darkened. "And the girl's father, Alexandre Vogel d'Ailly, was a lieutenant under Louis XV."

Bertrand read aloud. *"In the presence of His Majesty, Louis XV, Alexandre Vogel d'Ailly witnessed the peace signing of the Seven Years War."*

Madame Colére nodded. "The lieutenant, along with his wife, were killed in a coach accident the day of the king's funeral. The girl saw the entire thing. She was brought to Legros that evening. What a handful she was trying to run away. Opening the window to climb out. We had to tie her to the bed."

Bertrand took out a handkerchief and dabbed his brow. "And Nicole knows nothing of her heritage?"

"Why should she?" *Madame* Colére asked irritably. "She is an orphan. She had no living relatives. I considered it best to change her name. Nothing good could come from her knowing otherwise."

Bertrand sat back in his chair. "May I take these papers with me? In the name of the Cause."

"But of course, Citizen. Whatever will help our nation."

"Your generosity will not go unrecognized," Bertrand said, standing self-importantly. With a grim frown, he stacked the papers and slid them into the folder. "How unfortunate for the girl to discover her noble heritage, just as the winds of change have come."

***

Nicole and Antoine made their way along the *Quai de Gesvres*, both lost in thought as they took in the vista of the sun-filled river teeming with fishing boats. Nicole felt a miserable dampness under her arms from the strain of Antoine leaning on her for support and wondered if he was even weaker now than the day he'd come home.

"Let's stop for a moment," he said, dropping to a bench on the promenade. Sitting beside him, Nicole lifted her face to the sun, inhaling the mossy smell of the river. A sudden breeze offered a gust of coolness. Taking a few deep breaths, she tried to remember the last time she'd been in nature. She spent most of her time nursing Antoine. He rarely left his home, only a few times to attend a meeting of the National Assembly. It was a relief he'd agreed to walk like this.

Hearing a cluster of birds in a nearby tree, she closed her eyes and experienced a rare moment of peace. Her life didn't seem to belong to her anymore. Though she would never admit to anyone how imprisoned she felt. She longed for the freedom of riding a horse across green meadows and...

Reveling in the warmth of the sun on her eyelids, she allowed herself to finish the thought: She yearned for the love of a man who cared about the things she did. Family, nature, creativity, books. Joy. Her chest constricted. She could hardly bear it. Such a man did not exist. And such a life was not possible for her.

"Citizens.Citizens."

Her eyes popped open to see a young man running past, yelling. "Citizens. The villain Foulon de Doué has been captured."

Antoine bolted tall beside her. "Foulon de Doué? Incredible."

"Who is he?" Nicole asked, alarmed.

"The Controller-General of Finance. Nicknamed the *familiar demon*. He told the starving farmers to eat their hay if they were so hungry." Standing with the help of his cane, Antoine called after the man. "Citizen. Wait. You say Foulon is in our hands? Where?"

The man stopped and shouted back, "At the Place de Grève. Hurry. You can see the monster with your own eyes."

As news spread, the streets came alive with everyone rushing in the same direction. It was as if all of Paris had heard the news. Nicole could not fathom where they came from, men brandishing swords and rifles, others pitchforks and sticks. The young and strong charged side by side. Women abandoned their apple and flower carts to follow, tugging children behind. Along the route, red, white, and blue streamers fluttered from windows as people leaned out and shouted encouragement.

Nicole held up Antoine as he hobbled along with an energy she'd not seen since his injury. They were jostled through the triumphal arch at Porte Saint-Martin that led into a huge square before the Hotel de Ville, filled with a mob chanting, *"Liberté, Egalité, Fraternité."*

Antoine kept pushing, forcing their way toward the center of the square. Suddenly Nicole sensed a new urgency. The chants transformed to a roar of excitement as people pushed backward toward a cabriolet now making its way through the arch, its landau top shredded so that flaps of torn leather rippled in its wake.

"It's Bertier." The news spread through the crowd, growing into a thunderous uproar.

Nicole covered her ears. "What's happening?" she cried, growing frightened.

"They've got Foulon's father-in law, Bertier de Sauvigny," Antoine shouted over the roar. "The man responsible for the food shortages. It seems they'll both face the people's justice."

Nicole's mouth went dry. This madness was justice?

The cabriolet came to an abrupt halt in the center of the square. The door opened to the clamorous outcry of the crowd. Bertier de Sauvigny appeared on the coach step, a puffy-faced man stripped of his wig to reveal a bald head, his face bruised and bloodied. Horrified, Nicole looked away, toward the azure sky.

Then she saw it.

Floating above the crowd, atop a pike being brought for Bertier to see, his son-in-law's head, eyes bulging, tongue lolling.

"Oh, Antoine," she moaned, her stomach sour and tight so that she thought she might be sick.

Antoine took her arm. "Foulon de Doué has met his just end."

Nicole tried to object, to question, to express revulsion, but in all the tumult, not a sound escaped her lips.

The crowd surged forward. Bertier was lifted, and a noose slung around his neck. A youth scurried up a lamppost to secure the rope.

"*Liberté, Egalité, Fraternité.*" chanted the mob as Bertier struggled against the two men hoisting him up.

"No, no," Nicole murmured. This could not be happening, not in the open, not in Paris. She covered her ears to the chants.

The crowd quieted in expectation. Nicole felt nauseous as she waited, eyes clamped shut, listening to her own ragged breathing.

And then the crowd erupted in cheers.

Chapter Twenty-Nine

Little Jac's icy-blue eyes widened as Nicole poured a cup of sudsy water over his bare shoulders. "I see you like your bath, little man." He gave a happy shriek and splashed his palms on the water, wetting her blouse.

Aimée glided into the room, a towel in her arms. "All done?" she asked.

Nicole hefted the dripping baby over to his mother. "He is. Good as new."

"My sweet boy," Aimée crooned, enfolding Jac's slick body into the towel, kissing first one pink cheek then the other.

Nicole followed them to the dressing table with a bundle of clothes. "I see he's outgrown his swaddling," she said, handing over a dressing gown.

"He's growing so fast."

Nicole believed Aimée had never looked more lovely. Or happier. "What is motherhood really like?" she asked.

Aimée thought about the question. "Being a mother is the hardest thing I've ever loved." Her expert hands tucked a linen clout under Jac's bottom, wrapping it around his fat kicking legs. "I don't think I've slept more than two or three uninterrupted hours since he was born." She put first one chubby arm then the other into the long puffy sleeves, stood him and smoothed the garment that draped past his feet.

"Aren't you a happy one?" teased Nicole, taking Jac and holding him to her shoulder.

Smiling, Aimée slid a frilly lace bonnet Sarah had made onto Jac's bald little head, tying it under his double chin. She then tugged on crocheted booties, the handiwork of Auntie Nicole. "That he is." She laughed. "Except when he's ready to eat. Then, what lungs he has. A scream that splits the night."

As though Jac understood his mother's words, he let out a wail. "What did I tell you?" Aimée smiled and brought Jac to a wide-backed oak chair. "It's time for lunch." She eased into the chair that Jacques had crafted weeks before the birth. *A mother needs a comfortable chair to sit with her child*, he'd said proudly.

In the kitchen Nicole poured hot water into a teapot, humming and relishing the peaceful cocoon of Aimée's home, such a contrast to the chaos, the insanity, throughout the city. Sprigs of lavender perfumed the air. Cabbage soup bubbled on the stove. Before the baby, Aimée had been meticulous about cleaning, but now breakfast dishes sat in the sink, and dust and crumbs had gathered on the floor. Jacques didn't mind, even asked Aimée *not* to clean, insisting she rest when the baby was sleeping. Nicole believed Jacques's thoughtfulness continually grew, as did Aimée's love for him.

While the tea seeped, Nicole washed plates and swept the floor. But with each swish of the broom, her mind stubbornly wandered to a gloomy place. What about her own life? She might never have children of her own. Antoine didn't want a family. But that didn't matter. She'd grown firm. She wouldn't marry him. Even if he asked her again. Which was not likely. Antoine hadn't talked about a wedding, not with his head full of Revolution.

She put the broom away, but her melancholy thoughts persisted. Her fantasy of creating a life with the man she really loved was shattered. As she dried the dishes, a feeling of exhaustion swept through her. She must rid herself of this dreariness. With a sigh, she pulled her thoughts back to the sweetness of Aimée's life.

***

A block away, Luc guided his cabriolet along the street. In what seemed another lifetime, he had brought Nicole to the apartment building of her childhood friend Aimée Guerin. He hoped he could find it again. But where?

This morning he'd started on his way to *Les Saules*, for some peace from his growing worries: the violence in Paris, his difficulty in finding Éric to help Georgette, and his father's increasing anger and belligerence. Though foremost, he needed to escape his grief over Nicole. She wouldn't see him at Baston Millinery, but days ago he'd thought he might catch sight of her in her neighborhood, and he rode around to no avail. He even stepped into her parish church, the memory of that day they'd received the blessing from the priest striking him hard, but the pews were empty.

He'd gone to La Maison de Couture to ask Marchand, but the shop had been shut for good. He didn't have any way of knowing if Nicole had even read his letter. If she had, did she believe him?

The need to tell her everything became so overwhelming that he'd impulsively veered off from the road leading out of the city and made his way back, until, at last, he'd turned onto what be believed to be Aimée Guerin's street. From all he'd heard about the woman, she had a wisdom beyond her years, and a kindness that might possibly open up to help him.

He pulled the reins, slowing to scan rows of two-story buildings lining the narrow street, trying to locate the spot he'd dropped off Nicole that spring evening. The edifices all looked alike with crumbling plaster and similar doors. He eyed one two-story building with a wrought-iron balcony jutting over the street and pink geraniums draping down. Was that it? Upon closer scrutiny he realized…no.

But surely, he was close. He remembered green shutters. Or were they blue? He guided the horse slowly around a curve in the street, and there it was, on the right, the stone building with forest green shutters. Relieved, he pulled the cab to a halt and sat for a moment, watching the small front window shut off from the street by a drawn curtain. Maybe no one was home.

Climbing down, Luc wondered how to best conduct himself when meeting Aimée. Should he approach the subject of what happened the night at the restaurant? Or ask to have Nicole write him? Would Aimée—or maybe her husband would answer—send him away, as Gus had?

Luc rapped on the door, then removed his hat. He stood for what seemed far too long for anyone to be home. He rapped again.

The door swept open, and there stood Nicole.

His thoughts and breathing stopped. She was stunningly lovely, with the sleeves of her blouse pushed up, a towel tucked in the belt of her skirt, and loops of wheat-colored hair falling from her braids. Her complexion looked fairer and her skin dewy, as though she'd seen less sun these days. At the sight of him, her cheeks flushed.

"Nicole? I didn't expect to find you here."

At that moment he could feel her woundedness in her set mouth, her hardened green eyes. He was ashamed. To have hurt this beautiful, innocent creature felt sinful.

He'd known her vulnerability. She'd told him all the terrors she'd endured. And now, he was another betrayal piled onto her wall of defenses. He vowed to make it up, if it took a lifetime.

***

Shocked that Luc stood at the doorstep—handsome and tall in his riding cape and boots, his hair tied back from his tanned, angular face—Nicole felt her knees weaken. How could it be? Had he followed her? She took a step back to gird herself against a deep and wild instinct to throw her arms around him. Instead, she tightened her fingers on the doorknob.

"What are you doing here?" she demanded.

Luc leaned forward. "You wouldn't see me. I remembered your friend Aimée lived here and hoped she'd listen."

"You needn't have bothered. Nothing you say to Aimée or anyone will change how I feel. You should go home to your wife."

He took a step closer. "But that's not possible," he said, propping his arm on the doorframe and gazing into her eyes. "Did you not read my letter? You see, I'm not married."

This unexpected revelation washed over Nicole in a wave of disbelief. Then relief. And finally, confusion. All this time she'd imagined him standing at the altar, vowing to love and cherish Georgette Fontenay. And now, he wasn't married?

Yet none of it mattered. She had to clear her mind, get free of this man who brought nothing into her life but sadness and turmoil and pain.

"I don't care whether you're married or not. But—" She stopped, unable to stand another moment of his presence. This was the man who had betrayed Antoine. She made to slam the door, but Luc caught the edge and pulled against Nicole's struggles to push it shut.

"Why don't you leave me be?" she cried.

"Because I love you. I've loved you from the moment I first saw you."

Her breath caught in her throat. She released the door.

"It's true," he said, stepping closer. "My heart is yours, now and always will be. I've worried all these months about you. You would know that if only you'd read my letter."

Her arms and legs grew leaden. Who was this man who would make such a profound declaration on the doorstep, who would slide his grandmother's ring onto her finger, all the while scheming to send Antoine to prison? No. She'd not listen.

"Get out." She would not let his words enchant her. "You've nothing to say I want to hear. Go."

"Nicole, let me tell you what my letter said. If afterwards you wish me out of your life, I'll never trouble you again."

She wanted to close the door. But she could not. She'd wondered many times about his letter, how he could possibly explain. She needed to know. She deserved to. She dared not admit it, but she was weakening. And yet…no. Luc was a traitor. Never again would she fall under the spell of this treasonous man. But why wasn't he married? Why was he still coming to see her? She had to lean against the door.

"Please, Nicole. You once said you would trust me. Just this one last time."

His words touched something deep inside. An old memory. From another time. Another place. And then as if someone else were speaking, she heard herself saying, "Ten minutes, no more."

Luc let out a breath of relief. "That's all I ask."

"I'll join you," Nicole said, not wanting to involve Aimée. "Give me a moment." She turned, leaving the door ajar. Finding Aimée asleep with the baby in her arms, Nicole grabbed her wrap. From habit, she started to fuss with her hair in the mirror, but then made a face, swung around, and walked to the door.

Luc was standing in the street near the cabriolet, stroking the horse's neck. Seeing him, she paused at the threshold and watched. His gentle way with the animal flooded her with unwanted memories—flying on Hera through the flowery countryside, lying in his strong arms under the willows.

She banished the pictures from her mind. It was all a cruel mirage. She would never think of that day again. She would do anything to free herself from this man. She'd listen to him for the last time. And she'd confront him with the terrible truth. She'd come all this way. She'd not go back.

She strode out toward the cabriolet.

Luc held the door open for her, but she brushed by.

"I want to walk," she said as she started down the street.

Caught by surprise, Luc slammed the door and with long strides caught up. Nicole kept walking, eyes straight ahead. The idea that Antoine had suffered because of this man caused her to take longer steps. She would not look sideways at him. She would hear what he had to say, thank him, then ask him to leave. Forever.

Luc guided her to a shady spot beneath the eaves of a jewelry shop.

"And now," she said, inching back from him. "What do you wish to say that is so important?"

"Where would you like me to start?"

"Your marriage. Tell me about it."

"It was an arrangement. All planned before I met you. Georgette and I have known one another since childhood. Our families always supposed we'd wed. When Georgette became *enceinte*, they insisted on the engagement." Nicole looked away from him. Just hearing the word hurt.

"We'd been indiscreet, foolish. Only once, before I left for America. I'm not proud of my actions, nor any other indiscretions before I met you." He paused. "But it is *not* my child. If it were, it would have been born a month ago. As of yet, there is still no child. We know the father now. We're trying to bring them together. Georgette has always loved him. She was as caught in our parents' scheme as I. I think it's why she was so unkind to you. She was jealous of your freedom."

"I'm sorry. I wish I had known."

"That's why, in part, I waited before telling you. I wanted to spare you this ugly tale. I had to be sure about the child. For everyone's sake. I prayed I was right. And I was. Now, I can only pray you will forgive me."

All the while listening to him, a tiny bud of hope, of yearning, sprouted in her heart, then, remembering Antoine, she pushed herself away from the wall and stood straight. She didn't respond.

"Nicole. I should have told you all this. I know that now."

"Do you know I don't even care?" she said, her throat tight with tears. "It wasn't you I loved, Luc, I realize that now. It was the joy of being in love. It could have been with anyone."

Luc searched her face. "Do you try to convince me, or yourself?"

"I let myself be swept away by a man who lied to me, who destroyed any belief I had about truth and love."

"You allowed yourself to feel genuine emotions, and it was real. You know that. I know it. The love I have for you I will never feel for another woman. And somewhere inside, I know you feel the same."

Each word felt to Nicole like salve on a wound, and at the same time, so many drops of poison. None of this changed the hard truth of his betrayal of Antoine.

"How could you have been so cruel?" she asked, looking straight into his eyes. "So duplicitous?"

Luc frowned. "I was wrongheaded in how I handled this, I see that now. But...cruel? My God. I never meant to be, Nicole."

"Even now you lie. You betrayed Antoine as well as me. Your deceit, telling the police where to go and when, on the very night you made love to me and proposed with your grandmother's ring. It's beyond forgiveness."

Luc frowned. "What are you saying?"

Her head throbbed from a long pent-up anger. "That you are an informant."

Luc took a step back. "A what?"

"You've been discovered, Luc. How you and Philippe Montpellier conspired. How your betrayal sent Antoine to prison."

He turned, walked away, then looked back at her. "This is outrageous," he protested. He looked down at the pavement, apparently trying to absorb her words.

She grew apprehensive. He seemed truly shaken. He turned back toward her, but now his face filled with hurt and anger. "Do you really believe such a preposterous lie about me?"

She stepped back as he drew nearer. Was this the rage of injustice? Or a man faced with the truth?

"Nicole, look at me," he demanded. "Tell me you don't believe a word of this slander."

"Luc," she said, searching his face for some hint of truth or lie. "I don't know if I'll ever believe anything you say." She wanted to turn and run back to Aimée's house and breathe in the sweet innocence of Jac. But his vehement denial had confused her. It felt...believable.

"Nicole, think about it. Why would I do such a thing?"

She closed her eyes. Everything was spinning. "Money. Your family. Your father's connections. You and Philippe Montpellier both. You did this for your fathers."

He stared at her with disbelief. "Who's been spreading this deception? And why?" The answer to his own question appeared to strike him like lightning. "It was Bertrand," he said, with a sudden clarity in his eyes. "I can see by your face, Nicole. It was Bertrand." Luc paused. "But how is accusing me his gain? Why would he?"

Nicole wondered the same thing, and an unsettled feeling crept through her core. It was true that Bertrand had always seemed mean-spirited, particularly the night in his cabriolet and later, with Antoine at the café. Could this be about Bertrand hating Luc?

"Luc," she said cautiously, "do you swear you did not inform the authorities about Antoine?"

"Of course, I do. My God, Nicole, regardless of what you think about me as a libertine and blackguard, surely you can't believe such an accusation against me. My values of justice and equality reach to my core. It's who I *am*. It's who I thought you'd fallen in love with." He walked away from her, leaning his head back in frustration and anger. Then he turned and caught her eye. "And you truly see *me* as an *enemy* of these values?" Nicole had no answer. Luc drew nearer. "Did Bertrand tell you he is Georgette Fontenay's brother?"

Nicole felt her heart skip. Bertrand Le Mansec? The man smoking cheroots, his cocky cap, his patchwork of affable and uncouth ways...he was the *brother* of that ice princess? Her mind reeled. How could Antoine not know?

"But how?" she asked. "I don't understand."

"Few people understand Bertrand," Luc said darkly. "I've always tolerated his resentment, even sympathized with him. He's the son of a wealthy man, with few of the advantages Georgette enjoyed."

"Bertrand's father is *Monsieur* Fontenay? Bertrand Le Mansec?"

"He is Fontenay's *illegitimate* son. Élisabeth Le Mansec once served as chambermaid in the Fontenay household. *Madame* Fontenay banished her after the pregnancy became known. It was my father who found employment for her at Versailles, in the home of Count Montpellier."

Nicole stared at Luc as things became clearer.

"For decades my father has sold and bred horses to the Count," Luc explained. "Count Montpellier is a good man. He paid

Bertrand's mother well, and he sent Bertrand to university along with Philippe. They'd grown up together. In a way, they were like brothers. I've always known Bertrand lived both in and out of wealth. I don't think it served him well. Still, I never thought he'd go so far as this. *He's* the traitor."

"One night," she said, "Bertrand took me home from the café. I've not thought about it until now—" She looked squarely at Luc. "How did he know where I lived?"

Luc nodded. "He may have been gathering information on you as well."

"He knew about the print shop," Nicole went on, putting pieces together. "Antoine talked with Bertrand about him staying there after hours. That's how he was able to print his newspapers. It would take someone with that information to inform the police."

"Nicole," Luc said gently, "we will uncover the truth." He reached out and edged his thumb along her jaw. Warmth flooded her body. "Before I met you," he said, "I was skeptical about marriage, about love. With you, something came alive."

Their eyes met as if for the first time, as though no hurt existed between them, no struggle, no lies.

And then Nicole looked away. She had to give her mind and heart time to catch up with it all. "I must go back," she murmured. "Alone. Thank you for telling me this, Luc."

He nodded with understanding. "Only remember this, my love," he said. "I was a fool to withhold truths from you…but never have I told you a falsehood. Never have I betrayed Antoine, you, or the Cause."

She could say no more. Though it felt like pushing against a current, she turned from him and walked away.

Chapter Thirty

Lulu's small living quarters, located in one of the poorest sections of Paris, was a study in contrasts. Over a row of shops and cafés filled with sordid customers and questionable merchandise, up a flight of crumbling stairs and inside a flimsy door, she kept a one-room apartment. The high ceilings were covered with faded frescos of cupids frolicking in clouds. The bed served as the focal point of the room, crowned with a golden coronet from which a gossamer drape swept to the floor. A hand-painted *chinoiserie* dressing screen stood beside a tall chest, holding all the *accoutrements* of a lady, along with her washing *toilette*.

Bertrand stepped from behind the screen, adjusting his cuffs. Feeling a sense of contentment, he passed the bed where Lulu lay hidden under a mountain of silk and cashmere. He'd always considered Lulu beneath his station, one of Philippe's whores. But now he saw possibilities. He glanced about. Yes. He could live here. At least until better accommodations could be found. At that thought he slipped on his jacket, careful not to awaken Lulu. He had no desire to engage in pleasantries this morning. His mother awaited him in her new household. She'd arranged an introduction with the servants. He might even share a cup of coffee with them, make a good impression. Being late would not start this new adventure off well.

Out in the morning air, Bertrand took a deep breath, ridding his lungs of the apartment's perfume. He'd parked under a tree. Whistling, he untied the reins and gave the horse a pat on the neck. Behind the seat, he found a carrot and fed it to the horse, still whistling as the creature nuzzled it from his palm.

Suddenly a roar assaulted him. He was gripped by the shoulders and whirled about to face Luc Chatillon.

"Get in," Luc ordered. "I'm driving." He shoved Bertrand toward the cab.

"What's this about?" Bertrand demanded.

"I said, *get in,*" Luc snarled.

In silence, the two men settled in the tight space, both aware of the tension in the other. Luc whipped the horse forward.

"*Sacre,*" Bertrand complained, straightening his cravat. "By what right do you assault me? I could have you arrested."

"Really?" Luc challenged. "Even I never imagined you to be so heartless. For your own gain you would destroy people's lives?"

"This is absurd," Bertrand exploded. "I demand you stop and get out of my cab. I should challenge you to a duel for such an outrage."

"Don't think I'd not welcome settling this the old way," Luc said, a vein on his temple throbbing. "But that would be too easy. No, I'm taking you straight to Gilles Fontenay. Together we'll tell him what you've done. That you've accused me of informing on Antoine. An evil you did yourself. Then I'm taking you to face Antoine. You'll clear my name, or I may be forced to use pistols after all."

Bertrand reached in his pocket and pulled out his remaining cheroot. As they rumbled over the cobblestones, he fumbled with a match, trying to strike it against the breeze. "Luc, I don't know who has told you such lies," he said, finally lighting the cigar and taking a deep inhale. "Do you really think I would accuse you of spying? Why would I do so?"

"You tell me, Bertrand. I've always known you and I were not fast friends. I only now realize how you've despised me."

"This is mad. Someone has slandered *me*. I give my word, never have I accused you—"

"Enough of your lies. Nicole told me everything. That night of Antoine's arrest, you knew the way to her home. You knew the location of Antoine's print shop. You must have been plotting for months. Probably from the first time you insisted I come to *La Fenêtre*. Did you conspire with Georgette? What did you hope to gain?"

Bertrand clamped his cheroot between his teeth. "You should watch yourself, Luc. If you want to protect that little harlot of yours, Nicole Vogel."

Luc whipped his head toward Bertrand. "What is that supposed to mean?"

"There are those who would be quite interested in the little bitch. Careful, Luc. She's not who you think. Being associated with her will bring you no good."

Luc jerked the cabriolet to the side of the road, stopping on the edge of a field. He threw aside the reins and grabbed hold of Bertrand's collar and yanked him close so that their eyes were inches apart. "Tell me your meaning," he demanded. "This moment. Or we can settle this now without pistols."

Bertrand struggled to free himself. "If you go to Gilles Fontenay, or any other person, with what you think about me, I'll reveal her little secret to the authorities. It could mean her life."

"What are you saying?" Luc demanded.

In a burst of energy Bertrand flung Luc's arms away and, scrambling to open the door, jumped out. "I think I'll keep hold of the information about your *putain*." He adjusted his coat. "It might come to good use if you're foolish enough to say anything against me." Bertrand gave a laugh. "Keep the cab. I can't feed the horse anyway. You see, I'm desperate, Luc." His expression hardened. "So, don't cross me. You won't like me if you do." With a last nasty look, he turned and trudged into the field, murderously angry but knowing he'd get his revenge.

Chapter Thirty-One

In the lofty meeting hall of the National Assembly, the afternoon sun beat down from a row of windows. Deputies who sat sweltering in the upper balconies fanned themselves, not with the lacy and jeweled fans seen in court, but with folded newspapers, leaflets, anything to find relief from the heat.

Sitting on the main floor in a heavy jacket, Antoine seemed unaware of the heat as he leaned close to Nicole. "See that man there on the right balcony?" he said in a low voice. "Jacques-Pierre Brissot. He founded the Society of the Friends of Blacks. He's recently returned from America. He was the one who took the keys after the Bastille fell. He supports a constitutional monarchy."

Nicole nodded. "Having a constitution like England? That seems like a good solution."

"And keep a king? Never," Antoine said dismissively. "See those sitting on the left? They're Robespierre's men. They propose we abolish the crown altogether."

Nicole closely watched several of the deputies descend from the balconies and take their positions at a long table set up before the assemblage, each of them youthful and wearing self-styled military uniforms matching their affiliation.

She leaned toward Antoine. "One side against the other," she said. "This all seems like a play for power. The king has agreed to our demands to create a new constitution. Why isn't that enough?"

"Careful, Nicole, such thoughts are dangerous," Antoine admonished with a frown. "Keep them to yourself."

Keep her thoughts to herself? She'd never known Antoine to be so watchful of her opinions. After all their running through the night streets last winter, risking arrest, and keeping him company through the cold nights in the print shop...he'd listened to her then, even asked her for ideas. And now she was to have none?

But she *did* have opinions. Something virulent and deadly was spreading through the citizenry. She saw it in the mob hangings. And today, she felt it here, in this assembly. Too many people wanted revenge, not justice.

Antoine was part of it.

As the deputies settled into their places, Jacques-Pierre Brissot rose, a gentle-faced man, his graying hair tied back carelessly.

"Today," announced Brissot, gazing at the crowd, "the Assembly votes to adopt the Declaration of the Rights of Man and of the Citizen." He paused thoughtfully. "We are told by the Marquis de La Fayette that Louis has approved the text and will sign once ratified. This document is our best hope to bloodlessly create a government that guarantees the people of France equal opportunity, freedom of speech, popular sovereignty, and a representative government." His words were met with scattered shouts of approval on the main floor, and a thunderous applause from the right side of the balcony.

Antoine cupped his hand to Nicole's ear. "Popular sovereignty? A lie meant to keep a king." Nicole pulled away and politely clapped, approving of the calm wisdom in Brissot's words.

With the applause fading, another deputy came out from behind the table. Nicole detected a childlike quality in the man's round face and forehead that sloped below a white wig crimped at each temple. Although he looked official, wearing an impeccable navy wool jacket trimmed in military gold braid, he reminded her of a boy playing grown-up.

"Is that him?" she asked.

"Yes, Maximillian Robespierre," Antoine said with admiration.

Robespierre surveyed the crowd with an aloof air. "Reform under a constitutional monarchy can *never* be possible," he announced in a resounding voice. "Everyone in this room knows that the Crown and the Church will protect their power. If this assembly gives up gains that have been purchased with the lives lost at the Bastille," he paused, looking about the room all the way to the upper galleries, "then, Citizens, we will *never again* be in a position to make demands."

Over half the audience rose in wild applause. Robespierre basked in the ovation, then raised his hand for quiet.

"We demand the elimination of all titles, even royalty. Close the churches. All power goes to the citizens of France."

A thunderous applause erupted, and Antoine joined in with enthusiasm. Nicole sat, quietly troubled at such a radical notion. Antoine had suffered greatly, and nothing could change that. Of course, no one wanted to go back to the way things were. But Louis had agreed to their demands. More bloodshed could be avoided.

Robespierre raised his hand for quiet. "Today we are honored with the presence of someone who has suffered imprisonment by the royalists. I have asked him to come so we can see the evil we are fighting. Will that hero of the Nation please rise."

After a brief silence Antoine struggled to his feet from the crowded bench. Nicole thought he looked like a stranger standing in the middle of this huge assemblage.

Robespierre took in Antoine's pitiful condition then bowed to him. "Citizen, you honor us with your presence. Tell us your name."

"Antoine Durand."

"*Monsieur* Durand, what were your charges?"

"Sedition," Antoine replied in a clear voice. "My crime consisted of printing truths about the Throne."

"I assume you underwent torture from the royalists?"

"The rack. They destroyed my knees."

An angry rumble ran through the assemblage. Robespierre challenged the crowd with a question. "Do we not see here the handiwork of brutal tyrants? If left in power, this abuse will not stop. Each man and woman here will be endangered with such a fate. It is the sacrifices of men like *Monsieur* Durand that give us the power to make *our* demands heard." He raised his voice. "This is why we must abolish the monarchy."

Cheers erupted, swelling across the room as men and women stood and applauded with shouts of approval. Antoine turned to look to each side with wave of his hand, standing as tall as his broken body could manage. When the cheers quieted, he looked again at Robespierre.

"I care nothing for the Kingdom of France," he announced. "But I will fight to the death for the Nation of France."

An explosion of cheers mushroomed through the hall. Men and women rose, chanting *Liberty. Fraternity. Equality.* In the bedlam, Robespierre approached Antoine and stopped directly before him, laying his hand on Antoine's shoulder. "The citizens of France will forever be indebted to you," he murmured, then more intimately said, "We need you to join us tonight. It is most important. At eight."

It was then that Nicole felt everything shift. Something frightening was happening. Antoine had shut her out of his life.

Robespierre looked over at Nicole. His eyes were filled with an intensity that sent a chill through her. He broke the stare and made his way to the other released prisoners.

Nicole helped Antoine take his seat on the bench, noting how his hands trembled from excitement. "Say you'll not go tonight," she whispered. "You're unwell, Antoine. Let me take you home."

Antoine's stare followed Robespierre. "Don't you understand the importance of what we do?"

"Please," Nicole insisted. "You look exhausted. Let's leave."

Antoine nodded. "For now. But I will attend the meeting tonight."

"Of course," she murmured, supporting him as they rose and made their way along the crowded aisle. Seeing Antoine unsteady on his legs, she wondered if they should get a public coach, if there were any to be had.

Looking ahead toward the exit, she noticed a woman directly in front of them, an oddly familiar woman. Nicole looked closer. What was it about her...the narrow shoulders, the slight curve of her back...?

The woman suddenly turned and faced them. "Nicole Vogel. It is you, is it not?"

Nicole blinked. The room darkened and shrunk around her. A paralysis seeped into her body so that she could not breathe. Standing before her was the woman who had filled her childhood with terror. *Madame* Colére's gaunt face was surrounded by a white organza bonnet with a tricolor cockade pinned to the side.

"I see you remember me."

Nicole could not answer. *Madame*'s familiar smell of jasmine made her nauseous.

"You and I go back, don't we?"

"Who are you?" Antoine asked.

"I believe Nicole Vogel knows me."

Nicole finally found her voice, her wits. She coldly stared into the woman's face that was unchanged by the years. "What do you want, *Madame*?"

Madame Colére's coal-black eyes narrowed. "And so, you have not changed. Still as rude."

"What is this about?" Antoine demanded.

Madame Colére snapped her head toward him. "It's about your fiancée, Citizen." She looked down at Antoine's frail legs. "You see what tyrants do? Torture. What a pity. Such a young man, ruined. *Monsieur* Durand, do you not think the traitor who informed on you should receive the same fate?" She glanced back at Nicole. "What of you, Nicole Vogel? I'm sure you too remember the cruelty of the Throne. That day of the king's funeral?"

The words assaulted Nicole as alien and bizarre. It made no sense. She had to concentrate, to try to integrate them into the here and now. What was the woman saying?

"Do you have something to say to *Mademoiselle* Vogel?" Antoine demanded. "I insist you explain yourself."

Madame Colére's attention remained fixed on Nicole. "Of course, you remember that day of the funeral, don't you? The coach? It was a royal one. Did you know that? Oh, but how could you? You weren't yet five years of age. What a tragedy for one so young."

Nicole began breathing faster. The frightened child within wanted to run, but her feet were frozen. *Madame*'s words—they willed her to listen with a kind of macabre fascination. Mesmerized, she waited to hear more.

"Come, Nicole," Antoine insisted. "This woman's not in her right mind."

Madame Colére reached out and clasped her arm. "Oh, but Citizen Vogel knows I speak the truth." She leaned close and said, "I warn you, my dear, *all* the nobility will meet their rewards. You *do* remember that day, don't you? You always said you remembered. You can't deny it now."

"Take me from here," she whispered to Antoine, purposely turning her back on the woman of her nightmares. She didn't want to hear more of the vitriol and lies the woman constantly used against her.

For the first time since his release, Antoine became her pillar. She leaned onto him as he took her arm and hurried her out.

Outside in the light, Nicole felt as if she were awakening from a bad dream. And yet, there had been something…something *Madame* had said. Nicole stared ahead, remembering. Yes. There *had* been a coach. She closed her eyes, envisioning a doll's head rolling across cobblestones.

"My God," Antoine uttered, wrapping his arm around her. "That woman must be mad. Who is she? What coach? What funeral?"

Nicole pulled away from him. "The king's." She was remembering the crowds, the bells tolling. "It *was* my mother." Her breath caught. She felt as if wings had sprouted. She only had to think it and she could fly. "I *was* there. With my mother. I remember it all."

Chapter Thirty-Two

"Nicole, my dear," Aunt Charlotte said. "A good hot cup of tea will make you feel better. Antoine, look at you, your hair is damp with exhaustion. What has happened?"

"*Merci*," Nicole said, taking the cup Aunt Charlotte offered.

"I've never seen you look so pale, my dear," Aunt Charlotte said, taking a chair beside her.

"I met someone this afternoon," Nicole said softly. "Someone I've not seen in years. *Madame* Colére, the directress of the orphanage."

"For goodness sake, Nicole," Antoine said, taking a chair against the wall. "You act as if you'd seen a devil, not some crazed old woman."

Nicole glanced down at her cup. "*Madame* Colére brought back so many feelings. Pure fright to begin with," she said, her words so soft they almost couldn't be heard. "But also, *hope*." She looked up at Charlotte. "I remembered my mother."

"Your mother," Aunt Charlotte exclaimed, clapping her hands together. "That's wonderful."

"Yes, it is. But I can't help wonder why *Madame* Colére said all these things." She appealed to Antoine. "It was so odd. She called me your fiancée. How would she know that?"

Antoine shrugged. "The woman heard my name announced. She saw you and assumed we were engaged."

Nicole lifted her teacup to her lips. Antoine's explanation didn't sit right. "*Madame* said the royals had done something terrible. She asked if I remembered a royal coach."

"But how strange," Aunt Charlotte said. "What can it mean?"

"It's a memory. My mother and a coach. As a young girl, whenever I would ask *Madame* Colére about it, she would scold me for making up stories. She told me I'd been abandoned on a church step. She said it so often that one day I began believing her."

Antoine gave an impatient grunt. "Nicole, I've just been introduced to the assembly by *Robespierre*. He's asked me to join him tonight. And we're talking about a madwoman from your childhood."

Nicole threw him a look of protest. "Her cruelty *did* something to me, Antoine. It was as if a mass of tangled memories knotted up inside me. The mix-up of who I was, who I *am*... And now, I feel—" She looked up at the ceiling, trying to find words to make him understand. "I feel the mystery has begun to unravel."

"Nicole, you were a child. You'd lost your parents in a horrible accident. And from what this woman said, a royal coach killed them. And you saw it all through a child's grieving eyes. Of course you were confused."

"But I wasn't."

"Nicole, maybe you were."

"You would believe *Madame* Colére's words over mine?"

Aunt Charlotte rose and wrapped a protective arm around Nicole's shoulders. She glanced at Antoine with a chiding look. "Can you not see the dear girl speaks from her heart? Bad things happen to everyone. Sometimes the scars follow us throughout our lives. They destroy our hopes and dreams. You should understand that, Antoine. Isn't the pain of *your* mother's death the very thing that pushes you? Even tonight, to go to a meeting when you should be resting?"

"This is not about Nicole," Antoine erupted. "Have you all lost sight of the magnitude of this? We've toppled the monarchy."

"Yes, we have won," Nicole replied hotly. "The king has conceded. Now it's time to help him form a government."

"Do you believe such a fantasy? The First Estate will *never* agree to our demands. The queen's brother will send his army and imprison us all. Do you want that?"

At that moment, the door slammed open, and Sebaste bounded into the kitchen, sweaty from playing in the hot sun.

"*Sacré Dieu*, Sebaste," Aunt Charlotte scolded. "You look like you've been roasted."

Seeing Nicole, Sebaste rushed to her and threw his arms about her neck. "*Ça va*, Nicole."

Hugging him, Nicole felt her tensions fade. "*Bonjour*, Sebaste," she said, tenderly holding him at arm's length. "You seem to grow an inch a day."

Grinning, Sebaste pulled away and ran to the water bucket, dunked the dipper, and took a long draught. "I've been organizing a group," he said, looking up, wiping a dribble of water from his chin. "We're planning a memorial. For the boys our age who died at the Bastille fighting for the republic." He stood up and glanced at Antoine. "Antoine, did you make it to the assembly?"

Antoine nodded. "I did. I saw Robespierre. He's asked me to join his meeting tonight. Everything is changing."

Sebaste gave a shout of approval and ran to embrace him.

"Antoine, you really should not go out tonight," Aunt Charlotte admonished. "You're about to fall apart."

Sebaste brightened. "I'll go for you."

Antoine tussled his hair. "No, I'm going. This is my chance to make a name in the movement. To find justice."

"But this is not justice you're seeking," Nicole said, unable to hold her tongue. "This is revenge."

A flash of contempt brightened his eyes. "And do you say this to protect Luc Chatillon? His life of privilege is paid by taxing the poor." His anger taking over, Antoine couldn't stop his tirade. "You should know, Nicole, tonight's meeting is about men like Chatillon. I've seen a list being drawn up of those wanted for questioning."

"Questioning for what?" she asked, alarmed.

"For conspiring with the enemy. The nobility. Victor Chatillon's name is high on that list."

Nicole drew back. "What are you saying?"

"Are you really so naïve? Victor Chatillon is the Royal Equerry."

"But *Monsieur* Chatillon is not a member of the nobility."

"His wealth comes from them. They're all the same."

Nicole eased into her chair as understanding came. "Oh, Antoine, did *you* give *Monsieur* Chatillon's name?" As she studied him, her throat tightened. "You did, I can see it on your face."

Aunt Charlotte came to take Sebaste's arm. "Out you go. This is not for young ears."

"Leave him," Antoine said. "He might as well learn. Things will soon become different in Paris," he scoffed. "Nicole, your guileless support of Luc Chatillon is getting dangerous. It doesn't speak well for me. Robespierre plans to make me a deputy, perhaps tonight. Do you want to jeopardize my position in the party?"

Nicole lowered her head. "What's happened to you, Antoine?"

"And I might ask the same for you. Don't think I haven't noticed your change. Where is that young woman who hid from the Guet with me?"

Nicole looked up, her face drawn and tired. "She's still here. She stood with you against injustice. But now, you arrest someone for personal reasons? Is this where your revolution is going? To destroy lives out of anger and jealousy?"

Antoine's stare grew insolent. "None of the guilty will escape."

"But who are the guilty?" she asked. "Do you still believe Luc betrayed you? It wasn't him."

Antoine stared at her as if she had become a stranger. "What you are saying?" His voice filled with anger.

"Antoine," shushed Aunt Charlotte in alarm. "Lower your voice."

"It's Bertrand Le Mansec," Nicole blurted out. "Luc told me. I accused Luc. But he told me it's been Bertrand who has lied all this time. Bertrand is not who he says. He's the illegitimate son of a wealthy merchant. He's connived and maneuvered all his life." She stopped, seeing the look of disbelief and disgust on Antoine's face. "I couldn't believe it at first either, Antoine. But it's true."

Antoine rose, slowly and dramatically. "You saw Luc Chatillon? Without telling me? The man who betrayed me, the swine who did *this* to me," he shouted, indicating his legs.

"No, Antoine, he—"

"You believe his lies? His flattery? My God, Nicole. You let such a man convince you that our *friend*, Bertrand, who has done *nothing* but help us—you let a cur like Luc Chatillon convince you he betrayed me?"

Nicole shook her head. "Think on it. Only Bertrand knew you were working on your newspaper that night. He informed the police."

"Everyone in *La Fenêtre* knew that," Antoine shouted. "You take a rake's word over Bertrand's?" Antoine thudded the tip of his cane against the wall. "*Never* will I believe a word of this. Bertrand is a good man. I'll not let his name be disgraced. And I'll not let you say another—"

"Enough," Aunt Charlotte ordered.

Antoine turned to look at her. He was leaning on his cane, breathing heavily.

"Can't you see she's trying to help?" Aunt Charlotte said. "You can at least listen. It's not easy to know your enemies in this new France."

Nicole rose from her chair and came to take his hand. He pulled away. "Please," she insisted, taking his hand again. "Hear me on this, Antoine. Bertrand filled my head with lies about Luc—and he knew where I lived. How could that be?"

"If you *ever* see that traitor Luc Chatillon again," Antoine said. "I'll not have you even as a friend." With a flash of hatred in his eyes, he turned and limped out of the room. Sebaste, mouth agape, watched Antoine disappear, then turning to Nicole, he glared with pure malice before rushing after his brother.

"Don't fret, Nicole, everything will be all right," Aunt Charlotte said, wringing her hands. "Antoine's in such turmoil. You mustn't take this to heart. More than ever, he needs you now."

Chapter Thirty-Three

Luc was sitting by the window reading a book when Symon's knock sounded at the door.

"Yes?" he called without looking up.

Symon opened the door. "Sir, a young lady."

Luc glanced up. Seeing Nicole enter, he felt as if he were looking at an illusion. Tossing aside the book, he met her halfway. "Nicole," he uttered, so taken with the unexpectedness of her standing before him that he could scarcely find words. "What has happened? Are you well?"

"I had to come—" Her voice broke.

"*Ma chérie,*" he whispered, taking her hands. "Come. Sit." As she did, he knelt before her so that he stared into her eyes, pale and troubled, sweeping over his face with worry. He called over his shoulder, "Symon, bring the lady a glass of water."

Taking a deep breath, Nicole forced out the words. "I first want to say what I have to tell you is my fault. I've brought this calamity on your house."

"What are you talking about?"

"I've learned that your father may be arrested."

Never in his wildest imaginings would Luc have expected such an utterance—much less from Nicole.

"Arrested for what?" he asked incredulously. "What authority could do such a thing?"

"It's the Assembly. Robespierre is ordering all nobles be stopped at the city gates—and...oh God, Luc, anyone else who's been associated with the nobility. I'm so sorry—but Antoine put your father on their list. They intend to arrest him. And I don't believe any person detained by Robespierre will be released. I've seen the man, and I fear for anyone caught in his crosshairs."

Symon reentered with a glass of water on a silver tray. Luc watched as she took a sip, calming herself.

"Thank you, Symon," he said.

The servant tucked the tray under his arm and crossed to the door, tidily shutting it behind.

"Luc, I'm so sorry," Nicole said softly.

Luc walked to the window and looked out, trying to fathom such a nightmare. "How sure are you about this?"

"Very sure. It's frightening how Robespierre has filled Antoine's head with these dreadful ideas," she said. "And Bertrand has convinced him you're responsible for his arrest."

Staring at the trees rustling in the breeze, Luc considered how that would be easy for Antoine to believe. His gaze strayed to several children outside the gate throwing a stick to a dog then focused back on his reflection in the glass. It was a hard truth she'd brought. But he'd been suspicious for some time that something was coming. "Do you think they'll close the city gates?" he asked, turning to her.

"Perhaps they already have."

He strode across the room and took her hand.

"Luc, I understand if you hate me. I cannot ask forgiveness for what I've brought to your family. But, please, believe that I never meant this."

"Come," he said, helping her up, pulling her close to his side in alliance. "I would never hold you responsible. Now we must tell this to my father."

***

Luc drew Nicole into the salon. His mother was busy embroidering, ignoring his father's pacing as he muttered to himself in a cloud of frustration.

"Father. Mother," he announced. "You must meet someone. I would trust her with my life. She has something important to tell you." He brought Nicole forward. "May I present *Mademoiselle* Nicole Vogel."

"Why, you are the milliner," his mother remarked, her mouth softening in admiration. "My dear, I've purchased several of your wonderful creations. And I've had the pleasure of telling my friends that I discovered you. My son, though, should probably have that distinction."

Luc adored his mother for her cordial welcome. He could tell Nicole felt it, with the respectful tilt of her head. "*Madame* Chatillon, I thank you. But sadly, I fear that world has passed."

His father, though, was another story. His suspicious manner was not as welcoming. "What's this about, Luc?"

Luc took Nicole's arm into his. "*Mademoiselle* Vogel has come to bring us an extremely serious report." He appealed to her. "Shall I tell them?"

"No," she said, her face grave. "This is something I must do." She met his father's inquisitive glare. "*Monsieur* Chatillon, I learned today that your name has been put on a list of enemies of the revolution."

His father's mild curiosity flashed into outright astonishment. "That's absurd," he exclaimed. Who is suggesting such a thing? I've done nothing against this revolt. By God, I've admired the effort to reform the Crown." He stopped. "I admit, what's happened these last weeks has concerned me. And yes, I have been vocal in denouncing the notion of abolishing the monarchy. But it's an outrage to say I'm an enemy of the people."

"Have you heard the name Robespierre?" Luc asked.

The question seemed to take him off guard for an instant, before he went on the attack. "Of course, I have," he snapped, his fair skin reddening in agitation. "Everyone has heard of the man. His abuse of power will lead to anarchy…and, I tell you, will produce a real tyrant. Are you saying Robespierre has called for *my* arrest?"

"Anyone on Robespierre's list trying to leave the city will be detained," Nicole said. "Your name is on the list, *Monsieur* Chatillon."

His mother gave a cry of alarm. "Victor."

Luc at once came to his mother's side and placed a comforting arm around her shoulders. She clasped his hand, her frightened eyes sweeping the room as if trying to understand what was happening. "What shall we do?" she cried.

"Mother, this will be sorted through," Luc murmured.

"Pure madness, all of it," Victor thundered. "Why would I be considered an enemy?"

"Because of your livelihood," Nicole explained. "Breeding horses for the royal stables. They say your wealth came from taxing the poor. They're calling it treason."

"Treason," Victor exploded. "I've paid taxes all my life. More than most."

Luc had been watching his mother's growing alarm, and now this was too much for her. She rose, threw herself into his arms, and began to sob. He held her until his father came and drew her from him into his full embrace. "Don't be alarmed, my dear," he murmured, kissing her temple. "This is all some mistake."

"*Monsieur* Chatillon, I must confess," Nicole said, looking distressed. "It was my friendship with your son that angered a member of the National Constituent Assembly. A deputy. He's not going to stop until you're arrested, *Monsieur* Chatillon. Perhaps even Luc."

Luc came to her and raised her chin so that she looked into his eyes. "Do not for a moment believe this is your fault, Nicole. This is much larger than Antoine. If not him, it would be someone else."

A knock sounded at the door. Symon appeared with a newspaper folded on a tray. "*Messieurs,* the afternoon edition has arrived. I think you would want to read it."

"Bring it," Victor said, and Luc bolstered himself for the news. "What now?" his father asked. Luc waited as his father unfolded the paper. He read a moment, then looked up with an unhappy frown. "The arrests are beginning." He read on, shaking his head in disgust. "So many of these people I know. My God, here's Count Montpellier, as well as the Countess, both detained in their Paris apartment."

His mother gasped. "Henri? And Caroline? This is dreadful. And Philippe?"

Luc took the paper to check. "He isn't named here. I'd wager he's in hiding."

"Oh, Victor," he heard his mother's voice as he read down the page. Looking up, he saw her flee to his father's arms. "We must leave, Victor."

Luc glanced at Nicole. She looked miserable.

"I agree we should leave," Luc said. "In fact, I'm taking you both to *Les Saules.* We should leave at once."

His father stood thinking. "Yes," he said with calm resolve. "Your mother must be protected. But if the city gates are closed, we cannot use the carriage, even if we go in disguise. Not with the

Chatillon insignia on the door. Luc, take your mother in the cabriolet."

"But, Victor darling, what about you?" Gabriele beseeched. "Let me stay behind. They don't care about me. You can leave with Luc."

"We'll all go," Nicole said. Luc turned in surprise. His parents stared at her, almost as if they'd forgotten her presence. "This has happened because of me. You must let me help. Luc, you can accompany your mother. I can travel with you, *Monsieur* Chatillon."

Luc was taken aback at her suggestion. And obviously so were his parents. He was the one to at last speak. "No, Nicole," he said firmly. "You are not to blame for any of this. This is our family's onus. We alone must shoulder our misfortune."

"There's no other way," Nicole insisted. "*Monsieur* Chatillon, there will be less suspicion if you're traveling with a daughter."

What a surprising idea, he thought. It seemed to confuse his father at first, then, thinking about it, he looked at Nicole with a new respect.

"Of course," Victor said. "They must have a list of the family members. There'll be no daughter."

"I don't understand," Gabriele puzzled. "How will four of us travel without the carriage?"

Nicole glanced at Luc. He saw clearly an idea that was playing in her mind. "Two in the cabriolet," she said, "two on horseback." She waited for Luc to catch her meaning. And he did.

"You're right," he said with smile. "And if I remember correctly, Nicole Vogel, you are quite the horsewoman."

Chapter Thirty-Four

As the *cabriolet* carrying Luc and his mother proceeded down the well-traveled boulevards leading toward the main city gate, Nicole and Victor Chatillon rode the opposite way on horseback. So as not to draw attention, they trotted at an easy pace down back alleyways through some of the most squalid sections of the city. Taking the southern route along the Seine, they passed loggers floating their wood downriver. Farther out, they passed farmers leaving the city with empty carts. As the road became little more than a rutted pathway, they slowed as their horses made their way through flocks of sheep being herded along the dusty passage. No one paid them any mind, merely a father and daughter off for a ride in the country.

Victor Chatillon sat tall and relaxed in the saddle as they trotted along. He was different than Nicole had imagined, more vigorous and youthful. Nicole remembered Luc telling her the horse would follow his lead—and in spite of her clumsiness and inexperience as a rider, that was proving to be true.

Once well away from the city, Victor pointed to a tannery with white smoke curling from two brick smokestacks. "Here's where we leave the road." He led his horse into a vast field and quickened the gait, and soon he was galloping across the meadow toward a distant village, with Nicole struggling to keep up.

As she felt herself falling behind, fearsome thoughts and self-doubt replaced her earlier confidence. Could she really ride all the way to *Les Saules*? And what if Luc and *Madame* Chatillon were arrested? A chill ran through her. If only Antoine had not done this awful thing that put them in danger.

"Are you all right?" Victor called over his shoulder, slowing his pace.

Looking ahead, Nicole called out, "Yes," and urged her horse faster.

Soon, the horses slowed. "I'm sorry about the speed in the meadow back there," he said as she drew alongside. "Ahead there's a lane. It will be easier." The lane took them through a hamlet of cottages. Nicole inhaled a deep breath of country air. Her doubts and uneasiness faded as she saw children playing, flowers growing over garden walls, and everywhere, it seemed, smelled the scent of lavender. There was no revolution here.

"I wanted to reach *Les Saules* before dark," Victor said as they left the hamlet and trotted down a narrow road. "Hopefully we'll arrive before Luc and his mother."

She found his words, his quiet authority, comforting. She wondered about Luc's relationship with him. There were tensions, she knew. And yet, it would have been wonderful to have a father like this. He made her feel safe. Even in the midst of danger.

"You're doing well," Victor said. "How often have you ridden?"

"Just once. With Luc at *Les Saules*." She wondered if she should have revealed this bit of information—and what he thought of his son having brought her to his ancestral home.

Victor sat tall in the saddle to scan the horizon, his hand blocking the glaring sun. "We'll cross to the east. It shouldn't take long now."

"You've done this before?"

He gave a small laugh. "Many times. Mostly when I was younger and liked adventure. It's not much of a lane here—more a path for farmers' carts. It's a rough run, and you're impressing me. Luc seems to have taught you well."

"He's an excellent horseman," she replied.

"How did you meet my son?" he asked.

She turned to him, surprised he wanted to know. "We met at a café, last winter. I was with a group that had—ideas about freedom. Luc was the only one who'd been to America, and he had much to say about the colonists' self-rule. Never did I believe our lofty ideals would result in this." Her brows knitted unhappily. "I don't understand how those who hate despots can become tyrants themselves."

Victor turned his head toward her and, in that moment, Nicole saw hints of Luc's strong jaw and striking eyes. They were both handsome men. And yet, the father had a hardness about his mouth. Luc had his mother's smile.

"When people are wronged and angry," Victor told her, "they sometimes lose sight of their best interests."

"Then I hope wisdom prevails."

"Yes, let's hope," Victor responded, reaching to pat his stallion's neck. "Tell me Nicole—" It was the first time she'd heard him use her name, "about your business. Clearly *Madame* Chatillon thinks highly of your talents. Where did you learn the trade?"

"I'd always wanted to sew, to create, all through my childhood in the orphanage. I was fortunate to find an apprentice who helped my dreams come to life. GustaveGustaveGustave Baston is an excellent hatmaker." Nicole smiled. "Designing hats is a joy. There is nothing as wonderful as bringing beauty and happiness to people."

For a few moments, they rode in silence with only the sounds of the horses' snorts.

"It's a worthy aim, Nicole," Victor said at last.

Nicole was aware he'd been thinking about her words and recalled Antoine's anger at her profession. "And yet, some say it's vanity. Money wasted that should be spent on food."

"I'm not so sure I agree," Victor said. "What may seem frivolity, like fashion, can create wealth for workers, and a richer society. Look at the rise in our textile industry. And silk. These industries have helped raise our people out of farming. We need factories to make stockings and gowns and hats. What you do is valuable. People will always need hats." He smiled at her. "And they will always need horses."

Nicole nodded. His respect for her work impressed and surprised her. He'd drawn together both their livelihoods, as though their occupations were equal. "Perhaps our skills will be put to use in new ways," she mused.

"Indeed." He appeared lost in thought for a few moments and then said, "We need to make it before nightfall. Are you ready to pick up the pace?"

Readjusting herself in the saddle and making sure she had the proper hold of her reins, Nicole nodded. "I'm ready. Let's go."

***

Red streaked the indigo sky as they trotted through *Les Saules's* ivy-covered gates. Victor led Nicole through a scattering of squawking chickens to the back entrance of the chateau, where Luc had carried her in the rain. Together they navigated the worn and mossy stone steps. Not being dazzled by the rush of being in Luc's arms, Nicole was able to give her attention to the two-story chateau, the pretty pattern of stonework and the tall windows with faded blue shutters. It was lovely. Magical.

Inside, she expected to see *Madame* Lamont, or Coco, but neither were in the pantry or the kitchen. She and Victor made a solo entrance into the central corridor to the main salon.

Light from the setting sun shimmered through the tall windows, turning the walls a golden luster. Nicole found a spot upon a down sofa, worried as Victor paced the room, his hands clenched behind his back. In the silence they awaited the moment the cabriolet's wheels would come crunching down the drive.

When at last Victor stopped pacing and stood near the window, an old brown and white spaniel stumbled into the room and nosed up to Nicole. With a sigh, he thumped down at her feet.

"Well, hello there, *Vieil Homme*," Victor said, coming over and stroking the dog's ear.

"His name is Old Man? What did you call him when he was young?"

"He's always been Old Man." Victor laughed. "Even as a pup. It's been a while since I've seen him, but it seems he just may live forever."

"Do you have a dog in the city?" she asked, wondering if he loved animals as much as his son did.

Victor walked to the window and gazed out. "A dog never seemed—practical."

Before either could say more, the backyard hounds were all at once flying across the window-framed landscape, yapping with excitement.

"They're here," Victor exclaimed, his ruddy face brightening. The two of them rushed out the door in time to see the cabriolet drawing up.

Standing back, Nicole watched him greet his family. Victor helped Gabriele down and embraced her, held her at arm's length, then kissed each cheek. And then Luc stepped out.

Nicole stood leaden, realizing now how much she'd longed for him all day. He looked so handsome, so strong and confident as he approached his father. Her eyes teared as Victor reached out to him, but then, her breath caught as Luc hesitated. *Luc. Please, no. Don't turn away—*

In that instant, father and son came together in an awkward but heartfelt embrace—and just as quickly drew back. Nicole saw as Luc nodded in respect that no words need be said. She knew. They had reconciled.

Luc turned toward her. She stood breathlessly as he approached and stopped before her, and right there, in front of his parents, enveloped her in his arms, his lips nuzzling her hair. Unable to hold back tears any longer, she melted into him.

"Thank God," he whispered into her ear. "You're safe. My father. My mother…we owe everything to you, Nicole."

Chapter Thirty-Five

Nicole's senses were overcome with the beauty of the table setting, the blazing candles, the heavy silverware, the crystal glasses. Even with such short notice, *Madame* Lamont had prepared a feast of braised rabbit and a savory galette stuffed with cabbage. Victor opened a prized burgundy brought up from the wine cellar and made the rounds of the table, filling each glass. Nicole was sure he smiled at her as he did so. She was as sure *Madame* Chatillon's serene expression from the end of the table was one of gratitude.

Standing at his chair, Victor lifted his glass. "To having made a safe journey. And to Nicole Vogel, for her courage."

Nicole met Luc's eyes. His look told her everything: his pride in her, his admiration. She lifted her glass to him, to his parents, smiled, and took a sip.

"So, tell us, Luc," said Victor, taking his chair. "Exactly what happened when you reached the city gates."

"He was brilliant," answered Gabriele, who to Nicole looked beautiful in a formal robe *à la française*, her silvery-blond hair wrapped in an elegant chignon.

"I'd hoped we'd come to an unguarded gate and pass straight through," Luc said. "But Nicole, you were right—there were revolutionary soldiers everywhere, checking any cart or coach attempting to leave the city. One guard, not much out of his teens, asked who we were and where we were going."

"And that's when," Gabriele added dramatically, "Luc said to him, *I am Hugo Lamont and this is my mother, Madame Lamont. We're on our way home to Gentilly.*"

They all burst out laughing. Nicole felt a delirious happiness. Sharing joy at the table, she felt she belonged in this family. "Luc said it with such composure and clarity," Gabriele went on merrily, "that even *I* almost believed him."

"*Madame* Lamont," Victor jovially called to the next room, "did you hear that? You were an accomplice."

Madame Lamont poked her head through the doorway of the butler pantry. "I heard it all right," she said wryly.

"A moment, *Madame* Lamont," Victor called, his smile fading. "Can you join us? I'd like you to hear what I have to say."

His words were somber. Nicole felt something change almost at once, as did everyone in the room. *Madame* Lamont, her gray hair pulled back in a tight bun, a brown apron covering her ample body, stepped into the room. "Sir?"

"I've something important to say," Victor said, "and I'd like you to hear it too, *Madame* Lamont." He looked at the opposite end of the table. "Gabriele, my dear—" He turned to Luc. "And Luc. My only son." The room grew quiet. "I realize I have not said it before, but the two of you have always been at the center of my thoughts. If having concern is love, then I know I've always felt a deep love for you both."

Nicole's eyes flashed to Luc. He sat staring at his father, his face unsmiling.

"Tomorrow," Victor said to Luc, "your mother and I will be leaving for England."

There was a moment in which the words settled in each person's mind. Nicole stared blankly at the roses in the middle of the table. Luc put down his wineglass, his expression incredulous. "What are you saying? After we've gotten safely out of Paris?"

Victor cleared his throat. "Before dinner, your mother and I had a long discussion about what we should do, with the events in France being so unpredictable. Who knows where this will end? The king may rally troops and regain control. Things could go back to normal. But until then, your mother and I must leave the country. We will stay at Fernsby House with Lord Lindley."

"But *Les Saules* is safe," Luc protested.

"Things aren't so simple. Nicole has not been the first to warn me that trouble may lie ahead. The omens can no longer be ignored. The tribunal will seek me out. First in Paris, then here."

"Father—" Luc insisted.

"Don't try to dissuade me, Luc. *Les Saules* is in your name. And if you harbor me, I put you at risk. As well as *Madame* Lamont and the entire household. I will not allow anyone to be apprehended because of me."

"Mother?" Luc turned to her.

"Your father is right, my dear. Marguerite and William will be happy to help us. Fernsby House may be a country manor, but it's a grand one. We'll get lost in it." With a brave face she addressed the housemistress. "*Madame* Lamont, we will need you and Coco to help us prepare tonight."

Madame Lamont had been listening with a sad expression. "But of course, *Madame*," she responded. "I'll set Colleen to it at once."

"And so, it's settled," pronounced Victor. Pouring another glass of wine, he held it out for *Madame* Lamont. "I'd like to propose a toast to our beloved *Madame* Lamont. For all she has done so magnificently over these years—and will continue to do as headmistress of *Les Saules*."

As Nicole raised her glass, her throat tightened with sadness. They had to leave? Tomorrow? It wasn't fair. She'd only met them, and just as Luc and his father made amends, they were leaving. She could not imagine what Luc must be feeling. Her heart went out to him.

Luc looked over to her. She did not know what to read in his expression. Not sadness. Not fear. It was determination—as if he was filled with some inward conviction at that moment. He slowly rose. "And now, I have something to say," he announced.

Victor and Gabriele looked from one to the other then to Luc. Nicole could not imagine what he was thinking, what he was going to say. Surely not that he was going *with* them? *No. No.* He couldn't. Not now.

"Mother, Father," he said, addressing both. "I do not know when we shall be together again." He paused, letting everyone in the room take in such a momentous fact. Nicole felt a flood of relief. He wasn't leaving…

"And so, while we are, I would like to share with you my own hopes and dreams."

Victor and Gabriele sat spellbound, wineglasses in hand, waiting to hear their son's words.

"I wish to marry Nicole Vogel." He looked across at her. "Should she have me." Without waiting, he addressed his father. "And if she will, I ask for your blessing."

Nicole sat forward on the edge of her chair, clasping the table as her body began to tremble. *Oh Luc.* It couldn't be real. She forced herself to sit calmly. Luc was actually asking his parents' approval. She was overcome with love for him, for his parents, for *Madame* Lamont, even the stable hands and Coco. She belonged here. Her dream had come true.

Gabriele and Victor shared an intimate look, one that needed no words.

Victor took a deep breath. "I couldn't imagine a better wife for you, my son," he said.

"Nor could I imagine a finer *belle-fille*," added Gabriele. "I welcome you, my beautiful daughter."

Nicole could not think as Luc rose up and walked around the table and knelt at her side. He pulled the familiar black velvet box from his pocket.

"My dear Nicole," he said, opening it to reveal the ruby ring shining crimson in the candlelight. "I gave you this ring once before, and I pray you will accept it again—now, and forever." He took her hand. "I cannot promise you the future I'd once hoped for us, but as your husband I will always be at your side. Nicole Vogel, will you be my wife?"

"I will," she said, her eyes brimming with joyful tears. "Oh yes. I will."

Luc slid the ring onto her finger then brought her hand to his lips. "I'll love you forever," he whispered.

Gabriele sniffled into her handkerchief. Victor cleared his throat.

Realizing the house matron stood frozen in place, Luc turned to her and smiled. "*Madame* Lamont. What do you think of my choice of wife?"

"I think," she said, smiling, her voice breaking, "I should bring out the champagne."

***

The light of a bright moon guided the cabriolet back to Paris. With Nicole nestled at his side, Luc had never felt so many feelings at once: ecstasy that his parents approved of her, deep concern for their welfare, sadness to lose them to England—and an abiding joy that

Nicole would be his wife. He glanced at her sitting there as the dark countryside rolled past.

"What are you thinking, *ma chere?*"

"I'm thinking so many things," she said. "That I love you so much. And that even though we don't know what lies ahead, we can survive it together."

"I believe that, too."

Luc fell quiet for a few long minutes. "Fate is odd, isn't it? It moves us in ways we are unaware."

Nicole reached for his hand, twining her fingers between his. They rode that way in silence until they reached the city gates. Growing tense, they sat up taller, but the guard only waved them through with his torch.

Chapter Thirty-Six

"*Egad*, have you been on the streets? Everyone has gone insane," Bertrand declared, rushing into the Fontenay salon and yanking off his hat.

"My, my, what a surprise to see *you*," Georgette said with no real enthusiasm. "And why have you braved the mobs to honor us with a visit after all this time? To see my daughter?" She smirked. "Her name is Giselle."

Bertrand stood repulsed by the motherly scene of Georgette, her face devoid of makeup, and in her arms, a squirming, scarlet-faced baby. "Must you be so common, Georgette?" he said, tossing his cap onto the bureau. "You know I don't care for *enfants*."

"You really are heartless," she said. Her unpowdered hair was tied back simply. She wore a plain muslin gown with a white lace fichu modestly covering her breasts.

Bertrand pulled back the blanket and stared down. The infant's pink mouth yawned. "Well done, my dear," he said flatly. He sensed a change in the household, something more than Georgette's maternal dowdiness.

He turned toward *Madame* Fontenay, who sat knitting on a settee. "*Bonjour*, Helaine. There's a chill in the air. Shall I light the fire?"

"Do as you wish," she replied, her attention on her knitting.

Bertrand strode to the fireplace, knelt, and lit a match to the bundle of wood. God, he wished he had a cheroot. And by the looks of things here, there was no brandy either. Fashioning a broad smile, he rose and approached *Madame* Fontenay and kissed her cheek.

"Don't tell us you've arrived on foot," she murmured. "Where is your cab?"

"One does what one must. Such luxuries are not so easy to keep these days."

"I assume that means you have no money," Georgette said. "Don't bother coming to us." She rose and placed Giselle in her cradle. "It appears we're as destitute as you, Bertrand. If you're here for a handout, you'll have to wait in line...after the servants, that is. They've not been paid in weeks." She settled beside her mother and gave him an insincere smile.

"Destitute?" Bertrand uttered. "Now, there's a word. Everyone's having difficulty, of course, but to say our family is *destitute*? That's a bit harsh, don't you think?" He sensed a growing distance from this woman, with her stern face and her baby smell.

"Father is insolvent," Georgette said with an airy nonchalance as she reached for her knitting basket. "He's been unable to withstand the financial chaos." She picked up her needles, along with a pink knitted square of yarn. "All merchants and industrialists are at a standstill. Those with reserves will survive. But as we know—" she looked up, wrapping a string of yarn around her thumb, "—that was not the case with Father."

"Your father's mismanagement is a sickness," *Madame* Fontenay said with a frown. "As are his indiscretions."

"Ah yes," Georgette murmured. "But the latter didn't seem important until the first bankrupted us."

Bertrand chewed on his lip. It seemed motherhood had changed Georgette. While she'd lost that giddiness he'd so despised, any intrigue they'd shared was clearly no longer possible—not with her motherhood. Good. Let her fester. Unmarried, with a child. She was not getting younger and left in dire straits. Losing Luc had put her in a very bad place. Clearly, old Fontenay never thought about her future, or that of his wife. And now this grandchild. How then, could he, Bertrand Le Mansec, *a bastard,* expect anything from the squanderer? His presence in the household was now uncomfortable. And he'd always guessed that Helaine's acceptance of him had only served to annoy her husband.

"And where is our dear stable boy?" he asked, wanting to lay wreckage to Georgette's smug domestic scene.

Georgette looked up from her knitting. "Éric came to see the baby," she said. "He loves Giselle. And *me*. He wants us to leave Paris. Together."

Madame Fontenay set aside her knitting. "I, too, am leaving this monstrous city."

Bertrand closed his eyes. The finality of it all being over so quickly came as a shock. "Leaving?" he repeated. "Wherever are you going, darling?"

"To my sister Adelaide. She's in *Saverne*. I detest the dreary place, it's so cold. But what can poor relatives do?"

Bertrand went to the fireplace and placed both hands on the mantel. *Sacre*. It was all arranged. Without so much as a note sent to him. "Father?" he asked, looking into the flames.

"Gilles?" *Madame* Fontenay's lips tightened. "My dear sister detests my husband. She has not extended the invitation to him. I'm sure he's arranged a place to stay."

Georgette plopped her knitting in her lap. "Bertrand, several weeks ago Luc came to Father saying you were the one who had Antoine Durand arrested."

Bertrand's eyes grew guarded. He swallowed. What was this? "Luc's a liar. He's been spreading rumors about me. I wouldn't be surprised if he doesn't end up in prison himself. I have it on good authority he conspired against the citizens, spying for the monarchy."

"That's absurd," Georgette declared.

"It's all true," Bertrand said recklessly. "Do you remember Luc's whore? The hatmaker?"

"Nicole Vogel? Luc told me he's in love with her."

This caught him off guard. So, she knew that too? "It seems the little orphan schemer has played us all. She's actually a noble. Probably spying on us, along with Luc."

"What? The hat girl? A noble?"

"So it seems. This morning a deputy of the assembly asked me if I knew her address. I tell you, they're on to her."

"My God, Bertrand," Georgette said, standing up in alarm. "Say you didn't give it."

Bertrand shrugged. "How would I know where the strumpet lives? They'll find her. Then we'll see who believes whom. I don't need any of you, anyway. Frankly, it's a relief to have the lot of you out of my life, along with that worthless father of mine. I shall take pleasure in knowing this family will finally live like I always have. Insolvent. Don't come to me begging. I wouldn't give one of you a *sol*."

At that, he grabbed his cap and stormed out.

**

"Nicole, tell us," Aimée said, sitting on a blanket spread on Sarah's kitchen floor. Jac, strong like his father, was struggling to sit up by himself. A curious Midas sat nearby, watching his every move.

"How did Luc ask you to marry him?"

"It was so romantic," Nicole said, washing the supper plates. "His parents were there. There was a lovely meal with wine and conversation. And then—" She paused, remembering the scene. "Luc gave me his grandmother's ring." She held up her sudsy hand, showing off the ring for the tenth time since Aimée and Jacques had arrived this afternoon for the good news.

"It's a nice ending to a sad time for the Chatillon family," Gus said, taking his pipe from his pocket. Seeing Sarah's stern shake of her head *no*, her eyes indicating the baby on the floor, he sheepishly tucked the pipe away. "It's a disgrace," he said with a sigh. "Fine people like the Chatillons who've worked hard, being chased out. I like Luc, Nicolette. He's a fine man."

"And handsome," Sarah added, pulling herself up from the chair to clean the remains off the table. "And so polite, coming last night to ask Gus's permission to wed you." She stepped over Midas who, ears perked, watched the rattle in Jac's fist.

Aimée glanced up at her husband, who sat at the table. "I'm not sure if it's the time to tell them, Jacques. But should we?"

Jacques nodded, a smile slowly spreading across his face. "I think so."

Nicole turned from her dishes. Seeing the happy exchange between Aimée and Jacques, understanding dawned. "*Mon Dieu.*" She wiped her hands on her apron. "You're having another baby."

"You know me so well." Aimée grinned, patting her flat tummy.

Nicole rushed to Aimée. Kneeling beside her, she stared into her dearest friend's eyes. How she adored her. How thrilled she was for her. After a moment, they both burst out laughing and threw their arms around each other. "I'm so happy for you," Nicole whispered into Aimée's hair. "You deserve all of this. And more."

Gus rose from his chair. "Well, it seems we now have a double celebration. A wedding *and* a baby." He pulled a bottle of sherry from the cabinet. "I wish we had something better—"

"Gus, this is perfect," Nicole insisted, helping Aimée stand as Gus poured a few drops into each teacup. Jacques rose and gathered up his son, holding him aloft to take it all in.

Midas hopped on a chair and gave a loud meow. Everyone laughed and raised their cups.

"I wish Luc could be here," Nicole said wistfully. "He's helping the servants at their chateau find placements. He'll try to join us."

Gus took a cup from the wall rack and emptied the last few drops. "For Luc," he said, setting it before the empty chair. "And now, Nicolette, the honor is yours."

Nicole looked around at the circle of these beloved people. Her heart had never been fuller. "Here's to new life," she said, her eyes on Aimée. Then lifting her cup high she added, "And to love, persisting through all hardships."

With murmurs and smiles of agreement, they drank to her toast and were laughing at Jac's shrieks of happiness when, from below, a loud knock sounded at the door.

"It's Luc," Nicole exclaimed. Excited, she set aside her cup and flew from the kitchen downstairs and threw open the door with a joyous smile.

Standing before her was a young deputy of the tribunal wearing a blue coat and red knit hat bearing the tricolor cockade.

Her smile faded.

Behind him stood a uniformed guard, a rifle draped over his shoulder. "Nicole Vogel?" the deputy asked.

"Yes?" Her first thought was Antoine. Something had happened.

"Nicole Vogel, *née* Nicole Eugenie d'Ailly, you are under arrest by order of the French National Revolutionary Tribunal."

She couldn't quite take in his words.

Behind her, bootsteps clattered on the stairs. "What's this about?" boomed Gus, with Jacques following close on his heels. Seeing uniformed officers at his door, Gus stepped forward and wrapped his arm about Nicole's shoulders. "By what authority are you here?"

Sarah had ambled down and waddled forward. "What's happening?"

The guard eyed Gus and Sarah. His gaze lifted to the huge man, Jacques, standing tall and menacingly looking on. "Are you aware you are housing a member of the nobility?" He pointed at Nicole. "This woman."

Nicole wasn't sure she'd heard him correctly. "Nobility?" she said, her voice sounding not like her own.

"What lies are these?" exclaimed Gus, his face angry and frightened at the same time. "Nicole is no more nobility than me. Her name is Vogel. I should know. I signed the papers to take her from Legros orphanage. *That* is who she is. An orphan. She's spent her entire childhood in more want and need than either of you two. You were probably in your warm beds sleeping when she risked her life all last winter for your cause, pasting up posters for the revolution."

Without hesitation, the uniformed guard unshouldered his rifle and brought the gunstock down on the side of Gus's head. He slumped to the floor. Sarah screamed and rushed to him, kneeling and placing his head in her lap. Gus looked up with blood trickling down the side of his face. Upstairs, Jac began to screech. The guards glanced toward the upper floor. "Who's there?" With his massive body, Jacques moved to block their view. "My wife and child. Do you want to arrest them too?"

The guard frowned and clenched Nicole's arm. With a thunderous stare Jacques stepped forward, but the guard raised his rifle and wildly swept it over the room. "And the rest of you. Don't think you're not noted in my book."

Sarah had been dabbing Gus's temple with her handkerchief. She looked up with fright. "Where are you taking her?" she begged.

"Le Conciergerie," the deputy barked, stepping aside for the guard to lead Nicole away.

"Have faith, Nicole," Jacques called out in his deep voice. "We'll bring help."

"Wait," Sarah called. "One last good-bye." She labored up from Gus's side and rushed to grab Nicole's shoulders and hug her. "We'll come for you," she said, her voice quavering.

Nicole held her tightly, then, disengaging, slipped Luc's ring from her finger and pressed it into Sarah's hand. Sarah's eyes widened, but when she shook her head to say nothing, Sarah wrapped her fingers about the ring. "Don't worry, my dear," she said.

"That's enough. On with it," called the guard, grabbing Nicole's shoulders and shoving her to the door.

As they led her to the huge coach, Nicole tried to look back to say good-bye, but the guard forced her head down to duck into the coach. She was shoved onto the seat and the huge guard sat heavily beside her. How could this be happening?

"This is a mistake," she said, appealing to him.

He stayed silent. She looked hopelessly at the man's profile. The resolute determination on his face told her everything.

***

Hearing them leave, Aimée hurried down the stairs with the weight of Jac in her arms. "Oh my God, Nicole," she cried, running out the door as the coach pulled away. "We'll come for you," she called, waving until the coach turned the corner. She turned and fixed her eyes on Jacques. "What has happened? Where have they taken her?" Seeing Gus, she covered her mouth.

Gus slowly sat up, and with the help of Jacques struggled to stand. He let Sarah guide him to a chair, where he eased down and dropped his head in his hands. "I'm fine, I'm fine," he insisted as Sarah hovered over him. "But Nicole—there's a mistake."

Aimée felt herself ready to crumble. "We must go to Luc—" Her voice caught with emotion.

"How?" Jacques asked.

"Once Nicole showed me the Chatillon chateau," she said frantically. "It's on Faubourg Saint-Antoine. I know exactly where it is. Sarah, will you stay with Jac?"

"Yes, yes, of course," Sarah said, holding out her arms for the whimpering baby. "But hurry."

"Wait," said Gus, struggling for coins from his pocket. He handed the money to Jacques. "Cab fare."

"Luc will help. I know he will," Aimée cried as she and Jacques rushed out the door.

Chapter Thirty-Seven

Nicole huddled on the narrow bed, which was little more than a wooden slab jutting out from the wall. When she'd first arrived in the cell, the dark was so thick she could not see her hand before her face—though what she couldn't see, she felt, as a rat scampered across her shoes. From that moment on, she'd perched upon the thin mattress with her arms clasping her knees.

As her eyes adjusted, the floor became a shadowy reservoir of furtive movement. A mildew smell burned her throat. Moans sounded from somewhere. Some were close. Some far away. All were horrible.

But what troubled her most was her mind. It was playing tricks, confusing her. A swarm of unleashed memories swirled about in her head. The officiant had arrested her as *Nicole Vogel,* née *Nicole Eugenie d'Ailly.* That name—it was as if a door opened in her mind, illuminating a memory of her standing on the street, and in the distance, silhouetted against the sun, the outline of a man standing on the steps.

She was trying to sort it out when a rattling and jangling of keys made way into her thoughts, bringing her back to the cell. The sound of the gaoler approaching. She detested the fat little brute of a man. But she had little fear of him. She'd met bullies at Legros. She knew they were cowards at heart.

Her eyes strained toward the small opening in the cell door. A glow of lamplight appeared beyond the bars, followed by the gaoler's head, and behind him a second, taller figure. Nicole scooted back against the wall, suddenly frightened. The gaoler turned the lock, and with a heavy clank of the pin, pushed open the iron door.

"On yer feet, Citizen," he ordered gruffly. "Here's a visitor."

Nicole rose in slow motion as a woman entered the cell. The gaoler raised his heavy lamp, revealing the woman's face in the moving shadowy light. Nicole stared at her in bewilderment. *Madame* Colére? But why? How? Why was she here?

"Leave us," *Madame* Colére commanded.

The gaoler set the lamp on a ledge, the light illuminating *Madame* Colére's tall, emaciated figure. "She's not much to worry about," the man offered, his critical eyes apprising the dark corner where Nicole stood. "Still, I'll be down the corridor." With a loud sniff, he turned and pulled the iron door shut with a thud.

As the key clunked in the lock, Nicole stepped back in terror as *Madame* Colére approached her. "Come, come, my dear. No need to be frightened. I have important news for you." The woman reached out, and Nicole flinched as she felt skeletal fingers grab her arm. *Madame* Colére squeezed tighter, pulling Nicole into the light.

Nicole stared into *Madame* Colére's gaze as the pieces began falling into place. That day she'd seen her at the National Assembly. Robespierre wanting to meet Antoine. Her arrest under the name Nicole Eugenie d'Ailly.

"It was you who did this," she said at last, shaking her arm free from *Madame* Colére's grasp. "But who else would it be? What have you kept from me? Why did they arrest me as a noble? Nicole Eugenie d'Ailly."

"I think you already know."

"I know nothing about myself. All these years, I've been in the prison you created, *Madame*. Even as a child. I'd lost everything I loved—and you, who should have been my protector, mistreated me. What do you know about me?"

Madame Colére scoffed. "You never change, do you? Obstinate, even here in prison. But that will soon end. Already we are setting up trials for you and your kind."

The news struck Nicole to her core. "My kind?" Closing her eyes, she whispered, "Why have you hated me all these years?"

"You're mistaken. I've been more than patient with you—and all your high-horse superiority. You're like all your blood kin."

Nicole turned away, rubbing her temples in confusion. "I don't understand any of this. Are you saying my father was a *nobleman*?"

"I think you know. You've always known, haven't you?"

It was too much. Nicole turned back and stared at her enemy. "Yes," she accused. "I *am* beginning to remember. All those years you were so clever in wiping away who I was, destroying any sense of my identity, making me question my mind. And now I know why. My father was a member of the nobility."

Madame Colére stood rigidly with her arms at her side.

"Wasn't he?" Nicole demanded, drawing close.

Madame pulled back her head. "Indeed, your father was a lieutenant in the war. A nobleman. I have the proof. And I'll present it at your trial."

A hazy fog muddled Nicole's thinking. *A soldier. Yes. He wore a uniform.*

While she was trying to put together the bits and pieces of information, *Madame* Colére watched on with a crooked smile. "You should thank me, my dear," the woman said at last. "It was only from pity that I kept the truth from you." She reached out and touched her finger to Nicole's cheek.

Nicole flinched. "Don't touch me."

"The accident was *your* fault," *Madame* Colére murmured. "What a stupid child, stopping as you did in the street, in the path of a coach. Your mother and father saved you—"

Her eyes widened. She felt herself getting sick. No. No. It was not true. There was no coach. She lowered to sit on the bed, cradling her stomach with her arms, trying to take in what she'd heard.

Madame Colére loomed over her. "What a huge coach it was, too," she droned on. "Eight horses. I saw your parents in the morgue that night. Broken and bloodied. Pity. Your mother had hair like yours."

Nicole covered her ears. A gut-wrenching anguish spread through her as an image came to her…a doll's head, rolling across cobblestones to a dead stop. The flood of memory could not be stopped. It washed over her in a sickening wave of sorrow and pain. The doll's blue eyes. Staring up at the sky. She felt arms, felt herself swept up…then…darkness.

"And so you remember, my dear. You see how kind I was to help you forget?"

"The sun was shining," Nicole said dully to herself. "There were people filling the streets. Everyone was in black, all except my father. He wore a uniform, coming down the steps." She looked up at *Madame* Colére in astonishment. "I *do* remember. It was the king's funeral."

"Well, one of the funerals," the woman murmured. "There were two. The old king was buried at midnight, in secret at St. Denis Abbey."

"But it was daytime. I remember how sunny. How hot."

"Louis XV died of smallpox. The corpses of kings dead of smallpox are buried in secret, in lead coffins. No one mourned the internment of Louis XV. Except perhaps the ghouls that welcomed him when his lead coffin was placed in the sarcophagus. All that night a violent thunderstorm raged through Paris. Some say it was Beelzebub opening the doors of hell for one of his own. If one believes in such nonsense."

Nicole squeezed her eyes shut. "It can't be. The sky was blue..."

"You remember the state funeral. The second public one. In July. You came to Legros in July. By then the new Louis and his wicked Marie Antoinette had been on the throne for months."

"But my father—"

"Your father was a lieutenant for the old king—much decorated, it seems." *Madame* Colére bent so close that Nicole drew back from her sour breath. "Decorated for his service in the war. It was your father, the traitor, who allowed all those young men to be killed. It was his fault. Their blood is on his hands. And for that, they invited Lieutenant d'Ailly to view the king's coffin." *Madame* Colére looked about the prison cell, a strange gleam in her eyes. "An empty coffin, though." Her head snapped toward Nicole. "The real coffin had been entombed since May, solid lead beneath the oak, built for a king putrefied with smallpox."

Mercifully, she stopped her tirade as she clasped her narrow chest and sat on the cot. "It was by the justice of God that Lieutenant d'Ailly died at his own daughter's hand. God's justice for the men he killed."

Nicole felt as if she must run. Run from this woman. But there was no place to go. She began to pace the cell, and as she did so, it was as if a door opened onto a bright light as the memory washed over her.

The sun splashed across the icing-white buildings. The royal coaches were arriving. Her father stood across the broad avenue, wearing his uniform while everyone else was dressed in black. He was coming across the street to her. "Papa," she called, letting go of her mother's hand. She ran across the street to meet him, calling out, "Look at the doll maman bought me—"

A loud rumble, frantic calls, a gigantic coach, the monstrous horses—then screams as she was shoved to the cobblestones and a luminous burst of sunlight flooded her vison.

Everything shrank to her cheek on the cobblestone. Sounds came from far away. She lay there, looking at her doll's head, its blue eyes staring up at the blue sky—

Nicole stopped pacing. Her breaths were shallow.

"I see you remember," *Madame* Colére said from the shadows. "It was your fault they died, Nicole."

Amidst the despair and loss, a strength pushed through. Her fear of this woman was a child's fear, built on lies and deception and cruelty. But now she was a woman. Never again would *Madame* Colére frighten her. Even if they took her to the scaffold for her father's sins.

She turned her head toward the place the woman sat. "Deep in my young mind, I took on shame," Nicole said, walking toward the old woman, who looked up as she stopped before her. "And you kept me in confusion. I was buried inside the guilt of having done something horrible."

Madame Colére stood. "I did it to protect you."

Nicole straightened to her full height—a head taller than the old woman. "But now I thank you, for freeing me. No matter what fate awaits me, never again will I be that hurt child." She came closer so that *Madame* Colére stepped back. "I'm not the one who should be ashamed. You should be. My one question now is why have you hated me so?"

Madame Colére's thin rib cage rose and fell with emotion. "The next time I look at your face will be at your trial," she said hatefully.

"My family must have had a home," Nicole went on, her mind flooding with the realization that a world had been stolen from her. "There must have been money available to raise me," she said. She stopped, trying to understand. And then she knew. "You," she accused, looking squarely at *Madame* Colére. "*You* claimed it all. That's why you kept my identity hidden. So no one would discover what you'd done."

Madame Colére called for the guard. She brushed past Nicole then at the door turned back. "You think you know everything. Well, you don't. But you shall learn it all. At your trial. And you're right about one thing. I do hate you."

As the gaoler opened the door, *Madame* Colére pushed past him, not waiting for him as she made her way out.

Nicole was trembling with rage as *Madame* Colére's footsteps rang along the corridor.

It was the stare of the gaoler that brought her thoughts back to the cell. The man was insolently looking her up and down. "She's an important one," he said. "Knows Robespierre, they say. Think on that tonight, Citizen." He pulled shut the heavy door, leaving Nicole to stare after him.

***

Lulu poured Luc a cup of coffee. *"Mon Dieu, mon cher,"* she said. *"*I am so sorry, Luc, but I cannot help. The girls when they are arrested are always taken to the *Salpêtrière*. Ah, if your Nicole had been taken *there*, I know all the guards." She shrugged. "In fact, very well, eh? And they would do anything for me, you know. Oh, but your Nicole. That's another thing. The *Conciergerie* is a formidable prison."

Luc dropped his head into hands in frustration. "There must be something we can do." Lulu had been his thread of a chance to reach Nicole. And she could not help. He could hardly bear it a moment longer, not knowing why Nicole had been arrested, where she was taken, imagining the horrors she was enduring this very moment. He rose and paced. "There must be *someone* who can help," he insisted. "My God, we've got to do something. There must be somewhere to go. Some way to discover the charges."

Philippe, sitting in a chair by the window, looked up from his newspaper. "They don't need a reason for anything they do," he said, rattling the paper in disgust. "A handful of demoniacs are in control. Look at my mother and father. I've been trying to learn the charges against them. There are none, it seems. Only that they belong to the First Estate. But there are thousands of nobles. Do they plan to arrest us all?"

"Oh, such drama," Lulu said as she eased into a chair across from Luc. "Soon you'll imagine they'll be chopping off everyone's heads," she teased. "This will all pass. Count and Countess

Montpellier will be released." She poured herself coffee. "Come sit, my darling. You're making me nervous. Here, more coffee." She poured him a cup as he came and begrudgingly plopped into the chair across from her.

"I've got to do something," he said.

"But, Luc, I must confess. I do feel a little guilt about your fiancée, you know."

Lost in his thoughts, Luc gave a long pour of cream into his coffee. "Why would you say such a thing?"

"I think I know why your Nicole was arrested."

He thudded down the heavy silver creamer. "And whatever would make you say that?" he demanded. "You don't know Nicole. You've never even met her, Lulu. How could you possibly know why she was arrested? Why didn't you say something?"

"Wait, wait, slowly, slowly, Luc." She shrugged prettily. "I am not sure about this, darling. I just think I *may* know something. I could be wrong."

"Tell me."

"It's Bertrand," Lulu said, stirring sugar into her coffee with her pinky extended. "At the time I thought it was a man thing, you know. Bertrand is always after your conquests." She shrugged. "I thought nothing of it."

"What are you saying?" Simply hearing Bertrand's name filled Luc with rage. "You thought nothing of *what*? Tell me, Lulu."

She squirmed in her chair, fussing with feathers on the sleeves of her wrapper, avoiding his eyes. "Bertrand, you know, stayed here for a while. What could I do? He had no place to go. But he was so nervous, pacing around like a caged cat. I asked him to leave. He went to his mother."

A muscle twitched on Luc's jaw as he remembered the threat Bertrand had made about Nicole. Why hadn't he thought of it? "Did Bertrand say something to you about Nicole?" he asked. "Something to endanger her?"

"No, no, nothing like that. Not to me," Lulu said. Setting her dainty cup in the saucer, she extricated herself from the chair and with her gauzy robe flowing behind, walked to a bureau against the wall. "But he left some things," she said, rummaging through the drawer, then withdrawing a red portfolio. She turned to Luc. "This."

Puzzled, Luc rose and took the bound leather folder.

"I admit that, yes, I was naughty," Lulu said, watching Luc's expression as he jerked open the flap, pulled out a handful of papers and glanced at the first page. "I read through it when Bertrand left."

"Philippe," Luc murmured, reading. "You must come and look. *This* is why Nicole was arrested."

Chapter Thirty-Eight

Luc burst through the door. Antoine, standing at his typeset table arranging the type pieces onto his composing stick, looked up. Luc rushed him, despite the astonishment in Antoine's eyes as he took in Luc, along with Philippe and Lulu, invading his shop.

"Antoine, I've come—"

"Luc Chatillon," he bellowed. "What in hell is this about? Who are these people?"

"Just listen—"

Antoine approached his hands clenched in fists. "Traitor. You betrayed me. Sent me to *La Force*."

Luc had never seen the man's face twisted in anger. He was looking at a different person. "You must listen," Luc said in his calmest tone. "Nicole's been arrested. We need your help."

Antoine blanched at the news. His brows unfurled, and his eyes darted to Philippe and Lulu. "What are you saying? What is this?"

"Nicole has been arrested," Luc forced the words to sound coherent. "She's been taken to *La Conciergerie*."

Antoine stood rigidly, staring from him to Philippe and Lulu. Luc could see he was struggling to understand, to fathom such a thing. He came closer, willing himself to stay composed. "Forget what you think about me, Antoine. Think of Nicole. We must help her."

Antoine looked down, his face sagging into a mass of confusion. "Nicole arrested? That's impossible. She's done nothing wrong."

"And yet it's true," Luc said quietly. "She's been betrayed by the same person who turned *you* into the authorities. Bertrand Le Mansec."

Antoine stepped back, clearly unable to take it all in. "You're lying," he said, his lips beginning to tremble. "It can't be—it was *you*."

"Your arrest came as a blow to me," Luc said. "I had no idea how or why it happened. My friends here—Philippe Montpellier and Louise-Marie Bisset—knew it was Bertrand Le Mansec. Bertrand was the one who gave your name to the authorities. For money."

Philippe stepped forward and stood alongside Luc. "Bertrand came to me the day after your arrest. He seemed quite pleased with himself."

Shaking his head in denial, Antoine leaned against the table. "I don't believe this."

Lulu had been standing back, but now she spoke up, her charcoaled eyes fixed on Antoine. "I know Bertrand, you see. He's often talked about his resentment of Luc." She held out the red portfolio she'd carried during their hurried coach ride. "Bertrand had in his possession these papers. Read them, *Monsieur* Antoine. I think you'll understand everything."

Looking down at the folder she held out, Antoine wavered, then accepted it. He lifted the flap and peered inside.

"I regret to add," Philippe interjected, "that I paid Bertrand to gather information about Nicole Vogel. I was quite active in investigating revolutionaries before the Bastille. Lots of us were. We thought we were doing the right thing." He took a deep breath. "Never did I imagine it would come to this."

Numbly taking it all in, Antoine pulled out the documents. Luc reached over and tapped the top sheet. "I'm only learning this myself," Luc explained. "The truth is, Nicole came from an extraordinary heritage. These papers tell the story of a young girl whose father served as a lieutenant during the reign of Louis XV, leading a brigade in the war in the Americas."

Antoine read, his face growing more stunned with each word—and then he closed his eyes in anguish. "My God. Are you saying these papers have been at Legros all this time?

"Someone wanted to keep her identity from her," Luc said. "And now they're using it against her," he added grimly. "Her father's regiment was attacked in a raid. When the tribunal gets this information, they'll claim he was responsible for the casualties. He'll be found guilty of treason against the Citizens. And they'll find Nicole as guilty."

"I think I know…that woman, the directress, she's the one who has done this." Antoine's voice cracked. "Nicole told me about her. I didn't listen."

Luc held back a surge of anger. It wouldn't help to reprimand Antoine. He needed him. "I confronted Bertrand about giving your name to the authorities," he said. "He of course denied it. And he made threats about Nicole. He planned to use the information he'd gotten from Legros in some way. Perhaps for blackmail. Or to give it to the tribunal himself."

Antoine leafed through the papers. "Nicole warned me about Bertrand and—about the difference between justice and revenge."

Luc placed his hand on Antoine's shoulder. "Bertrand is not your friend, not *our* friend—and certainly not a friend of the Cause."

Antoine slumped to a chair, dropping his head in regret. "It's all my fault," he said. "My jealousy—" he looked up, "of you, Luc. I didn't want to lose her. I was blinded to the truth."

It was a simple admission. Luc was impressed and touched by the strength it took to say those words. "None of that matters," he said. "All we care about now is freeing Nicole. To do that we need your help."

***

Nicole couldn't take a bite of the stale bread, the only food she'd been given since her arrest. Throwing it aside, she paced. Surely by now Aimée and Jacques—or the Bastons—had gone to Luc. She rubbed her hands through her hair. Merely thinking of Luc made her ache. He would be desperate about her welfare, and his suffering hurt as much as her own.

Her thoughts leapt to Antoine. Perhaps he would help. She bit her nails, thinking of it. Or would he consider her a traitor? Perhaps testify against her at the trial? She closed her eyes, feeling helpless and alone.

Somewhere in the darkness a woman moaned. Shivering, Nicole lay down on her cot and pulled the meager blanket over her shoulders. The dark felt heavy and terrifying. She squeezed her eyes shut, forcing herself into another world. Images of her parents came to her—their kind faces soothing her. She breathed in their love and strength, willing herself to drift into the safe world of sleep.

The clanking of the key in the lock startled her awake. It took an instant to remember where she was. And then a deep voice from the darkness commanded her, "Citizen. Come with me."

Nicole's blood congealed. This was not the voice of the turnkey she knew.

A shadowy figure dangling a lamp from his hand entered. Before she could see the man, his breath stinking of herring assailed her. As she tried to sit up, he strong-armed her from the bed. "Let's go."

"I demand to know where you're taking me," she cried, twisting away from him.

Not answering, the whiskery-faced man clamped his fingers on her arm and shoved her out of the cell. Using the barrel of his musket, he goaded her down the dank corridor. "Tell me where we're going," Nicole insisted over her shoulder.

"Keep moving."

Growing sick with fear, she almost stumbled but caught herself as she felt the gun barrel press into her back. *My God. Is this to be the trial? Will I die today? Am I never to see Luc again?* She wanted to pray, but no words came. Nothing but the cold gun in her back. Coming before a wide wooden door, the guard grabbed her arm and yanked her to a halt.

"Please, what's happening—"

He forced her inside and released her with a shove. Entering a room flooded with sunlight streaming in through windows, Nicole squinted against the brightness. She was almost blinded. She'd been in the dark cell so long.

"The prisoner," announced the guard. "Citizen Vogel."

As her eyes began to adjust, two figures materialized, two men in uniform. She stumbled forward then jolted to a stop.

Had she lost her mind?

Impossible—but—could it be? Antoine? No. And yet, it was. He stood upright without a cane, wearing a gray and gold deputy's uniform, a black wig with a wide-brimmed tricorn hat and spectacles. And behind him—

She thought she would faint. Luc stood by the door, masquerading as a guard in a tattered uniform, with filthy white breeches, scuffed knee-high boots, and a tricorn hat covered in badges.

Her dumbfounded stare went back and forth between the two. They both glared at her, their eyes cautioning her to remain silent. She felt a moment of dizziness—then her pulse started racing. How could this be? What were they doing? They were all in danger.

Antoine, his face serious, held a document. "Citizen Vogel," he said in an official tone. "You must understand that the charges against you are grave. Several witnesses have submitted to the tribunal signed statements against you and your family. You are Nicole Vogel, *née* Nicole Eugenie d'Ailly, daughter of Alexandre d'Ailly, first lieutenant under the reign of Louis XV. Will you waive trial and sign this confession of your knowledge of this heritage, as well as knowledge of your father serving as commander of a military regiment in the Seven Years' War? If you do so, the time and expense of a hearing will be curtailed. You should know, such a consideration will be in your favor."

Nicole panicked for a moment until Antoine continued. "I thought not." He addressed the prison guard with authority: "We're escorting this prisoner to headquarters. The interview should take four or five hours. What is your procedure? Should we remove the prisoner through the main entrance?"

The guard drew up with self-importance. "It's always the way prisoners are removed from the building."

"And when we return her, should we use the same?"

"No. Prisoners are admitted at the north entrance. There will be a checkpoint."

"Good. You will have Citizen Vogel's name ready when we return?"

"I'm off this minute to give it to the clerk, Deputy—" The guard paused for the name.

"Deputy Thomas Mercier," Antoine said clearly. "And note that I'll be taking the prisoner directly to Robespierre."

The impressed guard nodded in the affirmative. In military fashion, he turned on his heel and marched out, banging the door shut behind him.

With him gone, Antoine went to the door to listen. He held his fingers to his lips. Nicole was frozen in place as a thousand butterflies fluttered in her chest. Her eyes flicked back and forth from Luc to Antoine, waiting for a cue. Was she breathing? No. She must. *Take a breath.* She waited.

Then, with Antoine's nod that all was clear, Luc came forward and wrapped his arm about her waist. "Well done, my love," he murmured, kissing her temple.

She collapsed into his strength. "Thank God you're here," she whispered, pressing her cheek to his chest.

Antoine remained listening at the door. He cracked it open, looked out, then motioned for Luc and Nicole to follow. They silently slipped out and passed along a long corridor, Antoine walking upright with little sign of his limp, Luc escorting Nicole. Nicole kept her eyes on the end of what seemed to be an endless corridor. Could they truly get away with this? She was in such a daze she could not anticipate what lay ahead. Guards? Would they be surrounded?

Turning a corner, Nicole found they had entered a vast reception room with fluted pillars reaching up to an arched ceiling ribbed with stone. Sitting at a small table were several guards engaged in some sort of game. Without a break in stride, she and Luc followed behind Antoine, their footsteps lost in the buzz of conversation.

Nicole's breath tightened as they passed the table, then approached several armed guards milling about, talking to one another. Without hesitation, Antoine kept pace, looking straight ahead with a frown, and beside her, Luc remained alert and official in his escort of the prisoner.

They halted before the posted guard. He saluted Antoine.

Antoine gave a curt nod. "We're taking the prisoner for questioning."

"Very good, sir." The guard lifted the latch and creaked open the oak door to a cerulean fall sky, dotted with cottony clouds.

***

Nicole sat stock still in her chair. It was as though her body hadn't caught up to the reality that she was here in Aunt Charlotte's kitchen. As she adjusted to the room filled with sunlight and tea scents, Antoine and Luc were in the bedroom doffing the outfits they'd worn, ready to be returned to Lulu, who had used her resources to procure such convincing disguises.

When they at last entered the kitchen, Nicole's eyes rested lovingly on Luc, handsome in his dark suit and his hair pulled into a queue.

"Tell me it's over," she said.

"You're safe," he assured her.

"For now," Antoine said, looking thoughtful and contrite. He took his chair. "Nicole," he said, meeting her eyes. "You tried to tell me the truth about Luc. And Madame Colére. But I wouldn't listen. Bertrand had me convinced." He turned to Luc. "And, Luc, you're not at all what I thought. I'll be forever grateful that you saved Nicole."

"It wouldn't have been possible without you," Luc replied.

Aunt Charlotte reached for Antoine's hand. He looked at her with such warmth and softness that the woman flushed with shyness. Nicole's eyes teared at Antoine's show of tenderness. She hadn't seen this side of him for a long, long time.

"I want you to know," Antoine announced, "Bertrand will be arrested. I have Robespierre's ear. Thanks to Lulu's disguises, no one can identify me as the guard who aided a prisoner's escape. And when I get back to the committee, I intend to use my authority to steer this revolt away from injustices like Nicole's arrest. I see we must enact the liberty and equality that we've fought so hard to gain. We must stop violence. This revolution is about justice. Not revenge." He smiled at Nicole. "I've learned that, Nicole."

"And *Madame* Colére?" Nicole asked. "Will she receive justice? Not only for my arrest. But what she's done all these years, to so many children in her care."

"I wish I could say so. But Marthe Colére was one of the women who marched on Versailles. She's become a heroine of the Revolution. There'll be little I can do."

Luc stood. "And now, Nicole, it's dangerous for you to remain here. They won't stop looking for you."

"It's true," Antoine said sadly. "You must leave Paris."

"Yes," said Luc. "And at once. I know just the place to take her." He reached over for Nicole's hand. "She's already agreed to marry me. And now I intend to take her to safety."

Aunt Charlotte rose from her chair and kissed Nicole's cheek. "Congratulations, my darling girl. I will miss you terribly. But I am so happy for you."

Nicole clasped Aunt Charlotte's hands. "I will never forget you," she said. She turned. "And you, Antoine. Thank you for risking your life for me. And—for all you've meant to me. I've loved you, Antoine. I always will." There would always be in her heart the memory of Antoine, hiding from the police behind a cart, how as his partner, she'd welcomed the thrill, the power, of rebellion.

"Antoine," she said, taking his hand. "I'm only beginning to understand your life's passion has always been the pursuit of justice."

"Justice for his mother," Aunt Charlotte said. "And for Sebaste."

"And for myself, a young boy who'd lost his family."

"Yes," Nicole said. "I see that, Antoine."

"I would have given my life for you, Nicole," Antoine said. "But what is happening in France is my journey. Thank you for letting me see that." He paused for a long moment, staring at her face as if trying to memorize it. Then he turned toward the door and called out, "Sebaste. You need to say good-bye to Nicole."

The boy came bounding into the room, and exclaimed, "What do you mean, good-bye?"

"I must leave Paris," Nicole said, holding out her arms. He came to her and let her hug him.

"Why, Nicole? You promised to always be in my life."

"You have Antoine. Aunt Charlotte. I'm going to be married. I will write, as often as I can. I hope you write back to me."

Sebaste untangled from Nicole's hug and glanced at Luc with saddened eyes. "To this man?"

Luc gave the boy a wink. "I'm very fortunate. I see you know that. You're a good judge of a person."

At the compliment, a tiny smile touched Sebaste's face. "I know."

"So, will you watch over your big brother?" Nicole asked

Sebaste ran over to Antoine and flopped across his brother's knees. "Of course, I will. I'm a man now." Nicole and Antoine shared a look of pride at the boy's strength and courage.

Antoine ruffled Sebaste's hair. "Well, then, between you and dear Aunt Charlotte, I feel well accounted for."

Sebaste's smile faded. "And Nicole, will you be all right? Nothing will happen to you?"

"That is now *this* man's work," Antoine said, gesturing to Luc with genuine fondness. "They belong together." He looked down to his little brother. "And I belong to you, and the Revolution."

Chapter Thirty-Nine

Bertrand Le Mansec came into the tribunal chamber. He stood at the door a moment, as if bewildered at the events that had brought him here. Antoine saw on his face the fear of a man who knew his guilt, but not the identity of his accuser.

A guard nudged him forward so that Bertrand slowly neared the table of four tribunal officials. He was wearing that absurd cap cocked to the side and looking about for clues as to what was happening to him. Antoine summoned every ounce of strength to refrain from leaping up and attacking the man. But he quelled the impulse and sat back passively, twirling a pencil in his hands. He waited for the sweet moment when Bertrand would notice him. Then, all at once it came. Bertrand abruptly halted. The color drained from his face.

"Take a chair," Antoine said.

Staring steadily at him, Bertrand eased into the solitary chair placed directly before the table.

Seated between the other officers, Antoine looked down at his notes. "Le Mansec, I have before me complaints that have been brought against you. Complaints that are quite serious, telling of your conspiracy against the Cause." Looking up at Bertrand, Antoine saw the expression that all accused prisoners wore. Confusion and innocence. As if they had no idea about the charges or the crime.

"There's been a misunderstanding," Bertrand said.

"You'll not speak until told to," Antoine said. He drew his finger down a paper spread out on the table. "It is stated here that on January fifth, seventeen eighty-nine, an informant approached Royal authorities with information about a subversive group responsible for distributing so-called treasonous pamphlets on the streets of Paris. These pamphlets were printed in the shop owned by Jules Tout." Antoine lifted his chin. "The printshop from which I made and distributed news about atrocities committed by the Monarchy. The shop wherein I was subsequently arrested by Royal guards. The shop then destroyed by those guards. Someone was an informant. Someone who knew I would be there."

Bertrand shook his head. "I have no knowledge of this."

"But you did know the location of the shop?"

"Of course, I did. We're friends, aren't we? I was there once or twice and helped you. You know that, Antoine. My God. How many nights did we sit and plan at *La Fenêtre*? Are you suggesting I was involved in your arrest?"

"I am." Antoine's eyes narrowed. "You were a traitor to our cause."

Bertrand ran his hand over his whiskery jaw. "It's true you were betrayed, Antoine. But not by me. By Luc Chatillon. I told you about Luc, if you remember—as soon as I was sure about him. Even though he was my friend. I even told your fiancée about Luc. I warned everyone."

"There is another person you spoke to about Luc. Philippe Montpellier."

At the name, Bertrand's body stiffened. Any pretense of confusion about the charges evaporated. Antoine propped his arms on the table. "No games, Le Mansec. Montpellier has told us everything." He nudged forward a paper. "It's all here. Philippe Montpellier's statement, telling how you were paid for information. How you sold every friend you had for money." His mouth tightened. "*Here*," he said in a steely cold voice. "Read it. Go on. Read and try to deny you've done all this." As Bertrand glanced down at the page, Antoine leaned forward, his face red. "*Deny* that you betrayed me. Had me sent to prison. Tortured." His eyes bored into Bertrand's. "For *money*, Bertrand. Our friendship meant nothing. And all that time I'd defended you. Against those who've suffered because of it." He pushed the paper directly in front of him. "*I said read it.*"

Bertrand's eyes flashed about the faces of the tribunal members. Sniffing, he leaned back with an incorrigible air. "I, a commoner, should read the accusations of a count's son?" he said lowly. He appealed to them, one by one. "My mother has been a servant of Lord Montpellier. She's given her life to the family, even abandoning me to do so. But he threw her out, with nothing. Philippe Montpellier is a noble, and you listen to *him*?"

"This information has been verified, Bertrand," Antoine said. "We know everything. Every contact. Every piece of information. All corroborated." He picked up the paper and thrust it at him. "Now, read it."

With all pretenses gone, pure hatred filled Bertrand's face. "That's how it is, then? Nothing changes. Power gets its way. I've always hated your Cause, *all of you*," he sneered, addressing the tribunal. "You've ruined France with your idiotic ideas of equality." He stared at Antoine. "And you. You and Luc are dreamers. I can almost understand you, Antoine. Look what it's gotten you. All this authority. When you were nothing." He frowned. "But Luc? My God, what a fool *he* is." He was rambling now. "He's ruined his own life. And why? So that new tyrants will take over? Steal away his father's fortune? What lunacy. What will have been gained? *What?*"

Antoine eased back in his chair. He was silent a long moment. "We have already signed orders for your arrest," he said quietly. "But not for your beliefs, Bertrand. We have fought against despotism. Cruelty. Tyrants. We have fought for liberty. I have no interest in arresting citizens for living the lives they were born into, be they nobles or not. But you, Bertrand, have betrayed the cause of liberty. I could more easily forgive your personal betrayal, than that."

"Antoine, can we not try—"

"Take the prisoner away," Antoine commanded, taking up his official stamp without looking at him. "To await sentencing."

He felt a release in his bones of the months of torture as he pounded the papers with the stamp, hard, one after another, sealing Bertrand's fate.

***

Nicole leaned against Luc as they sped through the city in the cabriolet, which was like an old friend. She'd ridden in it so many times with him. And now, she thought, looking out, this was the last time she would see Paris. The city had never looked more beautiful, glowing in the dusky twilight. Her eyes misted, remembering her life here, her nighttime swims in the Seine with Aimée, suppers in Sarah's kitchen, working side by side with Gus on their hats, and the exciting evenings with Antoine pasting up the propaganda that had led to a revolution.

Luc brought his cheek toward hers and took her hand. "We're approaching the gate. Be brave, my love."

Nicole sat straight. Seeing two carriages stopped in front of them, her heart jumped. "They're questioning the drivers," she said, her frightened eyes taking in several guards dressed in a motley assortment of uniforms.

"We'll get through this," Luc murmured as one approached. The guard stuck his boot on the footstep and looked inside. In the dim light, Nicole took in his youth, his thin adolescent body beneath an oversized military coat.

"Citizens," he demanded. "Show your identification."

Nicole tensed. She'd not expected this…had Luc? Ah yes, he had, she realized as he pulled folded papers from his pocket.

"Good evening, Citizen." Luc addressed the guard with a casual familiarity, as if he'd done this many times. "Hugo Lamont, and my wife, Victorine. We're returning home."

Nicole held her breath. Would *Madame* Lamont's documentation work for them?

The guard gave a cursory glance over the papers. His eyes flicked to the dark cabriolet interior. "What was your business in Paris?"

"I brought my wife to visit her mother."

"She lives in Paris?"

"Yes," Nicole said, leaning forward and speaking across Luc. "My mother is gravely ill. She lives with my brother, a member of the Jacobins."

The young man's face lit up, impressed. "Very well, Citizens," he said, returning the papers and stepping back. "*Viva la Republic.*"

Luc responded with the proper amount of enthusiasm. "*Merci* for your service."

As they pulled away, Luc stared ahead, one hand on the reins, the other firmly holding Nicole's hand. When they were well away from the city gate, he released his clasp and gave her an impressed look.

"It's frightening how well you can lie," he said with a smile.

"And you," Nicole replied, glancing back for assurance they were not being followed.

"It was easy," Luc said. "I feel as though you *are* my wife."

Amazed and grateful, Nicole leaned close and kissed his cheek. How could it be? This morning she'd awoken in a dank cell, and now she found herself with Luc, headed to the countryside she loved so much.

"Husband." She smiled, trying out the word.

He grinned. "In a way, Nicole, we have Bertrand to thank for all this happiness."

"Why would you say that? He caused everything."

"Think on it," Luc mused. "I met you because I came to the café with him. And later, he was paid by Philippe to learn as much about you as possible."

"So that's how he knew where I lived."

"And he went to Legros."

"Did he?" she asked in surprise. The thought of Bertrand at Legros sitting with *Madame* took a moment for her to grasp.

Luc went on. "The directress must have thought he was an ally. She gave him your entire family history. In a folder in her office."

Nicole shuddered. "It was always right there." It seemed impossible that for all those years her entire life had been within reach, in *Madame*'s dank office where she'd received so many punishments.

"*Madame* Colére wanted me to believe my memories were the fantasies of an abandoned child. But for years the same ones came again and again—in dreams. They were strange. A doll. Now I realize my mother had only that morning bought it for me. I wanted to show Papa, and ran across the street." She looked at her folded hands. "I never saw the coach."

"Nicole, I read through your father's papers fairly quickly. But I had enough time to see most of them were military documents. Some legal. There was a property deed. Your father's pension—"

"Pension?" Nicole repeated. "I received none of it. It must have gone to Legros. *Madame* called me a burden to the Crown." She took a sharp breath, quelling a long-held anger. "And you say my father had property?"

"Yes. Along with a bill of sale for it and all the household furnishings. Everything was sold years ago. After his death."

"My home," Nicole said, trying to fathom her lost world. "I've always had memories of it, dim ones…a blue room. I think a bedroom. And there was a large entry, with a soft rug. I remember sitting under a table, watching the adults' feet pass by." She paused, gazing at the flourish of purple in the evening sky. "*Madame* told me I'd been abandoned by my mother. I cannot understand how that woman could have been so cruel. To take it all from me," she whispered sadly.

"There's something else," Luc said. "Something that may shed light on why." From his pocket Luc took a page that had been folded into quarters, and with a meaningful look, handed it over to her.

With a sense of curiosity and foreboding, Nicole unfolded it, barely able to make out in the dim light what seemed to be an official document.

"Your father's official records."

Squinting, Nicole read at the top: *The Battle of La Belle-Famille. July 24, 1759. Deceased with Honor.*

Luc gave Nicole a moment to look it over. "It's a listing of men who were killed, apparently all from your father's troop," he explained. "This battle was a massacre. The British ambushed your father's troop with no warning. These names must have meant much to your father, to have kept this. There's even a marginal note. Perhaps in his hand."

Nicole felt a welling of hot tears as she traced the scrolled handwriting with her fingertip.

"My love," said Luc, turning to her. "You should know..." He paused.

"What? Tell me, Luc."

"One of the slain was Hadrian Colére."

The name struck Nicole like a blow. Stunned, she brought her hands to her lips and closed her eyes, trying to imagine what this meant in her life. And yet, she knew. "Colére? Someone related to *Madame* Colére?"

"Her husband."

"Oh my God."

Nicole held the paper to her breast as a barrage of memories came: the haircutting, the slaps, the locked, dark closet. "The woman held my father responsible for her husband's death. All her life, her hatred grew." A torrent of pity and understanding washed over her. "I cannot imagine what the woman felt when she learned my father had been killed and that his child was to be placed in her orphanage."

Luc stared ahead quietly. Nicole sat with her memories, her feelings.

At last, she turned to him. "These papers are all I have of the dear, dear papa I had almost forgotten. But I didn't. He was always there with me. But at last, I know who he was. And I have a small understanding of *Madame* Colére. She was a woman who lost her love." Nicole re-opened the paper on her lap and drew her finger down the list, stopping again at Hadrian Colére. "How ever did you get this?"

"Bertrand left your papers with someone who is quite dear to me, Louise-Marie Bisset. Nicole, I'm not going to lie to you that she's always been merely a friend. At another time in my life, she was perhaps a kind of refuge. But those days are past, and she's become one of my true allies, along with Philippe. They are the ones who helped persuade Antoine about Bertrand."

Taking it all in, filling with a deep-seated peace, Nicole leaned closer to Luc. "*Shh.* I care nothing about your past. Only our future." She folded the paper and tucked it into her vest, close to her heart. She closed her eyes to luxuriate in the knowledge of having a father—and feeling pride in him.

Luc stretched his arm around her shoulder, and as she snuggled into the warmth of his body, she gave in to the serenity that filled her, lulled by the rhythmic sounds of the horse's clomping hooves along the road, and now and then, a faraway hooting owl.

***

Luc climbed the grand staircase of *Les Saules* carrying a sleeping Nicole in his arms. Knowing she was exhausted, he laid her on his bed and watched her breathing. Pulling up a blanket to cover her, he sat on the edge of the mattress and smoothed back hair from her face. The ravages of her arrest had left a faint darkness about her eyes. Still, her beauty struck him to the core.

Assured that she was safe, Luc stood and unbuttoned his shirt, threw it and his britches on the floor, and dressed in riding clothes. He halted as Nicole turned over in sleep, waited for her to settle, then quietly pulled on his riding boots and made his way out of the room. He took from his pocket his grandmother's ring that Sarah had given to him and slipped it on her finger. She moaned and turned in her sleep. He bent and kissed her forehead.

Hurrying down the winding staircase, intent on his mission, Luc rushed to the back of the chateau. As he passed the kitchen, he heard a voice, one he knew well. Brightening, he changed direction and went inside to find Georgette sitting with *Madame* Lamont. The two women looked up, and with a gasp of delight, *Madame* Lamont rose and rushed to him. "Master Luc. We've been worried. Your message said you'd be here before nightfall. Is *Mademoiselle* Nicole with you?"

"She is. In my room sleeping. Tell Coco to watch for her. The lady will be famished when she wakes."

He turned to Georgette. She sat in her night-robe, her hair flowing about her shoulders, with a sleeping baby in her arms. Luc believed she'd never looked more content, her skin radiant, her eyes glittering.

"This is your child," he stated, staring down at the slumbering baby.

"Giselle," Georgette said with pride, pulling back the blanket for him to take a peek. "She looks like Éric, don't you think?"

"She looks like her mother. A charmer."

"I hardly feel charming," Georgette scoffed. "I've not had a smidge of makeup for months."

"Your face needs nothing but happiness, it seems. I've never seen you more lovely, Georgette."

She reached out and clasped his hand. "You found Éric," she said with wonder. "How can I thank you? He's changed, Luc. The moment he looked at the baby, he fell madly in love."

Luc tussled Georgette's hair. "Where is this new father?"

"With his other love," Georgette said with a smile. "His horse. Though I swear, I'm not jealous."

***

It was midnight when a four-horse wagon laden with hay rumbled into Paris. Éric clicked the reins while behind him Luc sat with his back propped up against the seat, hidden in a nest of straw. The streets were empty. Armed guards roamed about, with no obvious purpose other than to be a presence. As Éric headed toward Baston Millinery, the unwieldy wagon drew a few disinterested stares. Playing his role, Éric stared casually ahead, ever alert to Luc's directions, until Luc whispered, "Here. Stop."

As the two men approached the hat shop, the front door jerked open and Gus stood waiting. "What's taken so long?" Gus said, ushering them in. His hair was disheveled, his face drawn into a worried frown. "Where is Nicolette?"

"At my country house. Sleeping."

"Oh, merciful heaven," Aimée exclaimed. Luc looked around to see the others. A candle illuminated Sarah, huddled in her wool cape. And on the settee, Jacques shouldered his son, asleep under a blanket.

"We've been beside ourselves waiting to hear about her," Sarah exclaimed, coming to clasp Luc's hand. "She is not hurt, *Monsieur* Chatillon? They did nothing to her?"

"Please, Sarah, call me Luc. Nicole is fine," he assured her, covering her hand with his. "Thanks to Antoine. He was impressive in his masquerade. Black wig and all. They'll never identify him. But by now they've discovered the hoax. They could be here any moment looking for Nicole."

"We've been ready since your friends came to warn us," Gus said, herding the group toward the door. "Out now, everybody. We need to hurry."

On the street, Luc conducted them to the rear step of the wagon, helping the ladies climb up and into an interior hollow prepared by Éric and the stable boy, Pepe. But no sooner had they settled in, with Luc propped behind the driver's seat and Éric ready to click the reins, than from the back of the wagon Sarah let out a squeal. "Wait."

Luc flew out of his perch, rushing to the rear of the wagon to find Sarah trying to extricate herself from the wagon.

"We forgot Midas," she wailed, rushing back inside.

Luc watched her rush into the shop and back out, the fat orange cat sprawled in her arms.

Chapter Forty

"*Old Time is still a-flying*," Luc recited with a note of mirth, his arm encircling Nicole's waist. They stood in the willow grove where they'd first made love, but now the branches draped to the ground in glorious yellow and gold colors of autumn.

Nicole slipped her arms about his neck, a slow smile crossing her face. "I remember that afternoon. You'd asked my thoughts about seizing the day."

He pulled her closer. "And if I remember right, your response fairly shook me to my foundation."

"Hmmm," she murmured, tracing his lips with her finger. "I'm so glad it did."

"Making love to you has too long been a memory," Luc said. "Tonight, sweet Nicole, I plan to ravish my fiancée."

"Oh, do you?" she said naughtily. "And are you ready for a bit of ravishing yourself?"

"Do your best," Luc said, grinning. He released her and, taking off his coat, spread it upon the grass, then drew her down beside him. "And yet, *ma chérie*, we've a lifetime to make love and make babies and grow old together." He grew serious and smoothed back hair from her face. "But here, for now, we must prepare for the changes ahead."

"I know," Nicole said a bit sadly. "We can't stay here, can we, Luc?"

"No," he whispered.

"I'll go wherever you want. It doesn't matter. As long as I'm with you."

"I must tell you, Nicole, we'll need to find strength. It won't be easy."

"With you, I can be strong."

"I've always believed that. Would you like to hear my plan?"

"Tell me. I say yes. Yes to it all."

***

The setting sun cast an apricot glow into the main salon, warm and cozy with a blazing fire. The huge room with timber ceilings, rough-hewn doors, with a collection of antlers displayed on the walls had been the seat of Chatillon holidays and celebrations. It was where Luc's most fond memories had been created.

And now Luc had brought together here his new family. They expectantly gathered about on the collection of settees and chairs and footstools.

He stood before them, quieting everyone. "Nicole and I have asked you all to join in our joy," he began. His gaze touched Nicole, moved down to Coco perched on a footstool, then swept across to Aimée and Jacques, with Jac—fascinated with the brown and white dog—at their feet sitting on the floor, then to Georgette and Éric, baby Giselle propped on his chest, to the other side of the room where the Bastons sat shoulder to shoulder, their fat orange cat on Sarah's lap.

Finally, he turned and nodded to *Madame* Lamont.

"*Madame* Lamont," Luc said. "You've been with this family and this house as far back as I can remember. And it's my desire that you stay here as long as you wish. And as for you, Colette—" He motioned for Coco to stand. Blushing, she rose, suppressing a smile. "I'd like you all to know these two women have more knowledge about this house than perhaps anyone. It is their home."

Madame Lamont's eyes filled with concern. "Master Luc. Why are you saying this?"

He took Nicole's hand and pulled her to his side. "It's become clear that Nicole and I cannot stay in France," he said. "There's danger for her, with her parentage. As well as for me, being an accomplice in my parents' escape."

Madame Lamont frowned. "Master Luc—"

"However," Luc interrupted, seeing her concern, "Les Saules has within this room the new owners." He turned and walked to a table against the wall. From a drawer he withdrew a rolled document, tied with a faded green ribbon. Pausing, he looked up at the portrait of his grandparents, then returned to the group. "I hold here the deed to *Les Saules*. I have always loved it as my home, my refuge."

He surveyed the group. They looked curious, concerned, but mostly fascinated.

"My grandparents wanted *Les Saules* to be filled with family. Sadly, they did not see that wish fulfilled. But I know they would concur with the decision I've made. *Les Saules* is now the property of two of my fiancée's most beloved people, Jacques and Aimée Guerin."

A cry of surprise broke from Aimée's lips. Luc smiled at her, then at Nicole. Jacques's body seemed to have grown rigid with astonishment. Aimée jumped up and rushed to embrace Nicole, then she turned to Luc. "I cannot believe this. It is a blessing beyond anything I've ever dreamed. There is such peace and goodness here. How can we thank you?"

"By making *Les Saules* a home," he said softly.

Jacques slowly rose and approached. Luc admired the deep respect and honor on the man's face, but he knew he should be the one respecting and honoring this man.

"This is more generous than I can express," Jacques said in his deep voice. "And I think I speak for everyone here when I say we wish this could be otherwise."

Luc saw the pride on Aimée's face as she listened to her husband's eloquence, and indeed, even he was surprised by it.

"Our greatest desire," Jacques said, "is that you, Luc and Nicole, stay and raise your family here, as your grandparents wished. But I vow that we will honor your *Les Saules*." He paused, nodding solemnly. "And I will devote my life to keeping it a family home you'd be proud of. We profoundly thank you—and your ancestors."

Aimée slipped her arm into his. "I'm so happy and yet so sad," she said, her eyes wet. She looked at Nicole. "I know you must leave, Nicole…and Luc." She paused and swallowed. "But I'll never stop waiting for your return. France will not always be as it is now. I believe I will see you again, *ma sœur*, and your many, many children." She hugged Nicole, and the two seemed unable to part. Luc felt his own eyes moisten, watching the woman he loved filled with such devotion and loss. He vowed that Nicole would never feel loss again.

At that moment, Jac shrieked. Luc turned to him and chuckled as everyone's attention was suddenly on the child clamoring on all fours after the dog. Then the entire room broke into laughter. "He's crawling," Aimée exclaimed in delight.

At the ruckus, Midas jumped off Sarah's lap and ran under a settee. Little Giselle awoke with a start and began whimpering. Luc had never been happier. It's what he'd always wanted. A family, here in the place he loved so dearly.

A smile lighting up his face, Éric handed the baby to Georgette, then, with a deep breath stood and looked about.

"It's a night of many joys and announcements," Éric said. Luc glanced at Georgette, who he knew was about to become as happy as he and Nicole. "And it's time I jump in," Éric went on. "First, I thank Luc for giving me a position at Les Saules, and for offering the lake cottage to live in, as a freehold possession."

Luc nodded.

"I've known Raoul for years," Éric continued. "There's not a better man to work with, or a finer stable. And with such a position, and my own cottage, I need a family to fill it." He turned toward Georgette sitting beside him. "Though even without such a fine home, I'd be here asking this beautiful woman, the mother of my daughter, the same question I do now." He motioned for Nicole. Luc pressed her arm, knowing what was coming. She nodded and came forward to take Giselle from Georgette's arms.

Georgette's eyes flashed from Nicole to Eric, then to Luc. He winked at her. She grew still as Éric clasped her hand. "Gette, I may not be the man you deserve. I'm not proud of who and what I've been. But I'm ready to become a real man. To deserve a wife and child such as you and our beautiful Giselle. Your motherhood has brought out the loving woman I always knew was there. And I vow to deserve it."

Georgette brought her palms to her cheeks to wipe away the tears. Luc looked down. He'd never seen such pure emotion from her.

Hearing Georgette gasp, he looked up. Amid the delighted murmurs from the others, Éric was bent on his knee before her. "And so, Georgette, in witness of these good people, having already gotten permission from your father, no easy feat—" His words were met with titters of amusement. "And from your very happy mother—" He stopped for a few laughs, then grew serious. "I ask for your hand. Georgette, will you be my wife?"

Georgette cried out, "Yes. Yes." As he drew her up, she threw her arms around him, pressing her face against his chest while quietly sobbing.

Luc neared them. "May I congratulate the groom?"

"You may. And thank you, Luc."

He turned to Georgette. "And kiss the future bride?"

Georgette threw her arms about him. "Oh Luc," she whispered against his shoulder. "Thank you. Bless you."

After a quiet moment, Aimée approached them. Luc broke the embrace. "We shall be neighbors, Georgette," she said, "and new friends."

Smiling and nodding, Georgette said, "Call me Gette?"

"Yes." Aimée laughed and gave her a hug. "I love it."

Luc joined Nicole where they had a moment of privacy. "Can you believe it's come to this, darling?" he said.

"I remember the first day we met. How much I detested her. I even thought whoever married her was an unlucky man. I was wrong. Éric is very lucky."

"It's you," Luc said softly. "You've changed all our lives." He'd never said truer words.

Georgette was then passed about for best wishes, with the men shaking Éric's hand in congratulations.

"I'm so happy for you," Nicole said when Georgette came to her.

Georgette clasped her hands. "How can I make up for how I treated you, Nicole? I'm so ashamed, and so sorry for the problems I caused. Will you forgive me?" Briefly recalling Georgette's ugly scene here only months before, Luc smiled at the course of events.

Nicole shook her head. "It's all in the past. I'm glad you and your daughter can be with Éric, at *Les Saules*." She turned and pulled Aimée into their circle. "And you'll be with my most dear friend, who saved my life many times over when I was a child. I'm thrilled she'll be your friend. You'll never have a truer one." Watching it all, Luc was moved by Nicole's kindness.

He raised his hands. "And now, to celebrate." Almost on cue, *Madame* Lamont opened the door, holding a large cake aloft. Symon, Luc's chamber valet from Paris, entered carrying a tray filled with champagne, followed by a barrage of others including Raoul, a collection of kitchen helpers and maids from the Paris chateau, and a smattering of field hands from *Les Saules*. Last to enter was young Pepe, with his mother and father who worked as farmhands, all washed and clean from finishing the harvest.

Luc took Nicole by the hand and brought her beside Aimée. "Happy birthday, Nicole and Aimée," he said.

Nicole's eyes widened. "Had you forgotten?" Luc murmured.

"Not I," Aimée said with a teary smile. "*Bon anniversaire*, sister of my heart."

"*Bon anniversaire*, my twin," Nicole whispered back. The girls hugged long and hard.

"To friendship," Luc said loudly, raising his glass. Everyone toasted, and then plates of white frosted cake were passed about.

In the pandemonium, Luc felt compelled to say something. "Aimée, if there is ever anything, any danger from the revolution, you can contact my father."

Aimée nodded. "Thank you, Luc. For...all of it."

He thought it bittersweet she would say such a thing, when he was taking away her dearest friend.

Candles were being lit when Luc drew Nicole to the center of the room. He stood back as she raised her glass and tinkled her spoon for attention. Once everyone had quieted, she glanced at him, and with his nod of encouragement, she took a deep breath.

"Finding the identify of my father and mother has been both a blessing and a curse," she said. "Now that I know my ancestry, France will imprison me for who I am. And so, as you know, Luc and I must leave." Luc linked his arm through hers.

He wondered if he could say it. He would give anything for this night to last. But it couldn't. "It is our sadness to say," he said, "that tonight, my dear friends, Nicole and I spend our last night with you."

The celebratory mood sobered. "Where will you go?" Sarah asked, her eyes shining with tears.

He took Nicole's hand. He did not hesitate as she joined him, and in unison they proudly announced, "To America."

He wiped the tears from her eyes, embraced her, and lowered his head in a sweet, long kiss.

"Here, here," called *Madame* Lamont.

As their embrace broke, Nicole turned to Gus and Sarah. "And to the parents of my heart," she said, "I ask one last thing."

Luc knew this was the final piece. Knew the journey ahead. It would not be easy, but with Nicole at his side, he could do anything.

"After all that you've already given Nicole," he said to Gus and Sarah, "she has one last request."

Gus and Sarah stood still, watching them.

"My darling Gus and Sarah," Nicole said. "We will need your help getting there."

***

The moon glowed through the bedchamber window. Nicole felt this room told her everything about Luc's grandmother. The dusty-rose stucco walls, the limestone fireplace, the overstuffed cushioned chairs and settees—a room to be lived in, with a layering of comfort and love. She looked to the door as Luc entered wearing a soft robe, carelessly cinched and revealing his broad chest with tufts of dark hair.

She came to him, meeting him halfway. Smiling, she slipped off one thin strap of her nightgown, then the other, allowing it to slither to her feet in a fluid heap. Luc's passionate eyes took in her body, the firmness of her breasts, the curve of her waist, the way her skin fit her in a silken glove.

"My God, you're beautiful," he murmured, drawing so close she could feel his warm breath.

She reached out and unfastened the tie looped around his hips, then pushed back the robe to expose his shoulders, freeing his arms so that the robe dropped to the floor. His firm body awed her, his tanned skin, his broad chest with a ladder of muscles leading down his taut abdomen, and lower—

Her eyes flashed up to his. "My God, *you're* beautiful."

He grinned. "And you, my dear, are saucy."

She lowered her hand to his taut, velvety flesh. "You've only begun to see," she teased.

Luc's constraint ended. He drew her up into his arms so that Nicole clasped her hands around his neck, pressing her bare skin to his, thrilling to the warmth of his brawn. He carried her to a high-back velvet chair where, with both hands around her waist, he lifted her up then eased her down onto his lap, filling her with his passion.

"I've waited a lifetime for you," he whispered against her temple as she moaned in pleasure.

She opened wider to the robustness of his body possessing her. His tongue tickled and moistened her breasts, trailing and nibbling until she felt herself engulfed in a white light of ecstasy.

"Luc," she whispered. "I never knew it could be like this—" Her breath caught in a moan.

"My love," he answered huskily.

Her hips moved with his as their rhythm became one. She leaned forward, her hair falling about them in a silken tent as she held his face between her hands and their mouths met in deep, open kisses. "Luc," she sighed. "I love you—"

With a groan, he tucked his hands beneath her round bottom and meshed her movements to his. Again and again they pulsed together, with flutters of warmth consuming her, higher and higher until her insides grew molten.

And then, when she felt herself ready to melt, he powerfully pulled her up with him and carried her to the bed. As he laid her down and stepped back, her body mad with desire, she opened to him. He waited, watching her caressing herself to quell the passion he'd aroused, and still he watched her, taking in every inch of her body sprawled bare against the sheets. "Come," she whispered, reaching up to him. "Come love me."

He lowered his knee onto the bed at her hip, looking deeply into her eyes. "Now?" he asked gruffly, with his last thread of control.

"Yes, yes," she murmured, clutching at him, both pulling him to her and arching up to meet him so that together they lost themselves in a powerful discovery of passion and love.

***

Sitting propped against the pillows, Nicole held Luc in her arms, toying with tufts of chest hair as she gazed across the lovely room. "I wish I'd met them," she mused.

"My grandparents?"

"Yes. They seem like extraordinary people."

"I didn't know my grandfather well. But *Grand'mère* was the strongest woman I've ever met. She had an inner strength that comes from wisdom, something I'd never seen in another woman." He looked up. "Until I met you, my love."

Nicole drew him up so that he sat. "I know I said I'd be strong, Luc. But I'm afraid."

He frowned, drawing the back of his fingers down her jaw. "Whatever about, love?"

"Of tomorrow. Of leaving."

Luc kissed her temple. "You need never be afraid. Not with me beside you." He pulled back and held her by her shoulders. "There's something I have for you. To give you strength."

Nicole grew curious, and as Luc rose, she watched his remarkable body walk across the room. Bemused, her gaze dropped to his firm buttocks, a curve of a smile touching her lips. He opened a chest drawer and returned to her with something in his hands: a doll.

"It belonged to Françoise," he said, drawing on his robe and sitting on the mattress edge. "When you told me about the doll your mother gave you, I thought of this one. I know *Grand'mère* would want you to have it."

Nicole took the shiny wooden doll dressed in pink-striped jacket and culottes, the face painted with rosy cheeks, her blond hair tucked beneath a lacy white bonnet. She touched the bare wooden feet with painted toes. Her heart was overcome with love for the man who would think of such a gift.

"I'll always cherish her," she said, the girl inside rising up to meet the woman she was now. "Thank you, my beloved, for honoring my past—and for being my future."

Chapter Forty-One

A misty rain silvered the early dawn as two sturdy horses were harnessed to the old coach. Raoul and Éric had worked into the night oiling and patching the rig to prepare for the journey. While most of the inhabitants of *Les Saules* still slumbered, Luc, Nicole and the Bastons readied themselves and headed to the driveway. *Madame* Lamont hurried out into the dark morning and handed Éric a hamper stuffed with bread, cheese, and sausages.

"Wonderful, *Madame*," said Luc as she stood proudly, watching him inspect the contents. He'd helped Sarah and Nicole into the coach and they were ready. Gus was the last, hauling up a crate carrying the mewling Midas.

Éric, bundled in a heavy coat and hat, handed out blankets to tuck around their bodies, then walked round to pull himself into the driver's seat.

Madame Lamont remained watching, huddled in the cold, until Luc at last climbed into the door and slid onto the seat beside Nicole. "Everyone will be watching for your letters, Master Luc," she said, her voice awash with emotion.

"I know *Les Saules* is in the best of hands."

"It's an honor, Master Luc."

"The honor has been mine," Luc replied. "I will never forget you, *Madame* Lamont."

Éric flicked the lead horse and the coach pulled forward, crunching slowly over the gravel, away from the chateau, down the lane, past the willow trees. *Madame* Lamont watched until the coach lights faded—then she walked back inside, her thoughts filled with a little boy named Luc who'd loved books and horses.

***

The wearying trip took four long days. Nicole's body ached from the coach bouncing on rutted roads. From time to time, she worried they might be stopped, but there were no checkpoints, and no one paid them much mind as they rumbled through fields and past villages. Luc was steady as a rock, his eyes on the passing road, his hand caressing Nicole's beneath the blanket. Sarah and Gus seemed to be holding up well—and even Midas had settled into the rhythms of the journey. Every so often, Sarah took the cat from the crate and held him on her lap, scratching his ears, and Midas luxuriated in the attention, closing his eyes, his purrs filling the cabin. The rain came off and on, and though Éric was well protected in his sturdy clothing, Nicole made sure at each stop he had a drink and a dry change of kerchief to wrap around his neck.

It wasn't a journey without trials. The first night they had trouble finding lodging and so slept cramped in the coach under cover of a thick grove of trees. But the following night they came across a roadhouse with a tavern where they dined on a platter of roast chicken, followed by glasses of aniseed liqueur. Satiated and exhausted, they slept in the two available rooms, comfortable on feathered mattresses. The next two nights they were fortunate as well, being able to bed down at rustic inns.

At last, they pulled into the seaport of Le Havre, its impressive harbor looming in the distance filled with several seagoing vessels, but mostly fishing boats. Although it had been years since the Bastons had been to this city, Gus ably directed Éric down the streets, through the large public square, and along winding thoroughfares until at last they reached their destination: a row of stone houses.

"This one," Gus said, pointing out a honey-colored two-storied house with a red tile roof. The damp sea air felt heavy in the gray day. The group disembarked from the coach, stretching their stiff legs.

"You think she got the letter?" Sarah asked with concern.

"I'm sure," Nicole said, though she wondered.

"And do you think she wants us here?"

"Sarah, she will be delighted to have you again in her life."

Gus arrived first at the door, with Sarah coming more slowly behind. Nicole and Luc held back as Gus knocked. When she glanced sidelong at Luc, he squeezed her hand in assurance. The door was swung open by a tall girl with long, brown braids. Nicole saw in her face Sarah's wide-set eyes.

"*Grand'mère. Grand'Père.*"

With a shriek of joy, the girl flew into their arms. "You're here."

"My dear Sylvie," Sarah cried. She and Gus embraced the granddaughter who'd been a five-year-old when they'd last seen her, ten years ago. "You're so grown up," Sarah exclaimed in awe, unable to release the girl who was thin enough to get lost in the bearish hug.

A stout woman appeared in the doorway. Her face was gentle but strong, her hair covered by a scarf. Rosalie Baston Corbin.

On seeing her, Gus and Sarah disengaged from Sylvie. For a long moment, Gus's eyes met his daughter's. She stood before him in her freshly washed loose gown, a youthful glow about her skin.

"Rosalie," he said, holding out his hands.

She took his hands in hers, her steady gaze filled with warmth. "*Papa. Maman.* Welcome."

***

Luc had insisted Éric stay the night, but eager to return to his new life in the cottage with his beloved and baby daughter, he'd declined. And so, after unloading the baggage, he clasped Luc's arm, thanked him yet again, and amid everyone's well wishes and good-byes, rode away with a wave of his hat.

"You all must be exhausted," Rosalie said, ushering everyone into her low-ceilinged sitting room where Luc ducked to avoid the beams. She fortified them with coffee and biscuits. Sylvie pulled Midas from his basket, and the cat's huge round eyes took in all the corners of the room.

"Quint's at the restaurant," Rosalie said. "He's been preparing the feast for days. He's turned out to be a wonderful cook. It took him a while to accustom himself to cooking fish rather than catching it. But he's loving it. Wait until you taste his bouillabaisse." She turned to Luc and Nicole. "As soon as I received your message, *Monsieur* Chatillon, I spoke to Father Rayne. He's young and not stuck in the old ways. He's ready for tomorrow."

"That's wonderful, thank you," Nicole said.

"*Monsieur* Chatillon," Rosalie continued. "With the money you sent, Quint arranged the boat passage. You'll set sail for England the day after tomorrow, and then on to America. Boston harbor, I believe it is."

Nicole remembered when Luc had first mentioned that exotic port, and how she'd been inspired to make a hat named after the American city. Tomorrow she was journeying there with him. It seemed experiences were all entwined, like a thread woven through a fabric, seen only when one looked close.

"We're grateful...for everything." Luc tipped his head.

"You must be so excited," Sylvie said. "To be getting wed tomorrow."

"I am," Nicole replied with a smile.

"I can't wait until I'm a bride," Sylvie said with a wistful gaze. "Is your gown beautiful?"

"It is. Your grandmother made it."

"*Grand'mère*, you must make my gown, too."

Sarah grinned at her daughter. "Rosalie, is there something we don't know here?"

Rosalie shook her head. "I plan to keep my daughter single for a few more years. I was lucky. I married so young, but a woman's happiness in life has much to do with the husband she chooses. It takes time to learn who's the right one. Quint is a wonderful man."

"*Maman* worries too much, *Grand'mère*. I've not even been courted yet." Sylvie laughed. "Tell me, Nicole, how did you know he was the man you'd marry?"

"Sylvie," Rosalie scolded.

"It's all right," Nicole said. "I agree with your mother. It can take time. To really know each other." She flushed. "Luc, what can you tell this young lady?"

Little did she realize she'd put Luc in the center of the ladies' circle. He appealed to Gus, who suddenly became interested in stuffing tobacco in his pipe.

"I believe it's fate," Luc stated. "I have no other answer. That we're all here today—never could I have planned this as my life, though it's better than I could have imagined."

Thinking the time had come, Nicole rose from her chair. "If you'll excuse me." She hurried into the small entryway where she'd set her bag. Opening it, she reached down into her garments, feeling around, clasped the treasure, and rushed back to the group.

Nicole held out the velvet box to Rosalie. "Your mother hoped to give this to you one day."

"Oh my," Sarah said, recognizing the box. Overcome, she pulled a handkerchief from her apron. "Nicole, I had no idea you'd bring it all this way." She glanced at her daughter, uncertain how Rosalie would react.

With hesitation, Rosalie accepted the case and snapped open the lid. Her eyes widened at the intricate gold bracelet, a flower glowing at the center. "Goodness," she said. "I've never touched a thing so fine."

Nicole lifted the gold cuff from the box and slid it over Rosalie's chafed hand, onto her thick wrist. "It belongs to you," Nicole said. "A gift from your mother. She can tell you all about it one day."

***

The group stood overlooking the harbor, *Havre-de-Grâce*. Haven of Grace. The sky hung low and gray, the air rich with salty spray swirling in the wind. In her best muslin gown and the gold bracelet sparkling on her wrist, Rosalie stood next to Quint, a ruddy-faced fisherman, solemn and stiff in a brown suit. Sylvie, whose ringlets flew about in the wind, held a purring Midas against her chest. Gus and Sarah stood on either side of Luc and Nicole, who, hand in hand, faced the soft-eyed young priest, Father Rayne.

Clutching a purple and yellow posy bouquet, Nicole wore the midnight blue gown Sarah had made for her what seemed so long ago, gleaming like the sea as she moved. Sylvie had threaded matching blue ribbons into Nicole's hair, half upswept, half flowing down her shoulders. Luc stood tall and handsome in a black coat and dark blue vest, a white shirt and tie looped into a bow at his neck.

They listened soberly to the priest. Every word of their vows carried along the whistling wind, across the waves. At last, Luc took Nicole into his arms and they kissed, husband and wife. When Father Rayne sanctified them, Nicole knew Luc felt the blessing deep inside as she did, a bulwark to take them forward with their lives.

***

The bouillabaisse was every bit as rich and delicious as Rosalie had promised. It was served with thick bread, soft cheese, and plenty of wine, and everyone ate their fill. The restaurant brimmed with celebration, filled with a colorful assortment of fishermen and townspeople.

In the corner of the room, music struck up, a man playing a flute, another a violin. Luc held out his hand. She rose from the table and together they gave in to the dance, with complicated steps she didn't know. Laughing, Nicole signaled for Sylvie to join them. The girl giggled as they made a circle and whirled about. Then Rosalie and Quint were up, moving in a surprisingly graceful manner. And to Nicole's delight and astonishment, Sarah and Gus appeared on the dance floor, slow and easy, dancing careful steps. Soon, the room came alive with dozens of dancers whirling to the cheerful music.

When they had exhausted themselves, Luc and Nicole returned to their table, out of breath. Nicole gazed at the faces of those she knew, and of the many kind strangers. As she sat there, her eyes brimmed with tears at the thought of her friend, her twin sister, not sharing this day.

"What are you thinking, my love?" Luc whispered, his lips at her ear.

"Oh, Luc," she said, "I'm so happy. But I already miss Aimée. I wish she could be here."

"We will often miss those we leave behind."

"Yes," Nicole concurred. "Whenever we think of them, let's send them the gladness and love we feel in our hearts."

***

Standing on the ship deck, Luc's arm warming her against the cold, Nicole waved at Gus and Sarah. As the shore of her homeland receded, tears threatened to come but stopped when she looked at those who stood beside the Bastons: Rosalie, Quint, and Sylvie holding Midas. Their family was together at last.

Nicole gripped the handrail, blinking her eyes against the misty spray. That world was past, and her dream had come true. It hardly seemed possible. The events of the past weeks rose in a flood of images, filling her mind with wonder, sadness, and hope.

Of all the things that had happened, she remembered one moment above all others. Not her arrest. Not *Madame* Colére telling her the awful truth about her parents. Not saying good-bye to Antoine for the last time. Or Sarah and Gus. Not even Jacques...or Aimée. It was one moment that, to anyone else, would have passed as inconsequential in the magnitude of events: the night Luc had proposed.

Not when he'd slipped his grandmother's ring on her finger, but later, when they were preparing to leave. Luc had taken her hand and led her to the cabriolet. He'd stopped a moment to look at the night sky. "Have you ever wondered," he'd asked as he took in the sweep of stars overhead, "if we were destined to meet, or is it simply life, the simple crossing of paths? If not me, would you have married another young man who thinks he loves you as much as I do?"

She hadn't wanted to blurt out a quick rebuke of such an idea. He was asking her a serious question. "None of us can know this, but I think if I hadn't met you, I would have married. I would have had children. Maybe fate has been kind to me and brought me the love of my life. Maybe the angels felt I'd suffered so much as a child I deserved the bliss of being with the man who touches every part of my being, not only my body, or my humor, or my thoughts, or even my heart, but who I am. I am more, Luc, with you."

She knew the answer to be her truth. At that moment she knew it was his too by the way he stood at her side, taking her into his arms, lowering his lips to hers in a forging of devotion and promise.

And, she was right.

ABOUT THE AUTHORS

Mary-Kate Summers is the writing team of Mary Janelle Melvin and Kate Evans. Kate is an award-winning author of six books. Her writing has appeared in over 50 publications, including *Woman's Day* and *Good Housekeeping*. She holds a PhD and an MFA, and works as a writing coach and an editor. Mary Janelle holds an MA in English literature. Her textbook *Grammar Illustrated: Seeing How Language Works*, was published by Fountainhead Press. An avid history buff, she has been enmeshed in the French Revolution for many years. They are lifelong friends and former professors of English at San Jose State University.

Connect with Mary and Kate:

website: Kateevanswriter.com

blog: Beingandwriting.blogspot.com

facebook.com/MaryKateSummers/

twitter.com/kateevanswriter

linkedin.com/in/kateevansauthor/

www.BOROUGHSPUBLISHINGGROUP.com

If you enjoyed this book, please write a review. Our authors appreciate the feedback, and it helps future readers find books they love. We welcome your comments and invite you to send them to info@boroughspublishinggroup.com. Follow us on Facebook, Twitter and Instagram, and be sure to sign up for our newsletter for surprises and new releases from your favorite authors.

Are you an aspiring writer? Check out www.boroughspublishinggroup.com/submit and see if we can help you make your dreams come true.

Made in the USA
Monee, IL
27 February 2021

61459748R00184